A DELTA BOOK

A NOVEL BY

RONALD SUKENICK

Originally published by The Dial Press

Published by FC2
with support given by The English Department
Unit for Contemporary Literature of Illinois State University
and the Illinois Arts Council

Address all inquiries to:
FC2
Unit for Contemporary Literature
Campus Box 4241
Illinois State University
Normal, IL 61790-4241

ISBN: 1-57366-045-0 (paperback)

**Library of Congress Catalog Card Number
98-071789**

Cover Design: Todd Michael Bushman

Produced and Printed in the United States of America

THE WORST THING IS THE COLD. I've always hated being cold—maybe they know that. Outrage, humiliation and dread have all been absorbed into this one, final, petty discomfort. As I sit huddled over my knees on the stone floor, arms crossed over chest, shaken by spasms of shivering, the question of what they intend to do with us, or rather, of how they're going to dispose of us, seems an abstract consideration. I try to pull together the ill-fitting shirt of my pajamalike canvas suit, and I realize that our mortal denouement has become an academic point, even to myself.

1

I speak of "us," but as a matter of fact I'm quite solitary. I haven't seen anyone since we were herded into the large, white-tiled room that had so much the look of our common death chamber (a slight, bald man who broke down was quickly ushered out a side door—we heard one scream in the distance). There we were told to drop our valuables in a pile, ordered to strip (two nubile high school girls being obliged to disrobe, sobbing, along with the rest) and issued our harsh, gray anonymous canvas suits. Then I was led alone through a labyrinth of stairs, always descending, and corridors lit by an occasional naked bulb, to the bare stone cell with its heavy door—allowing through its tiny grill this minimum of damp light—where I still wonder how they managed to find a place so perfect a cliché of such places, even to the rusticated stone and a large iron ring clamped into one wall. Of modern improvements there is just one: at incalculable intervals the cell is filled with blinding fluorescent light, I hear a latch in the door grill open and, after a long minute close, the light is extinguished, and I'm left again in near-darkness that seems blacker than before.

I've long stopped speculating about the reasons for my being here—in fact, as soon as I recognized the situation, I knew that such speculation would be useless. At first I guessed the police wagon was bringing me, in the incidental company of a few routine suspects, to some garage where, perhaps, my car had been towed in consequence of a minor violation. Every time I asked a question the policemen, two oldish types who looked like they drank a lot of beer and were assigned to school crossings, nodded calmly, as if to reassure me regarding law and order. It was when we were handed over to the mild, businesslike men in quiet suits, and led, about eighty of us, to the open doors of a long, high trailer-truck, that I had my only moment of panic. Not merely my common sense—my body seemed on its own account to rebel against entering. But these ordinary men all about us, otherwise so bland, looked at you with expres-

2

sions of such terrible implicit power that, although they never showed a weapon, not one of us dared balk.

My first thought was that it had something to do with being Jewish, but it seemed hardly the case that all of us were, and then, after all, that was Hitler. The first shock over, some began talking about due process and habeas corpus, but by then I knew better. It was too much our possible fate, too much a death of my nightmares, to doubt or question. And now as I sit shivering in my cell I know without thinking about it what will happen next, and my organism is unable to concern itself with its approaching annihilation, because it's too cold, and the cold is so much more insistently unpleasant.

Why the hell don't they send up some heat?

I go turn on the stove, make some coffee while I'm at it.

On with the radio. Contra solipsism. Retreat from the ivory tower, so baleful and maladive. Contact with Outside essential to nerves—if there is an Outside and if this is a contact.

The administration categorically denies Moscow's charge that the American delegation is trying to systematically wreck the tentative negotiations for a preliminary meeting to discuss the possibility of top level talks on a temporary cessation of the bilateral boycott of the conference to probe resumption of the nuclear moratorium, Washington affirms. The time is one thirteen and a half. Henry Sliesinger reports the news.

Thanks. That lets me know where I stand. Nowhere. I go back to my cramped and littered desk.

THE ADVENTURES OF STROP BANALLY

the luxe office, his immense free-form desk
the girl, the look of a wanton adolescent

3

Strop Banally

blond, tanned, well-tailored, and baritoned, football build, strength and regularity of feature

(the time he spiked a sorority's spring party punch with Spanish fly, made boat fare to Europe selling old Dewey buttons, taught on several campuses without so much as a B.A., hit 110 on the Pasadena Freeway and talked the cop out of a ticket, posed as an artist in Paris and had a successful show without paintings, screwed in one household within twenty-four hours twin sisters simultaneously, and serially their mother, their old governess and an anonymous lady who had the wrong address, as well as at one time and place or another a countless assortment of sacrifices to a lust whose enormity demands memorial)

conner of con-men, sucker's scourge, effective, insouciant, at home in heaven or hell

Strop Banally, boy genius of the communications industry or, as he is known to some, the Albert Einstein of the pornographic film

he is on the phone

she, demure, curious to the point of compromise

he looks familiar, somebody seen in a tabloid, on a screen, in a cigarette ad. The fact is that Strop made up his past as he went along, so that by now it was impossible to separate the truth from the fiction. He has allegedly been a cowboy, a flyer, a fashion model, a yacht captain, an actor, an undercover agent, a stockbroker, an advertising executive, and an entrepreneur. Impossible to say whether any of it is true, but all of it is credible. Don't betray the discontinuity of experience.

The ripe grapes heavy melons palped canteloupes of her breasts, baby blue eyes

he smokes a pipe

actually she looks somewhat tired around the eyes, lines at the corners of her mouth. Sugarplum Downey—the "teen-queen sexpot" as her publicity used to ingeniously

4

put it. Back in Hollywood. Some years ago. In fact she'd be quite happy to compromise herself, given half a chance. To get what she wants, whatever it is— a job, a favor. A job.

 she wears an engagement ring, though not quite engaged
 she knows she's going to get laid, she wonders where
 on the desk

The mailman. All morning I've been glancing out the window, waiting for the day's one event involving me in official interaction with real life. I race down, dodging the garbage leavings on the stairs, to the hallway where the mailman is sorting between two banks of opened boxes.

"Faggiuli . . . Gomez . . . Sukenick . . ."

"That's me. Gimme."

"Wait a minute, wait minute. Don't grab. Interfering with the mails is a federal offense."

"But that's mine. I'm Sukenick."

"Oh yeah? How do I know that? How do I know you ain't Gomez, for example? Look, Jim, all I do is put the letters in the box. After that I don't care what happens. Read em, burn em, use em to wrap fish. Take my advice and relax. You'll get your mail. Only it's got to be done regular. I just work for the Post Office, I don't make up the rules. Okay Jim?"

"My name isn't Jim."

I wait hovering over my mailbox turning the key in its latch and whistling, just to make it uncomfortable for the bastard. New York's infantile, infuriating tit for tat. As soon as he closes the box, I open it. A bill from Con Ed including a pamphlet on the advantages of free enterprise. Coupons offering significant savings on a new cooking oil. The "Third National Bank Neighborhood Newsletter." "Manny's Meat Mart Memos." Everybody wants to sell you something. And a letter from who?—Ernie Slade. Upstairs I open Slade's letter:

5

Dear Sukenick, by the time you get this I'll be in New York at the beginning of a new phase. Phase. Slade always spoke of himself as if he were writing his own biography. I knew him from way back. He was an old Brooklyn friend, a high school pal. I've been meeting so many of them since I've come to New York that I sometimes feel like I'm back in Brooklyn again. God forbid. It's taken me ten years just to get across the damn bridge. But then Slade is always turning up in the same places as me. Come back to New York to get away from Brooklyn. The university phase is finished. Like Santayana I looked out a classroom window the other day and said screw. I walked out and left my section babbling. They're busy spreading a rumor that I had a nervous breakdown. It's not true. What I had was a nervous breakthrough. The university is no place for a young man. How did you do it? You must be old before your time. First of all, I'd been spending most of my energy up here not getting along with everybody. A few of the older types are sympathetic if rather removed from reality. The future of the body politic seems bright to them because they're Professors. They can't comprehend that the rest of the world has neither time nor tenure nor enough money to regard social problems enquote with patient objectivity. While talking about the possibility of meeting the threat of violence with the threat of violence in the South, one eminent old liberal told me, "While not sharing your impulse toward such radical solutions, I still have hopes that your generation will find means to redeem itself." His presumably did during the McCarthy era. As for the graduate students, they're simply training to be future flunkies of the State Department. The other day my chairman said he didn't know why I was preparing for an academic career. I said to store up intellectual capital in order to have an intelligible program for the revolution. He laughed at me. And he was right. There will never be a revolution if its would-be perpetrators are persuaded to

6

work within the academic institution. That's merely another way of serving the state. Try to influence the students, you may say. Nonsense. Of course there is a splendid minority these days, but they don't need any influence. The vast majority of students are never influenced because they never think. The student is my enemy. In five or ten years he's likely to be my persecutor. He's never taken anything he's learned in school seriously and he never will. What he takes seriously is making a buck, and I can't honestly tell him he's wrong. He's concerned with brass tacks: grades, the dollars and sense of a college education. And that's what he's supposed to be concerned with. The consequent staggering irrelevance of my position here is what I finally and absolutely saw the other day when I looked through the window like Santayana in the middle of a sentence about the Greek city-states and walked out of class. Actually what I saw was a lithe co-ed in a red sweater with her big boobs bouncing as she pranced across campus. Suddenly the possibility of communicating with my students seemed so farfetched as to be unreal while, sex being the lowest common denominator of reality, the girl seemed so palpable. All of which is simply a preface to what I'm really writing you about, that is, my new magazine. Slade's phases, since he was by inclination an activist, always blossomed into agitation. I met him as a result of his philosophy phase when, at fifteen, he started his Oswald Spengler Society, a discussion group that broke up in disorder at its organizational meeting when the members learned that Slade, who was also an admirer of Machiavelli, had already elected himself president. During his literary phase Slade worked his way into the editorship of the school newspaper, had his first issue entirely devoted to a novel he was writing, and was consequently deposed by the principal, who found its vaguely D. H. Lawrence tone not to the taste of the P.T.A. Then he turned to radical politics and, disillusioned with the fellow-traveling left at the height of the Wallace campaign, organized a Young

7

Independents Softball Team and invited the school's Y.P.A. cell to a Popular Front Picnic, at which he informed the Young Progressives, shortly thereafter dissolved, that his Softball Team would from that point attend all Y.P.A. meetings with baseball bats. So I wasn't startled by Slade's new editorial venture. *Secession* is to be an action-minded pacifist-anarchist quarterly, whose aim is to crystallize around itself the discouraged remnants of the nonacademic democratic Left, the fragments of the splintered peace movement, the more political civil rights elements, and all sincere civil libertarians, in order to formulate a program of aggressive, organized political and economic nonparticipation, including selective boycotts, don't-vote campaigns, peace marches and picketing, that will appeal to the confused, misinformed, misled, underdog masses, and lead the common man to find his own voice. *Secession* is to be run by the Committee of Seven, of which I am the chairman and as yet only member. We have already aroused considerable intellectual interest, I might even say enthusiasm, in radical circles, and we have a surprising amount of financial support, largely through the agency of one source whose faith and generosity are credible only after you meet her personally as I have reason to hope you soon will, since Marietta is leaving school to follow me to New York. He had always been helped by women—even in high school, when we were all dying for a piece of ass we never got, Slade had his exploits to report with maddening regularity, a series of feats, like the time he screwed the famous girl with the ninety-nine point eight average, performed with none of the sentimentality or self-conscious coarseness of adolescence, but because women were part of the program of his life, like his pretensions as a polymath, or his ambition to become school gym champ. "Leone Battista Alberti," he would tell us, "who revolutionized Western architecture and introduced perspective into painting, was a lawyer, musician, scientist, playwright, famous for his brilliant conver-

8

sation, and could jump over a man's head with his feet close together." As though Brooklyn and ultimately America didn't exist and he could, by concentrated effort, give birth to himself in an ambiance created by his heroic conception of his own personality. No need of a past. What Brooklyn? Among the figments of my imagination, the clack and rumble of the BMT. 42nd. 34th. Union Sq. Long wild screaming tube, umbilicus, Sea Beach, rock me to sleep, West End, give me a good ride, Brighton Express, a girl to soften the rush hour squeeze, gum machines, compañeros, keep me company late at night. Boro Hall. Pacific. De Kalb. Gravesend. A tin can in an empty lot. White smoke against gray sky. Buildings like faces in a subway. Cardboard people walking around as if they were flesh and blood. Afternoons the quality of cheap wallpaper. Unreal without an effort of recreation, an effort like that of a diver moving painfully in his leaden suit across the ocean floor. Gravesend is a precinct of the mind to one side of Flatbush, occupied extensively by old, overcrowded Jewish cemeteries, tenements of the dead. On their cramped lives was Gravesend built. Chapter for a novel. *The Autobiography of Roland Sycamore.* Come then, and let us pass a leisure hour in storytelling, and our story shall be the education of our heroes (*Repub.*, II, 376.) It isn't enough, though, for the kind of publication I have in mind, and I'm coming to New York to look for angels as well as writers. I contemplate a magazine that will reach beyond the intellectuals to publicize its cause among the more general, even popular, audience. It is my belief that the common man will understand his own interest if it is put to him plainly, that he is at heart peace-loving and always ready to rebel against the increasingly suffocating restrictions placed on him by the growing intrusions of government and oligarchy, that he is hamstrung by current American institutions and what's more only has to know it to rise up. I know you'll be sympathetic and I'm counting on your help. Get in

9

touch as soon as possible. I'll buy you a drink and we can talk about it. Incidentally, I heard you've run into my recent ex-wife. Don't listen to anything she tells you. She's a total paranoid schizophrenic with maniacal destructive instincts presently fastened on me. This is a very, very sad story, but it will have to wait till I see you.

Here a knock at the door.

"Hamstrung, for christ sake! Why the hell don't you send up some heat?"

A tall, bony, blue-eyed Swede, with hair as red as a radish and skin pale as a cadaver. Janitor's overalls and a dirty T-shirt that showed his long, flat muscles. Thor Hamstrung.

"I'm on vacation."

"What, again? Last week you were on vacation."

"No, no. I'm on vacation. Got to make a four-thirty plane back to Minnesota. Having a little celebration."

Every once in a while Hamstrung decided to take his vacation and go back to Minnesota. He called up and made a plane reservation, bought five or six quarts of bourbon and had a little celebration. By the time his plane left he was down in the basement completely stoned and having far too good a time to take any trips. Around the fourth bottle he started cursing and throwing furniture, threatened suicide on the fifth, passed out cold over the sixth, and nobody had any heat or hot water for the next twenty-four hours. Word that Hamstrung was going to Minnesota made everyone in the house edgy and irritable, especially in winter. Hamstrung hadn't been in Minnesota for twenty-five years and there was reason to doubt he ever would get to revisit his native state.

"Couldn't you stoke the furnace up a bit before starting for the old homestead?"

"No, no. I'm on vacation. Christmas take care of it."

Christmas was nominally the assistant janitor. He was a ninety year old rummy who came on like blackface and shuffle shoes, and he never took care of anything, least of

10

all himself. He was out all day looking for drink and came in at night to sleep on the coal pile, like an old cat. I could see that Hamstrung was already half crocked and beyond human influence on the subject of work.

"Why don't you come on down and have a drink?"

"Thanks, no. I'm busy," I told him.

"A friendly drink. Got some things to show you."

"Thanks, but it's too early. I just made a cup of coffee, and I'm writing, you should understand that. Besides, I have to go out soon to have tea with my aunt, and her mother don't like it when I smell of liquor. Not only that, I have a hangover."

"Sure, I understand, Dr. Sukenick, you being a professor and all. You're busy and you don't feel like a friendly drink with the filthy son of a bitch of a drunkard janitor."

"Cut it out."

Hamstrung grinned. Implication of mutual understanding, beyond position, beyond circumstances, beyond words even. Conspiracy of underdogs. He knew he had me.

Hamstrung's cellar. Fixed up with an old stove and icebox, a sagging cot, a bridge table. Since there were no windows it was always lit by a few bare bulbs. I liked it there because it reminded me—pocked concrete floor, coal grit, boarded walls—of a night-watchman job I had once near the downtown piers, where I sat from 12:30 to 7:00 A.M. reading Henry James and writing congested stories. Imagine writing like Henry James in the cellar of a dock-front warehouse. At 7:00 Rivers, the superintendent would show up, a short venomous man with a fat brutal body and a gravelly voice. I had to report to him each morning as soon as he came in and straighten up his office for him. Soon as he saw me he would toss his cigar on the floor, say, "Clean it up," and walk out. I was just a kid. When he came back he'd run his thumb over the top of his desk, hold it up, and say, "What are you, some kind of moron? And the toilets are filthy too. Do them over—I want them clean, understand?"

11

I would get the mop and start swabbing pools of muddy piss—because by that time the workers were back in the building—scrubbing shit smudge off porcelain and collecting used Kotex from the ladies' rooms, where I was frequently humiliated by the amused stares of the ladies as they walked in or out. Even then I felt a perverse admiration for Rivers. There was a kind of grandiose health in his casual brutality. I have since come to cherish my contact with Rivers as an encounter with an irreducible and problematic reality.

We sat down at the bridge table. Hamstrung opened a quart of milk and poured a drink for his huge red cat. Then he opened a quart of bourbon and poured two for ourselves.

"For the road," he said, as if he were about to gulp his drink and start hitchhiking to the airport. He did in fact gulp his drink, grunt, and help himself to another.

"Minnesota," he said, raising his glass. He held it at nose level, stared thoughtfully, furrowed his brow as if he were formulating a toast and, failing to do so, drank it anyway adding, "Don't know why I ever left."

I could have told him why he left. He left because he couldn't stand the place. But he would get around to that. When Hamstrung began cursing Minnesota, you knew it was time to leave.

"Say, listen. I want to ask you something before I go. How do you like this as a title: *Modern Vikings*."

"Sounds fine."

"But which is better, *Modern Vikings* or *Vikings of the Pacific?* I thought *Vikings of the Pacific* would get the idea across because the old Vikings never went into the Pacific. But then maybe people won't think of that. But *Modern Vikings* doesn't have anything about the Pacific. I don't know."

Hamstrung was a Seabee during World War II. He was obsessed with writing a novel about the Pacific campaign whose Scandinavian hero would be treated as the heir of the Viking spirit. As a matter of fact, Hamstrung never saw

12

the Pacific, having spent the duration in Fort Worth, and knew about as much of island warfare as I did from reading comic books when I was a kid. Moreover, since Hamstrung suffered certain debilities as a writer—sloth, ignorance, and stupidity, in the main—you wouldn't expect too much of his saga.

"What about *Modern Vikings of the Pacific*," I suggested.

"*Modern Vikings of the Pacific*. Well now, I knew you'd come up with something. Why didn't I think of that? Say, would you like to see how it begins?"

"No."

He handed me some papers.

"Be a sport. I want to know what you think."

I already knew what I thought, but I drank my bourbon and started reading.

When Fletch Swensen woke up in his foxhole that morning and found his buddy with his throat cut out, dead . . .

Another swallow of bourbon.

WhenFletchSwensenwokeupinhisfoxholethatmorningandfoundhisbuddywithhisthroatcutout, dead, he took a personal oath of vengeance against Big Stoop, the gigantic Hairy Ainu the Japs sent through the lines at night to cut up the G.I.'s which terrified them. There were many legends about Big Stoop among them being, he couldn't be killed. Fletch didn't believe you couldn't kill this terror that came at night.

Another swallow.

Tonight Big Stoop would come to cut up more G.I.'s. Fletch volunteered for an advance foxhole all the other G.I.'s were terrified of going into because of getting cut up.

To my surprise, I began enjoying myself as I glanced through the bloody pages of Hamstrung's fantasy—a cinematic awful-awful—Alan Ladd as Fletch, Anthony Quinn as Big Stoop, the tragic, misunderstood giant. Underdog

13

evil, rising from the swampy field in the dark to terrify the
G.I.'s. Dumb, offended Grendel, accursed force of darkness,
blundering through the foggy fens like Frankenstein, howling for gore. Hrothgar's men terrified of getting cut up,
Grendel's claws. Beowulf in Heorot where Grendel stalks,
swearing revenge. Hamstrung's Norse heritage. I began to
discover rude virtues. Another swallow of bourbon.

"Not bad," I said. "I especially like this part where
Fletch traps Quinn, I mean Big Stoop, with the flamethrower. 'Big Stoop was a screaming human torch, a flaming corpse who wouldn't go down.' Jack Dempsey against
Luis Firpo. 'Fletch could see his face twitch and sizzle. The
giant rushed at him, screaming, to catch him in his fiery
arms. Fletch pulled the pin of a grenade, and coolly waiting
till the last second, threw at the monster point blank and
flopped. The explosion caught Big Stoop in the belly and
he disappeared in a flash of light and smoke. Fletch was
showered with bloody guts, bits of shrapnel, and chunks of
burning flesh. He rose up, ignoring his wounds, and probed
the charred remains of the monster with his bloody bayonet.
Big Stoop was no more. Fletch had taken his revenge.'
Full of raw power."

"It's only the beginning," said Hamstrung modestly.
"Fill 'er up."

"The world hasn't done well enough by you, Hamstrung. Thanks." Seabee, sailor, jack of all trades. Crude
intellectual gropings. A handsome man in his way—high
brow, flaming widow's peak, blue eyes, straight nose, wide
mouth, firm jaw—Jack London hero.

"Go on Ronnie. I've never been what you'd call a go-
getter. Rather stay down here in my hole, mind my own
business, keep my nose clean. There aren't many people who
get what they deserve anyhow. Come on what are you
talking about? Country run by lawyers, a poor man don't
stand a chance. Help yourself."

Hamstrung had a real sense of justice. "Thanks."

14

"What's a lawyer but a professional hypocrite. We know what's what. Never believe what they tell you. Look at this."

He picked up a tabloid and read.

"Cops trap Park Avenue sex fiend. What are you talking about? What happened was some poor horny bastard had a few and propositioned a girl in the wrong place without taking a shave. Kennedy gets tough with Brazilian reds. What's that in plain English? It means some rich guys just lost a pile and don't want to lose any more. Congress schedules tax cuts. What's that mean? To me it won't mean a damn thing."

"Go fight Capitol Hill."

"Sure, it's all the big boys, who are you kidding? They own the country and they're gonna run it, so what's the use? Last time I voted was for Roosevelt in forty, and all it got me was five years in the service. Listen. Why go around the corner to mix in a dog fight? You can't win. Step on somebody else to get ahead. And then where are you? Still ten guys standing on your back."

Hamstrung was a little surly but he had good instincts.

"Losers are the nicest guys," I said.

"Sure. They have to be. But don't you worry, I get my finger in lots of things."

And sharp enough where it came to his own lookout too.

"You'd be surprised if you knew everything went on in a house. Keep your eyes open and things come your way. Help yourself."

"Thanks. I'm good."

"Before I started working for that cheap kike bastard Slumski, no offense meant . . ."

"That's all right. He's not Jewish."

"He's a cheap kike bastard all the same. I had a good job in a building on West 13th Street, nice professional people, you could expect a decent haul every Christmas.

15

One day I go up to 3A, Rubgass, a psychologist, to look at the kitchen sink. Christ, nobody there but the daughter home from boarding school, no more than fourteen but she could have been twenty, blonde, sunburned and stacked. Oh boy I'm telling you. I'm telling you. Just out of bed, hair down, nothing on but a kind of slip that ended half-way up her thighs and a rabbit's foot hanging down from her neck on a long chain. Please come in she says. Right away I knew something was up and it wasn't only me. I got a sort of sixth sense about that. She must have had a real bug because she couldn't stand still and kept touching me and skipping away. One of those sexy brats liable to start rubbing against you any minute like a cat in heat. I don't know what they teach them at those boarding schools, but it's a damn shame. So there I am under the sink, and she's eating breakfast over the sink, and let me tell you I'm not looking at the pipes. One of those innocent jobs, you know? Like nothing's happening. Am I in your way, that's okay miss, whoops sorry, not at all, could you just move a little this way, that way, my hankie just fell down here, I just have to reach over there, no need to move, don't mention it, would you like to touch my rabbit's foot, sorry, didn't mean to, just slipped, could you see if I twisted my knee, yes, that's good, if you could just lift, open, excuse me, I just have to get my prick in here, ah, oh, quite all right, oh, oh, oh, right on the kitchen floor. I swear to god. What a chance I took christ, what are you talking about, her mother walking in, no rubbers or nothing. Later on we made it on the living room couch. What a great piece. And on top of that Rubgass gave me two bucks for fixing the sink."

"No thanks, no more for me."

"After that she used to ring me when her parents weren't home. Every time I saw 3A light up I'd grab my rubbers and run. No kidding, the brat nearly gave me a heart attack. I'd get up there, she'd pull down her pants, we'd

16

start in, and then she'd say, Hurry, Mommy went to the store and said she'd be back in five minutes. Then she got hold of some sex book by whatsisname, Arthur Miller about the tropics, and she starts in with all *kinds* of crap—she wants to do it on the table, she wants to do it in the john, she wants to do it with three other people, she wants to do it on the front lawn, she wants her little brother to watch, she wants to do it in the elevator—and all I want to do is do it without winding up in prison for statutory rape. That was on my mind all the time, so you can imagine what I told her when she comes down to the basement one morning and asks me would I mind if she told her mommy all about us. After I get done telling her what would happen if she told her mommy she looks up at me like I'd insulted her and says, Well I'm sorry, I already told her. Well, I didn't even say anything, I just started looking for my suitcase. I had this friend in mind with a chicken farm near Great Barrington. Where's your mommy now, I ask. She's right outside, she says, she says she wants to talk to you alone. Out goes the kid, in comes Mrs. Rubgass, not a bad piece herself, about thirty-five, dressed nice. Eyes me up and down and what do you know she don't look angry at all. You know my daughter's at a difficult age—not so difficult, I was thinking—what with the impact of the I think we may speak frankly sexual drive and all, and I want to say that unconventional as it may seem this does a great deal for her emotional stability and self-confidence because it's been some time since she's been aching to get planked, or words to that effect. And moreover, she says giving me a fishy look, she's told me some very flattering things about you. Get that. Well, no shit, it turns out Mrs. 's been in on the secret for a week or two already, working herself into a lather till she can't stand it and has to come knocking at my door herself. Well, there I am, Barnacle Bill the Sailor. I know you don't believe it, but it's the god's honest truth. Well, what could I do but make myself agreeable. And that

17

was where I made my mistake. The trouble with me is I'm always being too nice. Because after all a man can handle just so much and the Mrs. turns out to be even livelier than the kid, and what it comes down to is there are no two ways about it, when I'm screwing one I can't be screwing the other and vice versa. So one day the brat has a jealous fit and spills everything to Rubgass and that's it. They make out like I made indecent proposals to the old lady, wife and mother, and I'm out a good job and no references either. Just because of those two bitches. There's no getting around it, a poor man is always fucked in the end, guilty or innocent. Good thing I picked up some of their jewelry when I had a chance. It saw me through."

Hamstrung shook his martyred head and spat disheartenedly at the cat who was pawing the milk bottle, falling far short in aim and dribbling strings of sputum from chin to shirt front.

"Miserable ungrateful beast," he grumbled. "Now ain't that one for the books? There's no justice."

I saw he really had his heart in it so I asked him why he didn't put that down instead of the stuff he broke his balls to make up.

"Put it down! What do you think I want to do, write dirty stories?"

"Sorry."

"I got ways of making money before it comes to that. If I had to depend on that kike bastard Slumski for a living—no offense . . . Tell you what. What I do with that son-a-bitch?"

Mumbling and fumbling through his pockets, he pulls a wristwatch out by an end of its strap and holds it up.

"This here just come to me yesterday is worth a good forty fifty bucks. I can give it to you for fifteen. Antimagnetic and all. Here, take a look."

"Thanks no. Got a watch. A bar-mitzvah present. I always get it repaired, it's a superstition."

18

"Sweep hand, see here. Ten dollars as a friend. What you say? Keep it in mind. You never know when your watch might get hooked. Maybe you need some cheap razor blades? No? Or cut-rate rubbers, a bachelor like you? Hey? I seen that blonde you been bringing here. Bet you could use two dozen a week. Go on. Interested in transistor radios, nylon stockings, they sell good. Wholesale bubble gum? Dirty two-language comic books, Spanish-English, these jerks buy anything. Feel like a clean young piece, ten bucks a throw? Need seaman's papers for a hundred dollars? Want to know where to fix a parking ticket? Maybe you like spicy pictures, Gigi and her St. Bernard. No. You ain't interested. Neither am I. You be surprised all the people like that kind of stuff."

"No I wouldn't."

"Sure. Tell you what it is. One woman gets just like another. You got to spice it up. Some guys go in for young stuff, some like it two at a time. All kinds. I used to know a guy was crazy for fat whores. And his brother-in-law had this thing where he just liked to watch. I once heard about this fella who photographed pussies. Had hundreds of them all different. Used to make enlargements the size of a wall. The bright boys forget about women altogether. That's going a little too far maybe. Lots of you eggheads like that, ain't you? Like some guys in the Seabees, after it all the time. Grab it while you're pissing if you don't look out."

"Yeah."

"Yeah. Once in a while now, that's a different story. A nice-looking young guy like you must be getting propositions all the time. All sorts of creeps and perverts. Got to watch your step. Can't trust every jerk you meet in a bar. Some cute fella's liable to pull a blackjack first thing you turn your head. You got to know who you're talking to. How's about it, Ronnie?"

"You got the wrong guy."

"Now don't get *me* wrong. You know me, Ronnie. It's

19

just that the world's getting so damn full of queers you need a program. Can't tell the fish from the fruits. It's these fucking intellectuals, coming around taking advantage of young sailors—I seen enough of that when I was shipping out. Don't tell me buddy. I seen it, I seen it. They say New York is all tied up by faggots . . . interior decorating, publicity . . . Madison Avenue pricks running everything . . . them and the fruity Harvard eggheads, a poor horny bastard don't stand a chance if he's straight. It's you smart-aleck college fruits and slick New York Jew banker fairy beatniks, getting us into wars to make the world safe for Wall Street and starting all this pinko miscegenation with the colored moving into every neighborhood they god damn please . . . not that I got anything against jigs . . . just let them stay out of my house . . . I don't care what language they speak, Spanish, Zulu, or Siamese. If you wise guys just leave honest working people alone without trying to improve the world, maybe it wouldn't get worse every day. One thing I don't like is a guy can't mind his own business . . . always sticking his nose where he ain't wanted . . . coming down here . . . drink a man's good whiskey . . . come on like a fucking queer . . . acting like king shit . . . who the hell you think you are?"

He banged his fist on the table, tried to get up, and fell back into his chair. Beard stubbled his face like flecks of blood. "Drop the bomb," he muttered, "bomb them to hell, bomb the shit out of them." Let's get out of here. Air of an underdog with the instincts of a degenerate. Not on our side.

Going through the entrance hall I glimpsed Slumski the landlord skulking around a corner. He didn't like to show himself at the house—afraid of tenants asking for things. I never heard him say anything but no. Walk up to him and say, "Hello, nice . . ." "No!" he yells before you

20

can get it out. Reported he also says "rent," "evict," and "What's in it for me," but I never heard him. "No!" Definitely not on our side.

Retreat to the ivory tower. No one ever visits me here. You'd think I was living in the North Pole for all the people I've seen in the last two weeks. A can of sardines and coffee. I count my money. A five and three singles in my wallet plus two nickels and five pennies, eight fifteen I have and my bank book has ten twenty-seven equals eighteen forty-two from my last and final check. After which find work. I must borrow money.

Dear Dr. Sukenick:

I think it might be advisable should you find the opportunity to drop into my office if you would want to discuss a certain matter regarding a Mr. Moosoff this afternoon at one o'clock sharp.

Q. Whitebread Blackhead, Acting Chairman

"In the matter of style," I say in answer to a question, "the basic virtues, for all ordinary purposes, are clarity, directness, and concision. In realizing these qualities, we must first of all give our attention to diction, or the choice of words. Diction is a fundamental part of rhetoric . . ." The students listen, take notes, stare out the window. One kid, slouched in a seat at the back, regards me with a permanent sarcastic sneer. Another, not too bright, tries to catch my eye with an ostentatious gaze in order to show his earnestness. A girl who comes to class dressed like a French whore indulges a conditioned reflex to smirk at her neighbors every time I open my mouth. The receptive girl in the front row is doing deep-breathing exercises again, and working her legs up to expose her attentive thighs. She stares

21

at me with big drippy eyes which advertise awe, lust, virginity, and a desire for self-immolation. I would like to keep her, mildly drugged, in my apartment for a week, then quietly sell her into the white slave market.

After class a few students gather around my desk to exhibit their interest. "Dr. Sukenick, don't you think that diction is a fundamental part of rhetoric. . . ?"

I was walking to my office when Whitebread Blackhead stuck his head out a door and beckoned me with his ponderous wink. He liked to make a sporty impression. Your friend and mine. We went into his office. I had no use for this two-bit academic Machiavelli, but we got along in a certain way. Whitebread Blackhead was an administration shill. He didn't quite regard teachers as a dime a dozen, but he wished they were. He ran the department as if he were dealing with a collection of con-men and this, in the circumstances, corresponded to my sense of being a furtive interloper.

"Well, Mr.—ah—Suchanitch."

"Sukenick."

"Yes. Of course. We have such a large staff this year. You have two Composition courses, is that correct?"

"Yes."

"And we have finished your round of class observations this semester, I believe."

My classes had been inspected six times in the last two weeks.

"I suppose you are interested in the—ah—suggestions that developed in the course of observation?" He thumbed through a folder on his desk.

"Certainly. There's always room for improvement isn't there?"

"In your case . . . um. On the whole though . . . you were hired at the last minute, were you not?"

"That's right."

22

"Yes. Well, the report is not bad, not bad. Not too bad. One observer remarks a certain spontaneity in your classroom style."

"Really."

"Yes. He suggests you prepare your lectures more thoroughly. Another observation is that you seem to have a grasp of the subject matter. Very nice. Very nice. I see that one man found your classes—as he puts it—boring."

"After all, they're Composition courses. I find them a little boring myself sometimes. I mean we all do. Don't we? Now and then?"

Whitebread Blackhead laughed briefly. He is the only person I've ever known who could maintain a straight face while laughing.

"I see one remark here that you don't give the impression of being very interested in teaching?"

"I can't understand that."

"That you are in the habit of making irrelevant humorous digressions from the subject matter?"

"Only by way of illustration."

"And it seems that during one session you forgot to take attendance. You know we can't tolerate that sort of thing, Mr. Subenitch."

"It must have slipped my mind. I'll see to it."

"Do. For a young instructor, you're not doing too badly. With some effort you should come along, you should come right along, and if registration doesn't drop next semester . . . You don't mind this observation business, by the way? None of us like it, of course. It's just one of those things."

"Well, it's for our own good, really, isn't it?"

"One of the observers seemed to think you might have resented his presence. I don't know what led him to suspect that. He mentions certain arch comments to the class."

23

"My sense of humor, no doubt."

"Well, try to keep it under control. Now. What's all this about Mr. Moosoff? He plagiarized Hemingway on his Hemingway imitation?"

"It was the best thing he wrote all term," I explained. "The rest of his work was worthless."

"But, he was—admittedly—cheating?"

"I don't completely condemn cheating," I began. "First of all you can't prevent it. Secondly, I find if often requires more effort by the student, and certainly more ingenuity. Third he sometimes learns more despite himself through cheating than he would by cramming."

The fact is I empathize with cheating, a childish and perverse tendency to find greater satisfaction in cheating than in winning being undoubtedly one of the things that unsuits me for practical life.

"But, you don't think—in any case—he's qualified to pass?"

"No."

"Then. Why not fail him?"

"If my classes are going to be filled with unqualified students I can't see much point in failing them. Besides, if I failed him he wouldn't be able to play football, and that's what he's here for, to play football."

Whitebread Blackhead chuckled. It was his famous judicious chuckle which he always chucked when he was about to give somebody the shaft.

"Of course, final decision in such matters always rests with the instructor. But nota bene, Mr. Suckanitch, nota bene: while you take it upon yourself to wrongfully defend malefactors from authority, who—one wonders—will take the trouble to defend you; particularly in this faculty where your position is—allow me to point out—practically non-existent, and, chuck-chuck, rapidly becoming more so. Mark me, and take counsel for another day."

He meant I could forget about next semester. I was fired. So much the better. We parted on the best terms, he cordial, me smiling—you would have thought he'd just given me tenure. The truth is I like to get fired. The times I've been fired—all too few by my reckoning—I remember vividly and count among the happiest in my life. There's an art to getting fired—a matter of knowing how to maneuver yourself into a delicate position between working and malingering. It's really an act of economic suicide for the sake of personal salvation. So long, Professor, and thanks.

Space race experts claim to have theoretically overcome all barriers to cosmic travel, except the incalculable effect of total isolation on the human organism. Henry Sliesinger reports the news.

Roger. The view from here is magnificent, magnificent (see tinted snapshot verso). I have only been traveling a week but it already seems like light years. Our little earth there looks like a minor invention of Rand-McNally and the sun is the small change of the universe. The sky is deep black and swarms with stars big as silver dollars. The planets glow each with its peculiar color; e.g., Venus saffron, Earth pistachio, Mars lavender. The frequent displays of dazzling interstellar light are something that can only be seen: they include none of the shades in our earthly spectrum. What is that smell? I am very worried about current events. I listen regularly to Henry Sliesinger reports the news and let me tell you things are going from bad to worse. Generally speaking though my mental state is euphoric to say the least. Talk of peace and quiet! Only would you please stop sending me those messages about the instruments. What do I care about the instruments? Oh boy. The hell with instruments.

What is that, did those jokers ship some Limburger

25

cheese or what is it? This wasn't programmed. I don't want anything going on up here that isn't programmed. No surprises, get it? Do you read me? Over. It's probably another one of their lousy experiments. That's one hell of a damn nudnick trick. Wise guys. How do I know they're just putting me through a few fast orbits around Mars? That's what they said, yeah. I'll bet. Before they locked me up in here. Why bother bringing me back to Earth when for the same trouble they could probably shoot me all the way out to Saturn? Sure. Why spend all that money just to retrieve a lousy colonel? They got all the colonels they need, what do they care? I should never have taken this job.

Instruments. What instruments. With all the worries I got they think I have time to fool with instruments? They must be cracked. What I need is a nice piece of ass. Like that secretary, what was her name, who we all laid after the space travel convention, Cookie, when I slipped the Spanish fly in her martini. That was a hell of a thing to do, the girl nearly killed herself. Oh well, it would have been a beautiful death. What a son of a bitch I am. Me and Fatty Arbuckle. Some piece she was, we had fun with her that time all the same. What I wouldn't do to her if she were here right now, so help me. Christ, there's not even enough room in here to masturbate. They might have thought of that, the cocks. And the food! I mean, I'm not fussy, but couldn't they think of anything better than this toothpaste? A little Jello or something, a nice can of soup. Do you read me? Over. Over. A little Jello. Do you hear me? You fuckups? Wise guys. Are they just stupid or are they out to get me? What did I do? Why me? All right so maybe I was a little cocky with the general. I'm a space man, ain't I? It makes good copy. I know, he thinks I'm horning in on his endorsements. But is that any reason to hang me up like this? After all, what are we in this business for?

Hello. Hello. What time is it at least? I keep forgetting to wind my watch. Do you read me? Over. Losing track. Over. Over. Can't get a decent night's sleep. Over. Night. When is that? Do you read me? Over.

Drinking too many tubes of coffee. Over.

I think I'm having a heart attack. Over. Over.

Everything is very slow. Over. Over.

Amnesia of the universe, thought without memory.

no   syntax

27

uP

over

over

over

over

a   l   p   h   a

b

e

t

uP

s

o

u

P

THE ADVENTURES OF STROP BANALLY

Strop put down the phone and switched his attention to the girl with his unvarying bold smile, that fixed grimace which is simultaneously a challenge, an insult, and a gesture of complicity.

"Old times' sake?" he asked, laying on the table the appeal with which she had implicitly come.

"You could put it that way."

"La Cienega. Wilshire and Western."

"I'm going to be married," she said.

"Wonderful. Congratulations." He stopped and tapped his finger on the desk, looking at her. She seemed nervous.

"I got to New York a few months ago," she said finally. "It's a tough town."

"Sure. Anything at all. Consider it done. Now," he said without batting an eyelash, "how would you like it? The desk is big enough, but the rug is nice and soft."

She frowned. "The price of admission," she remarked. She got up and walked smiling to his side of the desk. "You haven't changed," she said. "Remember the tar pits where we did it the first time?"

his coarse, familiar laughter

—the one obvious vulgarity of his demeanor

his bright green eyes

TEEN PUNKS TERRORIZE STRAPHANGERS

It was on the Seventh Avenue local, about two o'clock. I was sitting reading my paper when I noticed a commotion at the other end of the car. As I watched I heard a yelp of anguish that pierced the roar of the subway. Approaching the scene I became aware of muffled groans, an occasional thud, and the stomp and howl of rock 'n' roll. I saw a white-haired, balding old man on his hands and knees,

30

bleeding from his eyes and mouth. Just as I came up a
young fellow swung his heavy booted leg and caught the
old guy at the top of his breast bone with a crunching
sound. I wanted to leap at him but found myself barred by
a crowd of young hoods exactly like the one standing over
the old guy. The kick had turned him over on his back
and blood was bubbling out of his mouth. The kicker
punched one of his buddies on the arm threateningly and
said, "Come on, chicken shit." Then they all started jumping on the old guy, kicking him, grinding into him with
their heels. The crowd looked on, terrified. I turned to
them and screamed, "Do something! Let's do something!" They looked at me with horror-struck, helpless eyes.
The kids were finishing the job, kicking and stomping to the
rhythm of the rock 'n' roll which had loudened to a volume
that drowned out the noise of the subway. I ran to the
kid who seemed to be the instigator, shaking him as hard as
I could by the shoulder. "Why did you do that?" I shouted.
He shrugged and said, "He looked at me." Then he turned
his back and I noticed that he and all the kids wore black
jackets lettered in white: "The Roundtable Gents." As we
pulled into the next station the Gents posted themselves at
the doors to hold them open and prevent the train from
starting. They had zip guns, ice picks, lead pipes, switch
knives, tire chains, blackjacks, baseball bats, sharpened
umbrella sticks, sawed off shotguns, straight razors, .22
rifles, Molotov cocktails, brick-loaded stockings and garri-
son belts with knife-sharp buckles. They herded us out
onto the platform in single file. A fine old gentleman with
a straw hat brandished his cane indignantly at one of the
kids: "See here. I'm on my way to my broker. What do you
mean?"

"Say Stoopnagel," said the kid, "the old fart wants to
know what we mean." They knocked off his hat and split
his skull with a lead pipe for his trouble. They looked for
approval to the one who seemed to be their chief. Stoop-

31

nagel was much bigger than the rest. Now and then he nodded almost imperceptibly at something they had done. He kept his head cocked to a transistor radio that the tinny throb of the rock 'n' roll came from. He held the radio next to his ear and on his pocked and pimpled face a thick leer gleamed as his eyes shone with the blank delight of an idiot.

"Okay, folks," one of the Gents said. "We think you folks is a little dirty, so we're gonna do you a big favor and give you a bath."

They lined us up in front of a foul smelling men's room and made us drop our wallets and valuables in a heap at the door as they herded us in. On line in front of me was a pretty and well-bred young co-ed. As we approached the door one of the Gents came over and looked her up and down with a sneer.

"How's about you and me bein' friends," he said. The girl moved her lips but was too scared to talk. The Gent pulled out a zip gun and shoved it up under her skirt, working it around.

"We're gonna be friends," he said. "Doncha like that?"

"Y-y-yes," the girl managed to say. He ordered her to where a group of Gents were standing around a table. They made her strip at point of knife, reaching out to sample her breasts now and then, sneering and moistening their lips. They had made her lie down on the table and were having a great time getting her to utter wanton obscenities, when a mounted policeman clattered up shouting, "I'll teach you young punks. The law is officers first—and then their horses." With that he ripped open his fly whence burst a titanic cock erect that he grasped with his strong right hand and, plying it like a billy club, scattered the Gents hither and yon. As they ran to and fro in confusion, an immense woman in blackface and bandanna appeared on the scene and, to whines and plaints of "Mammy," and "We wuz only havin' fun," hauled them off harum-scarum while

32

chanting in a fine and emphatic contralto, "Mah o *mah,* but you evah-lovin boll weevils is gonna *ketch* it."

RED OR DEAD

The monthly meeting of the Committee Against Nuclear Holocaust was called to order on the question of whether to ban Communists from the organization. The negative side was argued by the radical wing consisting largely of undergraduates and women in menopause. They were opposed by a group of respectable and level-headed men and women who, judging by appearance, were members of the liberal professional community. Also present was a conspicuously unobtrusive fellow in spectacles who said nothing but took notes assiduously, and who I at the time assumed was the group secretary. One of the representatives of the Infantile Left rose to charge his opposition with attempting to administer a loyalty test, and complained about the right of association, freedom of speech, the Fifth Amendment, bills of attainder, the Alien and Sedition Laws, the Test Acts, the Court of the Star Chamber, and the characteristic timidity of the liberal bourgeois humanitarian. A distinguished gentleman, at a guess a New Deal lawyer who had made his pile, replied that much as he fervently sympathized with the young man's idealistic point of view, the practical complexities of the situation did not permit a simple commitment, and one could not be too careful about the legitimacy of the movement in the eyes of the public. A feverish spinster with hooked nose, jagged teeth, and pointy chin was understandably worried about witch hunts. A short man with a German accent called for restraint on both sides and threatened to walk out unless the resolution were approved. At this a pregnant redhead jumped up to say she didn't care beans for understanding when her child was liable to be born with two heads, and what did we intend to do about it?

33

Here a fat gent who looked like a professor emeritus rose to urge patience for, if there was one thing history taught us, it was that on the whole, as had been written, all things come to pass, and concluded with a senile chuckle. An Ivy League type wanted to talk about the motives of the national steering committee in proposing the resolution, but after much deliberation this was ruled irrelevant to the question on a point of order. Here the advocates of civil liberties became thoroughly aroused, the spirit of caution shook his mighty locks, the question was called, and I, totally exasperated, was on my feet babbling that as far as I was concerned I was of the party of cowards, that if they intended to make us choose both liberty and death I would be the first to come and lick our masters' hands, tail wagging, that if anything, I agreed with the woman with the two heads about her baby, and that I intended to go out and prostitute my principles, my ideals, and my way of life to the first comer who found within the dictates of his creed, that he could afford to let us stay alive.

This outburst was received with neither applause nor abuse but with what I gathered was a tolerant silence, which I counted as an opportunity, if not an invitation, to leave the meeting.

PEACE MONGERS SOFT ON PINKS?

Before I had taken many steps I heard someone calling to me: "Mr. Sukenick. Wait up a minute." It was the nondescript individual from the meeting, the note taker.

"Mind if I walk with you?" he asked.

"It's a public thoroughfare."

"My name's Gerald."

"All right Gerald." He was so innocuous looking that it was hard to believe he was really there. I figured him as a minor executive in a big company.

"I was pretty interested in what you were saying in there."

"Good."

"It struck me as about the only really forceful thing to be said all evening. It's a pretty incompetent group, don't you think?"

I looked him over again, but was enlightened only to the extent of verifying his presence.

"Impotent," I said. "Impotence is the word for them. But I don't hold it against them. It's the common fate. Impotence and futility."

"The monolithic state? Corporate capitalism? The cold war?"

"Just so," said I, looking at him with increased curiosity.

"What about the open society, pluralism, enlightened self-interest? What about the Gross National Product?"

"All nonsense," I said, deciding on shock tactics.

"Isn't that interesting?" he marveled. "Could you elaborate a little?"

"It's simple," I said. "Madmen. Assassins. Judo and small arms practice. Chalk slogans in the subway, stick decals on auto bumpers: 'Join the American Revolution.' Write letters to the *Times*. Infiltrate the Boy Scouts, Hadassah, the American Legion. Win over the toilers, especially in sensitive industries. Get them to steal the nuclear warheads and hide them in their attics. Picket the Pentagon. Kidnap Everett Dirksen, quietly, so his absence isn't noticed. Hold mass demonstrations. Terror. Arson. Devastation. Anarchy. Annihilation."

"Isn't that something? Well, what do you know? By an odd coincidence we seem to be in front of my apartment building. Allow me to invite you up for a few minutes."

"Well, I don't know . . ."

"Come on," he said, putting his arm around my shoulders. "You can't disappoint me."

He conducted me into the elevator and twenty floors

up where I was ushered into a windowless, metal-walled room with a desk and two chairs, the door clicking shut behind me. Gerald sat down and motioned me to the other chair. He then reached for his wallet and opened it on the desk, allowing me, before he snapped it shut, a glimpse of a badge that might for all I know have been FBI, CIA, Internal Revenue, or Captain Midnight's Secret Squadron.

"Say now, Gerald," I said, "what's going on?"

He looked down, slipped off his glasses, and I found myself staring at two pale blue marbles whose glance would have paralyzed a snake.

"That's Mr. Gerald," he said. "Now, let's go over some of that ground again, can we? Did you say force and violence?"

"Wait a minute. Wait. I was only kidding. Can't you fellows take a joke?"

"Look here, Ronnie . . ."

"That's Mr. Sukenick."

"Sukenick. What would that be? Polish? Russian, possibly?"

"It's Jewish."

"That right. As I was saying, you don't have to answer any questions, if you don't want to. You're not under oath. Yet. You can just sit there all night if you feel like it and waste your time and mine. I don't care. I get paid for this. But I want to point out you're in a tight spot. I, personally, have nothing against you, you understand that. I'd just as well see you get out of this. But let me tell you, my friend, you better give me some straight answers because we know all about you, see?"

"And what's going to prevent me from walking right out of here?"

"You intellectuals are pretty smart, aren't you?" He opened a drawer, took out a dossier, and began looking through the papers. "Born July fourteenth, hey. Fall of the Bastille? Liberation? Revolution? You admit to that?"

"I was born July fourteenth, yeah."

"I think you have what we call tendencies, Ronnie. Definite tendencies. Now let's get down to the nitty gritty. In 1944, at Camp Wackanooky, they caught you, little Ronnie, playing with yourself in the toilet."

"I was only twelve."

"Around 1950, almost arrested for feeling up a girl on the BMT."

"It was rush hour, I couldn't help it. She was touchy."

"Seduction of your friend's wife in the bathroom during a party."

"He wasn't my friend. She asked for it."

"More recently, the corruption of the pubescent daughter of a colleague—and I'm skipping."

"I deny that. There was no question of corruption."

"Then there was Nanette. Remember Nanette?" he asked, regarding me with his stony eyes.

"That was Paris. It was a different country."

"And speaking of Paris, what about Marie?"

"Marie!" I broke into a sweat. "I never heard of her. I swear. I was only watching. It was the Beaux Arts Ball. Everybody knows what goes on there."

"Scratch an intellectual and find a pervert. Never fails. Everybody's got something to hide."

"All right, all right, I admit it. A spy, a lecher, anything you like."

"Force and violence? Conspiring to overthrow?"

"Conspiring to overthow, advocating to conspire, overthrowing to advocate. Now tell me what you want or let me go."

"Just a minute, my friend, not so fast," he said, rubbing his throat in a peculiar way. "Now that I know exactly where you stand," he continued, lowering his face, "I can reveal my true identity." And suddenly he sprouted a bushy black beard, a set of blackened, broken teeth as he slowly peeled the skin of his face, a rubber mask!

37

"Now, comrade, you see me as I am," he said in a thick Slavic accent and, whipping out a bottle of vodka, added, "Let us drink. *Za vashe zdorovye!*" Then time snapped to a stop, his arm froze in mid-air, his neck stiffened, his hand was caught raised in a perpetual toast, and he was left with his expansive smile fixed on eternity, nostalgic and slightly absurd, like a photo in an old newspaper.

The Adventures of Strop Banally

By RONALD SUKENICK

This first novel by an obviously talented and intelligent young writer is another one of those tales in the manner of what has aptly been termed "rebellious farce," introduced with so much success by such as J. P. Donleavy and Joseph Heller. It concerns the adventures—sexual, financial and, finally, political—of a ferocious rascal who trades on his irresistible sexual appeal, his All-American appearance (he looks like he could have stepped out of a cigarette ad), and an incredible competitive drive for power that he seems to indulge not for the sake of conquest but simply for the pleasure of exercising it. Surely to equal Strop Banally in sheer rapacity one would have to go to the annals of the great "robber barons" of American industry, or perhaps to the annals of our own age, if they are ever written.

Strop Banally, when we first see him, is known as a "boy genius" in the communications industry—which seems to mean that he has his adroit finger in advertising, public relations, television, movies and publishing; but he is also known to some as "the Albert Einstein of the pornographic film." Nobody knows exactly where he came from, for, as the author informs us, he makes up his past as he goes along so that by now nobody can tell the truth from the fiction. From here on we are treated to a wild series of comic feats, improbable *coups*, unbelievable conquests, and gratuitous crafty machinations. We learn how Banally

38

masquerades as a college professor, turns a sorority party into a bacchanale, seduces women of all ages and conditions, plots to corner the Persian melon market (perhaps the hilarious highpoint of the novel), hucksters dubious securities in a manner worthy of P. T. Barnum, peddles political influence he doesn't have, and gulls a Congressional investigating committee.

Plot and machination are most characteristic of Banally, for he is a con-man in the spirit of Melville and Felix Krull, and it is the confidence game that intrigues him above all. It is never enough, for example, that he seduce the cloistered daughter—he must conquer the furious mother as well, and then defraud her innocent, well-meaning husband. Why? The string of *fabliaux* which constitute Strop Banally's picaresque career could comprise a handbook to success in our society, to success, that is, as a never-ending end in itself, pure, aimless ambition gone wild and feeding on its own substance.

It is his fantastic success that distinguishes Banally from the ordinary picaro. The picaresque hero traditionally has been used in the novel to reveal the contradictions and hypocrisies of society by exposure to a cynical outsider eager to exploit them. But Banally is not outside society: he is in it; in fact he is practically on top of it. His is not the cynicism of the rock bottom but the cynicism of the top. He is an infinitely more knowing Gatsby, Gatsby without illusions, Gatsby "wised up" with the experience of the last forty years. None of the sentimental yearnings of Fitzgerald's quixotic hero. He is not Quijote, he is Sancho and he knows what he is about. How should he not? Sancho has governed us for a hundred years, after all, and as a practical man, he knows his business. And yet, Sukenick seems to be telling us, through one of the minor ironies of history, he, the practical man, his pragmatism inadequate to grasp the complexities of contemporary reality, has suddenly become the antic dreamer, leading us all to catastrophe after catas-

39

trophe while Quijote, the poet, the scholar, the visionary, stands by comprehending it all quite well, but powerless to do anything except deliver fruitless warnings and offer solace after the debacle.

The novel employs the by now quite conventional artifice of the plot narrative that no longer believes in itself as a means of approaching reality, and is not, therefore, meant to be taken very seriously. The main device is the hero whose implausible series of exploits (do we discern sardonic echoes of Augie March?) is used to test and expose society. It is necessarily on the characterization of Strop Banally that the book stands or falls.

One regrets to say that it falls. "Blinded by envy and contempt," the author writes, "I with exasperating ineptitude begin groping my way into the identity of my incredible hero. Keeping him with desperate concentration before my mind's eye, struggling to feel how it would be to be Strop Banally, I seek to capture his reality, to imagine him." In fact the author never succeeds in entering imaginatively into the identity of his hero. One wonders why he could ever wish to do so. "Why do I keep coming back to Strop Banally?" the narrator asks at the outset. "Why am I fascinated by the dirty story of his life?" Pertinently, he speaks of himself as "utterly sick of my narcissism, my paranoid distortions, the life I have reduced to the limits of my own mind and which is suffocating there." At the heart of Sukenick's envy of Banally is the ease, indeed the mindless gusto with which Strop sails through life. Banally is described as "effective, insouciant, at home in heaven or hell." May one venture to suggest that basically the author's compelling drive is to feel at home somewhere, anywhere at all in fact, and that this accounts for his obsession with his hero's predatory nature.

Is the game worth the candle? We are bound to say that under the circumstances one could hardly expect Banally to come to life. For in seeking to identify with his hero, the author seeks nothing less than a prostitution of himself and the rape of what he desires. We do not deny the author's sincerity in seeking these things; indeed, in his book we can say that he finds them. For Strop Banally remains a gross and empty character, offensive as a practical joke, and the novel has the effect of a crude and obvious anecdote.

At the end we find the disillusioned narrator bitterly taking leave of his hero and retreating from the world, not indeed to the charterhouse or the ivory tower but, being more up to date, to indulge himself "in the immediacy of desire, in the fulfillments of revery, in the excitement of dissolution" (there are some nuggets here). But Banally's complete triumph is his creator's defeat, for Strop remains a symbol, an abstraction, unreal. It could not be otherwise. We must conclude that it would have been better had the book gone unwritten or, at least, unpublished.

I'd been told that she had des jolies fesses. I'd also heard she was a prostitute by choice, not necessity, and that caught my interest. I knew at a glance that my instinct had been right. It wasn't that she was beautiful. She wasn't beautiful but sexually appetizing. There are beautiful women who don't stir the penis. You look at them as if they were designs, abstractions. They don't appeal to the sexual imagination. But one look at this girl and I went, hopping with lust, to take her arm and follow wherever she might lead me.

She was one of those Paris Américaines who refuse to speak English even with a compatriot because they want to perfectionner la langue. This familiar tropisme is usually due less to linguistic ardor than a desire to obliterate one's own despised genesis and start new in a superior soil. Though she wasn't dressed for her part, her clothes revealed a promising souplesse. Her tailored shirt was

41

covered by a somewhat collegiate-looking sweater, loose around the waist, but showing up the rise and division of her breasts. Under a short, tight skirt, that was neither too tight, nor too short, her jolies fesses undulated like a suave animal. No lipstick, fresh-faced, without makeup of any kind, très jeune fille. In fact she gave an impression of innocence, of défense de toucher, même, with her brown tennis court hair, her childish eyes, her healthy freckles and her well-bred nose. Why have I always refused to learn what money can buy? All you have to do to get what you want is put down the price. It was so easy I'd never thought of it before. Just open your wallet and pay for it, simple as that. The idea was so powerful that at a certain point, walking with her on my arm, I could have wept for the time I had wasted.

"How much further?" I asked her.

"Pas loin," she said. Her accent was almost as bad as mine.

We went through an obscure street near Châtelet to a dark hotel and climbed to an impoverished chambre meublée. It was like stepping into an erotic fantasy. The walls were covered with large, obscene photographs. They exhibited fornication in every conceivable form, position and combination, a variety that might have stupefied a Hindu sect. Cocks were shoved into every available orifice of the human anatomy, cunts, ass-holes, mouths, armpits. There were complicated daisy chains of from three to what looked like about ten. There were crowds of men going at one woman and crowds of women going at a man. There were orgies, gang-bangs, women with women, with apes, with donkeys, with St. Bernards, with basset hounds, with chihuahuas. I sat down on the iron-frame bed that was practically the only piece of furniture in the room, and as I did so I realized that a good many of the photos were of my petite amie.

She sat down next to me, her wide mouth fixed in a

42

smile tense with license. I grabbed her arm and abruptly pulled her toward me. Her head landed in my lap and she began biting my cock through my pants. It was like touching a trigger. I had a short orgasm right there, then cautiously pushed her away—I wanted to make sure I got my money's worth. She leaned back and looked at herself in a mirror, patting her hair. Then, as if we were meeting at a thé dansant, she said, "Je m'appelle Nanette. Et vous?"

"Waldo," I answered immediately, for some reason withholding my right name. On second thought, this seemed a little corny, so I added, "Mais on m'appelle Nifty."

"Très bien Neeftee. Vous le voudriez tout de suite, ou préfériez-vous voir les films d'abord?"

"Mais ne perdras-tu pas de temps?" I asked. After paying her I was near flat broke and didn't want her charging me time and a half plus a surcharge for the audio-visual aids.

"Ça ne fait rien. Je ne travaille que pour me plaire. C'est importé des Etats-Unis," she added with a wink. "Ils fabriquent en plus les meilleures capotes."

She switched off the lights. A square of radiant white appeared in the darkened room, was filled with flashing numbers, geometrical fragments, then steadied to the image of a luxe modern office, a long free-form desk, and speaking on the phone behind it (I've seen this before) a young, hip-looking executive, knowing, debonair. A door is opened by a chic secretary who admits a young girl (she looks familiar) and exits. She is a mere teen-ager, sexy, flirtatious, virginal. She takes a seat at the other side of the desk, fingers her pocketbook, looking uncomfortable on the ascetic modern chair. The man nods to her, covers the mouthpiece of the phone, says something, speaks into the phone, looks her over in an obvious way while he puffs on a pipe. She is speaking, smiling, looking shy. He nods understandingly, says something with an encouraging smile. She speaks again. She

43

apparently wants something, a job maybe. He hangs up, speaks, gestures toward the desk and the floor with clear lascivious intent (I know them both). She looks shocked, coy, thoughtful. Gets up and walks over to him with a lewd smile. He laughs, points to the desk. She lies down. He says something. She lifts up her sweater exposing her bare breasts. He's still sitting behind the desk, refrains from touching her, gives another order, and in a minute she's completely naked. He makes her go and get something from the other side of the room. It's a pair of handcuffs. He shackles her to the desk, and, while her mouth repeatedly shapes the word no, he stands up, unzips his fly, and sticks it in. After a few thrusts he withdraws to relight his pipe. By now she's wriggling on the desk with her legs spread, asking for it. He gives her a quick one. She asks for more. The secretary enters and, at a word, takes off her clothes and stands passive like a drugged slave. He makes the secretary, who I now recognize as Nanette, play with the girl on the desk while he sits in his chair and caresses them both. Nanette responds with the dreamy obedience of a hypnotic, then has what appears to be an extended epileptic fit, and sinks exhausted to the floor. By this time the girl on the desk is performing surprising gymnastic feats, begging and pleading and moaning. The man rings a buzzer. Enter a junior executive type. He responds to her entreaties with lusty gusto after which she shows her gratitude by lapping his limp and dripping organ. The two men light cigars and make her do it with the office boy as they laugh and applaud. Then they show her the concealed movie camera that has been recording the whole scene and release her from the desk. They laugh and punch one another on the arm. Heedless, Sugarplum gets up and leaps for the junior executive's fly. The office boy jumps Nanette, the projector speeds up, Strop goes for the office boy and there is a mad chase and jumble of flesh during which everyone turns to butter as the reel runs off and out.

44

When Nanette turned on the light she was nude. She put her hands behind her head to emphasize the thrust of her breasts. Her nipples were stiff and plump. They quivered as she walked toward me. "Qu'est-ce que vous pensez? J'aime prendre les poses comme ça pour les photographies. Mais," she says very politely, "voulez-vous que je vous suce un peu . . . ou bien peut-être—" and reaching into her night table hands me a short, mean-looking cat o'nine tails, and throws herself face down across my lap. I flip her onto the bed and pull off my pants, she lies flat, opens her arms, wriggles her pelvis, and says in a stage whisper, "Allons, chéri."

It was like the climax of an orgasm which had begun an hour before when I first saw her. The girl never had a chance. One plunge and Boom, it was over, more of a detonation than an ejaculation. I came out feeling a little guilty on her account, but why worry about it, what did I think I was paying her for? Therefore I was surprised when she opened her eyes on me and said in English: "I suppose *you* enjoyed yourself."

"What the fuck do you think I'm doing here," I told her. It was something I always wanted to say to a woman— this time I supposed I had the right.

No sooner were the words out of my mouth than tears started oozing from her eyes. "That's right," she said, "I'm nothing but a whore. Go on. You can talk to me like that. You paid for the privilege. But just don't forget that if you hadn't paid for it you could never have laid a hand on me and you know it. I wouldn't even have acknowledged your existence. Ordinarily I wouldn't spit on the likes of you. This isn't my life. I do this for fun. All I want out of you is your cock, and it's a pretty feeble one too. I make you pay because I'm using you, I enjoy that." She fumbled in the night-table drawer and threw some bills at me. "Go on, take it. You have to pay for your women, you may need it. I could buy and sell you, or any man I pleased, but no one

45

touches me unless he pays for it first. If you think that means I'll get down on my hands and knees and suck your cock, or let you stick it up my ass, or hold a gang-bang for your friends, or screw your pet dog, or pose for dirty pictures just because you say so, you're making a mistake. Why, I wouldn't let a man hold my hand without making him beg. I see them on the street looking at me like dogs in heat just because I don't wear any underwear, trying to see my breasts, imagining how it would feel to run their hands up my thigh—it's disgusting. I like to screw and I get it when I like it, otherwise nobody gets near my ass. Once in boarding school two sailors picked me up when I was hitchhiking. They took me to a cabin and had me tied to the bed for twelve hours. I was a virgin. I couldn't move my hands and one of them would hold my legs apart while the other gave it to me. They were drinking and they gave it to me over and over again, one after the other or sometimes just taking turns sticking their cocks in. They did everything to me, they made me say things, sometimes they hurt me because it got them excited. After a while they started playing games with me, getting me hot without doing it so I had to beg, crawl, pay for it . . ."

By this time I was quivering with rage and lust. I made a grab for her but she eluded me.

"Keep away from me," she lisped in a scornful baby voice, "I don't play with little Jew boys."

She's going to do the whole bit, I thought.

I gave her a hard slap in the face. She started sobbing to beat the band: "Don't hurt me, I'll do anything you want, please don't hurt me."

"Open your legs," I told her. The whole bit.

"No, no, please."

I got on top of her. She was whimpering and babbling, no, no, please, she couldn't stand it, she was frightened, I shouldn't force her. The whole bit. When I shoved it in she gave a long sigh ending in a groan and said as she closed her eyes, "You're raping me." Shortly her sobs and whimpers

46

turned to grunts and moans. Her vagina was a volcano erupting in a spastic flow of molten ooze, and my cock kept turning from white-hot metal to liquid fire and back again. She was grunting encouragement, moaning endearments, spurring me on: "Have fun with me, come on, give it to me, what cock, I love it, rape me, hurt me, ram it in."

Brilliant light, a long, soundless roar reverberating in silence, then blank. A pause. From somewhere outside, beyond, a tiny, high-pitched fluting expands in volume, blossoms into a wail, hopeless, lost, fractures into dry sobs, spasms of hysteria. Oh no. She was lying on the bed next to me, tears pouring off of her, writhing, choking, making queer vomity sounds in her throat. I didn't know whether to grab my pants and beat it or go look for a doctor.

"Now, take it easy. Try to relax. I mean, I didn't mean . . ."

"What? What is it? Who? Ah. Ah, ah. Oui. Mais qu'est-ce vous faites ici maintenant? Vous n'êtes pas fini? Vous n'êtes pas satisfait?" She began to breathe more easily. "Mais ça m'a vachement plu, mon dieu. Ça m'a fait du bien." She sighed and stretched slowly, catlike. "Vous vous êtes amusé bien, n'est-ce pas? Voulez-vous me donner un petit cadeau?" Her lips shaped a coquettish smile. "C'est vrai le service est compris, mais quand même, comme petit souvenir. Renseignez vos amis, au moins. Vous connaissez le rendezvous . . ."

I was completely disgusted by the time I got out of there. Twenty-four hours later I walked through every back street of the quartier Hôtel de Ville vainly searching for that rendezvous. Which leads me sometimes to consider whether any of this really happened and why it doesn't much matter since, if it didn't, I would have made it up.

What a circus.

I seem to have developed a kind of technical curiosity about the thing. Not that it matters. But do they force a rubber ball into your mouth, for example? Rubashov was spared that. Your hands would be tied behind you, of course, but do they offer you a black handkerchief? Would I want one? Would they take it from the lifeless but presumably staring eyes of the preceding victim, taken from the preceding victim from the preceding victim? Suppose you refuse to walk? Do they drag you out or give it to you then and there? I think I'd prefer to walk. Will it be far? How do the executioners relate to the condemned: respect? vindictiveness? consideration? indifference? Will they wear uniforms? Will they have the common, familiar faces of passersby? Will it be indoors or under the sky, big difference. What time will it be?

The method of execution I already know. They've been at it for an hour at least, pulling them out of the cells, every once in a while a man or woman sobbing, and then at various intervals a burst of tommy gun fire or some such automatic weapon. Good. Quick and sure. I can face a tommy gun. Indifference to a fact. Soon, soon, this is it, now. Compulsion to look down gun barrels. Curiosity about death. The key in the lock, the door swings open, "Let's go, fellas," I say, "I'm freezing." No chance for a quip—who would care? The important thing is sphincter control.

Perhaps not everyone today, very possibly not everyone today, a certain number per day more likely. How do they decide who? Or maybe it's a different group. Alphabetical order? Or do they even know who I am, documents destroyed, no identification. Tend to forget your own past here, how long has it been? Just don't think about it somehow, in the grip of the present, the stones of the cell, the cold, when will they come, what difference—still, not today perhaps, certainly there'll be some time. Will I be asked to affirm my guilt?—why not?—I'd admit anything just to hear the sound of my name, invent infamous episodes, what does it matter, god knows I have enough to draw on—but here I have no name, what matter, rag on a stick, the veritable

48

thing, Lear—guilt is an illusion of the ego. Kafka was an optimist.

I don't really believe it. Lapse of sound, lapse of light, of pressure, cities gone, buildings, people, solid ground, lost in a blank, a final absence of mind. Unimaginable. Too much to expect. They come. They lead me out. They push me to the ground like a sick dog and put a gun barrel to my head. No. Impossible. Cursing, they tie me to a post with two twitching, witless wretches on either side, the one pissing in his pants, the other mumbling and crossing himself, never seen them before, never see them again. Scene from Goya, wide eyes, gaping mouths, faceless executioners. They open the door. One gestures matter of factly with his thumb, indicating the corridor. I walk ahead. The corridor is long and winding, impossible to see where it leads. The floor is large stone block, uneven and dusty. A shallow, irregular hole in the wall to the left. Our footfalls echo slightly. A roach scuttles across the stones. An overhead bulb is out. I feel them not more than two feet behind. One in, exhales heavily, a mouth breather. One grunts. One raises his pistol, slowly, till it's at arm's length, two inches from the nape of my neck. A creak and widening rectangle of light as the door swings open—four tired business-men with the preoccupied look of hurried commuters—"Let's go"—"Me?"—"Come on get going"—one draws a pistol, another gives me a shove—"Wait, I have to go to the bathroom"—"Move, we're behind schedule"—"What's with this jerk? Get with it, huh. A little teamwork"—"But, what . . ."—"Cooperate!"—along the corridor, quickly, through a steel grill that locks shut again behind, through a heavy door too fast into a wind early smelling predawn lit open death court shivering—"Over there"—brilliance of many candle power eye glare can't—"Wait, I, wait, I"—see bowel spasms what's happening to me—"Okay"—"Right"—"Let's go"—want to machine gun tripod no fast—"Look at the birdie"—say name explain wherefrom whatage first remem-

ber all can explain complete life in ten detail seconds as
see will too late now shit understand—

"And smile."

"Actually, in the long run, we're all comic characters.
You can't beat it. I did everything I could to screw up. I
refused to study for a degree. I expressed my contempt for
academe at every opportunity. I ignored my colleagues. I
publicly attacked Whitebread Blackhead's famous thesis on
the fart in Chaucer. And finally, at the faculty-graduate
seminar, in complete exasperation I attacked the profession
as a resort for mean-spirited middle-class time servers. And
what happens? Everybody eats it up. They love it. They call
me a firebrand. All I wanted was to make a few bucks and
remain a free agent, an itinerant intellectual, so to speak,
and suddenly, of all things I never wanted to be, I'm Professor Bernard Marsh. I'm institutionalized. And I can't
turn it down actually, because everything I want they give
me, till I'm afraid to ask for any more. Now every time I
open my mouth I have to think twice, because I too have
become official."

I had just congratulated Bernie on his appointment as
Assistant Professor. Finding it in the end impossible to live
without people and in particular—being down to seven
dollars and change—without people to borrow from, I had
finally got myself to abandon my shabby ivory tower and
come uptown to Bernie's smooth-walled, well-carpeted,
modern-furnished, new-kitchened, elevatored and doorman-
ned apartment.

"Have you resigned yourself to failure?" I asked.

"Don't kid me. One thing I can ask at least when you
come around borrowing money is not to kid me for having
it. Especially a guy like you who's bound to wind up
on the bounty of his friends. The trouble with you is you
don't fit in anywhere. Well, maybe that's your genius actu-

50

ally, if you have any. Of course, I'll give you as much as you want. Only why do you have to show up just when I have a big insurance payment due?"

"What insurance payment? You have an insurance policy?"

Bernie's pouty face sharpened to an acute grin.

"Of course. For years."

"But who's the beneficiary?" Not only was Bernie unmarried but, as far as I know, and I've known him a long time, he'd never—with one exception—dated a girl for anything but intellectual companionship.

"My mother, actually."

"Your mother!"

"What other beneficiary do I have? Not that I expect to knock off and leave her a fortune. It's simply that it pays to understand and, as far as possible, pursue the means of accumulating and preserving wealth in the capitalist economy. We may not like it, but there's essentially no reason to be crushed by it. Do as the Romans do actually, until you convince them to do otherwise, heh-heh. Did I tell you about my stock market coup? Fantastic. Some guy put me in touch with a broker handling this Canadian oil stock with a terrific PR ratio and a lot of smart money behind it. Went up thirty points in two months. I just sit on my ass and read the papers to see how rich I'm getting. Nothing big of course, not yet. I'm hedging with a few gilt-edge investments to keep a balanced portfolio, as they say. You know making money is a fascinating business."

"Few would disagree."

"Of course this is exactly the hypocrisy of the middle-class left. Make a mint and subscribe to *Dissent*. It's ridiculous. But essentially it's the only realistic point of view. It's the Cold War. Our hands are tied and everybody's sick of the old alienation crap. Why play the shrinking violet and wither away? For what? Essentially our generation has to maintain a series of small, even personal holding actions.

51

Endure and fructify the young. Little children shall lead us. Besides my position is not radical so much in the political sense—I'm a cultural radical, more like D. H. Lawrence."

"Don't apologize to me. I don't give a shit about your position."

"No, you don't. You just sit around playing straight man to your friends like a god damned psychiatrist waiting to pounce. I know your game. I know you for too long to let you get away with that. You creative types who live in the imagination don't know what it is to commit yourselves to something in this miserable world. Sometimes I don't know whether I'm living or dead. What is the good life, let me ask you? Is it to live in Westport and own a yacht after all? Believe me, stupidity is not confined to the complacent nor malice to the rapacious. I won't even mention the academic life, even at its best—

> *The Ivy League, the Ivy League,*
> *Where tweedy poets die and rot,*
> *Where scholars learn to lift the nose,*
> *And drown in their own snot.*

Old song. I'm thinking of the so-called intellectual life as expressed in the reviews and quarterlies we've been raised on where scholarship and art and politics supposedly come together in what is nowadays called a dialogue worthy of the humane intelligence. Christ, I remember as a kid in the Great Gobi Desert of Brooklyn living on the hope that maybe someday I too could participate in this enlightened exchange. So now I do. Big deal. What remains of the intellectual reviews these days but an obsessive style, the critical twitch and analytical stutter of a leftover ideology, a habitual nasty snideness deprived of content and situation. Frederick Engels on sabbatical. It comes out like sour-tempered trivia. Hatchet jobs by snot-nosed careerists on their betters or stale grudges from the thirties."

Bernie's puffy face sagged with depression.

"By the way," he added with new interest, "have you seen my latest article?"

He handed me one of the standard reviews opened to an article entitled, " 'Boy Scouts and Cojones: Hemingway and the Cold War' by Bernard Marsh. The suicide of Ernest Hemingway, now the tragic lamentations of the Luce publications have subsided, may in time come to be seen as a symbolically fitting end of America's most popular and, in many ways, most suspect, culture hero."

"I'll finish it later," I said.

"Sure. This is always compensation. There's nothing like seeing one's name in print. Still, do you think I like writing one of those things? Actually, I go through slow torture, sentence by sentence, every time I write a review. And the filth you have to read," he exclaimed, slapping himself on the forehead. "Contemporary fiction is nothing but a tissue of petty lies. This is the real trouble. Naturally there are exceptions. Negroes, queers and junkies. Through no fault of their own they happen to have inescapable points of view. Narrow, but permitting a bare minimum of evasion. As for the rest, it's enough to make you physically sick."

He rubbed his chin nervously, as if feeling for a beard that wasn't there. His pasty face was fixed in a familiar sarcastic smirk. He looked unhealthy. First of all he was too fat. And then he had a crewcut left over from undergraduate days that gave him the air of a fugitive from day camp, fat legs and dirty knees.

"I tell you I don't know whether I'm living or dying. Do you ever have palpitations?"

"Even astronauts have palpitations."

"No, I mean the kind where you actually can't breathe for a minute. As if something hit you in the chest. God, sometimes I really think I have heart trouble."

"Why don't you see a doctor?"

"I did. Twice."

53

"What did he say?"

"He said it's just palpitations. But it gets on my nerves. Remember that guy in high school who dropped dead just as he was about to enter Harvard on a scholarship? It can happen to anyone, you know. Anywhere, anytime. Besides I'm not that young any more. I'm getting close to thirty. You begin to feel it. You need more rest. The hair starts falling off your head and growing out your nose. I already have a couple of false teeth. I get these strange shooting pains in my side and left arm, headaches, and my eyes are going bad. Sometimes I'm actually terrified of having a brain tumor. The brain can't feel its own pain, you know. What about this All-American halfback who just died of leukemia? Do you think I should see a brain specialist?"

"What's a brain specialist going to tell you? To see a psychiatrist?"

"All right, I know I'm a hypochondriac. I've been to psychiatrists. Sometimes I live in absolute terror of losing my mind. If I ever become completely certain of going mad I'll kill myself. I've thought about it. Carbon monoxide is probably the easiest way. Attach a hose to the exhaust, run it through an air vent, and take a handful of sleeping pills. I'd rather go that way than like this guy I once saw in the subway. Standing right next to me in the middle of rush hour and suddenly his face turned gray and he collapsed. He didn't even have space to fall down. Christ, nobody wanted to help him, least of all me. I've actually written a suicide note. It's twenty-five pages. I'm revising it. I think it's quite good actually. I'll show it to you when I type it up."

"You're not serious."

"Why not? More than ten Americans in a hundred thousand are serious about it. It's far more popular than homicide. And the rate is four times as high for men as for women, which says something about the deal men get in this country, it seems to me. In any case the ratio is lowest among people who never marry and people who stay married, so my advice is don't get married at all and then you don't run any risk. Also, don't keep any guns around because that's by far the most popular method. Hanging comes next but I can't see hanging at all. In my opinion people who are willing to hang themselves deserve it. Drowning and jumping only account for 4.5 and 3.2 percent. Obviously people are afraid of water and height. Actually, suicide is a very indicative business. Read Durkheim. Believe me, I've done the research. It's worth an article. That reminds me, I ran across a story of yours in a magazine."

"Which one?"

" 'The Permanent Crisis.' "

"Oh yeah. How did you like it?"

"First of all," he said, "I appreciate what you're trying to do, but frankly I don't understand why you want to publish your practice work."

"What do you mean?"

"Well it's not bad writing, actually, but it's not yet literature—in the best sense, of course. See what I mean?"

"I see the distinction."

"And then the long sentence. I don't quite see it."

"Well, it just sounded good, Bernie."

"Yes, but essentially you haven't digested Proust, Joyce, Faulkner—they all had some point in writing long sentences. Not to mention Virginia Woolf, Sterne, Rabelais and others. This is a tiresome list, but the thing is that pointless innovation always sounds like an echo, a weak imitation."

"Yes, I can see that."

"Another thing. You understand, as a friend I was terribly interested in your piece. Don't get me wrong. I liked it—as a friend. But this is just the thing you see. After all, fiction isn't confession. You and I may be interested in your tribulations and so on. But the reader. To the reader this sounds like a maudlin exercise in group therapy. Of course

55

you can say all fiction is confession. But that's just playing with words. Once you forgo the element of artifice, the assumption of fiction—precisely the advantage of objective form—your words are judged as experience rather than literature. And then who are you? What's Bloom's Odyssey, after all, compared to Marco Polo's or even, say, the average Marine's in the Pacific war? I mean this is just the essential irony of all art, isn't it?"

"I didn't think about that."

"But essentially these are only minor criticisms. I don't want to quibble. The real trouble is that you're still writing about the middle class. The tortured forms of Thomas Mann's books are the grotesque tombstones of the bourgeois novel. For a half a century the novel has been struggling to get free of the middle class just as you and I have spent our lives trying to do the same thing. Don't ask me for any answers. There is no answer. There's no place to go. There's nothing to do but wait, and there's not time enough to wait. Our generation is a sacrifice to history. When a creative writing student asks me what to write about I answer: Amuse yourself. There's nothing to write about."

"I ought to burn my notebook."

"I see what you're trying for. Writing as self-expression and all that. The Romantic gambit. But you can't go back. Between crisis and catastrophe who cares about your ego? Your complaint, your indignation, your outrage—your boils, your hangnails, your stomach aches. It turns to self-pity. This just bores us, we have the same problems. You ought to stick to comedy."

"You're absolutely right, Bernie. In fact, I don't know why I was ever born."

"Now don't go and blame yourself. This is just the trouble. You're helpless. It's history. It's politics. It's capitalism. It's the literary situation. We're all paralyzed. I envy you in a way. You're a real writer. If I thought it were possible to write something worthwhile, I'd drop teaching at the end of the semester, get a cheap pad in Hoboken, and start a novel. I ought to do it anyway, if only out of self-respect. Something in the first person, as if Bloom were writing Proust in order to recapture the American myth, like Faulkner."

The old man, spats and cravat, elegant as an old photo, one of my ghosts, strokes his goatish beard white yellowed and lights a cigar butt moving with the slight discontinuity of a home movie, lips shaping words I don't hear, laughs soundlessly, coughs, cleans his pince-nez, folds his Yiddish paper, folds his German paper, folds his Russian paper, belches, drops them in a wastebasket and, with the aid of a bamboo cane, grunting, rises, taller than all my uncles, taller than my father, straight, pot-bellied, thin, goes to the kitchen shelf, takes from a Jewish starred tumbler once filled with sacred candle wax several loose rolled dollar bills, counts them, stuffs them in his vest pocket, reaches down to pat me on the head, takes my hand and walks me to the stairs, follows me down leaning on his cane, me hanging on the banister two steps a stair, stops downstairs speaking to my mother, aunt Theda and grandmother who was, they say, a saint, who answers shaking her fist in Yiddish I don't hear except for two stray words that sound like "gunisht," and "horsemadel," which I don't understand, and the old man turns red, throws his cigar on the floor, raises his cane like a staff and defies his family like one of the prophets, then points to me and signals for silence, puts his hand on my shoulder and draws me to the stairs, down to the cellar to his work table where he picks up his tools one after another and puts them down, talking again but this time not to me, and still talking goes to the cesspool in the corner, kicks off the wooden top, looks down into it, spits, and speaks the only words that memory repeats: "Do you see it? That's dreck. Tell that to grandma when she asks where

57

I am"; and with that opens the cellar door, puts his finger to his lips, winks, waves his cane, and disappears.

"Stewart. What do you say?"

No answer. It was a house full of problems—the old man upstairs dying, my aunt in her usual state of sustained hysteria, my uncle complaining about money and fighting with his kids—but the worst of it was that my cousin had retreated into the god damned bathroom for the summer and nobody could get him out. It was enough to make you constipated for life.

"Stewart. For christ sake, in plain language, I have to take a shit!"

"Oh my god."

Aunt Theda waddled out of her bedroom.

Oh my god. What is it now? More trouble? More conflict? What's he up to now? Tell me. I can't stand any more. What's he done now? I have enough. I can't take another bit. What with your grandfather upstairs and your uncle half crazy over business I literally don't know where the next dollar is going to come from, I don't know where we're going to get it. Stewart dear. What's the trouble? What is it?"

"Lemme alone," came the answer through the bathroom door.

"You see? What can I do. He won't even talk to me. What do you think of a boy who won't talk to his own mother? I'm worried about him, Ronnie. He never talks. He never does anything. He doesn't take an interest. I'm afraid he's going to grow up to be one of these neurotics. And we used to be so intimate you can't imagine. He used to tell me everything."

"Well, gee, he's past fifteen, Aunt Theda."

"So what. What's that got to do with it. Your Aunt Yetta's boy, Douglas, is nineteen and he doesn't blow his nose without asking his mother's advice. Stewart dear. What are you doing in there? What's he been doing in there, two and a half hours by the clock. Tell me."

"Reading?" He was probably masturbating but she wouldn't have believed it if I'd told her.

"You know he doesn't read. He doesn't even watch television. Ronnie, I'm worried about him. Maybe he talks to you. Give me your opinion. What should I do with him?"

"Give him ten bucks and send him to a cat house."

"What's that?" She cupped her hand behind her ear in an exaggerated display of deaf incomprehension.

"I don't know, Aunt Theda. He doesn't talk to me either. Maybe you should ask his friends."

"He doesn't have any friends. He doesn't do anything, he doesn't talk to anybody. He just sits on the toilet all day. I'm at a loss. You'd think the child wasn't normal. Stewart dear. Talk to me."

Leaning against the wall, she forced her blubbery body to bend till her eye was at the level of the keyhole.

"He's put paper in the keyhole," she said, panting. "He doesn't trust his mother. Stewart dear. Why don't you trust your mother? Talk to me. I'll call the police. What can I do? Go upstairs."

I didn't like to go upstairs. I was afraid of death. Not so much afraid as profoundly discouraged by it. Here in this house. At the hospital it was a different story.

Snippick, the practical nurse, was on her way down the stairs. The old man was pinching her again. She wasn't going to stand for it again. She was walking out again. As a matter of fact she looked like Tony Galento and was probably quite flattered to get pinched now and then. Grandpa knew it. He used to pinch the hell out of her. Foxy grandpa. It was his insults she couldn't take. He hated her guts and loved to get her sore. He said she was trying to kill him.

"She's at it again," I could hear him yelling as I went upstairs. "What do they want from me, a dying man? A dying man," he sobbed.

59

Never mind. I went back downstairs. During that summer the secret in the house was that the old man was going to die. It was a secret to everyone but himself, who complained endlessly that they knew he was dying, that they were letting him die, that he didn't want to and wasn't going to die, until everyone secretly wished him dead and buried as soon as possible.

The old man was always someone I imagined rather than someone I knew. My memory of him at that time is hopelessly confused with my summer's job in the maternity ward. I think of him as a fetus, helpless, a coil of needs gestating in the womb of life, awaiting the spasm of annihilation. His wail is the wail of the women in the traffic jam of waiting stretchers that lined the corridor of Obstetrics day after day, is the wail of infants from the delivery rooms surrounding my desk, his pain is their pain, shocking, inescapable. It was a devastating reality for an eighteen-year-old who looked at women in terms of a few romantic high school girls and one thrill-hunting Bohemian type, to begin a day by disposing of accumulated placentas, abortions and still-births, then sit down amidst that female curse and bellow, I, with my superstitious fear of sanitary napkins, to total up the night's get, the births, the nonbirths, and the occasional deaths. I began to look at things in terms of obstetrics and in small ways my life was permanently altered. Once I dropped a placenta in the elevator and, without describing what it looked like, I will say that I could never get myself to eat soft boiled eggs again. And besides, my situation in Gravesend that summer was such that I could hardly avoid, even then, the symbolic relevance of my job to the state of my life. I knew I was one of the unborn, I was convinced that my real life had a substance I had barely begun to imagine, and which would emerge only after complete severance from the stunted shadow world of my Brooklyn childhood.

From the roof of the hospital, fifteen floors up, you

could see Brooklyn in all its deadly reality, pinned like a corpse between the parachute jump in Coney Island and the Dime Savings tower downtown, crushingly plain, impervious to glamour, flatly what it seemed—the sum total of its right-angled streets and right-angled houses. The only thing of interest on the horizon was the skyline of Manhattan.

The memory of this roof gets me salivating. It was a perfect place for lunch, as far as I was concerned, good, oily sardine sandwiches from a paper bag, tough-crusted rye, cheap, sunny, solitary. One o'clock. I take the elevator down to Obstetrics. Brown, male, and Martinez, female, children of grudging municipal charity, have been born in my absence. This was one of those giant city hospitals where the children of the poor are brought into the world, that prenatally disinherited surplus of humanity that constitutes most of the earth's population. I tick them off. Make it official. I was in a position to deny life, officially speaking, to hundreds of newly-borns. I could have created a new breed, unofficial man, entirely personal, stripped to his profoundest intentions so complicated and diffused in the workaday specimen—but, young as I was, I missed my chance.

My desk is strewn with order forms, specimen jars, stool samples, and test tubes containing various organic fluids, requiring trips to the lab, pharmacy, and autoclave, with a stop for blood on the way back ("I drink it," I tell them in the blood bank. "I'm a vampire"). I set out with my little cart, a load of blood, shit, and urine, bound for the clinical underworld, a network of dim tunnels, steamy workrooms, laboratories, and stores, that holds the fate of every inmate up above. I wait for the elevator. The door slides open and I'm looking at a rolling stretcher bearing a corpse. It's draped from head to foot with white sheets. "Come on in," calls one of its attendants. "Plenty of room for everybody," adds another. It makes for some reason a mountainous

61

bulge under the sheet at about what must be the abdomen. There seem to be three attendants. They're playing a game of salugi with a wad of paper around, over the stretcher. Laughing, dodging, jumping, they're having a hell of a good time. They wear white coats. They're Negroes and the dark of their weaving forearms and bobbing faces against the white coats and sheets makes a graphic picture. The wad of paper drops on the bulge of the sheet and bounces off. They look at me and at one another and quiet down.

I roll my cart off at the basement. I turn to the left. I'm coasting down the long, warm, humid, dim, sloping tube that runs under the breadth of the hospital. You can't see the end of this tunnel—only the horizontals of the steam pipes on either side joining in the distant merged glare of the yellow bulbs placed every twenty feet in both walls. It was a warm summer night, one of those nights with all the windows open when indoors is simply an extension of outdoors. I was sitting up late reading when she walked into the room, a silly kid, I thought, but not bad for a high school junior, in short pajamas with her hair down and sat holding one knee and rocking herself slightly on my bed.

"Can you sleep?" she asked.

"I'm not trying."

She was just back from a date, I knew. I'd heard her arrive in a cascade of giggles a half hour before, and the voice of Chet Vance, a Cornell fraternity type and one of her main boyfriends, as he gunned the motor of his new convertible, and zoomed off to Rockville Centre whence he came.

"I can't fall asleep," she said.

"Did you have a nice time?"

"Not bad." She made a sour little face. "We had fun. Chet's silly. I'd do practically anything for a ride in his convertible. I love driving fast. But after I get home I feel sort of sad."

"How come?"

"I don't know."

She got up and walked around the room. Nice brown hair and nice legs, but her face was regular to the point of anonymity thanks to what Theda called a plastic, blessing her with, as Theda said, a starlet nose. You could see her nipples under thin cloth bobbing up and down as she walked.

"What are you reading?" She stopped next to my chair. A lolloping pair of buttocks for a kid her age.

"*Ulysses.*"

"Isn't that some kind of dirty book?"

"What do you know about it?"

"A boy showed me the good parts. He goes to college."

"Is that what he learns in college?"

"The parts he showed me weren't that sexy. They were too hard."

"It's not that hard either."

"You're a smart boy, Ronnie." She sat on the arm of my chair. Nice, chubby thighs. "I can talk to you. But why are you always so quiet? Don't you like me?"

"What do you mean, Sugar?"

"Where does he think he's going?"

"Hey, where do you think you're going? Wake up and live."

"Hah hah."

"Hah hah hah."

Les misérables. I'd forgotten to turn off at the autoclave.

"Maybe he thinks they moved the autoclave to the morgue," says Hunch.

"Hah hah hah," adds Zip.

I turn my cart around. They were three workers who always hung around a bunch of crates and cartons at a junction of the tunnel. I have the idea they must be charity cases, marginal types given city jobs through pull or municipal pity. Hunch, whose body looks like a question mark, is

63

despite his low brow and jut jaw the only one who could pass an intelligence test for a street cleaner. Borneo, a short wide guy, is just plain stupid, and Zip is so little there I feel sorry for him. I take the corridor to the autoclave.

"What do you mean, Sugar? You're my favorite cousin. I'll talk to you any time you want."

At that moment Stewart came in.

"Get the hell out of here, Sugar. You got your own room." He was a skinny kid with a snaky body and a narrow face that came to a point at the middle of his upper lip.

"Oh," said Sugar. "The insect. You know what they call him at school? The insect. Nobody likes him. I'm ashamed to admit he's my brother."

"Yeah, that's right. Everybody likes you, Sugar. Especially the boys. Now get the hell out. It's enough I got *him* in here. I told you to stay the hell out."

"Just what do you mean? What do you mean by that?"

"You know god damn well what I mean. Who was elected most popular girl by the men's room wall vote? Now come on. One guest is enough. Or maybe you'd like him living in your room. Maybe you would."

"Where've you been, Stewart?" I ask, trying to break up the argument.

"Times Square, what's it to you?"

"Oh," said Sugar on the way out. "I thought he was in the bathroom."

The autoclave stands in my memory as the center of the hospital. It was nothing but a hole in the wall with a round door like a safe, a huge sterilizer that I had to visit at least twice a day to keep Obstetrics in rubber gloves. But the utilitarian aspect of the instrument was as nothing to me. As soon as I enter the room I'm overtaken by a sense of mystery, as if I were about to take part in an elemental rite. The white-coated attendant takes my bags of soiled gloves, looks at my order form, and opens the heavy round door. Clouds of steam, a rush of moist heat, depth, darkness. He

64

reaches in with a hooked pole, takes out the cloth cases containing the gloves, and that's all. More gloves would be used, more babies would be born, and before long another penetration of the autoclave would be called for. Was it I who was in some way creating all these children? Was I in some way responsible or was I simply mistaking effect for cause? The attendant gave me no answer other than my quota of gloves.

I'm going through the emergency ward on my way back to Obstetrics. Suddenly a woman starts screaming, high, flat, unmodulated cries of utter shock. A young woman, under thirty, quite tall. She just stands there in the middle of the floor screaming like that for no apparent reason. In no time she's surrounded by nurses and orderlies trying to lead her away. She won't let anyone near her. Screaming, she fights them off. When they manage to pin her arms she starts kicking and biting. Four orderlies finally wrestle her to the floor, howling and moaning, and administer a hypodermic.

I ask around to find out what happened. "They just told her her husband died," an orderly says. "She brought him in yesterday for observation and he was still okay. Last night he developed a fever that went up to 109 and this morning he was dead. They don't know what happened. Lucky he died though. When they come back from a temperature like that they're never the same."

The nurse is just bringing Henrietta McCann out of the delivery room as I get back to my desk. She looks at me from the nurse's arm as I check her off, her head sticking out of the blanket, big, dazzled, pale blue eyes, an air of protest suspended by amazement. I'm astounded to find in her stare an intense curiosity that seems quite feminine. It hits me that I'm confronting a real person—one who didn't exist four or five minutes ago. This revelation made me shaky for the rest of the day.

"Health," said Uncle Julius, and drank from a glass of

65

beer in confirmation. He had the face of a crafty butcher, broad cheeks, flat nose, pig eyes, fat neck, balding brow under straight, reddish hair. Out of the corners of his shifty eyes he sought an echo of his toast.

Sugar yawned, lit a cigarette, and looked out the window. Stewart stared into his plate.

"Health," I said, and took another drink of beer. Julius glanced at me suspiciously.

Theda got up and came back with an oven pan. "Croutons?" she asked. "Who would like croutons?"

Nobody answered.

"Have some croutons Ronnie." I took some croutons.

"How did it go?" asked Theda.

"Sold a car," said Julius. He owned a used-car lot in the Bronx.

"That's good."

"Sure it's good. It's a lousy season. Nobody's buying. I spoke to Schwartz today. He hasn't sold a car in three weeks."

"Did you decide about getting that Ford?" asked Sugar.

Julius grunted.

"Wouldn't you like to learn how to drive?" Sugar asked Stewart. "A Ford convertible?"

Stewart, getting the feel of an almost ripe pimple on his cheek with thumb and forefinger, ignored her.

"He's too young," said Theda.

"He is not," insisted Sugar. "He could get a Long Island permit. I'll teach him, Daddy. Soon as I get my license."

"Please," said Theda. "No conflict."

Julius, finished with soup, lifted his heavy body, took the *Post* from the seat beneath him, and started opening it.

"Julius," said Theda.

He sighed, put it back, and relit a cigar butt.

"How's your father?" he asked.

66

"He makes such a problem of himself. He complains, but Snippick says he's better. What can you expect at his age?" She got up with some dishes and went to the kitchen. Julius got his newspaper out and started reading. Sugar went to the television set and tuned in. Stewart lit a cigarette and stared vindictively into the living room as if he were planning to set the house on fire. It was perfectly clear as soon as Theda turned her back that the rest of the family wanted nothing better than to get away from one another. I was chewing nervously on a seeded onion roll. I was terribly full. I couldn't possibly eat another course. We were in an alcove facing the living room—a bulging couch and two easy chairs of Victorian dimensions, thick Persian imitation rug, a miscellany of fake antique chairs and tea tables, two big mirrors in gilt-scabbed frames, a large television set, a giant AM-FM-short-wave-console-radio-phonograph, a small television set, a huge photograph of Stewart's famous bar mitzvah at the Waldorf, air conditioner, drapes, venetian blinds, knickknacks, end tables, cigarette boxes, humidors, Dresden statuettes, cabinets, shelves, niches, candy dishes, doilies, coasters, candlestick holders, vases, lampshades, cut-glass decanters, hassocks, chinaware . . .

Theda came in with a leg of lamb surrounded by roast potatoes and carrots.

"Stewart," she wailed. "You smoke too much. Julius! Sugar, turn that set off."

Stewart was served first. "Too much," he said, staring at his plate as Theda set it before him.

"Eat, Stewart," she said. "He doesn't eat. He smokes too much."

"Stewart, put out your cigarette," commanded Julius. Stewart went on smoking. "Ah, leave him alone," says Julius. "You think he listens? Pass the vegetables, will you? Ronnie, take more lamb. Give Ronnie more lamb."

67

I take some more lamb. I'm drowning. I can't think, I can barely speak.

"I can't eat any more," says Stewart.

"Ah, quiet," says Julius. "Eat your dinner."

Stewart glares at his father and doesn't eat his dinner. Julius is panting, putting away slice after slice of lamb. His cigar butt smokes in the ashtray. Sugar is the only one who can keep up with her father. She has a tremendous appetite. It all goes to her breasts and ass. I can see them getting bigger day by day.

"Julius," says Theda. "Put out your cigar. It's not nice."

He brings up an ostentatious belch and crushes the cigar. This Theda chooses not to hear. "How's the lamb?" she asks.

"Oh, wonderful, delicious. Have some more lamb Ronnie."

For a while nothing but smacks and grunts. Soon I'm going to roll off my chair and settle on the floor like a sack of meal. I'm getting seasick. The click-click of utensils on china becomes strangely abstract, bells, Santa Claus with his bursting bag disappearing across the Arctic waste, bare, desolate, barren, white, clean, empty . . .

I'm staring at a spot of blood on the white enamel of the counter where the nurse is working. It's surprisingly red, about the size of a quarter, with a jagged circumference. I'm fascinated, although I handle blood all day in the hospital. To see blood there, wet and red, unenclosed in jars, slides or test tubes, is extraordinary. The nurse is pouring placentas from nickel-plated basins into large glass jars. The room glistens with nickel, steel, glass and enamel, sterilizers, sinks, refrigerators, cabinets, instruments, ranks of test tubes, everything in order. It's the sterility of the hospital that gets me down, white, metallic, smelling of alcohol and disinfectant. In this asepsis, where an unaccountable spot of blood is so blatant, death, decay and

68

infection are more shocking than in the world outside. This is a test tube reality, calculated to render incontrovertibly certain essential facts. Here there's no evasion, no waste, every event is measured, every response is meaningful. An aseptic world with no tolerance for the fictions people whisper to themselves. It's a relief. Still it depresses me. It's not human.

We have a bumper crop of placentas today. Those I bring to the laboratory are enclosed in glass jars, but the ones intended for disposal are in large tin containers, old fruit-salad cans without covers. They always get me nervous. On top of that I have a dead baby to bring over to the morgue. They've packed it nicely for me in a large cardboard box tied with a string. Just like a pair of shoes. As I put it on my cart I can feel it bumping around inside. It's heavier than it looks. Down in the lab an orderly from surgery is chatting with one of the technicians. "Oh, yeah. No rush on these tests. They opened him up this morning and he's full of cancer." He turns to me and winks. "The knife don't lie," he grins.

I'm coasting down the long, warm, humid tube that runs under the hospital. It was a hot evening. Sugar was waiting to use the shower. Two boys had just brought her back from Jones Beach and she'd come into my room to wait. She was still wearing her bathing suit, a loose two-piece cotton thing that looked like it was made for an eight-year-old, a loose bikini really. It occurred to me that a bathing suit on the beach and a bathing suit in the intimacy of a house were two different matters. She had a nice reddish tan and reminded me of a ripe peach. What fascinated me were the heavy white half-moons between the fringe of her trunks and the deep creases under her buttocks.

"How long's he been in there?" she asked.

"Don't know."

I knew a girl in Manhattan that summer who was usually good for a lay, but I didn't get to see her too often.

69

"Why doesn't he find a girl friend," she asked petulantly, "instead of fooling with himself all day?"

"What do you mean?"

She puffed her cheeks in exasperation and looked up at the ceiling in a bored way.

"Why don't you introduce him to a sexy fourteen-year-old?" I said. "A lot of good that would do."

She took a pack of cigarettes from the pocket of the beach robe she was carrying and offered me one. I took it and the matches. She bent over me so the depth of her breasts swung into view as I lit hers.

"You got a nice figure," I observed.

"Why Ronnie!" she minced. "I bet you know a lot of girls."

She gave me a hard stare of informed curiosity. I felt she was estimating the size and capacity of my penis.

"Did you have a good time at the beach?"

"I always have a good time," she said, puffing on her cigarette.

Theda called that dinner was on the table. Stewart came out of the bathroom and gave us a venomous glance as he passed the door.

"Now there's not time for a shower," she said. "That brat. I'm all sticky. Do you think it's okay if I eat in my robe?"

"Okay with me."

She walked across the room, turned her back to me and unhooked the top of her bathing suit.

"Don't look," she said.

Like hell. She took her top off, put the robe around her shoulders and stooped to take off the bottoms.

"Hadja like one a them college girls to do anything you want?"

"Like what?" asks Borneo, gulping and salivating.

"You know a lot a college girls, doncha?" asks Hunch, ignoring him. "I bet they do anything you want."

70

"Like what?" asks Borneo.

I'm waiting for the elevator. Hunch is sitting on a chair, the other two on crates. I'm making a quick detour for the morgue. I want to get rid of the little corpse on my cart. I'm not crazy about wheeling it all over the hospital. I can hear it bumping around inside the box.

"Like you get her with her clothes off," says Hunch, grinning and wetting his lips.

"Yeah," says Zip.

"And you tell her to get down on all fours. And you're sitting on a chair like this."

He spreads his legs. He's panting and staring hard at a naked co-ed on the floor about ten feet away. I look, but she's not there.

"And you make her crawl over slow and then you stick it right in her mouth." He slaps the chair between his legs and laughs.

"That's right," says Zip, his round, empty eyes not really understanding. "Hah hah hah."

"You shut up," says Hunch viciously. "Who the hell asked you?"

The elevator comes. Nobody says anything. Nobody gives away a thought or even thinks it. Nobody talks but Theda. Sugar always has a cigarette going. Stewart is tight-lipped, pale. Julius communicates with grunts and nods. His official attitude is that he's there to eat and if anything else is going on besides eating, he doesn't know about it. We eat. The food is delicious: chopped liver, tomatoes, endive, avocados, lettuce, huge baked potatoes with nuggets of butter melting in their cross-split tops, pot roast, meat loaf, chopped creamed spinach, and stewed carrots and celery. Julius is stupendous. The bread he eats is alone enough to gorge an ox. As he chews and gulps his eyes never stop moving around the table, looking for the next thing to eat, for a sign of possible trouble. He has the appearance of a man looking three ways at once while juggling

71

on a tight rope. The instant conversation gives a hint of danger an expression of secret craft flickers across his broad, dumb face, and in his blunt manner he directs attention back to the food spread before us.

"Take some more pickles Ronnie. We can't get rid of 'em. Stewart. You don't like your mother's cooking?"

"No."

This Theda chooses not to hear.

"Of course he likes it," says Julius. "Now shut up and eat your food."

"Leave the boy alone," says Theda blandly. "More roast, Stewart dear?"

Stewart doesn't answer.

"What time did you get in last night?" asks Theda.

"Who, me?" says Sugar.

"We need more bread," says Julius.

"Your father didn't hear you come in, but I did."

"More bread," says Julius.

"Three o'clock, Julius. The young lady came in at three o'clock. Seventeen years old."

"What! Three o'clock! What the hell were you doing till three o'clock?"

"I was out with Henny Stein."

"Stein?" says Theda. "From Great Neck? Stein's Supermarkets."

"I'll take a strap to her. What the hell was she doing till three o'clock?"

"It's not so awful, Julius. It's a good family. I used to know a cousin. Did you meet the parents?"

"Yes," says Sugar. "I found them quite charming."

"But three o'clock."

"No conflict, Julius. Try to get home a little earlier, dear. It don't look good."

"Nobody saw us."

"More bread," says Julius.

I was on a rush for some whole blood from the blood

72

bank. I didn't even bother to take my cart. I get back to the ward in a record fifteen minutes. My arms ache from hugging three jars of blood in fear of dropping them.

"Here it is," I tell the nurse breathlessly.

"Here what is?"

"The rush."

"Oh. Never mind, she's dead."

I sit down at my desk. In one of the delivery rooms a woman is straining in the stirrups that elevate her legs. She's covered to the hips with a sheet. Between spasms she looks for some reason over her belly through the parenthesis of her thighs out at me. Quite a view I have. The doctors are urging her on, young interns or I don't know what they are: "Come on mother, come on now, push, that's it, push hard . . ." The woman makes desperate mooing sounds, tears out spasmodic bovine screams. Now and then the doctors crack a joke and laugh. "Mother," they call her. Callous young snots.

I have a lot of paper work on new births. Sixteen kids born that morning and it's only eleven o'clock. The ward has been a mad scene of screaming women and squalling kids, all the delivery rooms going at once and women already in labor waiting on stretchers lined up in the corridor, doctors doubling up and doing two births at a time. The continuous exhibition of fecundity here appalls me. All day all night the women fill the delivery rooms, the kids are brought out, the world is populated, populated, overpopulated, each baby another individual, another person, and this only one of twenty city hospitals, hundreds of private hospitals in a single city. All day and all night it goes on, three shifts of personnel can't keep up with them.

I check into the nurses' workroom to see what they have for me. There among the placenta basins and specimen jars I spot the unmistakable box of oversized shoes.

73

"What's going on. I just brought that down to the morgue."

"They sent it back," a nurse informs me. "It goes to the lab."

I pick it up and head for the elevator. This is no joke. It's a hot day and the box is heavy. Sweat is pouring off me and I was already tired when I came in this morning. The corpse is beginning to smell or so I imagine. I can feel it bumping around inside so I try to hold the box steady in front of me. It takes a good twenty minutes to get downstairs, under the hospital, and up to the lab on the other side. Soon my arms are tired. It must be a giant baby, fifteen pounds at least. I wish I'd brought the cart. I try holding it under one arm but it bumps too much. The air is so close in the tunnel I feel I'm suffocating. I hold the box up to my nose and sniff at the lid. It's beginning to smell, I'm sure of it.

The guy at the lab takes the box from me and undoes the string.

"What you got here? Your lunch? Hey wait a minute."

"What."

"I can't take this."

"Why not?"

"It's too old. I can't take no cadaver. This here is a cadaver. This goes to the morgue."

"The morgue just sent it back."

"What do you mean? They got to take it. This is a cadaver."

He closes the box. I pick up the cadaver and we both go over to the morgue. The guy in the morgue is a prick from the word go. A sharp type who looked like a bookie, and very up on what was his job and what was yours.

"It ain't a cadaver," he insists. "It's a fetus."

"That's no fetus—it's all developed," says the guy from the lab.

"If it's a cadaver where's its death certificate?"

74

"It don't have a death certificate," I say.

"Then as far as I know it's still alive. Take it away."

"It's not alive," says the guy from the lab. "It don't have a birth certificate. It was never born."

"In that case it don't exist," says the guy from the morgue.

That stumped them. I slip out while I have the chance and leave them looking at each other. I head back to Obstetrics. If it doesn't exist I'm not going to worry about it.

This time it beats me back up there. When I get to the ward I find the shoe box waiting for me on my desk. I go into the head nurse's office—Miss Amnion.

"I'm quitting," I tell her.

"Why, aren't you happy here?"

"It's too much. I'm not used to this kind of thing. It gets on my nerves."

"Can't take it, hey."

"No." She was a squat article, Miss Amnion, looked like a member of the Anti-Saloon League.

"Look," she says. "Obstetrics isn't a place for sick people. You should work in some of the other wards. Surgery, for instance. This is a happy ward. Maternity is a normal, healthy business. Of course, there may be a still-birth now and then, even a death. That's just the facts of life."

"I know all that. But I'm sick of it. Leave maternity to mothers. I'm quitting."

"No you're not quitting. This is no ordinary job. You can't just walk out and leave me short a worker. It takes weeks to break somebody in. I didn't ask you to take this job. You came here and asked for it"—she pointed her finger at me—"and now you've got it. You are needed here," she said, poking me in the chest. "Who do you think you are?"

"All right," I said. "All right. All right, all right."

I think this was the first time I had ever been con-

75

fronted with a pure moral imperative. It was an irresistible onslaught, and I knew it. When I got back to my desk the shoe box wasn't there. It had disappeared. I don't know what happened to it. I never asked.

I had to go up to the maternity. ward where the newborns were sent from the delivery rooms. The babies were kept together in large temperature-controlled atmosphere-regulated wards separated from the corridors by plate-glassed partitions. They lay in canvas cradles, near a hundred to a room, sleeping, crying, sucking, retching, cooing, kicking, gurgling, coughing, playing with their toes. Relatives and friends stand in front of the plate glass, pointing, tapping, laughing, waving. It's feeding time and most of the babies are awake. Their hundreds of tiny cries, the mews, the coos, the bleats, the high-pitched wails send through the glass an innocent melody of delight that is irresistible. I stop entranced. There is absolutely nothing like it. Music for the pastures of paradise.

Dinner at my aunt's that night began with creamed herring. There were olives, celery, pickles, rolls, butter, pumpernickel, and caraway rye on the table. I was already full by the time Theda brought the chicken noodle soup, but I encouraged my stomach with a glass of beer.

"We're ready for the steak, Theda. Put it on the table."

"What steak? Chicken. I told you Stewart don't eat steak."

"I thought he don't eat chop meat."

"Stewart doesn't eat anything," puts in Sugar.

"Good, chicken," says Julius. "Nothing like a juicy chicken, right Stew?"

"We had chicken yesterday," answers Stewart.

"You're so agreeable," says Sugar.

"Sugar," says Theda. "Please, no conflict."

Stewart stares into his plate. The thin line of his mouth tightens, his pale face gets a degree more rigid. I admire the little bastard. He has a capacity for resentment that is prodigious, a talent for repression that amounts to genius. One day soon he's going to blow his top and I hope I'm not around.

The chicken comes with stuffing, carrots, and roast potatoes. It looks delicious but I'm so full I can't taste anything. Alongside the chicken Theda puts a plate of sliced roast beef and a large bowl of green beans. She serves Stewart, then passes the platter around. Stewart looks at the food in his plate and sneers.

"Wonderful spread, hey Ron," says Julius abruptly.

"Great," I answer. "Pass the chicken."

"Stewart," says Theda. "You're not eating. He doesn't eat anything."

"Do we have to eat chicken every day?"

"Take some cold roast beef," says Julius. "It's good. See." He takes some roast beef. "Ronnie. Take some cold roast beef." I take some roast beef.

"I don't want roast beef," says Stewart.

"What do you want?" asks Theda. "What does he want? You need a fortune-teller. How am I supposed to know what he wants? Tell me what he wants and I'll give it to him."

"Stewart. Eat what your mother tells you. You don't want to be a god damned runt, do you?"

"I'm not hungry."

"He's not hungry, Theda. Leave the boy alone."

"He's not hungry? What do you mean he's not hungry. He never eats anything. What do you take me for? He does it for spite, that's what it is. I'm no fool. He hates his mother!"

"Now you've guessed," says Stewart coolly.

Theda gives a little scream.

"Eat your damn food you little son of a bitch," yells Julius, half rising in his chair.

Stewart gets up quietly and walks out.

"Exit the insect," say Sugar.

77

"You shut your trap," says Theda. "The way she makes fun of her brother."

During this eruption I've eaten a chicken leg and a slice of roast beef without even noticing. I feel like I'm going to roll off my chair. The wallpaper makes me nauseous—a pattern of graceful ladies and gents playing shepherd, pink on green, very eighteenth-century. I've often thought that if someone had put a Klee in that dining room the house would have exploded.

There is a congealed silence in which a tacit agreement crystallizes that nothing has happened. Continents can disintegrate and races disappear, but in this house nothing ever happens.

"Help yourself to salad Ronnie," says Theda.

"How's your father," asks Julius.

"Fine. The same. Snippick says he's getting better but won't admit it. What a problem he makes himself. After all he's an old man. He's not reasonable. He can't expect perfect health anymore."

My aunt gets up to put dessert on the table—cheese, fruit, ice cream, apple pie, chocolate cake, Danish pastry, and coffee.

"Say," says Julius suddenly. "What's wrong with you?"

"Who?" says Sugar. "Me? Nothing's wrong with me."

"You look funny. What did you do to yourself?"

"Oh. You mean my hair. I bleached my hair yesterday. Haven't you noticed?" She patted her hair and revolved her head. She was blonde. Yesterday she was light brunette.

"My little movie star, hey? What you all dressed up for? A party?"

"Me. I'm not dressed up."

She was wearing lipstick, eye makeup, a red raw-silk sleeveless blouse with costume jewelry, Bermuda shorts, and a silver charm bracelet.

"You should see me when I get dressed up," she said.

78

Julius laughed. "What did you do today puss?" he asked his daughter.

"Went shopping."

"Shopping again?"

"A girl her age needs clothes, Julius," says Theda. "There was a sale. A few pairs of gloves, some shoes, a bathing suit—a real saving . . ."

"Another bathing suit?"

"Wait till you see it on, Daddy. It's real sexy."

Julius laughed. Suddenly we heard a cry from upstairs, a series of protesting bellows, infantile in their insistence. We looked at one another. Then the familiar sound of Snippick thumping down the stairs.

"Help! He's trying to get out of bed again. He's after me."

And the old man from the head of the stairs:

"Bitch! She's trying to kill me. She's letting me die. You're all in on it. I'm dying. I'm in pain. She won't even give me a needle. A dying man."

My aunt and uncle ran upstairs.

"Grandpa's such a pain," sighed Sugar.

I headed for the bathroom. I had a stomach ache and reached the john about ready to faint. Bloody murder, he beat me to it. All day and all night. The insect. At it again.

Dentine Johnson, girl, 7½ pounds, born 11 A.M., July 27, 1951, face all mouth, was screaming her head off next to my ear as I put down the necessary statistics in my birthday book. She had reason to complain. She had no father, her mother was fourteen, and she was a Negro. The paperwork in such cases for Welfare and the police got on my nerves. Just born and already on relief with a police record. It made me angry. A while later they roll the kid out, the mother I mean, looking confused. She'd probably be back in here before she was sixteen, I'd seen a lot of that. Every time I send one of these papers to the police I get anxious. What do they do with such children? I feel like tearing the

79

thing up and throwing it in the wastebasket—nobody would ever know the difference. Anyway they could at least use a little more anesthetic in the delivery rooms—it would be easier on my ears. They didn't believe in using anesthetic, they claimed it was better that way. It was cheaper too.

I take my cart and make the rounds of the soiled glove receptacles in the ward. I collect the gloves, the rubber stained and slimy, in a large burlap bag—a job I always put off as long as possible.

Monstrously pregnant women are shuffling back and forth through the corridor in their sloppy hospital robes. Women of all ages from puberty to menopause, matrons, prostitutes, adolescents raped by their uncles, grandmothers on their tenth child. I spot Jimmy, my predecessor on this job, joking with a couple of nurses at the other end of the ward, a small, nice-looking, energetic guy, a Negro. Jimmy is popular here. He had been a good worker, happy at the job, glad to have it, three things I am not. He had to leave when I applied as a summer replacement, because he couldn't pass a civil-service exam I'd dashed off the day I was hired. I used to get nervous when he was breaking me in, nice though he was, because he'd look at me as if he wished I'd just somehow disappear. I knew he had come around to see if it happened yet. I can see his disappointed look when he catches sight of me.

Just then a woman in labor starts screaming and yelling in Spanish. Most of the Obstetrics patients are Puerto Rican or Negro. Nobody in the ward understands Spanish and if a woman doesn't speak any English they don't know whether she's yelling for pain, grief, or exercise.

"Don't let it get you down," says Jimmy. "The Puerto Ricans always yell the most. Them and the Italians. White Protestants are the quietest."

"You seen many white Protestants in here?"

"There was one of em in here once," he said defensively. "She never said a word." He laughed.

80

"Did you find a job?"

"Don't let it worry your head, man."

He must hate my guts. I could never tell for sure whether Jimmy was being considerate or nasty, jovial or suspicious. Sometimes I thought we were pals and suddenly I'd realize it was only me who was pals. Then I'd think it was all my imagination, Jimmy was just another guy I worked with. And then I'd have to admit I couldn't tell a god damned thing about Jimmy at all.

Later on I was waiting in the long corridor of the basement for the elevator. Zip and Borneo were sitting around on some big cartons that had just been delivered. Borneo was hiding a cigarette cupped in the palm of his hand. Zip pulled a kaleidoscope out of his back pocket and put it to his goggling eye. The instrument's tube was colored like a circus elephant. As he pointed it to the light and turned the casing, his mouth formed a gaping smile.

"That jerk's been playin with that all morning," says Borneo, nodding in tolerant ridicule.

"Hey, let's see," I say. "Where did you get that?" I happen to like kaleidoscopes.

"From my mother," says Zip, handing it to me. "It's pretty."

It was pretty. In fact it was one of the nicest kaleidoscopes I've ever seen. Just then Hunch appears.

"Hey, let's see that," he demands.

I give it back to Zip.

"Give it here," says Hunch.

Zip hands it over. Hunch takes it, drops it on the floor and steps on it, first with one foot, then rocking back and forth on it with both. This is too much for Borneo. He breaks up in loud thigh-slapping guffaws. Zip hasn't yet registered what's happened.

"What did you do that for?" I ask.

Hunch swings around to face me, legs apart, fists

81

clenched. His small, porcine eyes burn at me beneath the hump of his massive neck and shoulders.

"What a you got to do with it. What's it to you. You wanna make something out of it? You got a complaint? Go on, kid. Get the hell out a here."

The elevator came and I got the hell out of there. Last I saw, Zip was still looking down at the ruined carcass of his toy, and Hunch, as he shifted his body to look at him, turned toward me the grotesque question mark of his silhouette.

I was on my way to the morgue to deliver a death certificate. As I stepped through the door I saw two men holding up the corpse of a young woman, staring intently at her naked torso. The rubber sheet that enveloped her was drawn back to the navel. Her skin was the color of clay and jeweled with drops of moisture, the arms fell stiffly back and out, as if in a gesture of surrender, and her face, wreathed in wild, Medusa hair, the mouth slightly open, had an expression of abandon and release. I immediately assumed she had drowned herself in the river. In a split second I had a story, a whole biography composed of the squalor, misery, and misfortune I had seen at the hospital. Her body was shapely, the exposed breasts voluptuous, and her face, apparently handsome to begin with, was spiritualized in death to a haunting beauty. I hesitated on the threshold, repulsed by a strange shock of terror mixed with sexual impropriety, and drawn by a trembling curiosity. At that moment the two attendants looked up at the same time and, seeing me, quickly re-enveloped the corpse in its rubber sheet with a haste that seemed furtive —out of prudery, or clinical ethics, or simply because of the expression that must have been on my face, I do not know. With a few efficient motions the bundle was packed away in one of the giant refrigerated file drawers where the cadavers were kept, the drawer was shut, and nothing was spoken.

"How do you do. My name's Bill Davies."

A slim blond guy, crewcut, pipe, big Adam's apple, madras jacket, cord pants, tennis sneakers, hands in pockets, subtle pelvis thrust, languid Midwestern Ivy-League fruit.

"Hello."

"You're the writer, aren't you?" He was swaying gently with his martini, like a lily in a lake bottom. "How groovy. I used to write a little myself, you know. I mean before I became an account exec."

"Really."

"You're a New Yorker, aren't you? I'm from St. Louis myself. The capital and the provinces. Nothing really happens outside of New York. I'm a New Yorker by adoption. That's the only genuine kind."

"I'm from Brooklyn. I don't know whether that's genuine or not."

"Oh, really, Brooklyn. How cool. Do your parents, I mean uh, are they originally from Brooklyn? I mean, do you like lox and bagels?"

"Why?"

"Well, I really dig Jewish cooking. I think it's the grooviest. Stuffed derma, hot bialys, tsimmis, kreplach, gefulte fish, kugel, frozen blintzes . . . your mother make that stuff?"

"No."

"Your grandmother? She from Brooklyn too? I mean, Sukenick. Are you a"—he winked—"an M.O.T.?"

"I'm Jewish, yes."

"Well, mazel tov. You don't look. You know, I'm a great admirer of the Brooklyn Renaissance. Miller, Mailer, Malamud, Roth, Bellow, Salinger . . . you could make a minyan."

"They're not all from Brooklyn."

"So what, they're Jewish aren't they?"

"Are you?"

83

"Well, I'm not exactly a Cohan or Levi. I mean, strictly speaking, I'm a goy. But I've always felt strongly attracted by Yiddish culture. You know . . . Yiddishkeit. It's so full of vitality, so kreftic, to use an old French expression. I mean like shiksahs are so wishy-washy, aren't they? And the Yiddish sense of humor, that really knocks me out. You know the one about Moskowitz and Goldberg? Moskowitz meets this guy on Seventh Avenue and says, Goldboig, oy vay, you're looking vonderful, tventy years younger, a real mensch, a different poisson, he says, vat a you just get beck from Miami Bitch, how come, vat's cookin? Notting, the guy says, I ain't Goldboig. See what I mean? That wry wisdom, tempered by suffering. It's almost existential."

"That's a pretty thick Yiddish accent you have there."

"Oh, you pick it up. I like to go down to Delancey Street for a nosh and kibitz with the nudnicks in Yonah Schimmel's. You think you got troubles? You should go down there and talk to some of those schnorrers. Still, what chutzbah. It's like the Jewish moral sense, emerging from all that tsuris. Like if one of my goyishe friends starts knocking the Jews, I tell him, look, don't hock me a chinic, just to show him what side of the fence I'm on you know. What's that definition, Jewish gentlemen are kikes who just have to leave the room or something like that. But what am I whipping up a sturm? You tell me. What's it like to grow up in Brooklyn? It must be real hamishe. Lot's of rich, warm Jewish life. Lot's of zoftic girls, hey? It must be just nifty. Did you know any of the writers?"

"Oh, sure," I told him, wondering what the hell he was talking about. "Bernie Malamud lived right around the corner. Arthur Miller is practically a relative."

Meanwhile I was trying to decide whether he was putting me on, or whether I was putting him on. The conversation was beginning to give me that weird feeling you get from certain astigmatics who, while looking at you, are really speaking to somebody else. I ain't Goldboig.

84

NOSTALGIC BROOKLYN:
YOUTH'S SEETHE AND QUIVER

We sat down on the couch and prepared for the struggle. For about a half hour we talked. Actually we weren't talking so much as listening nervously for creaking stairs, sounds from the floor above. We talked about the colleges we might go to, about the movie we had just seen, sometimes about friends or books or music. We never talked about sex, which was the only thing really on our minds.

She got up to make coffee. I followed her to the kitchen where I embraced her from behind as she filled the coffeepot. I knew I could always get away with that. As long as she had something to do she could pretend to ignore the way I was handling her. I used to make out with her a lot when she was doing her homework. She would sit on that damn couch reading and writing with bland concentration while I, panting, caressed her breasts or worked my hand between her thighs. She used to get it all done too. Her marks were always a lot better than mine.

We went back to the couch. It was a little past twelve. We held hands and listened cautiously. The house seemed quiet. Her little brother was by now asleep, her parents in bed presumably for the night. I began by telling her I loved her. I did, too. True, I was a little self-conscious about saying so and maybe I didn't quite believe it myself. But, what the hell, the feeling I had for Nancy, whatever it may have been, was very immediate and very urgent—more real than anything else I can remember in the shadow world of my adolescence.

Nancy rarely returned my professions of love. Instead she responded with a particular expression, vexingly oblique compared to my profusions, a gallant smile, intimate, comradely, ironic, that seemed to imply she didn't believe a word of what I said, yet understood, and accepted it. That

85

glance of comprehension distinguished her from any girl I had ever known. And Nancy was different from any girl I knew. She was in some manner privileged, liberated even, in a way that seemed to me essentially non-Jewish, and not only non-Jewish, but completely foreign to Gravesend, something beyond Brooklyn altogether.

I put my arm around her and we began the nocturnal struggle that persisted week after week, Friday and Saturday, Friday and Saturday, Friday and Saturday. I put a cigarette in my mouth and she lit it. I inhaled, blew smoke out my nose, stared across the room and looked pained.

"What's the matter?" she asked after a while.

"Nothing," I answered, my voice submerged in melancholy.

"Then how come you don't say anything?"

"I am saying something." Actually I was depressed by my foregone failure at seduction.

"Should I put on some music?"

"Why not."

She pulled out *The Well-Tempered Clavier* and put it on the turntable. We used to sneer at anything more romantic than Mozart. We kept the volume very low so no one, god forbid, would wake up and come downstairs. She came back to the couch, stood before me, and took a puff on my cigarette. She was wearing a cardigan buttoned up the back and a tight little skirt, tall, thin but incongruously large breasts. Bending over, she grazed my lips with hers, then settled into my lap. I immediately turned all hot and eager, ready to say anything, employ every resource. I gave her a long hard kiss, using the time to run my hands tentatively over her body. She seemed not to notice.

"Before I met you," I told her, "my opinion of women hadn't changed since I was twelve." At that time I always called girls women.

"Oh?"

"I thought they were silly. Not with school and all that

stuff, but basically dumb." I slipped a hand down toward her breast.

"Don't," she said. I retreated.

"Especially the pretty ones. Like you."

She was pretty, extraordinarily so I thought. She had full lips, a high Jewish nose, dark eyes, but fair brows, her hair quite blond. Her father was a Sephardic Jew come from Tangier in his infancy, a shrewd, dark, nervous man, an important liberal lawyer, full of circumstance and high sentence, political pronouncements, quotes from Shakespeare and the Talmud, a born rug merchant who sometimes reminded me of Peter Lorre, and who I instinctively distrusted. The fair complexion came from her mother whose parents were German Jews, a tall, stately, frigid woman with an air of cultivation and—what was in fact remarkable for that generation—a college degree, which was always, incidentally, somehow implicit. From her also no doubt Nancy's grace of movement, a sort of half-conscious finesse of deportment, as if manners were part of beauty and beauty really important.

"You know," I said casually, "Slade loaned me a copy of Reich's *Function of the Orgasm* he borrowed from somebody." I began working one hand under her arm around to her breast.

"Who's Reich?" she asked suspiciously. "I don't like your friends."

"You always say that. You hardly know them." By bending my wrist sharply I could just about reach.

"I don't want to know them. They're too smart for me."

"Come on."

"I mean all they ever talk about is politics. Just like my father. Don't. Always catching on to some new crackpot book and complaining about the bourgeoisie. When there isn't even a bourgeoisie in this country and if there is we're it. It all seems very pseudo to me. Don't."

87

"First of all, your father isn't really a radical." That seemed decisive to me. I thought she had entirely too much respect for her father. I felt it hurt our "relationship," as we called it. "He isn't really a liberal if you ask me. He even sees virtues in this guy McCarthy. What kind of liberal is that?" By bending my wrist almost at a right angle I just managed to brush the bottom and side of her breast with the fore-knuckles of two of my fingers.

"Leave my father out of it. Let's not get into that again. What's this Reich book?"

Apparently she hadn't noticed yet this time. But my wrist was beginning to ache.

"Reich. He believes in love, work, and knowledge."

"What's so unusual about that?"

"By love he means sex."

"I knew it would come to that." She giggled. By flexing my wrist with heroic effort I managed to press my knuckles ever so slightly into the softness and resiliency of her breast. She must have felt that so I knew she was letting me do it. That was tremendously exciting. But the pain in my wrist was so acute I didn't know if I could stand it. I groaned. She must have mistaken the motive of the sound because she suddenly kissed me. It was a delicate situation. I didn't dare make any abrupt advance because that would destroy our mutual subterfuge that nothing was happening. But I couldn't withdraw because that would ruin whatever advantage I'd already gained. I kept talking.

"But he doesn't just mean sex. He means that people should do it whenever they want. He says that Puritanism is just a form of destructive social repression and that sex is a revolutionary force. Frustration just makes you neurotic. He believes you should do it just for pleasure. Otherwise you get sick. You get armored against it and if you don't do it, after a while you won't be able to do it at all."

"Do what?"

88

My wrist was so painful I couldn't stand it any longer. I made a desperate lunge, caught her nipple between my fingers and squeezed as hard as I could.

"Make love. Fuck."

"Ouch!" she screamed and jumped off my lap. "Do you have to use such vulgar language?"

"What's wrong with vulgar language? It's just your damn middle-class prejudice against calling a thing what it really is."

"There you go again. Why do you always attack me as if I were the only representative of the middle class?"

"Because you are. As far as I'm concerned because I love you."

A smile, not quite successfully suppressed, broke through the anger in her face.

"Oh Ronnie. Let's not fight."

I shrugged. "Sit down," I said.

She sat down beside me.

"Nice music," she said.

"Yeah."

"Tell me more about the book."

"What do you say we turn out the light?"

"Suppose my parents come down and find the light out? They'll think we're necking."

"And we will be too. So what. Tell them we're saving electricity."

She laughed, reached over, and turned off the light. In the half light coming from the hall I put my arm around her and let my hand dangle over her shoulder so that it occasionally grazed her breast. Darkness always weighed in my favor. In the dark her eyes were not obliged to notice what her body felt.

"You were saying about the book."

"Oh, uh, yeah." Just then my palm made contact with her nipple. "Reich discovered the orgone box."

"Where?" she asked absently.

89

"He invented it." She grabbed my hand, pulled it away, pressed it back.

"What's an orgone box?"

"It accumulates orgones."

"What are orgones?"

"Sexual energy."

"How interesting." Suddenly she pulled my hand away. "Why do you always have to bring in sex? Don't you ever think about anything else?"

"Rarely." I pushed my hand back. She sighed.

"Why can't you be more like normal boys? Sometimes I think you're obsessed."

"You're right. I am." I clamped my hand on good and solid.

"Don't," she said. She squirmed and gave me a kiss. I started unbuttoning the back of her sweater.

"What are you doing?"

"Nothing." I already had it half unbuttoned.

"Cut it out." She pulled away from me and started buttoning it again. I grabbed her hands and held them in front of her.

"Are you going to regress to middle-class morality again?"

"No."

"You'd think this was our first date."

"I'm sorry."

"You know it's just another fraudulent hypocrisy they try to pound into our skulls, don't you?"

"Yes, I know. But they've already pounded it in. What am I supposed to do?"

"You ought to go to an analyst. You're sick."

"Well we all are, aren't we? That's your theory. Why pick on me?"

"It's no reason not to make an effort. You want to be sick all your life?"

"No."

90

"Well then, relax." I started on the rest of the buttons.

"Cut it out!" She grabbed my hand. I pulled her arm in front of her and caught both wrists in one hand. While she struggled to free herself I undid the rest of the buttons, slipped my hand under her sweater and started rubbing her breasts through her brassiere. Her body tensed, then relaxed. She threw her arms around me and we kissed for a long time. I started feeling for the clasp of her brassiere.

"Do you have to?" she complained.

"Look, I love you. I'm not trying to take you for a ride." I was working at the clasp with one hand while the other was busy with her breasts.

"Do you love me or do you love my body?"

"I love you and I love your body." With unheard-of manual dexterity I managed to undo one of her brassiere hooks. "You don't believe in virginity, do you?"

She gave me a push that sent me flying to the other end of the couch. "No. But I never heard you say anything about marrying me, either."

"Marrying you. Isn't it enough that I love you? And even if I didn't so what?"

"That's easy for you to say."

"Christ! You've got the soul of a television set."

I gave up. I leaned back against the arm of the couch, exhausted. The hell with it.

"Ronnie. Don't say things like that. Ronnie, please. Come back."

"Go to hell."

Suddenly she smiled her knowing smile, reached behind her, undid the clasp, and threw her arms along the back of the couch. I couldn't believe it. I moved toward her and slipped my hands under her clothing, pondering the heaviness of her breasts, tickling my palms with her nipples. Her eyes were closed. She embraced me, swaying back and forth,

91

and started making appreciative sounds in her throat as if she were delectating some new, incredible ice cream delight. I grabbed her sweater and began pulling it off.

"Oh no," she said.

"Why not?"

"No. Just no. That's all."

"Yes."

"No."

She tried to push me but I was ready. I caught her hands and held them. She was squirming and panting, trying to hit me with her elbows and knees. I twisted her arms, forced her down to the couch, and held her legs in a scissor lock. I caught the edge of her sweater in my teeth and started pulling it off. She hit me in the cheek with her shoulder and I nearly bit my tongue off. I managed to get both her wrists in one hand. She bit me on the fore arm and I smothered a cry of pain. Neither of us dared make a sound her parents might hear. She got a hand free and scratched my cheek. I jumped on top of her and, straddling her body, caught her wrists again. With my free hand I grabbed her sweater and brassiere together and pulled with all my might. Something ripped and I went flying back off the couch onto the floor with her clothing in my hand.

She was sitting on the couch bare to the waist, sobbing and covering her breasts with her hands. I sat down next to her and put my arm around her naked shoulders. "Don't cry," I begged. "Don't cry. I won't do anything you don't want." She pushed her face against my shoulder, wetting my collar with tears. I caressed her naked body, held her breasts in my hands. We kissed. I hardly knew what I was doing. My hand was under her skirt, moist and smooth, petting, squeezing, trying to loosen her knees. Somehow my leg was around her waist, forcing her down. She wriggled out from under me, then lay on top of me, pushing her breasts into my face. Her skirt was up around her abdomen. I was massaging the insides of her thighs. They were cov-

92

ered with a warm film of perspiration. I ran my hand under her pants and squeezed her buttocks. "It hurts," she said, out of breath. I felt in my watch pocket for the ragged tinfoil of the three Trojans I had bought eight months ago. Then I slipped one hand under the elastic of her pants and with the other forced her hand onto my tortured penis. Suddenly she was in rigor mortis, stiff, cold, and limp all over.

"No," she said. And I knew she meant no. She didn't fight but just lay rigid. From there on in I knew it would be a question of cold-blooded rape. At that age I wasn't up to it, especially since I wasn't exactly sure what to do next. "Why?" I asked. "What's the matter. There's nothing wrong with it."

"I know. I know. I don't know."

We got up. She was crying, sobbing in bitter spasms that shook her body. I rocked her in my arms and ran my hand up and down her long back. After a while she calmed down, wiped her tears and put her arms around me. I put my head between her breasts, I licked her nipples. She stared into space, absorbed, expressionless. She moved onto my lap. We were calm, sad, fraternal in defeat, cradled together in a melancholy equilibrium of lust and misery. I sighed and looked up. In the doorway I saw, barefoot in a strange, old-fashioned white nightshirt, hairy legs, skinny neck, his fringe of hair tangled his glasses askew, her father, silent, motionless, staring at us with a look impossible to decipher. Without saying a word, without changing his expression, he looked at me, turned, and disappeared up the stairs.

Putting her sweater on, straightening her skirt, quickly, no time to talk about anything, in a panic, she hurried me to the door. Before I knew what was happening I was outside in the sad Brooklyn night fumbling with my tie. I could have vomited on the doorstep. I should have. And they call this a free country.

93

"Loan?" repeated Finch. "You want a loan? You have no job? I don't get it. Wait a minute. Henry Miller. The whole bit. I see, I see, you want a loan."

"That's what I said, yeah."

"That's what you said, but is that what you really want? Let me give you some good advice. Forget these literary notions. They're not practical. You came to the right person. My life is nothing but a series of loans. I live from one loan to the next. Borrow from Peter to pay Paul. Borrow from the bank to pay my installments, borrow on my house to pay for my car, borrow from my in-laws to pay the bank. You want to hear my latest coup? My car breaks down completely before I even finish the payments. So I go back to the dealer and he says he'll allow so much for a trade on a new car. But I don't have enough money for a new car. Does that faze me? Not at all, because long ago I figured out the key to the American economy. There's no such thing as money. There's only credit. So I get a bill of sale from the dealer, go to the bank, borrow money on my new car, start payments for it, and have a neat sum left over as profit. Don't get involved in this kind of thing. It uses up all your energy. It's a way of life. Take a practical suggestion. Stay out of debt. You're in great danger. You're on the verge of a step that could change the course of your whole life. Look at that piece over there. Don't I know her from somewhere?"

We were sitting in a bar on the Lower East Side.

"How would I know?"

"I thought she looked like someone we used to know in high school. Not that I'm interested in women, you understand. Especially with Arlene in her ninth month, god forbid, the mere fact I haven't got laid in seven or eight months—no, she reminds me of my mother, that's all it is, remarkable resemblance."

It was his manner to say everything in a tone of satire so you could never be sure whether he was kidding or not.

94

"I know what your mother looks like, Finch, and she doesn't look like any piece, especially that one."

"Leave my mother out of it. No, seriously, I'm just kidding."

"Of course I realize you might be short about now."

"Short? How?"

"On money. With Arlene pregnant and all your debts."

"Oh, my debts. Forget about them. I live on debts. I believe in deficit spending. Don't worry about me. I'll get along."

"Well, gee, I hope so Len. And in case you ever get into a hole remember your credit is always good with me. Meanwhile maybe you can let me have two bits or so toward a square meal."

"You're kidding me again. Why can't you ever be serious? Now look at that. All alone at the table. Just as a theoretical thing, how would you get yourself across to a girl like that if you were interested?"

"Go and ask her if she wants to hump."

"No, seriously. It's a problem in public relations. All these years writing ad copy and I still haven't learned how to sell myself. In modern life publicity is a central art—probably the central art. That's why copywriting requires creative talent. I speak with heartbreaking sincerity. Advertising is a kind of poetry. It's the perfect expression of.popular desire, it discovers our heart's profoundest images, and it creates a gratifying dream world whose power seduces the imagination. And everybody makes a mint. Did I ever tell you my theory of anti-ideas?"

"No."

"Sure. Since you can't take what you're doing seriously you turn it into parody. It's a doctrine of no-think. Nobody with any intelligence believes anything any more."

"Believes anything or believes in anything?"

"Both."

"That so?"

95

"Sure. It's the spirit of U-2 and the Bay of Pigs. People like you still talk about selling out."

"I never said anything about selling out."

"I didn't say you did. I said people like you are always shooting off about that kind of thing. You and your artist friends. So-called radicals, intellectuals, Bernie for example. All you pure types. Sell what out? I haven't got anything to sell out. And neither have you. We're all in the same boat. Bernie don't believe in Socialism any more than I believe in honest income tax returns. We all say one thing and do another. I won't buy it. You guys are suckers, that's all there is to it. Well if you like to live on peanuts, go on, but don't expect me to pay for it. How much do you need?"

"Fifteen dollars?"

"Fifteen dollars. How long do I have to work for fifteen dollars? You know, it's stupendous. Five years at this business and I'm still making seven thousand. It's unbelievable. I don't know how I do it. You know who I'm working for now? My former assistant. I must be the lowest paid man in the industry. Here, take twenty-five. What can you buy for fifteen dollars?"

"Thanks."

"Forget it. Just don't forget to return it, like some other guys I know. Why don't you go and get a job."

"I got fired."

"You fraud. I know you. It's the not-working stage, the poverty bit. You'll straighten out. Wait till you run out of friends to mooch off. You know the one honest guy I ever knew? Remember Yssis?"

"Yssis the pervert. What ever happened to him?"

"I couldn't stand him, but I respect him. He got into cybernetics and went to work for some kind of computer corporation, market research, I don't know what."

"No. Why?"

"Why. Because he's a wealthy man by now, that's why. He's a fellow I really admire."

YSSIS THE PERVERT, AND HIS
MERRY PRANKS

Once there was a finished basement. And in this basement there were three boys. The first boy was named Len Fink later called Finch and he was the first boy because it was his basement. The second boy was named Herbie Yssis later called Yssis the Pervert for his Merry Pranks. And the third boy was Ronnie our hero later called Suchanitch Suckanitch Subanitch Sookenack Bookenack Sackanook and so on.

Now this basement was an illustrious basement that gained in its time much renown. It was built of the most precious materials its builders could conjure, such as knotty pine, linoleum tile, prefabricated plaster board, leopard leatherette, aluminum TV tables, Van Gogh reproductions, and beer hall mottoes on plaques illustrated with drawings of busty nudes. There was even a bar with a beer tap and real bar stools. Built into one wall was a bookcase at the disposal of guests that they might refresh their spirits, which sheltered such dusty tomes as *Lydia Bailey, The Carpetbaggers, Green Dolphin Street, Dave Dawson With the R.A.F., The Power of Positive Thinking, This Is My Beloved, The Complete Works of Shakespeare, The Vixens, Black Beauty, Life Begins at Forty, Gone With the Wind, Little Women, The Heller, The Razor's Edge, Plato's Republic, A Tree Grows in Brooklyn, The Good Earth, Of Human Bondage, Forever Amber, The Great Snow, The Kama Sutra, Kant's Works,* and *The Hardy Boys Go Fishing.* A friendly refrigerator always kept at the ready ranks of frosty beer bottles for the thirsty wanderer on behalf of the Finks' ungrudging hospitality. All and all a fine place to go and stay out of trouble when Fink's parents weren't home. It kept us off the streetcorners, you see.

Now as the three boys sat together in this basement Len the first boy opened his mouth and, behold, he spoke.

"I don't know why I get mixed up with you intellectual shmucks," said Len. "It's all a lot of crap to me. Come on Yssis, what's the story. You want to run for something? What's the idea?"

"Pick my nose," replied Yssis, in the light-hearted manner that was his wont. "No idea. I don't believe in ideas. It's un-American."

As when mighty Etna, after much subterranean growling and grumbling, precipitantly releases his pent-up force, or risen from the fishy depths and shaking his mountainous shoulders, the leviathan breathes like a waterspout hissing on the ocean swell, so did restive Len, at this juncture, exhale.

"All I'm allowed to say is it's a cabal," Yssis revealed. "I'm liaison from central to the Gravesend-Flatbush-Bensonhurst cell."

"What cell. What do you mean cell. For what?"

"For the cabal."

"What cabal."

"Cabal, cabal," fumed madcap Yssis. "A cabal is a secret. Do you think I'm fool enough to leak a thing like that? A slip of the lip sinks a ship. There's some that leak and some that don't. I'm not one of your leaky fellows, or leakies as we call them in the trade. I have the highest security clearance, ten to the tenth power. Only the best credentials. Mum's the word. Bring your own armpits."

"Ah I think it's all a lot of crap," foamed irrepressible Len. His agile tennis-champ figure fidgeted over Yssis' head as if he were ready to pick him up and fling him from Dan to Beersheba but for some magic bubble that Yssis, like one of your wizards of olden times, managed to project about himself. Yssis was a miniature boy, much smaller than other boys his age, with thick, childish glasses, shiny cherub cheeks, and hairless face, all which often convened with his getting into movies at half price. But his stature, and indeed his relative youth, never diminished a kind of intellectual legerdemain he exercised among us, for his precocity was such that he was acknowledged a prodigy by all who encountered him, not excluding his teachers at Brooklyn Tech. And in faith it cannot be denied that he was marvelously aggressive in all his pursuits, which included the espousal and dissemination of such dark matters as the Cabala, Swedenborg, E.S.P., yoga, necromancy, metempsychosis, animal magnetism, scatological science, L. Ron Hubbard's Dianetics, and the Baconian heresy. In everything he did he revealed a blatant craving for converts, followers, audience, even enemies, a lust for attention.

It so fell out this Friday night, for Friday night it was, that Kenny Malcolm made his way to Fink's basement at an hour earlier than many, though not so early as some, who indeed were already present. Now Kenny was a big boy who had forgone the glory of an athletic scholarship by quitting the school football team. He was a guileless youth who, though constantly pursued by wenches, was so innocent of his own magnetism as to be confused rather than gratified by it.

"I just heard Marv Gilman got a scholarship to Yale," Kenny informed us in his furry baritone.

"That shmuck?" Len exploded. "What's his average?"

"I don't know," said feckless Ronnie who, in reaction to the general tone of things, made a point of not knowing the average of anyone in his high school, even his own. It was a thing of wonder throughout the borough, that everyone in our school of competitive importance knew the average of everyone else of competitive importance, and that all girls in the running knew all such averages to three decimal places.

99

"You know Marv," said Kenny. "He never even takes time off for a movie."

"Shmuck!" insisted Len. "He even studied for his I.Q. test. The shmucks inherit the earth."

"I hope you do as well," said mild-mannered Kenny.

"Drop dead," said candid Len. "All I want to do is make a lot of money and live like a king."

"Then why don't you do what Marv does?" asked Kenny.

"Because he's a shmuck," said Len.

"Be a shmuck," Kenny advised. "If you want to be a shmuck, be a shmuck."

"Ah, it's all a lot of crap," said Len.

There was something unspeakable saintly in poor Kenny's address. Gentle, maladroit Kenny, benign to the point of stupidity, you could imagine him in sackcloth and sandals, his blond hair curling over his forehead, begging his way along some dusty archaic road as of yore. He was an innocent among worldly seventeen-year-olds. As a pacifist, he was planning to risk jail rather than register for the draft, a position more sophisticated high school pacifists considered extreme, if not foolhardy.

Ed Roach, one of Yssis' retinue, made his entry. Roach was counted among Yssis' disciples. He was a barbarian from Red Hook whose tutelage the puissant one had undertaken. In consequence of his master's influence he had recently been suspended for pilfering materials from chem lab. With them Yssis had constructed what he called an infernal machine that when detonated had emptied a floor of his high school because of its stink, which was one of his Merry Pranks.

"Let's hear the letters, Herbie," importuned impatient Roach.

"Letters?" puzzled Len.

"Herbie's got some spastic letters from Sybil," revealed racy Roach. "They're pen pals."

100

"Come on, Sybil?" demurred dubious Len.

Fat Sybil the Stalinist, every man's poison, was not one to engage in frivolous exchanges with a member of the opposite sex. Grim Amazon, globous Diana, the people's delegate was known to indulge herself only in occasional young progressive amusements, and mainly in militant minstrelsy of the proletarian mode. You could find her in some unpopular corner of any gathering, strumming and humming about scabs and pinks and company finks. Wonderful also our youthful scribe's epistolary venture inasmuch as it was well known, and thought a defect in him by some, that Yssis hated the sex, and liked to frighten women on the street at night, which was one of his Merry Pranks. Indeed, women he counted little better than animals, and he loved to torment animals—whence also came Much Merry Pranking.

Sly Herbie clicked his heels together, snapped to attention, and raised his chubby hand in the Nazi salute. "Heil Hitler!" he barked. Then, drawing a scroll from his pocket and opening it with a graceful flourish, he began to read, lowering his own pubescent tenor in approximation of Sybil's hoarse contralto.

"Friend and comrade. I tell you frankly that I am highly ambivalent about your letter, and must ask you to clarify your position which to my knowledge has always been one of infantile negativism. It would be paradoxical if, while corresponding with you in the expectation of concrete discussion, I were merely indulging your juvenile deviations. Your proposal regarding the utility of mass mesmerism I refuse to take seriously. Though your interest in hypnosis is well known, I consider it nothing more than an example of the latent fascist tendencies in the habitual self-aggrandizing character of the typical bourgeois individualist."

"Ah go home," erupted Len. "These damn pinkos." Irascible Len was one of Yssis' most successful subjects in his pursuit of the drowsy art, as indeed we had all felt the

101

power of the maestro's spell in some degree one way or another.

"Silence in the courtroom," demanded chubby Herbie. "Likewise it seems obvious," he continued in sybilant mimicry, "that while objectively you show a certain amount of intelligence in penetrating the mystifications of the bourgeois mentality, from the point of view of history you and your friends must be considered reactionary hypocrites. Finally, I warn you against any kind of sentimentality that may have motivated your letter. I have no patience with that kind of opportunism, and I categorically reject your existence as a man. However, should you wish to arrange a meeting for a frank exchange of views, I would not be completely unapproachable. Signed fat Sybil," concluded Yssis in his own boyish tenor. "Ain't that enough to make you jerk off?"

"I can hardly control myself," remarked Roach.

"Spastic. Don't," advised permissive Yssis.

"What about the answer?" urged Roach.

"Do we have to?" inquired Len.

"What's the point?" pursued inquisitive Ken.

"May you contract the hairy lupus. The point is to be as disgusting as possible." Childe Herbie unrolled a second scroll. "I quote. Comrade. I find your missive very concrete. Let us hope it will cement the bricks of our friendship and become the mortar of a fruitful alliance. However, as you rightly guess, my letter was partly a ruse disguising a fatal attraction to the pendulous blubber of your flesh reeking, as it does, with a subtle hint of attar of armpits. I hope you won't consider my natural curiosity about your heavenly person too intime or indelicate to favor me with answers to a few irrepressible inquiries. Is it true, as is rumored, that as a babe you ate your own afterbirth, that your chest is as hairy as your crotch, and that (ah) you shit turds ten inches long? Awaiting your answer, oh fat, I will continue to hope and to dream of that moment when my sweaty, smelly toe slides into your quivering, expectant sphincter. Signed, the Enema of the People."

"Whew! Who farted?" exclaimed bluff Len.

"You're not really going to send that Herbie?" asked awestruck Ken.

"Only after I puke on it," was Yssis' droll rejoinder.

"You're sick," giggled goggling Roach.

"No, just got the rag on," flashed Yssis in snappy repartee.

"I don't know why we hang around with you," wondered clean-cut Ken.

"My finger," was the downy-dimpled spellbinder's oblique reply, as he raised his middle finger, knuckles out, in front of his nose. "Watch the finger, keep your eye on the finger, and I'll tell you. Why do the good boys play with naughty Herbie? Watch the finger," he repeated, waving it sinuously before Ken's fascinated features. "Because Herbie loves the dark that the good boys are afraid of, because Herbie loves the fecal corruption of its ghouls and vampires, because he knows the lost art of puking and shitting at the same time, because the good boys come to Herbie when they're fed up and he puts one finger down their throats and another up their anuses because he knows how to make them do their duty and they love him. Because repulsive like you, he loves the repulsive and knows its power. Because through it you become a walking insult, an affront, an ugliness, a pimple on the nose of society. Because the good people get mad and prefer all kinds of nastiness to the wretch that makes them gag and vomit and consider their own feculence. So hail to the wretch! Let us all rise in tribute and join together in a chorus of the wretches' anthem. To the tune of 'Gaudeamus igitur,' a-one, a-two, a-three:

> *Pimples, puss, and pubic hair,*
> *Uncle Mommy must be there,*

103

The Hairy Lady's dripping snot,
While Spastic Dan licks out her twat,
The scabs are brought by Sphincter Pete,
With other pukey things to eat,
And all the wretches twitch and prance,
To make good folk shit in their pants.

And now Kenny will lead us in a session of mutual regurgitation and fun with turds. Already he's starting to look nice and nauseous."

And indeed, gentle Kenny, staring at Yssis hand on throat and tongue protruding, suddenly shook his head and turned away exclaiming, "Christ! Someone hand me a beer."

"Yeah, make it two," said Slade, who came in at that moment. He was wearing tight pants, pointed black shoes, electric blue jacket, and pink shirt with open collar. He walked as if he were wearing boots. "Hey, what's all this crap with Yssis?" Slade asked dazzled Ronnie.

"Don't know. He won't tell anybody. What are you all dressed up about?"

"Going to the Palladium. Then maybe slip over to Bop City and listen in on Diz. I got my girl friend's car."

"Which girl friend?" asked innocent Ron.

"Is there any difference?" answered airy Slade.

A train of winsome youths walked in together, followed shortly by others in ones and twos, Bernie, with his stiff, awkward gait, Goodwine in beret and tennis sneakers, unshaven, Eugene the positivist, who went around crushed by the idea of determinism, the poet Belinsky who had invented his own language, Fein the nonentity, Goldberg the blue grass singer, Agajian the poker player, Harvey who talked through his nose, rabbity Shneck who played shortstop, pale McManus the Catholic mystic, Ratner who knew everyone, fat Barry, Weiss the rabbinical student, Kane who liked cars, Rabinowitz the math genius who perfected a way of cheating on the College Boards, Irwin the pianist,

104

ugly Weintraub who once memorized an abridged edition of Roget's Thesaurus, and ubiquitous Melnick who was always around.

"Well," said Bernie, with the sarcasm that for him passed as good humor, "this is about as demoralized a bunch of perverts as I've ever seen assembled under one roof."

"Let's break out the cards," said Len, who was handing around some beer.

"You heard from colleges yet?" Bernie asked.

"No scholarship at Columbia," said unlucky Ronnie. "Rejected by Lehigh. That leaves Vermont."

"But you're not an engineer. Why Lehigh?"

"People keep asking me that. Ask our college adviser. Why Vermont for that matter."

"Looks like Brooklyn College, hey?" said Slade. He had been accepted by Stanford and Cornell, and was waiting to hear about a scholarship to Harvard.

"Over my dead body," vowed hapless Ronnie.

"Wrong Way Sukenick," said Bernie. "You have a schizoid genius for getting fouled up in the meshes of bureaucracy. Fortunately you also have a schizoid genius for lucky blunders, convenient ignorance, accidental last-minute narrow escapes, and a knack for doing everything ass-backwards. Why can't you do things the easy way, you subversive bastard? What are you some kind of trouble-maker?"

"Things happen to me that way," mumbled Wrong Way Ron.

"Say," said Slade, "what do you think of this new stuff in the Hiss case? Looks like he's going to get another trial, hey?"

"What, the business about the typewriter?" said Bernie. "It doesn't prove a thing."

"What do you mean it don't prove anything," objected Slade. "It proves he was framed."

105

"Come on. That's all ambiguous as hell. And even if he was framed, he was up to his neck in the Party anyway."

"It strikes me," said Slade with a definitive air, "that you have a very fuck-ass attitude toward witch burning."

"It's a dichotomy," said Bernie. "I'm not talking about red herrings. But if there are witches, I'm in favor of burning them."

"And you're the guy who practically ran for class president on the Wallace-Taylor ticket."

"That was a popular front," shrugged Bernie.

"Recidivist," accused Slade.

"Recidivist my ass," said Len. "What the fuck are they talking about?"

Slade looked at him with grand contempt.

"Say Ernie," Ratner asked, "is it true what they say about you and Myrna Melman?"

Suddenly everybody was paying attention. Myrna Melman was a myth among us, the girl with the ninety-nine point eight average. It was not merely her fabulous school record, nor even that she was in addition rather pretty in her mild, doll-faced way. The thing that really intrigued us was that she never talked. After four years of high school no one, neither girl nor boy, knew the least thing about her. She sat in our classes not talking year after year, simply remembering everything and getting a hundred on every test. She rarely went out on dates, and when she did conversation was limited to the most polite formalities which she uttered, in her blank little voice, with the utmost gravity. And now a rumor was abroad, started I have no doubt by Slade himself, that he had seduced this mild-mannered sphinx.

"Is what true?" asked Slade with excessive innocence.

"That you laid her," said Ratner.

"No comment," said Slade.

"Come on, Ernie," urged Fein.

106

"Well," said Slade, "let's put it this way. I won't deny it."

"Cut the crap, Slade," said Rabinowitz. "Let's have the story."

"All right," said Slade reluctantly. "If you insist. But this is just between us, understand?"

"Sure, sure."

"Well," said Slade, "there's really not much to tell. I was on the bus coming back from school. It was a little crowded, see, and I noticed I was rubbing against this girl. Well, you know I'm not hard up for that kind of thing, so I stepped back a little. Well, she stepped back too and then I noticed it was Myrna so I stayed where I was. So we went along like that for a while. What a surprise. Finally I said, 'Hi Myrna.' No answer. 'How did you like Social Studies today?' No answer. Suddenly she says, 'I get off next stop. Want to walk me home?' So I get off and walk her home. Meanwhile I'm carrying on an absolutely brilliant one way conversation but I can't get her to say anymore than yes, no, or really. Now and then she turns her head and smiles at me—you know that harmless little smile she has? When we get to her house it turns out nobody's home. By now I've got an idea about what's going on, but I can't believe it. She hangs up her coat and says let's go up to her room. When we get to her room she shuts the door and I grab her hand. But she moves away and says, 'Would you like a drink?' So I say yeah. Three minutes later she comes back with two glasses of cognac and she's in her bathrobe. 'I see you've changed,' I said. 'Yes,' she says. She sits down on her bed, I sit next to her, we drink our drinks, I give her a kiss and then I lay her out, just like that. That's all there is to it."

There was a silence.

"How was it?" asked Belinsky.

"It was great."

"Well, I mean, did she say anything?" pursued Belinsky.

"Yeah, she did."

"What."

"Well, after I laid her she opened her eyes, pulled her robe back on, and said: 'Would you like to borrow my Biology notes?'"

"Ah, come on."

"No kidding. So I told her I didn't need her Bio notes and then I asked her when she wanted to see me again. She just looked at me with that blank look and said, 'Don't be compulsive.' How do you like that? Don't be compulsive. So I zipped up my pants, said thank you, and left."

"Was she cherry?" asked Kane.

"Are you kidding? Hell no. It was the biggest surprise of my life. And you know something. When she sees me in school now she acts like she doesn't know who I am."

There was another silence.

"Bullshit," said Len finally.

"I don't believe it," said Ratner.

"Me neither," said Bernie.

"Neither do I," said Slade. "And yet it happened."

But we insisted we didn't believe it. Not too hard though, because we did.

Now while the big boys were talking, little Herbie Yssis had climbed up onto the bar all by himself. And what do you suppose little Herbie did after he had climbed up onto the bar all by himself while the big boys were talking? Didums scream for momsy? Cry he wah-wah for sucky bottle? Baby makee bad wet in diaper? Maybe. Certain it is that no sooner had young Yssis attained this vantage than he immediately assumed the lotos posture, a posture which he had only with the greatest difficulty brought back from the Orient, and swaying slightly on the rectal axis, began to grunt and groan in a strangely familiar manner.

"Wait," said Goodwine. "The guru prepares to speak. The terrible infant rocks in his vatic cradle."

Hirsute Goodwine, Yssis' closest companion, was a lusty fun-loving fellow, which had been the cause of his ejection

108

from a high school and two prep schools around about the city, and made for his wealthy parents some incommodity in discovering an institution that would grant him a diploma. The young heir apparent professed a mighty interest in the curious cultivation of the pinky nail of his left hand, which was two inches long, and which he admired, according to the censorious, with overmuch ostentation. His presence always spurred Yssis to heightened extravagancy. It was a matter for speculation as to which of them dominated the other. Goodwine's rather effeminate flourish did not diminish the ambiguity of their friendship.

Goodwine took a couple of joss sticks out of his pocket, lit them, and set them in beer glasses on either side of Yssis. The smell of incense filled the room.

"Christ," said Len, "do we have to? Open the window."

Slade took a bright red tie out of his breast pocket and started knotting it under his collar. "Rank decadence," he said. "The decline of the West. I'm going to the Palladium. Want to come? You can always pick up a piece of ass Friday night."

Lovelorn Ronnie looked at Slade's racy smile, his aggressive chin, his long sideburns. Morosely he pictured Slade strutting through the Palladium as if it were his own cock yard.

"I think I'll stick around for a while," answered lackluster Ron.

"It's your funeral," he said. He made a thumbs-up sign derived from Victor McLaglan in *The Informer*, put on his trench coat, and left.

"Children of the cosmos," said Yssis. "I come before you in my earthly manifestation as an emissary from central. Our transmogrifications bear the *Good Housekeeping* Seal of Approval as advertised nationally in *Life, Look*, the *Retail Sausage Dealers' Newsletter*, all the best places. Only this morning I received vibrations to organize the

109

Gravesend-Flatbush-Bensonhurst cell. Are your astral bodies smothered in karma? Shuffle off that mortal coil. Try COS-MOS, the Committee On Spherical Migration Of Soma. It's big. It's the cosmic conspiracy. Clear your engrams, let COSMOS take over. Money-back guarantee. Contains latakia, lanolin, chlorophyll, charcoal, monosodium glutamate, H_2O, sodium floride, rhinoceros hormones, polecat semen, monkey duty, radioactive cobalt, and hot fuming sulphuric acid. It cleans your teeth right down your throat. A-1, ten to tenth power. Spontaneous paid testimonials. Our candidates in every ward with direct pulsations from central. Tomorrow the cosmos. Undermine, pervert, demoralize. Nothing but irregular procedures. Triple agents our sexual specialty, sixty-nine peachy flavors. We can do it, girls. I'm so excited. But so much for that. It is time to ask ourselves the Four Questions.

"What must we believe?

"Feces are taboo, and by extrapolation, all feculence.

"What must we abominate?

"Video is fecal matter. Linoleum is fecal matter. Freezers are fecal matter. Mixers are fecal matter. Canasta is fecal matter. Xavier Cugat is fecal matter. Southern Comfort is fecal matter. Chromium is fecal matter. Plastic is fecal matter. The *Sunday Times* is fecal matter. Frank Yerby is fecal matter. Girl Scout Cookies are fecal matter. Buicks are fecal matter. The Hit Parade is fecal matter. Nose jobs are fecal matter. The Academy Award is fecal matter. Not to put it too bluntly, boys, we're drowning in shit.

"What must we do?

"We must function as social laxatives. Elimination is our duty.

"Who is the chosen one?

"By virtue of his long struggle against the forces of determinism, and after careful examination of his stool, central has chosen a candidate who we will support by all means

110

in the forthcoming senior class poll. The fatal finger falls on Eugene."

"Who, me?"

Swart Eugene was a sullen lad who suffered from what might be called negative charisma. There was that about him one would be hard put to define, an ineffable *je ne sais quoi* of personality that was flatly repellent. In his presence conversation waned, wit turned sour, animation disappeared. He had long consolidated all his suffering in one fundamental grief—lack of free will. "We're the robots of fate," he liked to observe when he was especially gloomy. His theory was that man's only recourse under the circumstances lay in pitting his mind against the cosmic mechanism in order to gain some foresight of its machinations. To this end he charted the future carefully, estimated chance like a horseplayer, calculated probabilities, prepared schedules, graphs, itineraries, extrapolations, prognostications, lists, composed meticulous plots, but somehow always managed to fuck up in the end. As if in reflection of his mechanistic view of things, the movements of his body resembled the jerky awkwardness of a marionette and his mind worked with a weird absence of subtlety that might be found in a cybernetics machine.

"Fate, with its unerring telescope, has singled you out," intoned Yssis. "Few are chosen. Do you accept our candidacy?"

"For what?"

"Boy Most Likely to Succeed," pronounced sage Yssis.

This was the occasion of extensive jocularity among the company. Eugene gave no sign of cognizance. Eugene the schlemiel.

"An intriguing proposition," he said, considering within himself. "Should I run? On the one hand, I might lose. It's a ten-to-one probability. On the other hand, people are always in favor of the underdog. I could be a dark-horse candidate. I might win a long-shot victory."

111

"Why don't you just run for dark horse?" said one in sly inquiry. This made much merriment.

"How much effort will it take?" Eugene continued. "Is it worth the risk? It might be interesting," he pondered, stroking his chin and pronouncing every syllable of the word, "to make a study of the situation."

"I forgot to tell you," specified nimble Yssis, "this is a draft."

"Draft? That presents a problem. I might refuse a draft. On the other hand . . ."

"We have five fingers," concluded a certain wit.

"The hell with him," said Goodwine. "Hire a schwarze."

"On the other hand," Eugene continued, "if I refused a draft you could put me on the ballot anyway. I think I can safely say that if you draft me I'd have to run. I cannot refuse the mandate of destiny," he concluded with a grimace intended as an ironic smile.

Cheers and guffaws.

"Eureka!" exclaimed Yssis. "Let us proceed with the rites of initiation."

"Is that absolutely necessary?" inquired Eugene.

"Do you want to be most likely to succeed?" returned Yssis, trading question for question with typical Yankee acumen.

"It would look good on my record," considered Eugene.

"Assume the lotos posture," the guru instructed. "Do what I do, say what I say. Together we shall chant the magic syllables."

Eugene lifted himself to the bar beside Yssis who, swaying back and forth, began once more to grunt and groan in that strangely familiar manner. Then the maestro began to incant in his forthright funloving fervent fascinating foolish foulmouthed fashion: "Ga-ga ca-ca (grunt) ga-ga ca-ca (groan) ga-ga ca-ca (grunt, groan) ga-ga ca-ca (moan) a-a-a-h! Ga-ga ca-ca (grunt) ga-ga ca-ca (grunt) ga-ga ca-ca (moan) whew!"

Eftsoons demurrers rose up from amongst the congregation.

"What's all this crap?"

"Come on Yssis, cut the shit."

"Sniff it and bury it."

"Wipe it and weigh it."

"Can it and sell it."

Meanwhile the prodigious babe sustained his potent prattle, with Eugene, from the lotos posture, echoing the chant to the good-natured merriment and nauseous disgust of all that gentle company gathered together there.

Bernie tapped Ron on the arm. "I think I've had enough," he said. I nodded. As we left, Yssis was urging Eugene, who had taken over the chant: "Push, come on, push, harder, push." Several of the listeners were giving way to a giggling hysteria of an oddly infantile kind.

"How depressing," said Bernie as we walked away from Fink's house. "Between Yssis and the healthy, normal shmucks you could get completely schizoid. Not that I'm not neurotic to begin with. I mean I have trouble relating to people. I withdraw. I'm so tense I can't sleep at night. My mother says I think too much. She says it doesn't pay to be too smart. She keeps nagging me to go pre-med or at least pre-law. I tell her I don't care about making a lot of money. She tells me I'm too idealistic. She tells me not to be an altruist. Who's an altruist? It's just that that kind of life is so stupid, so narrow, so . . ." he groped for the word with convulsions of his palm, "so hollow. I'm sure it's all very oedipal, but I have no doubt that I'm totally maladjusted."

"There's only one answer," I told him. "Get out."

"Well, I'm getting out, thank god. Soon we'll all be getting out. And some time I'll look back and say, Remember Brooklyn? Those weren't the days. The pressure is terrific. I feel like I'm going to burst apart. If only I can hold it in a while longer. I've got to have a cognitive reorganization.

113

All right, so I'm maladjusted, so I'm insecure. The hell with security. I have to remember that money and prestige would be no relief. I have to forget all that. And above all I have to forget about success. If only I can get my scholarship to Columbia, I'm all set."

We were walking by the side of the big cemetery that borders Gravesend. It was a cloudy night, warmish and damp. In the street lights the tombstones glittered like rows of teeth. Bernie pointed to the cemetery.

"There," he said in his most pedantic tone, "there you have an objective correlative for all the clichés we learned in grammar school. The New World, the Melting Pot, the American Dream. Dead and buried."

But I was used to Bernie's doom-driven prophecies. Here we parted company, he taking his way, I mine along the side of the cemetery.

At such times, slowly walking home alone in the early morning, I frequently encountered a strange apparition. This was nothing more than an old man with a pushcart, hurrying through the streets to god knows what destination at that hour, in all kinds of weather, to gather and sell the kind of flattened box cardboard of which his cart was always half full. This man frightened me. He filled me with awe and even, it would not be too much to say, a kind of reverence. Now from far off I again heard the hollow rattle of his cart in the quiet night, louder and louder, till our paths crossed abruptly in the lamplight of a streetcorner. Pushing the cart with quick steps he rattled past, a short slight man with a narrow immigrant face, aging, slightly foreign in a worker's cap that looked European and a tattered, outmoded overcoat, bent over the handles of the cart looking neither to right nor left he hurried on. He seemed more than real and less than real, startling as he emerged from among the stolid apartment buildings and smug two-story houses, and totally isolated from them. Never, till now, have I been able to understand the effect

114

that poor figure always had on me, till now when he rolls through my imagination as vivid as ever, driven, deprived, the soul of Brooklyn itself, maniacal in its intensity, sapped by the mercenary scurry, in life and death condemned to cheap pathos.

Suddenly I caught the fresh smell of earth coming up from the cemetery, cool and dank. For a moment I felt a sharp empathy with the vitality of decay, the life-lust of ghouls and vampires, their hunger for the damp earth before dawn, their nocturnal glee in terror, assassination, depravity.

With that I remember my bowels were gripped by a loosening pang that moved me to quicken my steps homeward, even as the same moving sensation quickens my words of it now.

La Guerra Contra Los Ratos. A practical problem. Night after night I heard them scuttling in the walls. Then the scratching began. Incredibly loud, incredibly persistent. I kept thinking of long fingernails, a corpse trying to escape from a tin coffin. Finally I went down to see Hamstrung. He was fending off an old woman who was complaining about the heat. The three houses Hamstrung nominally took care of were full of Puerto Ricans and old people living alone, a lot of them on welfare. The old ones tended to get a bit strange, especially the women. Some of them really belonged in Matteawan—walking through the streets mumbling and shouting, scaring children, drunks some of them with no teeth and scabby faces, whining and aggravating the local storekeepers for groceries till the next welfare check, horrible old types. This lady, a Pole, lived next door to me. All I knew about her was that she had a heart attack last year, worked as a seamstress, and occasionally got some money from a daughter on the West Coast.

115

"Not only my radiators don't work," she was saying. "My pipes are broken. I hardly got any hot water."

"Well, it's an old house," said Hamstrung. "What do you expect?"

"Why don't you fix the pipes? You don't do nothing."

"It's not the pipes. That's not the trouble. Your trouble is you're too old. You can't feel the heat when it comes up."

"I'm going to call the landlord," she said, backing out the door and shaking her fist. "I'm going to call the Rent Control."

"Good. Call the landlord. Call Rent Control. Call the mayor. What the hell do I care who you call. You old bat."

"These old bags are the worst," he said to me. "Always complaining. It's their hobby. Can't do a god damn thing for themselves. They expect me to go around and wipe their noses for them. And do you think anybody in this house would ever give me a tip for anything? Fat chance. If she wants to start with the plumbing let her call Slumski and get a plumber. She'll be in her grave first. Besides, between you and me, Slumski wants these old people out of here. They been here too long. They're still paying the same rent they did in the forties when they put in rent control. Slumski wants them out so he can raise the rent. He told me not to give them too much service. Fine with me. What can I do for you, Ronnie?"

"I think we've got rats in the house," I said.

"Oh yeah, we got em all right," he said, looking around apprehensively as if it were me and him against them. "What are you doing about them?"

"That's what I'm down here for. What are you going to do about them?"

"Ronnie, there are rats all over the East Side, all over New York, all over the world. Wherever you go you find rats. They got rats on Park Avenue just like down here. There's nothing anybody can do about them."

"Come on, Hamstrung."

116

"Well," he says, "you want to loan my cat?"

"Is that the best you can do?"

"It's the best anybody can do. Cats are the best thing in the world for rats. I'll tell you what. Are they in your apartment?"

"They're digging through."

"Good. That's what you want. Let them dig right through. And as soon as you find a hole, you go and buy yourself some real big traps, not mousetraps, they wouldn't even stub their toes on them, and get some real smelly cheese, and you put those traps right around that hole. That's just what you want. Let them get out and expose themselves where you can get at them. Then once you catch one or two they'll never come back again, because rats are smart. They won't come around where they know they're going to get picked off all the time."

"What about an exterminator?"

"Sure. Call Slumski. You got his number?"

"Yeah, I got it. Thanks for the help."

"Any time, Ronnie."

I know better than to call Slumski. First of all he was never in. Secondly, when you got hold of him on the phone he'd agree to anything you wanted, and that was the last you'd hear about it. If you tried to remind him in person he'd yell "No!" and beat it. I went upstairs to call the Rent Control office.

As I reached my landing I saw that the old man who lived across the hall from me had his door open again. This always depressed me. He was about seventy, very decrepit, rarely went out of his apartment and as far as I could see never talked to anybody. Sometimes in nice weather he made his way downstairs—one hand on the banister the other on his cane—to sit on the stoop. He had the habit of keeping the door open when he sat at his table to read his paper, which he always did in his undershirt, so that anyone crossing the landing was treated to a first-class view

117

of the leathery flesh hanging from his skeleton. The room was tiny. It contained a sink, stove, bathtub, cot and the table where the old man sat. The walls were an unnameable stain of yellow-gray streaked with black, the ceiling cracked and plaster peeled. The place couldn't have been painted in the last twenty years. He sat over his paper with a magnifying glass shaping the words with his lips. It took him all day to get through the paper. When he was done he shut the door. These old rejects go on like that for years. Then one day an ambulance from Bellevue pulls up, a few people gather on the stoop to gawk and joke with the driver, the attendants come out with a bundle of rags on a stretcher, the ambulance pulls away, and that's all. It's the next best thing to evaporation. Very convenient all around.

I called Rent Control.

"I have rats in my apartment. What can I do about it?"

"You can make out a complaint," said a woman with a nasal voice.

"How do I do that?"

"I can send you the forms."

"The forms? But I have rats in my apartment."

"Do you want me to send you the forms or not?"

"Well how long does it take a complaint to go through?"

"A complaint usually takes several months to process."

"Look, I have rats running back and forth here. In several months they'll process my whole apartment."

"I'm telling you the procedures for making a complaint. If you want to make a complaint you can follow the procedures. If not you can try the Health Department. Or the Buildings Department. We're very busy here." Her voice was getting more and more nasal.

"The Buildings inspector's already been here. He told me to call you."

"Try Health."

"What will they do?"

"I wouldn't know."

"What happens once the complaint goes through?"

"We are not allowed to speculate on complaints. We're very busy here. Why don't you try Buildings?"

"Why don't you try having your adenoids removed you cunt."

I hung up. The hell with that. Self-reliance. I got a piece of tin and nailed it over the spot beneath the sink where they were breaking through the plaster. Next day I got up to find plaster all over the kitchen floor and a big hole at one side of the tin sheet. That night I heard the pitter-patter of scratchy little feet. When I got up and turned on the light there'd be a quick scurrying in the direction of the kitchen sink and nothing to be seen. That went on all night. Next day I borrowed Hamstrung's big red cat but the first thing it did was piss on the floor so I kicked it out and bought three huge rat traps. I baited them and set them around the hole. When I got up next day to go to the bathroom I felt something furry glide over my foot. There was a whiz and scurry in the direction of the kitchen. I waited for the solid snap that I knew was coming. Nothing happened. He must be one hell of a broken field runner.

Yesterday I bought three more traps. The area under the sink is one solid mass of rat traps. This morning the garbage bag was gnawed to pieces and the traps were just as I'd left them. Meantime, I'm afraid of springing the traps by accident. One of those things could break your toe off with no trouble at all.

WHERE'S THE SHMUCK?

I was talking to Sugar when Stewart came in.

"Where's the shmuck?" he said.

"Why?" asked Sugar.

"I have to get my allowance. Come on. Where's the shmuck?"

119

"He's inside with Mother. They're having a big conference with the Silverfish. I'm afraid you'll have to wait."

"Ah, for christ sake," said Stewart.

"What's the conference?" I asked.

"How to get you into college. I thought you knew."

"How would I know. Nobody told me."

I was pretty pissed off and immediately headed for the living room to barge in. The Silverfish were relatives from Aunt Theda's side whom she liked to consult on important occasions. Theda valued their advice because she believed they knew how to "do things," and she had great confidence in what she considered their pull and connections. Actually, she enjoyed confiding in the Silverfish because they were rich, and Aunt Theda had a childlike faith in rich people. She had the notion—ridiculed by Uncle Julius—that if she were only nice enough to the Silverfish they would reciprocate by using their pull and their connections to "do something" for her children. If they ever did it's not on record.

"Oh!" exclaimed Theda as I walked in. "We were talking about you. Say hello to Aunt Irma and Uncle Herm."

"Hello," I said.

Aunt Irma exposed her perfect set of false teeth in a smile that wrinkled the highly rouged parchment of her face.

"Don't you want to give your Aunt Irma a kiss?" asked Theda.

"Oh . . . yes."

I went over and aimed a quick peck at the loose skin of her cheek—not quick enough though, because before I could get away she threw her arms around my neck and planted a wet one on the corner of my mouth. "That's a good boy," she said. She spoke in a gravelly baritone.

"Have a seat," said Julius.

I sat down. Aunt Irma was wearing her perennial low-cut dress, exposing the maximum amount of sunken, freckled flesh below her diamond necklace. She must have been about sixty. Her hair was dyed a kind of blue-gray, set in high curls around a jeweled tiara. I took out my handkerchief and wiped my mouth. It was smeared with lipstick. Disgusting.

"So this is the genius," said Uncle Herm.

He was a little fat man with a long, crooked nose and mal-occluding teeth that thrust his jaw forward when he closed his mouth. Uncle Herm was Aunt Irma's second husband. He was considerably shorter than she, and considerably younger too. In contrast with his wife, his voice was a thin, obstinate tenor, a little like Hitler's.

"If you're so smart," said Uncle Herm, "how come you can't get into college?"

"Shut up," said Aunt Irma. "Nobody asked your opinion."

"Shut up yourself," answered Uncle Herm. "When I was a boy, kids his age didn't even think of going to college. If I'd of told my father I wanted to go to college he would have thrown me down the stairs."

"You were too stupid to go to college," said Aunt Irma.

"I wasn't too stupid to make a lot of money," said Uncle Herm.

"No," said Aunt Irma. "But you were too stupid to hold on to it."

"What do you want from me? Go spit on the grave of my first wife's father, the lousy thief. I made it back twice over."

"What a man!" sneered Aunt Irma. "A regular mental giant. He made it back because he married me, that's how he made it back. With my money. What a man. Look at him. The fat pig. Do you think he's capable of making a penny of his own?"

"What did you think I married you for, your good looks?" said Uncle Herm. "You're no spring chicken you

121

know. You old corpse. They should have buried you years ago."

"I'll spit in his face. All he knows how to do is eat, the old skinflint. Every time he has to spend a penny he cries. You should see the way he treats his son. If it wasn't for me his own son would have killed him with his bare hands. He had his hands around his throat. I'm only sorry I interfered."

"Please, Irma," said Theda timidly. "That was ten years ago. The boy's in an institution now."

"Where he god damn well belongs," said Uncle Herm. "He's psycho, that's what he is. Just like his lousy mother."

"You should know, you drove her crazy," said Aunt Irma. "You killed her just like you're trying to kill me. Well you won't do it. I'm too tough for you. You bit off more than you can chew this time, you son of a bitch. I'll see you dead. You'll never inherit my money. I'll see you in your grave first. I wouldn't be surprised if he tried to put some arsenic in my coffee one of these days. If he thought he could get away with it."

"It's not a bad idea," said Uncle Herm.

Julius emitted a loud belch. "Excuse me," he said.

"Julius," said Theda.

"I said excuse me."

Uncle Herm took out an enormous cigar, bit off the end, and spat it on the floor. Rotating the tip in his wet lips, he put a match to the long green-brown spiraled wrapper.

"So you're the genius," he said, puffing and chewing on the cigar.

"Shut up," said Aunt Irma.

"Shut up yourself," said Uncle Herm, unperturbed.

"Weren't we talking about the scholarship?" Theda asked.

"Yes, of course," said Aunt Irma in a tone of dowager

122

beneficence. "Let me talk to the boy. So you want a scholarship to college, do you?"

"I could use one."

"I suppose you want to be a doctor?"

"No."

"A lawyer?"

"No."

"An accountant?"

"No."

"Well, what do you want to go to college for?"

"I just want to go to college."

"He just wants to go to college," said Uncle Herm. "You see. What did I tell you."

"They all go to college these days," said Theda.

"What do you want to take up?" asked Aunt Irma.

"I don't know," I said.

"He doesn't know," said Uncle Herm.

"Quiet," said Aunt Irma. "Let me talk to the boy." She held a lorgnette to her eyes and peered at me. "A nice-looking boy," she said. "Looks a little like my side of the family."

"That's his tough luck," said Uncle Herm.

"You fat pig," said Aunt Irma. "I suppose you're a regular Adonis."

"They're all ugly on that side," continued Uncle Herm. "And if they're not ugly they're feeble-minded."

"You talk about feeble-minded with your maniac of a son," said Aunt Irma. "They had to put him away. Why you're cracked yourself you senile old idiot. You should see him, he can't remember whether he has to piss anymore. I ought to have him shot like an old horse."

"Irma, please," said Theda. "No conflict."

"You mind your own business," snapped Aunt Irma. "Your children are no bargain either, the way the girl goes running around. Especially that boy of yours."

"He's not normal," said Uncle Herm. "He's got an un-

123

healthy look in his eye. I'll never forget the time he kicked me in my rheumatic leg, the little bastard."

"He was only seven years old," said Theda.

"What do you mean by running around?" demanded Julius. "You leave my kids out of it."

"Please Julius," said Theda. She was on the verge of tears. "There's nothing wrong with Stewart. He's going through a stage."

"Sometimes I think he's not happy to see his Aunt Irma. That's not natural."

"Of course he is, Irma. He's just shy. He'll grow out of it. Now Ronnie, tell your aunt and uncle what you're thinking of doing in college."

"He's thinking of being a sponger, that's my opinion," said Uncle Herm.

"I'm not asking for any of your money," I told him.

"That's right," said Aunt Irma. "Don't let the old moron bully you. The boy's got spirit. Would you like to go to school out of town? Travel is very educational, you know. I've done an awful lot of traveling myself. What you ought to do is go to Europe. Paris is such a marvelous city. I remember when I first went there after the war. The flaming twenties, you know. The stores were simply magnificent in those days, I can't tell you. It was with my brother . . ."

"Don't mention that crook to me," said Uncle Herm.

"My brother was a very fine man."

"Your brother was a very fine crook."

"I suppose it wasn't all black market money to begin with?"

"Go on. Everything was black market during the war. A crook is a crook, the son of a bitch."

"Well he's gone now," said Theda. "Let him rest in peace."

"Let him burn in hell," said Uncle Herm.

124

"For christ sake," said Julius, "the kid's waiting to hear about his scholarship."

"Yes, that's just what I'm trying to get at," said Aunt Irma. "Now let's see how much the boy knows. Have you read *The Good Earth?*"

"No."

"You haven't read *The Good Earth?* He hasn't read *The Good Earth.* What has he read?"

"Tell your Aunt Irma what you've read, Ronnie," said Theda.

The hell with them, I thought. I didn't answer.

"He's reading all the time," said Theda. "You should see his room, always full of books."

"But I mean *The Good Earth*," said Aunt Irma. "That's by Pearl Buck you know. She won a Nobel Prize after all. It's about China."

"Well, after all," said Theda. "It's not what you know, it's who you know. You know that as well as I do, Irma. It's all pull."

"That's right," said Aunt Irma. "Take my advice, Ronnie. As you go through life you'll find what really counts is knowing the right people."

"People, hell," said Uncle Herm. "Money talks. That's the beginning and end of it."

"Well, Theda," said Aunt Irma, "we'll try. The most we can do is try."

"How good of you," said Theda. "And when your Aunt Irma decides to try something, she always succeeds."

"And if she don't succeed," said Uncle Herm, "at least she makes a big stink."

"You shut up," said Aunt Irma.

"Shut up yourself," said Uncle Herm.

Two weeks later we got a call from the Silverfish. It was all set. Someone in the Democratic Party who owed Uncle Herm a favor. Connections with some school in the

125

Midwest. They weren't sure exactly what school, but all I had to do was go see the man and get the details straightened out.

The man was a liberal politician whose name I'd seen in the papers. He was a small, energetic person with an egalitarian attitude that included receiving me at home in suspenders while finishing a bowl of pot cheese and sour cream.

"So you're Herman Silverfish's boy?"

"Well, his nephew, more or less."

"A very substantial man, Herman Silverfish. You're very fortunate he's taken an interest in you."

"I know."

"Very strong on Israel. Hates unions though. Well, he's a self-made man."

"I know."

"Do you hate unions?"

"No. Not me."

"Good. I can see you're the right kind. I place my faith in the younger generation. We ought to lower the voting age. Now about this school. I'm afraid it's not very well known. It's a small medical school not far from St. Louis."

"Medical school?"

"Yes. Don't you want to go to medical school?"

"But I'm not even out of high school."

"What do you mean? They all want to get into medical school. Didn't he tell me you want to go to medical school?"

"No. I just want to get into college."

"These young kids," he exploded in a spatter of pot cheese. "They don't know what they want. They got no sense. You mean to tell me I wasted my time and effort?"

"I'm sorry."

"I'm a busy man you know. Do my time and effort mean nothing to you?"

"I'm sorry. I didn't mean it." I wasn't sure what I didn't mean, but I felt horrible. Besides, my face was splattered with sour cream that I didn't dare wipe off for fear of seeming rude.

"All right, son," he said. "Let's forget about it. I guess we just didn't make contact this time, okay? Shake. And listen, wipe the sour cream off your face, will you?"

He got up, put his arm around my shoulders, and before I knew it I was thanking him and out the door. When I told Julius about it he said: "Sure. If you'd told him you wanted to get into medical school he would have got you into college. Politicians are no damn good."

The next Silverfish lead I tried was a wealthy old doctor who didn't seem to know exactly what he was to do with me. I didn't either so we stumbled through a series of vague generalities for about half an hour. He ended up by giving me advice on contraception.

Finally Theda came to me one day and said with conviction, "It's all arranged. You're going to Columbia."

Well I was a little skeptical by this time, but since Columbia was where I really wanted to go I couldn't help getting excited.

This time it was an address in the Wall Street area. An office on the thirty-third floor. Inside the quiet elevator with its liveried pilot, I had the sensation that I was being sucked up into another world. And it was another world. It was Wall Street, the same Wall Street that my radical friends deplored, exploitation and vested interests. But this was different of course. I was just trying to get into college, and the elevator was opening into Theda's vague but important world of "connections" and "influence" to which the Silverfish had some uncertain entry. I walked timidly through the carpeted corridor till I came to the right door: LOACH AND TENCH, CONSULTANTS. Consultants for what, I wondered.

"Yes?" asked a good-looking receptionist, regarding me with suave disdain.

I gave her my name.

127

"Of course," she said. "Won't you have a seat?"

I sat down in a deep leather easy chair. The walls were lined with wood paneling and there was a thick wall-to-wall carpet on the floor. The receptionist finished typing a letter, then took out a compact and carefully examined her face in its mirror, adding a dab of powder here and there. Then she picked up the intercom, spoke a few words, and said with a cold little smile: "Won't you go in now?"

I walked through the paneled door. For a moment I was dazzled by the sunlight pouring in through the two windows opposite me. By comparison with this stream of light the rest of the room seemed dark.

"Good morning," said a deep, smooth voice. "Sit down."

In the direction of the voice I made out an easy chair, a desk, and a man behind it. As I walked to the chair I saw through the windows spread out before me an enormous panorama of the harbor, the upper bay, the Narrows, the lower bay, ships, docks, islands, the Statue of Liberty, a liner cutting its slow wake through tiny ripples, all glittering in the sun. I almost gasped—maybe I did.

The easy chair, covered in leather like the one outside, was extremely low. The desk, a large, heavy affair, was situated to one side of the window so the man's face was partly in shadow. I had to look up over the desk at an angle to see him at all. He was smoking a pipe and rocking easily in an upholstered swivel chair.

"Mr. Loach?" I asked.

"Mr. Loach isn't here today."

"Mr. Tench, perhaps?"

"Mr. Tench passed away some years ago."

"Oh, sorry."

The room seemed old-fashioned to me: the paneling, bulky furniture, big floor lamps, Persian rugs, heavy ashtrays. Everything was made of wood, even the filing cabinets. The paintings on the walls were modern though—I even thought I recognized a Picasso.

"Tell me a little about yourself," the man said. He had dark blond hair, beginning to recede, regular features, seemed to be good-looking. A youthful forty-five maybe. I noticed he was suntanned.

"Well, I'm a senior in high school now, I'm a co-feature editor of my school paper, and I'd like to get into a good college."

"Is it a public high school?"

"Yes."

"That makes things a bit more difficult, doesn't it? Have you applied to colleges?"

"Yes, but I applied to the wrong ones. You see they only allow you three applications, though kids whose parents complain make a lot more, and our college advisor is an ex-gym-teacher who doesn't know much about colleges and neither did I. So I applied to one engineering school and one school that seems to have a lot of agriculture. I've already been rejected by Columbia—I need a scholarship."

"And you don't want to be an engineer or a farmer." He smiled.

"No. And you see my marks aren't bad but they aren't the best either. There's a lot of competition in my school and I didn't like it, so I didn't work as hard as I could have. And besides I don't believe in marks because I know they don't really show who the smartest people are. But I feel pretty guilty about trying to use pull to get into college anyway."

"I wouldn't use that word. There are channels, channels that can be arranged for exceptional students. What are you interested in studying?"

"Well, I'll probably major in Social Science. But the truth is I really want to be a writer. I've always wanted to be a writer."

"I see. Well the social sciences would seem to be a good background for journalism."

"No. I mean a creative writer."

129

"Oh. I find that quite an admirable goal. Have you done any writing?"

"Well, as I said I'm co-feature editor of my high school paper and I was also the sports editor of a neighborhood paper, though I didn't get paid for it. And I write stories and poems on my own."

"I understand. And you think Columbia will help you attain this goal."

"Yes."

"Now you see, I have certain friends at Columbia. People on the board, for example. I think I will be able to help you. Your cause seems a worthy one. But you realize, of course, there are many such deserving young men and women these days. You are aware, no doubt, that there are certain standard quotas that apply to many applicants from the New York City area."

"Yes, I know."

"Now the question arises, how are we to choose among so many qualified young people?"

"Real merit?"

"Yes, if it were only that simple. But you see, my channels are limited. And you need a scholarship. It takes a good deal of time and effort. I'm quite a busy man you know."

"Yes, I know."

"I think I may say I do wield considerable weight in such matters. But one has to be selective."

"Of course."

"You want to be a journalist?"

"A writer."

"A very fine goal."

There was a pause.

"I would have to put in a good deal of time and effort, you know."

"Yes, I know."

"There are many, many people who are eager for my good offices in this regard."

130

"It's very kind of you."

"Thousands apply, few are chosen, as Pope long since pointed out. Have you read Pope?"

"No, not yet."

There was a pause.

"Did . . . were you given anything for me?" he asked.

"For you?"

"Anything to give me?"

"Like what?"

"Well, an envelope, for example."

"Oh, an envelope. No."

"Or a note?"

"No. No note."

"I see. Well it's of small importance. So you want to be a journalist. A very admirable goal. How old are you?"

"Almost eighteen."

"Well you have plenty of time anyway, don't you. We will see what we can do. I can't promise anything of course, but we'll see. We can only do our best, right? And if it works out, why, you'll be hearing about it. Fair enough?"

"That's very kind of you. Thank you very much."

"Not at all, not at all." He looked at his watch. I stood up, thanked him again, shook hands, got another look out the windows and left.

I was still optimistic when I told Julius what had happened. But he thought about it for a minute and concluded bluntly: "He wanted money." As he said it I knew myself a fool. And I was mortified by a degrading illumination of the world we lived in and my own callow complicity in it.

Herm and Irma, since both of you are dead, how can I express my gratitude for those humiliations?

I turned the light out and lay back, listening carefully for the familiar scuttering sound in the walls. I thought I noticed a peculiar smell, a fetid odor. The plumbing? Speak to Hamstrung. The rats seemed to have disappeared

131

in the last day or two. Scared off by the traps? I doubted it. You can keep them out but you never get rid of them. Always two more for every one you kill. They sound like shades gibbering in the underworld, squeaking and scratching at the imponderable membrane that denies them existence. Dámelo. There is no place that does not see you. I rolled over and tried to forget about them. Then I knew it was going to be a hard night. I recognized the signs. Imperceptibly, my subversive mind had begun its insomniac agitation, throwing up its mordant ghosts, its flotsam of desire, the day's remainders, ends of thought, image fragments, lines of verse, phantasmal enactments and compulsive reenactments, useless calculations, sterile epiphanies, ambiguous cardiac fantasies, tubercular flights, cancerous excursions and alarms, snowman fear, scalding apparitions of guilt, and doubt, the false fiend—feverish symptoms of a disordered imagination. I tried to resist this morbid acceleration. A jet snarled overhead. Switch to jet, cutting through the air like a sovereign gesture, a perfect swing on a perfect strike, smack of ash on horsehide, a perfect arc into the cheering grandstands. Slow, heavy DC-3, streamlined silver gleaming in the sunlight of the empty 1937 sky. The first all-metal transport plane, a remarkable machine, they still use them. Wrong Way Corrigan, my hero then and for a long time, who took off for California and landed in Dublin, magnificent blunder. It was foggy and he was watching the wrong hand of the compass, he said, so he wound up flying east instead of west. He had already flown from California to New York cruising at 85 m.p.h. and dodging under thunderstorms by flying through mountain valleys. But he was having trouble getting a license to fly over the ocean because of what happened to Amelia Earhart. So he decided to fly back to California, he said. He knew the gas tank was leaking, but it would have taken a week to fix it, so he just took off. The gas leaked into the

132

cabin and rose to cover the tops of his shoes, but he took a screwdriver and punched a hole in the floor. When the weather cleared and he saw he was over water he figured he must have made a mistake. He said. But there was nothing to do then but keep going and, besides, they can't hang a man for making a mistake.

A herd of fire engines stampede down Avenue B, bellowing and screaming like hysterical rhinoceri. When does it stop? Drunks shouting all night in seven languages, busses snorting by, frantic truck fart shifting gears. All day all night. For Hispanic people loud sound is like bright color. Dámelo. Bohemian sex mother wheeling her baby carriage, no brassiere. Breast bounce like Nancy. Wanted to run out and follow her just to look, the bitch. Dámelo, dámelo, mamita. I marry you. I love you baby. Llévame. Traígame. Dámelo. The old man pinching nurses on his death bed must be where I get it from. Incredibly loud, incredibly persistent, a corpse with long fingernails. Keep far hence the rat that's foe to men,/or with his nails he'll tear your heart open. The death of my parents came before I was prepared for it. In such phenomena lies the origin of ghosts. One is rarely prepared for death. For the old man it was too late. He wanted to crawl backward through his life and die by being born in reverse. There is no place that does not see you. Helpless, a coil of needs gestating in the womb of life. He asked for a cigarette. "They don't allow me, the bastards." I offered him one. It wasn't my business not to allow. He drew out a cigarette and kept the pack. "Give your grandpa a few cigarettes he shouldn't die without the taste of tobacco in his mouth." I lit his cigarette and gave him the matches. He hid the pack and the matches under his sheet. His beard was a thin white fringe, his hair a line of surf receding from the crown of his head. Under the bulging veins of his scalp his skull looked like a specimen in the Museum of Natural History. In the nursing home he

133

was already the star patient, crying and complaining, arguing with the director, cursing the nurses, or trying to coax them within reach. When he got his hands on one he held on for dear life. They had to pry him loose. This was the end of a journey for him that began one evening when he dressed himself, evaded Snippick, slipped down the back stairs out the cellar door and, before anyone knew he was gone dragged himself nobody knew how to the Lower East Side where he had lived forty years where he came from Vienna where he came as a boy from Cracow and where he learned his trade, a gem setter, known and sought in the business for his skill, working when he wanted and half the time off in Saratoga, the Catskills, Asbury Park, with his gold watch, his cane, his ruby stickpin and big cigar, coming home to fight with his wife, curse his sons and bully his daughters, and the police found him wandering dazed in the streets and he didn't know what he wanted and he didn't remember where he lived, collapsed in the emergency room with senile eyes and spittle in the corner of his mouth, Theda hysterical begging the doctors to save his life, going from specialist to specialist until one took out his kidney and one cut off his leg and they told her with luck he might live six months or a year.

"Not enough I'm going to die," he said, "they have to cut me to pieces first. What do they want with my kidney? Criminals, they're robbing my guts. Already they took away my leg so I can't walk. Next they'll want my arms. Wait, I'll die a basket case yet." He coughed over his cigarette, a dry, desperate cough in mounting crescendoes that stopped only to begin all over again. "All for what?" he resumed. "For what? For nothing. To die in pain. Everything wasted. I could have made millions. I could have married wealth, ten thousand dollars a Williamsburg contractor for his daughter. I could have had my own business. I could have bought into Hollywood on the ground

134

floor, I missed my chance. Coca-Cola stock I sneezed at. For what? To marry a poor man's daughter who brought a sour tongue for dowry, to find a crooked partner, Lipke, my best friend, to raise two weakling sons to die before their time and one who wouldn't give me a nickel in my old age I should sue him for support. To Vienna I went, in Vienna I should have stayed. Here everything fails. I made money and I threw it away. Something else I wanted. What was it? Listen, let me tell you." His voice dropped to a grating whisper. "Let me tell you. You think I'm an old man. You think I lived my life. You think I'm tired. Let me tell you, I don't want to die. I don't want to die. I want to go back. My father was a rabbi, a learned man. When he walked through the Sukiennice, everyone knew who he was. And am I nothing but an old cripple dying on charity, treated like a child by snot-nose doctors? I want to go back," he wailed. "I'm not ready to die. I'm afraid," he sobbed. "You think because I'm an old man I'm not afraid? Let the young ones die if they're so brave. Somebody do something. Speak to your Aunt Theda. The doctors are trying to kill me. They won't let me smoke. I have to scream with pain before they give me a needle, the nurses. For this you have to work and slave. They tell you work hard, get married, have children, be important. Don't listen. You know what means *dreck*? It means don't listen. Everything fails. I have to go back. Something I wanted, I can't remember. What was it?"

He stared past the foot of the bed with glazed, pink-rimmed eyes. After a while he said, "You know what it means from Polish, Sukenick? It means falcon hunter."

It means cloth worker.

"Pop." Theda's quaver. "What's this I hear? Why do you cause trouble? I can't stand any more. I can't take it. I'm not a strong woman. I'm going to have a nervous break-down. Here, I brought the papers." She put newspapers in

135

various languages on a table next to the bed. "And a little fruit, maybe the doctor will let you eat a piece."

"Leave me alone, I'm tired," he said. "You don't see I'm tired? I don't eat nothing. I'm not hungry. A few cigars why don't you bring? Because that's what I want? No, you'll bring another doctor he should cut off another leg."

"It was for your own good they did it. What could I do? You're a very sick man."

"Of course I'm a sick man. I'm going to die. So leave me in peace."

"Pop, please. Why do you say that? It's not true. You're convalescing. The doctors said so."

"The doctors lie. The doctors don't say so. They don't know what they're talking about. I say it's true."

"Pop, please. No conflict. After all, you're not a young man any more. What can you expect?"

"I don't expect. I know."

"What do you know? You don't know. You don't know how I run from doctor to doctor, pleading. Only today I spoke to a big pancreas man, I had to beg him to come in from Manhattan. And this is the thanks you give me."

"Another doctor? What now? They come like sharks. Let them feed on their own flesh. This is your doing. Leave me in peace. When I'm dead you can give my body for dissection."

"Don't say that to me. It's for your sake. You don't know what's good for you."

"Don't tell me I don't know. You're trying to kill me. But I'm going to disappoint you. I won't die. I'm not going to die. I don't want to die. And when you're crying over my corpse," he shouted, pointing a bony accusing finger, "you'll know who murdered me."

Theda began to weep.

"Poppa, please. Tell me what you want me to do. Tell me what to do and I'll do it. Anything. Anything. Please poppa." She was sobbing like a little girl. "It's not my fault.

136

I didn't do anything. Forgive. You always had something against me. Tell me what it is." In tears, she sat suddenly deflated on the edge of the bed.

"Get her out of here. They're all out to get me. That bastard Lipke with his smooth talk, my son-of-a-bitch sons, and this one, always on the side of my wife the bitch, she can't wait till I'm dead before they cut me apart. Let her leave me in peace, at least. A dying man. A dying man," he sobbed.

"Pop. Tell me you love me. Poppa, please."

But he turned his head and refused to speak.

At that moment Old Dutchik shuffled through the door on his cane and sclerotic legs. Old Dutchik was a humble man, ill-dressed, ill-washed, without any apparent means of financial support. He had always been around my relatives and he had always been so. Nobody was sure anymore exactly what his connection was with the family. He seemed to have a fathomless admiration for my grandfather, who regarded him in return with blatant contempt. Dutchik spoke about seven languages, none of them well and all of them at once, in a polyglot mumble it was impossible to understand. Every day he would come from a great distance to visit the old man and every day my grandfather would greet him with multilingual abuse and tell him to get out. Each time Dutchik would simply tip his black hat, shuffle to a chair in the corner, sit there quietly for an hour by the clock, get up, shuffle to the door, mumble something and leave. As soon as he sat down the old man would ring for the nurse and tell her to throw him out. When she refused he would begin a harangue in Yiddish, Polish, Russian, and German that seemed to be full of spite, venom, complaint, and lamentation. Dutchik would sit in his corner nodding, sighing, shrugging, raising his eyebrows, and occasionally mumbling. Gradually the old man began looking forward to his visits until one day when Dutchik didn't show up I actually heard him say, "So what happened to that schle-

137

miel Dutchik?" It was the only time in my life I ever heard my grandfather indicate concern for anyone but himself.

At Dutchik's entry, then, we got up to leave him.

"It's very serious," Theda, weeping, told me outside confidentially. "I had a big nose and throat man in the other day. I didn't want to say anything. He may have to remove the larynx."

Then I understood it's a fight to the death. I've seen it many times since. I see it in Slim. What is that smell? Long fingernails scratching. Machine guns and the smell of death every morning, then all day the incinerators like burning meat. I couldn't sleep because they always came before dawn and you never knew. Was it pure luck or was there some method in it, alphabetical order or what? One time the click slap of their boots down the corridor, closer, louder, silence, the rattle of a key as my heart stopped but it was the next cell. What made it unbearable was that I needed just a little more time, another week maybe, before I dug through. After days of effort I had managed to loosen the heel of my shoe, and from the heel to remove a small nail, and with the nail I had with weeks of careful work pried the mortar from around a stone block in the wall below my cot so that I could with minute patience pull it away from the wall and push it back into place, slowly mining the earth behind the wall with the nail and with my fingers, training myself to look while I dug as though I were sleeping with an arm trailing off one side of the cot, digging slowly, desperately each night for months eating the earth as it came loose to hide any traces, my fingertips bloody, till I had dug almost through the shallow barrier to the ordure pit beneath the adjoining latrine, from there through a long half-flooded sewer two feet in diameter where I was terrified of getting stuck to a stream down which I could float underwater using a reed to breathe air from the surface hiding in the mud by day eating roots grasses acorns insects dead fish murdering passersby for clothes money identification life free-

138

dom wide blue sky jet snarl overhead out of Idlewild
hurling themselves through the air fantastic to see. Pok:
smack of ash on horsehide. A surge of sound breaking like
surf on a hesitation of silence. Screaming Stukas dive like
iron gulls. Death snout P-40's drill through the air. Machine guns like robot typists etching relentless stories. Spit-
fire zoom, St. Paul's lit by incendiaries, Hawker Hurricanes
weaving through beams of light, ack-ack syncopation, tracers
over Threadneedle Street, blunt Brewster Buffaloes barrel
over Farmingdale, massive Thunderbolts crash through
nervous schools of Jap-winged Zeros pursued by twin-boom
Lightnings into green coral lagoons while Eddie Basinski
plays the violin on second base, slow flak-bitten B-17 For-
tress death squadrons massing, 2,000 horse-power Pratt and
Whitney aircooled Mustang devastation rakes the European overcast, Messerschmitts redden, bloom, fragment,
descend like industrial snowflakes over Stuttgart, fall in
crippled spirals, eccentric spins, meteor dives into gray
stubble fields, Superfort con-trails scribble milk run rubble
fires, Dresden kaputt Hamburg kaputt Köln kaputt Mün-
chen kaputt keine Ausgang: denn da ist keine Stelle, die
dich nicht sieht—achtung, achtung, mach schnell bitte, du
musst dein Leben ändern—for there is no place/that does
not see you. You must change your life:

> get up earlier
> drink less coffee
> stop borrowing money
> diminish self-involvement
> plaster rat-hole
> relax sphincter
> do exercises
> finish Proust
> avoid trivia
> buy milk
> eliminate narcissistic fantasy meanderings
> reduce compulsive political exacerbation

139

stop reading newspapers
stop listening to radio
stop seeing Nancy
stop seeing neurotic friends
develop official personality
be more politic
show an interest
evade controversy
find job
live more in world
analyze paranoia
examine obsessive death angst
breathe deeply
eat more fruit
take walks
go back to CORE meetings
be more responsive to friends
get things straightened out with Nancy
be less selfish when making love
be open
risk ego
avoid false situations
eschew self-deception
say what you think
act spontaneously
live carelessly
love lavishly
get up earlier
drink less coffee
stop borrowing money
diminish self-involvement
plaster rat-hole
relax sphincter
keep thy hand out of placket holes
defy the foul fiend
what is that fecal smell garbage plumbing

fresh dogshit old piece of Limburger cheese you never know what they're going to drop outside your door they never drop in all caught New York isolation pockets always I call I meet ego defense fear in cool envy holes hang me up in persecution vacuum they have it in for me the hell with them

six and change I need two I need two two fifty milk in morning sardines lunch spaghetti dinner two or three days at two two fifty I need thirty a week bookstore janitor dish-washing Warren Street must borrow money

"While you take it upon yourself to wrongfully defend malefactors from authority, who—one wonders—will take the trouble to defend you . . ."

"First of all, let me say I consider it not only legitimate but a high calling to defend malefactors from authority. I refer you to the Constitution or, if you prefer, to the New Testament or, if you prefer, to the Prophets or, if you prefer, to *Antigone* or the *Oresteia* or Plato's *Apology*. Further-more I would remind you that there are two judgments to be made in such a case, one concerning the malefactor and one concerning the authority, for authority is not always legitimate and may be abused. This is in fact the case when authority is degraded to the status of a mere tool serving the ambitions of self-seeking bureaucrats. The more so when bureaucracy with its heavy official hand attempts to regu-late a relation by nature as delicate and inviolable as that between lawyer and client or doctor and patient. There can be no official standard for the quality of teaching other than its effect on the students. For the fact is that teaching is not a matter of orthodoxy or of routine, which indeed stifle it, but is a continual agitation in the mind of the teacher effect-ing a continual revolution in the mind of the student. Its ways are unpredictable, its consequences diverse, and its condition is freedom. I do not speak of technical curricula, but of the Humanities where the subject matter is equally what is to be learned and he who is to learn it. A scholar

141

cannot be standardized for convenience of production, like a can of beans. I speak of the humane scholar, not the professional hack. And while I do not presume to judge the quality of your own scholarship, may I say sir, that your relation to literature which, though you do not like it, you profess to teach, seems overmuch conditioned by your famous study of the fart in Chaucer which, though you never smelled it, you strive to comprehend. Thank you, Professor, and good day."

"Splut splut," said Whitebread Blackhead.

BANALLY AND BANALLY, CONSULTANTS, read the discreet sign on the paneling. I pushed open the door and went in. The secretary sat in front of a picture window that framed a panorama of the harbor and three or four states. She was quite a picture herself, blonde, mannerly, alert, with a hint of a British accent. There was an open copy of Wittgenstein's *Tractatus Logico-Philosophicus* on her desk. "Whom do you wish to see?" she asked, taking off her glasses. "I'm 34-22-34. I just graduated from Sarah Lawrence."

"I'd like to see Mr. Banally."

"I'm sorry, Mr. Banally is busy. Did you have an appointment?"

"No, but send in my name." My name was written on my tie in block letters which lit up when I pressed a button in my pocket. I pressed the button.

"Oh, go right in sir," she said, obviously impressed.

A section of wood paneling slid open revealing Strop Banally standing in an insouciant pose before his enormous desk with that unvarying bold smile, that fixed grimace which is simultaneously a challenge, an insult, and a gesture of complicity.

"Hello, sweetheart," he hailed me. "What's the bad news? Say, sweetie pie," he yelled to his secretary. "You didn't keep Mr. Sukenick waiting, did you? You better watch out if you know what's good for you or I'll have to give you another spanking."

"Whatever you say Mr. Banally sir."

142

She giggled. The door slid shut. Strop shook his head and winked. He was trim and suntanned and as he talked he puffed on a pipe in the corner of his mouth. His tight pants bulged at the crotch as if he were wearing a codpiece.

"Well, old sport. What do you think of the layout? How do you like my real Picassos?" He pointed to three paintings on a wall, two blue periods, one rose.

"Drink?" A Japanese houseboy appeared with a martini on a tray. I shook my head. He evaporated.

"What can I do for you? Have a seat."

He sat down in a high thronelike swivel chair behind his desk and indicated a leather armchair facing him. The chair was deceptively low so that I had to crane my neck at a forty-five degree angle to see him over the massive desk. He lifted one of a bank of telephone receivers. "Say what's A T & T today?" he asked. "Good. Pick me up about five thousand shares will you baby? That's right and step on it. And listen, tell your boy, send up a BLT on toast along with. Fine, you're a sweetheart." He hung up. "Don't mind me," he said. "Just keep talking. I got two ears." He picked up another phone. "Hey what's-your-name, blondie, get me my bank in Switzerland, will you cookie? That's a good girl."

"Well, Strop, it's like this," I began. I told him all about Whitebread Blackhead.

"So that's all it is," he said. "That crud. I think I might have a little influence up there, a few friends on the board." He picked up a phone and asked for a number. "We'll just fix his wagon before he knows what's happening to him. Hello. Yeah. This is Banally. Listen, you got a crud working for you up there name of Whitebread Blackhead? Well look it up will you and tell him to give me a ring right away. It's about a friend of mine named Sukenick. Sukenick. I don't know how you spell it—just say it. And listen, I mean right away, okay man? I'm waiting. Much obliged." He hung up. "You see that's the way we do things in our world. You just pick up the phone."

143

A red light on his desk blinked on. He pressed a button and the secretary stepped through the sliding door with a bacon lettuce and tomato sandwich on toast. She put it on his desk.

"Thanks, honey pot. Say, wait a minute, come here will you?" She came and stood near his chair. "Hey, you want to see something?" he asked me. "Look at this." He slid his hand up the back of her leg and lifted her skirt above her buttocks. She wasn't wearing any underwear. "How do you like this?" he said. "How would you like a piece off of that?" The girl looked at me and tried to smile. Strop closed his big brown hand hard on one tender blond buttock and gave it a vibrating squeeze. "Mmm-um," he said, "I love it." He took a big bite out of his sandwich. The girl groaned. "What do you say, thigh pie?" Strop asked. "What do you say, saucy chops? Say, give me a hot stiff one, Mr. Banally. Ask politely." "Yes, Mr. Banally," the girl answered. Strop slapped his desk in raucous laughter. "Say it," he insisted. Just then the phone rang. "Hello," said Strop. "Yeah, who's speaking? What kind of name is that? Get to the point, who do you want to talk to. Yeah wait a minute, he's waiting for your call."

Strop handed me the phone. "Hello, Dr. Sukenick. This is Professor Whitebread Blackhead. I had no idea, Dr. Sukenick. The President just called me . . . if you had only mentioned . . . if you would just take the trouble to drop in to my office . . . please forgive . . . I think we might arrange . . . terribly stupid of me . . . had I only realized . . ."

"Okay, okay," I cut him off. "Now, look, you want to get over here right away please? My shoes need shining."

The girl set a couple of drinks on an end table and stood over me as I sat on the couch. "You're not a bad-looking boy," she said. "How come you're so quiet. I bet you know a lot of girls."

144

"Oh, you bet," I said, trying to seem rakish. Oola Wonderleigh was a high school Bohemian of considerable renown, widely celebrated for the size of her breasts. She was the teen sex princess of MacDougal Street, where her countless exploits included a famous sweet sixteen orgy of fabulous bisexual abandon with a well known TV comic and his wife. I'd run into her in the Village after she was stood up by one of her married boyfriends, and she'd taken me back home with her to Brooklyn.

She was wearing tight jeans and a loose sweater with a heavy leather-thonged pendant that emphasized the division of her breasts. She worked her way between my knees and hung over me so her nipples bobbed enticingly on either side of my nose.

"Well like come on," she said. "Let's go. I mean my parents will be coming home after a while."

Long conditioned by Nancy's necking habits, I was somewhat disoriented by Oola's direct approach. I didn't know where to begin.

Oola straightened up. She turned around, unzipped her dungarees, and pulled them down below her buttocks. She smiled at me over her shoulder.

"How do you like this?" she asked.

I liked it. I grabbed it and pulled her down across my lap. We squirmed lengthwise on the couch, groping for one another's bodies, not kissing, she as eager for my flesh as I was for hers. What a revelation. Naturally I didn't have any contraceptives. She cursed at this, but took the initiative in a number of to me surprising accommodations. For the first time in my life the sensual reflexes of my body went on totally beyond my control. I had no idea what was going to happen next until finally I was overcome by a spasm that carried me beyond the peak of pleasure.

"You son of a bitch," she said, getting up off the couch. "Put your clothes on."

"What did I do?" I asked, still lying there comfortably.

145

I had no idea whether officially speaking I was still a virgin or not, but I felt that I wasn't.

"Come on, get up and put your clothes on. Oh my god, look what you did, you got it all over the couch. You clumsy jerk. My mother just had it reupholstered. Shit. How am I going to get that out before they come home? You idiot. Wait a minute."

She ran off to the kitchen and came back with a couple of soapy sponges. "Here," she said. "Start rubbing. It's going to stain, I know it is. Come on, rub."

"Tell them you spilled something on it."

"I'm sure they'll guess. Oh god, it'll never dry. What'll I do?"

Just then the phone rang. From her side of the conversation I gathered it was her boyfriend with apologies and a good excuse for not meeting her. When she came back she was in a better mood.

"Look," she said, "you can go now. I'll finish this myself."

I shrugged. "Okay," I said. "Can I finish my drink?" I gulped the liquor I hadn't touched before. Then she showed me out.

"So long," I said on the doorstep. "And thanks," I added hesitantly.

"Oh yeah. Sure." Suddenly she gave me a quick kiss on the cheek, the only kiss between us. "So long," she said.

There was a prolonged explosion and the gleaming tower seemed to float on billows of smoke expanding around its base then with a slow roar began to lift itself ponderously inexorably rising with huge effort on a boiling cloud pillar gaining momentum imperceptibly piercing some invisible barrier flung itself straight up blasting into the sky shrinking motionless perpendicular uncertain ballistic dot receding plume lost splash in engulfing blue the parachute opened with a slap city noises floating up B-29 rose lazy banking back over sea green coral basin beach ripple small

146

arms jungle staccato sick grenade puffs hang gray in dead air rank leaves drip poison on rusting helmets slit trench littered with thick-fingered dead mauve faces buried in liquid ocher steaming flesh from open Seabee shirts like sweating horses flimsy made in japan bullets ping off bulldozer shovels leveling pillboxes like anthills sneaking yellow-belly knife attacks butcher G.I. meat to night bird scream doors open daily 11:45.

"We've got to go after Big Stoop, Fletch. He's cutting us to pieces. The men can't get any shut-eye. They're getting jumpy."

"I understand, sir. When do I start?"

"You may not come back Fletch."

"I'll take that chance, Captain."

screen fade skeletal barbed wire corpses hang impaled on electric fence stiffen naked in snow robbed of canvas inmate pajamas lie denuded in charnel stockpiles fill the trenches clog the ovens bridgework gone wedding rings hair clipped wooden legs piled in stacks all day all night black stench rising smears Europe death clerks tick off blue stenciled flesh accounts long typhoid dormitory small window wooden crowded sleeping shelves animal lapping from spoonless dog bowls no toilet paper ex lawyer masturbates for bread crust huge eyed man kneels under gun muzzle staring at brink of slaughter pit naked girls kiss swastikas in slave brothels soap lampshades pillow stuffing babies hanged in rows from coat hooks queues at all hours line up at neat murder cottage shivering and hiding genitals for extermination showers heart injections gas rooms vivisection machine guns carbon monoxide trucks box car suffocation gestapo truncheons incineration squealing and fighting in death traps scratch marks in concrete walls and ceilings no escape assiduous slave captains choose victims till themselves are picked at any hour on any day by what method chance chronology alphabetical order jews slavs gypsies rebels deviants misfits non conformists priests professors crooks milk-

147

men peddlers schoolboys bankers violinists housewives dry goods salesmen ancient women with shameful exposed bellies a tailor's wife eight months pregnant an old lottery ticket vendor who asked what he had to do with it a young woman with perfect breasts glimpsed among the garbage tangle of naked arms and legs tumbling before the plow into the common grave

"Juden," he barked. "Come with me."

He carried a submachine gun under his arm. The two of us marched ahead of him around to the back of the barracks.

"Please," said the other prisoner. He was a short middle-aged man who had recently come into the camp and kept asking about his wife.

"Be quiet," snapped the officer. He looked casually at each of us, then nodded at the other.

"You," he said. "Turn around."

"Why me?" he asked. A corner of his mouth was jerking spastically. I thought he was going to cry.

"Why not?" replied the officer. He wore rimless glasses and looked like a clerk. "Do as I say."

The other turned his back. "Please," he said. "I'm healthy. I can work."

"Kneel," said the officer. He pulled a Luger from his holster and examined the chamber. "One bullet," he said. He threw the Luger on the ground between myself and the other.

"Turn around," he told me, "and pick up the pistol." He held the submachine gun in both hands ready to fire. I did as he said.

"Shoot him," said the officer. "Or shoot yourself."

"Please," said the other, but without hope. He was on his knees with his back to me. I aimed at his head and pulled the trigger. With surprising immediacy his skull exploded in a splash of pink jelly. The trunk pitched forward and lay twitching on the ground. The remaining portion

148

of the head looked like fresh hamburger mixed with tufts of hair. I turned and pointed the gun at the officer.

He was placing a cigarette in an ivory holder. Looking up he smiled thinly. "Fool. It's empty. Drop it on the ground." He was wearing fine high boots, thick soled and very shiny. With slow arrogance he pulled a matchbox from his pocket and still smiling lit a match. I pulled the trigger. The machine gun dropped from under his arm. "Fool," he said. "It's empty." The cigarette holder fell from his surprised mouth and he slumped awkwardly to the ground, still holding the burning match. Quickly I stripped him of his boots his trousers his tunic his coat his visored cap his cigarette holder, clothing myself as I denuded him, and after rolling the naked corpse under the barracks, I pried the matchbox from its hand and finished lighting the cigarette. Then I picked up the submachine gun and walked to the headquarters building. Soldiers and prisoners heiled me as I passed. Inside the boys were cutting up in their usual rough-hewn way, clattering about in hobnail boots slopping beer on the floor singing out of key arms around one another's shoulders uniforms askew faces raised in loud phlegmy laughter acknowledging me with loutish salutes as I strode crisply into the room. A drunken storm trooper was pissing in a corner swaying back and forth as the yellow stream hissed against the wall, two others sat on a bench embracing thick lecherous smiles bloating their boozy faces. Canailles. Boisterous laughter came from a group in the middle of the room that made way as I approached, the men leering significantly. There naked on a table lay a young but nubile girl, her blond pathetic genitalia helplessly open by the way the ropes bound her mired thighs. Her eyes were shut as if by pain, bruise marks covered her body and you could distinguish the articulations of the rib cage under her bluish skin. Her arms were incredibly thin. An inferior officer ventured to punch me jocularly on the arm. I gave him a withering glance. At that moment the girl's lids flut-

149

tered in her stained face and she looked directly into my eyes. "Kill me," she said. I surveyed the men with a slow scathing gaze. The circle around the table involuntarily fell back. "Swine," I hissed. "Obscene rabble," I rasped with measured contempt. The men flattened themselves against the walls or slunk silently toward the door. "Insects!" I yelped stamping my foot. "This is headquarters not the camp brothel. Your uniforms are a disgrace. You will be disciplined. Besides, the regulations are officers first. Then noncommissioned officers, then squad leaders. Form an orderly line behind me. Size places." With that I ripped open my fly whence burst a titanic cock erect, heavy, club-like, flexible as a blackjack. The men looked at it and cowered, then at one another eyebrows raised incredulously, murmuring. "A Jew," someone said. "A Jew," came the rising echo. "A Jew, a Jew, a Jew," they clamored, closing in. I raised the tommy gun and fired in a deliberate arc around the room ak-ak-ak-ak-ak-ak-ak-ak-ak-ak-ak-ak, then a dull blow from behind, a falling numbness, and I awoke naked on a stone slab, impossible to move. "Conscious?" asked a man in a white surgeon's uniform. "Good. What we're going to do to you. It's going to hurt. I can assure you, you're going to have quite a little bit of pain before you die. Heinie," he snapped. "The scalpel." "Ja, Herr Doktor."

ambiguous groin pain kidney stone gall bladder syphilitic harbinger bleeding gums possible leukemia symptom strange memory lapse brain tumor headache consumptive sore throat stop smoking emphysema gasp dull back pain spontaneous pneumothorax spastic fibrosis nerve twitch know early check up symptoms sudden left arm twinge syncopated heart jump slow angina quick coronary clot you don't feel quite right you take an aspirin you tell someone you have a peculiar feeling and before you can finish the sentence a throbbing in your back your chest a spasm a blinding pain you hear of those things cutting a steak feeling a girl signing a check stepping off a curb into oblivion

150

you never know helpless nothing to be done all mowed down by death's machine gun

what is that spicy sweat stink of rush hour smell of b.o. walls in seedy motels smell of stale piss like rotting spinach in cheap french hotels smell of decaying blood in andalusian carnicerías smell of mortality east side on a hot day old garbage cat piss incinerators like burning fingernails smear of soot fall yellowed walls layers of buckled linoleum with brown newspaper strata circa battle of verdun brown speckled plaster scars glued with roach bits d.d.t. smell you never get rid of them interesting question whether venus fly traps would eat roaches or get indigestion because of the hard shells

slumbago ache of slum life

army of giant waterbugs crawls out of sewers antennae groping for revenge acute insect faces visible eyes steel neck sinews glistening backs teeming roach phalanxes apex in with anti-d.d.t. mutations baby scream chokes under mounting rat squeal packs of starving alley cats attack passersby gaunt dogs lope the streets muzzles ravening squads of horrible old women vent loneliness with bricks and beer bottles cackling arthritics masturbate and commit arson psychopaths stalk with gleeful machine guns sobbing kids drop molotov cocktails from roof tops commit incest knife one another hysterically people tired of everything take to the streets and erupt in waves of total exasperation panic grabs the suburbs brokers make desperate reservations for Toronto for Zurich fathers bludgeon children with golf clubs housewives loot supermarkets conduct orgies in fall-out shelters cops barricade themselves in liquor stores tanks roll down Fifth Avenue glamor generals hatch sinister plots air raid sirens madden the precincts sick of public relations sick of traffic jams sick of wife complaints sick of girdle ads sick of hypocrite jobs sick of kindness to animals sick of media tease sick of packaging sick of insurance salesmen sick of plastic sick of journalism sick of voting sick of marriage sick of adultery sick of poverty sick of affluence sick of ambition sick of health drives sick of what's good for them sick of life sick of death sick of no joy sick of no splendor.

they picked me up soon as I got off the bus and put me into the police car a bulge belly type rolls of nape fat sweat stained pits the sheriff and his deputy a young nervous guy at the wheel ah yew a nigga lova son you maht as well admit it raht away who me no I just come down for an american legion convention what convention yew know of any convention in town harry yew not makin fun a the american legion ah yew let's go harry we drove out of town down the highway my suitcase still with me their mistake then lights dimmed turned down a dark bumpy road stopping in the woods told me to get out now ah yew a nigga lova yew from the north ain't yew son ah sayed answer me yes no he punched me in the face yew mean yessuh nosuh ain't yew got no manners son now ah yew a nigga lova nosuh he punched me in the face that's wheah lyin's gonna getcha son now ah yew a commie who me no a jew no no he's lyin what we waitin for the others don't get edgy we'll take care a this nigga lova another car bumped down the road men in shirt sleeves rifles behind it another I jump in police car motor still running jerk emergency jam gas pedal car peels out bullet smashes back window shots ch-ch-ch bumping along the road with a head start lights way behind going too fast hit a rock out of control smash into a tree crawl out and run into woods still holding suitcase dogs behind me baying on the scent I stop open the suitcase and wait they came breaking through underbrush fang snout german shepherds drooling bloodhounds man eating dobermans red eyed I pull the pin of special hand grenade concealed in three pounds flank steak they leap on it snarling one big squirming ball of dog snapping at the meat KA-BOOM shower of paws snouts bloody carcass parts still running they zero in cut me off I duck behind boulder come out a theah yew nigga lovin bayastid or we'll shoot yew out

152

ch-ch-ch pistol shots k-chu-ping of rifle I open my suitcase full of hand grenades pick one pull the pin count and throw KA-BOOM that gives them something to think about for a while then suddenly ak-ak-ak-ak-ak-ak a tommy gun come on outa theah yew ain't got a chance the sheriff's voice I pull a grenade pin count and throw KA-BOOM ch ch-ch k-chu-ping ak-ak-ak-ak-ak-ak-ak-ak-ak k-chu k-chu-ping ch ch ch-ch-ch k-chu ak-ak-ak-ak-ak KA-BOOM k-chu-ping k-chu-ping ak-ak-ak-ak KA-BOOM ch-ch-ch ch k-chu k-chu ch-ch ch ch-ch k-chu-ping I must have hit the bastard with the tommy gun KA-BOOM k-chu-k-chu ch ch ch KA-BOOM ch ch-ch-ch KA-BOOM ch ch KA-BOOM ch KA-BOOM KA-BOOM KA-BOOM Whitebread Blackhead KA-BOOM Loach and Tench KA-BOOM Herm and Irma KA-BOOM Nancy's father KA-BOOM Henry Sliesinger KA-BOOM Gerald KA-BOOM Slumski KA-BOOM Hamstrung KA-BOOM

pok: smack of ash on horsehide

can't I get any peace what's he up to he's going to get in trouble with that temper now he thinks he can get his way by throwing tantrums I can't even read my paper not a minute's peace not a minute's peace he has no respect

do we have to go through it all again can I get no rest

why don't you go out and play my god when I was a kid you had to fight every time you wanted to walk down the street

still at it are you I don't understand him always with books you're not practical Ronnie he'll ruin his eyes stubborn you were always stubborn I remember as a baby sulky stubborn unless you had your own way your mother always giving in to you that was the beginning of it I used to argue with her no discipline

and were you grateful that's the thing

it's my own fault I should have taken the strap to him but I couldn't do it because I

I refuse to be disturbed I want to finish my paper it's

153

been ten years and I haven't been able to finish my paper if you realized how painful it was the effort to look up to speak he should have walked him he had no right to pitch to Musial with two on they don't swing they just stand there and look at it go by I don't know just like his mother always trying to resurrect the past what's gone is gone and nothing you can do about it dead and buried finished but you were always a selfish child bothering your mother all the time there are other people in the world besides you you know always too demanding a real mother's boy I would have taught you how to box a boy has to know how to defend himself of course your mother is right it's best to stay out of fights remember how I took you to Coney Island just you and me and I bought you all the hot dogs and ice cream and Cracker Jacks and cotton candy then you had to get sick when you got home boy did she give me hell you did it for spite anything to get her on your side what a brat always playing by himself too smart for his own good him and his pansy friends it's my own fault I should have taken the strap to him but I couldn't because I because I knew they shouldn't have pitched to him with two on they just stand there and look at it go by

aggravation aggravation all I ask of life is to be able to sit down and read my paper I work hard all day you'll be the death of me look at the way you treat your mother he'll give me a coronary yet for ten years I've been trying to read this paper that's all I ask it's your fault she could have lived ten years after me nothing but aggravation oh I don't blame you for myself these things happen suddenly after years of not being able to read my paper and they just stand there with their bats on their shoulders

I think I can expect a little consideration from you now that I'm gone at least for myself I don't care but your mother was a different story though of course you never gave a damn for anything but getting your own way you were the death of her just as you killed me oh I don't blame you after years of aggravation but did you ever show any gratitude that's all I ask a little common decency

I should have taken the strap to you but I couldn't because I thought you understood when I gave you the bat I suppose I should have said you have to step up there and swing or told you about contraception and more and much more but I couldn't because she always took your side and I just wanted to read the paper if you only realized how painful it was they should never have pitched to him never with two on they should have walked him the damn fools it's too late now what's done is done dead and buried finished all I want to do is read my paper I think I can expect that of you a little peace I worked hard after all

and did I ever ask any thanks for it that's all I want to know

he's too smart for his own good
he needs a good spanking
I'm at my wits' end I'm telling your father
now I'm going to give it to him
now he's going to get it
he'll have to learn to curb that temper
at last wait till I get my hands on him

but I couldn't do it because I couldn't look up and speak because I couldn't read my paper because I just stood there and watched it go by because they should have walked him with two on the damn fools too late now what's done is done it's your own fault you were always too stubborn you could have come to me after all you could have said they don't swing at it with your pansy friends ruining your eyes with books for spite and a little respect taking you to Coney Island for a minute's peace so you can throw a tantrum and read the newspaper for his own good because god knows I wanted aggravation every time I walked down the street getting into trouble with Musial for ten years consideration common respect mother thanks she because blame pitched to of course you understood coronary nevertheless to dis-

155

turb to rest because I the swing finished to up the is again all explain remember remember remember me remember me remember me

then I see him as he turns away from me arm raised he begins to run he's running for a bus he's too old to run like that painful ungainly gasping then his stride evens he shouts waves at the bus runs faster shouting waving as the bus pulls away no chance now but he runs faster lumbering after the bus like a heavy animal then more gracefully faster digs into his pace shouting waving cursing the bus pulls away running now with the smooth velocity of a fullback fast as the bus faster narrowing the gap running waving laughing leaping into the air skipping turning cartwheels shouting for the devil of it throwing rocks to make the driver shake his fist lithe fleet laughing a boy's wild laugh he disappears in the distance

pok: smack of ash on horsehide
jet snarl out of Idlewild
mammoth flinging themselves into the air
over the misery of boroughs
over the yearning of boroughs
Bliss Street Utopia Parkway Mount Eden Avenue Olympia Heights
you must change your life
dry noon heat contracts skin loosens muscles stillness of painted eucalyptus crickets dozing nothing moves against the slow equanimity of occasional careless wavelets except beyond amidst the glitter a lateen sail bobbing and a quarter of an inch above the Pacific or Mediterranean horizon hangs a low lying merchant vessel of unknown flag rust colored preceded by the greasy smudge from its stack

noon quiet of cypress cedar eucalyptus lizard slips over garden wall glides across flagstones damp mausoleum smell of shade clay roots mortality thirst heat vibrations off rock and sand barbaric green of palm foliage clarity of Pacific or Mediterranean sky

156

a woman appears slim dark moving across the terrace with measured stride wearing a loose garment of white linen or miracle fiber black hair falls over shoulders she smiles balances a vessel in offering to me then sets the drink down on a table I following the mobile arabesques of her obviously unbound body

we embrace I ponder the softness of her breasts rub my palm against her hardening nipple

what is your name I ask

two others enter the woman blonde tall as a viking heroic breast and profile hair pulled back

the man very much like me I grasp his hand firmly he puts his arm around my shoulders in fraternal recognition

the woman advances her body molding the severe lines of her wine purple robe her blond brow gleaming we embrace she grasps my swelling penis looks steadily into my eyes hers gray full of solemn clarity

she smiles disengages herself the other man still holding the swarthy woman glued to him caressing her long back and buttocks

I take the arm of the gray-eyed woman stately I lead her beneath a spreading cedar benches near a low table in depth of shade

there come the olive complected woman dark lips arched nose the man much like myself we join hands in knowing contact smiling a circle of intimacy

a girl brings fruit serves demitasse sets on the table a pitcher of clear water

the swarthy woman arches her delicate wrist exposing her palm as though offering a gift says do we not in view of this sea think of Valéry's words masse de calme et visible réserve eau sourcilleuse

and perhaps the man smiles anticipate when le vent se lève since il faut tenter de vivre

to live says the gray-eyed woman isn't that just it as we

157

sit here do we not sit at the very center of life amidst the poise of the elements

the poise of the elements the sun a friend the ocean a lover whispering calm assurance I reach down and sift the reddish earth between my fingers Baudelaire's cat glides by gray mysterious

. it is almost she went on as if we could speak of the old categories truth order beauty

or indulge in the new ones the man smiles raising his cup pleasure excitement spontaneity

one feels a loss sighs the swarthy woman

I feel no loss I say caressing with my thumb the wood grain of the table top I was born here beside the sea on a very hot day they plucked me from the reeds the mermaids sang at my circumcision I grew up sucking olive pits and collecting the stones of the country gabbro wad haarkies sard horneblende orpiment pudding-stone dogtooth-spar turkey-fat-ore toad's-eye-tin tiger's-eye gneiss verd-antique obsidian which I licked nibbled and rubbed against my skin and even now overwhelmed as by a lover with color heat wellbeing I feel dilations of a vast internal grandeur full of power compared to which the explosion of a supernova is a minor energy phenomenon with enormous clouds of inter-galaxy dust measurable at $HR = 3 \times 10^{-8}E$ for the first fifty million years whose curvatures make M_0C^2 look a little silly to say the least if you're talking of fluctuations through six orders of magnitude boiling in the dark nebulae we have known vast shock waves sweeping through the ocean at speeds of up to five hundred miles an hour though measuring as little as two feet from trough to crest suddenly on approaching shore rear out of a quiet sea to a height of one hundred feet or more over helpless sunbathers trans-fixed by the huge beachy withdrawing suck and hiss of their gathering doom

screw churning greasy smoke boiling from the funnel rusty prow heaving through the swell rigid mast sway low

lying decks awash flag unknown the freighter moves in-
shore

I was sitting in the mouth of a giant with sour stomach
and decaying teeth each time he belches I faint in a foul
wind of fermenting vomit and fecal rot growing nauseous
in the putrid humidity as I struggle to remember my name

Why am I sitting in the mouth of a giant? Absurd. I'm
not sitting in the mouth of a giant. I turn on the light,
blinking and sniffing. A rat. I leap off the bed. I smell a rat.
Some idiot had decided to use rat poison and the smell
was by now unmistakably that of a dead rat corrupting in
the walls.

I turned on the radio and tuned in to some Muzak,
impossible to sleep. I didn't dare breathe too deeply because of the smell. I felt my diaphragm about to convulse
in spasms of nausea, and my head was stuffed with dirty
laundry. I wanted to throw open the windows of my mind.

Henry Sliesinger Reports: One of the practical problems that still confront space-race scientists is that of elimination. Each day the body secretes a quantity of waste in
the amount of a pound or more. The dead skin, old hair,
and fingernail clippings, not to mention the ordinary solid
and fluid waste, which the body normally eliminates, would
soon clog the limited area available in a space cabin, and
smother the hapless astronaut in his own secretions.

I opened the windows. I moved to the room farthest
from the source of the smell, I held a handkerchief over
my face and, finally, I put my clothes on and went out.

It was a clear night. A cold breeze had blown away the
normal congestion of atmosphere over the East Side. I
drew a deep breath, a second, and a third. I could have
gone on like that all night. Then, lungs clear and mind
clearing, I crossed the street to a bar whose owner, a nervous modern version of Chaucer's canny host, had culti-
vated a lumpenintelligentsia clientele whose beards had
totally displaced the red noses of indigenous Polack rum-

159

mies. His name, an arc of small gilt letters, vowels obliterated, smiled from plate glass like the gold teeth of an impoverished immigrant. The bar was an old establishment, and he had taken care to preserve the woodwork and glasswork of the manly, mustachioed nineties. I moved through the beer-laced mist of tobacco smoke to find a place at the bar and asked for an ale. As I started my drink, one foot on the brass rail and my elbow resting on the bar, I became aware of a feeling that seemed to flow from the well-worn wood into my body, a feeling that was induced by mere physical contact with the heavy, graceful piece of furniture supporting me. I was filled with a comforting sense of assurance that seemed to inhere through the long mass of the bar by virtue of its solidity, by virtue of its age, by the beauty of its wood, by its sheen of long use. In being so absolutely *there*, the bar communicated to me an absolute sense of my own presence. It was a feeling very similar to the one from which derived a peculiar hobby of mine, that of collecting photographs of myself. I also sometimes got it after a good lay. But not always. I thought of Nancy.

"Cigarette?"

My neighbor, who was holding out a pack of cigarettes, was a clean-cut straight-backed fellow with neatly clipped blond hair and an all-American face, wearing a jacket and white shirt with a quiet narrow tie.

"Thanks," I said, and took one.

"Here, let me light it for you."

He obviously worked for his father on Wall Street and went religiously to reunions at the Yale Club. He gave the impression of being slightly uncomfortable in this environment, although I had seen him here before.

"Do you come here often?" he asked me.

"Well, I live across the street. Do you?"

"Me?" He laughed, a little affectedly I thought. "Oh no. I've never been here before."

160

"Really? I could have sworn I'd seen you in here."

"Not me. It must have been two other fellows. God, look at that specimen over there."

He nodded toward a guy with long curly blond locks down his back, bushy blond mustache, flat Western hat, long-fringed kidskin jacket, boots, and skinny jeans.

"Yeah," I said. "The Daniel Boone set. Where you from?"

"New York."

"Brought up here?"

"Well I came here from Germany if you have to know. They sent me there from Czechoslovakia."

"Who did?"

"The Nazis. They didn't like Jews. Perhaps you've heard."

"I'm a Jew myself you know."

"Don't make me laugh. You Americans, you don't know what it is to be a Jew. I spent my childhood in a concentration camp. Not one of the more famous ones, I'm sorry to say, but on the other hand it was located near a very picturesque medieval town. Landsbeck. Hitler was imprisoned there after the Munich putsch. In the foothills of the Bavarian Alps. Slave labor. Very pleasant, I can assure you."

"Really." I was highly dubious.

"Of course you don't believe me. Very good. Very acute. Actually I work in my father's bank and just graduated from Yale. Fils de papa. I'm enormously wealthy and was born and raised in Montclair, New Jersey. You decide. What do you think? I'm sincerely interested in your opinion."

At that moment a guy pushed in next to me and I was confronted by a dark visage with a toothy Pullman car smile. He grinned at me sheepishly, pulled his ear, scratched his cheek, rubbed his nose, and looking over my shoulder said: "Scuse me, boss, would you happen to have a match?

161

I sure would like to light this here cigarette." I thought he was going to break into a buck and wing.

"Sure thing, son," I said. But when I took a good look at him I noticed he was about my own age and dressed not in overalls but in neat Ivy League style meticulous to the point of exaggeration. I gave him a skeptical look, left him with a pack of matches and moved on down the bar, stopping in front of a girl who had just come in and was standing uncertainly in the middle of the floor. She stepped aside to let me pass, smiling apologetically. She had straw-colored hair and wore a camel's hair coat and a cotton dress that looked like she ordered it from an ad on the back of Mary Marvel Comics. She must have been from some small town in the Midwest where they taught girls to smile at strangers. Definitely not one of the cool chicks from this neighborhood.

"Want to have a beer?" I asked.

"Shir," she said.

"Pardon me?"

"Thanks, shir."

I ordered a couple of beers.

"Well, who are you? Do you go to college?" I asked.

"Goodness, no." She giggled.

"Why, don't you want to go to college?"

"Well, Dad wanted me to go to college. Dad went to Princeton."

"Really."

"Eas. But college is so square. Don't you think so? I mean like, teachers."

"Oh, of course. There's nothing as square as college. College is a real drag."

"Of curse. So I quit."

"And what do you do now?"

"I'm a palmist."

"A what?"

"I read palms."

162

"No kidding. Would you like to read mine?"

"I knew you'd ask that. They all do."

Someone tapped my shoulder.

"Oh, I say there old boy. Thanks for giving me the matches. Much obliged."

"Quite all right," I said.

"Do you know who I am? Who am I?"

"You're the guy who I gave the matches to."

"Oh, capital. Quite good. Splendid memory old boy."

"Nothing to it, really."

"Oh, I say. She's not giving you that bloody line about palmistry, is she?"

"Well, as a matter of fact, yes," I said. "What's wrong with that?"

"Nothing at all, nothing at all. It's just her simple way of making friends." He slipped his arm around her shoulders. "Ain it baby."

"Don't make me do it here," she said.

"My, but it's hot in here," he said. He unbuttoned his shirt and took off his tie. "Haven't I seen you down at CORE meetings?"

"You could have."

"Sure I did. Let me get this round. Three mugs, Charlie."

"Thanks."

"You know this chick and me are old pals. I don't suppose you know that."

"No."

"You bet, baby. We been on a long freedom ride together."

"That so ?"

"No. I mean a real freedom ride, down South and all. That's right. And let me tell you, baby, it was no joke. I mean I spent one night in a Georgia jail that I won't soon forget. That old sheriff made me strip naked and we had a little conversation with his hunting knife right under my

163

balls. I could feel the edge, man. She knows it. She was watching. Sure, they made her watch. And the deputy who kept saying, You know ah ain't gelded myself a nigger these five years since. And she kept saying I demand my constitutional right to call my attorney. Constitution, shit. Look here girl, the sheriff told her, it's a damn lucky thing for you that you're dealing with gentlemen. I hadn't noticed. Hey. What you say, baby."

He went off with a group of goateed friends.

"My, the way he makes up those starries," said the girl. "He's never been south of the Bad-ery."

She drifted off in the chatter-filled haze.

"I see you've been ignoring me."

It was my Yale Club friend. I started to protest.

"That's all right," he went on. "Don't apologize. Let me buy you a beer. Cigarette?"

I took one. His match swayed through several arcs in front of my nose before it managed to reach the tip of my cigarette. Or maybe it was me who swayed. In any case I saw he was considerably drunker than before. That was all right. So was I.

"I don't blame you for avoiding me. Not in the least. As a matter of fact I'm a rather obnoxious fellow beneath this bland exterior. I would go so far as to say that your avoiding me indicates an innate good taste and strength of character. That's why I like you."

"I'm sure you're not as bad as all that."

"Don't contradict me. I make a statement in all sincerity I expect you to accept it as such. I've had enough of your patronizing crap."

"Well, okay, okay."

"Let's be frank," he said, putting his hand on my shoulder. "Do you know who I am?"

"No. Who?"

"None of your god damn business. I'll bet you think I'm some kind of nut, hey? Go on, say it. I'm some kind of nut. Go on, say it. But look, what I mean to say is, what does it matter who I am? Or what I do or any of that crap. Right? Pals are pals, right? Bottoms up." He drank his beer. "You want another round?"

"Let me get this one."

"No, no. It's on me. I don't have to worry about money. You don't suppose I have to worry about money, do you? Look at that guy, dressed up like the Prince of Wales. He probably doesn't know who's going to buy his next beer. These jerks. It's a regular masquerade party. Not for me. I am I, and you are you, and that's all there is to it. Right, friend?"

"Right. What's your name?"

"Ronnie."

"What a coincidence. That's my name."

"You must be making some mistake. That's my name."

"No, no. I mean it's my name too."

"Look, you're not getting funny, are you. I say it's my name."

"I understand that. But it happens to be my name too."

"Look here, mister. I don't know who you are, or what your game is. All I know is I'm drinking quietly at the bar and you come over and ask me for a cigarette. Then you start asking me snoopy questions about my past, my family and my religion, and when I answer them you as much as call me a liar. Suppose I am a liar? What business is that of yours? I buy you a few beers and you think that gives you the right to pass judgment on my character and life history. And would you even have the courtesy to pay for a round? No, not you. Do you think I'm made of money? What the hell do you think this is, freeloader's paradise? And on top of everything else you start getting funny about my name? Oh no. Now one last time. I say my name is Ronnie. What's yours?"

"Okay. Okay. My name is Homer."

165

"Homer, hey. That's a nice, harmless name."

"Yeah, I'm glad you like it. Well I think I have to go now."

"Yeah. A nice, harmless name. Only I don't believe it. Come on now mister. What's your *real* name. What are you, F.B.I. or something?"

Suddenly this Negro guy in beret and dark glasses comes over and gives me a shove.

"Say, you know who I am, man? Who am I?"

"How the hell do I know? And take it easy."

"Come on, man. You know who I am. Who am I?"

"I told you I don't know."

"I'll give you a hint. Freedom ride."

"Oh. Aren't you the guy who went on the freedom ride?"

"What freedom ride?"

"With the girl, the palmist."

"What girl? What palmist? You putting me on, man?"

"No, look, this guy was telling me about going down South."

"You mean a colored fella? About my height? Looked just about like me?"

"Yeah. That's right."

"Oh, I get it. We all look alike, is that it? Like crows on a clothes line. Can't tell one from another."

"No. I just thought that was you."

Just then the blond palmist yaws over and says to no one in particular, "Hey, there's a guy over there showing dirty pictures of his girl friend."

"So what," says the guy in the beret.

"I'm his girl friend."

"You're my girl friend," says the guy in the beret. He put his arm around her shoulders. "Ain that right, baby."

"Don't make me do it here," she said.

He pulled her close and started swaying to the rhythm of the jukebox. "Let's rock honey."

166

"Not here," she said.

"That's the girl," I said.

"What do you want?" he said.

"That's the girl, the palmist."

"What about it?"

"She told me you made up the story about the freedom ride."

"She's a liar, don't you know that yet? I never made up no story."

"The one about the sheriff?"

"Yeah, that's right, the one about the sheriff. Or any other story she says I made up. These white chicks just lie and lie. She wouldn't know the truth if you shoved it in her face and made her eat it. And I have. That's why I love you, honey. Cause you don't know who I am. Ain that right white girl." He put his hand on her breast and squeezed.

"Don't," she said. "It's too obvious."

"That's who I am. A black hand on a white tit. Any black hand. I hate her guts."

"Hey, get your hands off that girl," said the Yale type.

"Leave them alone," I say. "She likes it."

"Don't," she said. "It's humiliating." She gave him a long kiss.

"What do you mean, she likes it. You like it. You're as good as a nigger yourself."

They were in a clinch against the wall. The guy was feeling her up and whispering in her ear. "Don't," she said. "It's obscene."

"Are you just going to stand there and let this shine do that to her?" said the Yale type. "You're no white man."

"I heard what he said," said the guy in the beret. "I heard that. I wouldn't let that go by, man. Are you going to stand there and take that kind of crap?"

"Well, I mean, I was just taking your side."

"What do you mean my side. My side is black. I hate your white guts."

167

The Yale type sneered at the blonde. "You're disgusting," he said.

"Of course she's disgusting," said the guy in the beret. "She's a pig."

"When'd you bleach your hair last honey," said the Yale type. "Dark are the roots. No offense," he said to the guy in the beret. "I'm a married man myself you know. My husband's waiting at home."

"Sure thing baby. Come up and see me some time. Who's your creepy friend?"

"His name is Homer. I hear he's a cop."

"A cop hey. You better tell him to get the hell out of here."

"I think he's a fag, myself. Are you a fag?" he asked me.

"I loathe homosexuals," said the blonde, staring at me with infinite contempt.

"I don't care for bitches myself," I said.

"A typical queer response," said the Yale type. "Haven't you got anything better to do than go around insulting young ladies?"

"That's right, man. Watch how you talk to my girl. Do you know who I am?" He gave me a hard shove. "Who am I?"

"I don't give a crap who you are and watch your shoving."

"Well you better give a crap baby because my name is Joseph 4X and I carry a big razor. I'm warning you Homer." He gave me a shove.

"My name isn't Homer."

"I don't give a hot shit what your name is Homer. I'm warning you."

"Are you calling me a liar?" said the Yale type.

"You're damn right I'm calling you a liar."

"Are you looking for a fight Homer?" asked the Yale type.

"No, I'm not looking for a fight, but . . ."

"Well you're going to get one if you don't apologize, Homer."

"Why don't you fight like a man?" said the blonde.

"Because he's not a man. He's a chicken," said the guy in the beret.

"What are you anyway?" said the blonde.

"Fish nor flesh," said the guy in the beret.

"Perhaps you'd like to step outside," said the Yale type.

"You're fucking right I'd like to step outside," I said. "Come on, let's go."

I spoke quietly, but with a deadly certainty. I was filled with an invincible rage. I knew with total inner assurance that I was going to wipe him out. I could see the precise spot on his jaw where I was going to smash him, and I could feel the concussion of my knuckles on his bone. For once I was going to argue in a language nobody could contradict.

He followed me to the door. I was moving in a dream. I stepped out the door into the dark air, turned around, and next thing I knew I was flat on my ass in the cold street, no one in sight, and a terrific ache throbbing in the right side of my face. Who am I?

A BRIEF EROTIC AUTOBIOGRAPHY

This should actually begin when I was eleven. As a matter of fact it should begin when I was two and a half, with certain gratifying incidents of my naughty nonage which I chuckle to recall. But allow me my few rags of modesty. You remember that on page 69 I let drop how I knew a girl in Manhattan that summer between high school and college "who was usually good for a lay." Actually, that was a lie. Not exactly a lie since it was true for other guys though not for me. Let's call it a half truth in which I was included in the other half. That was the way I put it at the time: "Usually good for a lay." Pure

169

adolescent braggadocio to assuage my delicate ego. Of course there had been that ambiguous encounter with Oola Wonderleigh, but basically my erotic nature had been conditioned through my long, exhausting relation with frightened Nancy, maddening Nancy. To the demi-vierges of Brooklyn, may you fall early victims to odious sex crimes.

My escape to college did not, at first, help very much. At the last minute through a kind of fluke I was awarded a scholarship to attend the heterodox Aaron Burr School on the West Coast, an ephemeral experiment in the education of young intellectuals, that had opened shortly before I came and closed shortly after I left. A capsule of educational enlightenment, Burr did much to cultivate the mind, but little to develop the organ here in question. I walked a pale ghost among the glowing nymphs of Beverly Hills, thirsting to share a careless sensuality with those who, on the rare occasions when I became momentarily visible, seemed appalled by my presence. Letters of the period reveal in retrospect a piquant irony. For a while I sustained a correspondence with Nancy:

Dearest Nancy,

Yesterday R—— R—— (a famous actor) arranged passes for us to come and watch the shooting on his set—an adolescent piece of sentimentality full of saccharine love confessions in which everyone gets married at the end and lives happily ever after. It's amazing how these vivacious and pragmatic people can step into their celluloid unreality and become simpering dolls with such facility—I can understand why they say that the best American actors are always the ones who simply play themselves. Oh Nancy, if only I too could play myself, and end the endless masquerade which I am forced to play here, in this alien city. Nancy dear, if only I could send you a real kiss, not just an X on a piece of paper, and take you in my arms, I would become my real self again. Simply to touch your hand would make me

170

happy. And now that we're a little older and more mature, I think it might be a happiness that would last—as long as happiness can last in this unhappy world. XXXXX

All my love, Ronnie.

Note the celluloid quality of the emotion here—more Hollywood than Hollywood. There it is, the artist as a young American. By the time I had transferred to a big Ivy League school and finally joined, in some sense, the mainstream of civilization, my situation was acute. I had passed into a stage where I was a little brutish toward girls. Sick and tired of the conventional drivel they expected, my technique with dates amounted to a sullen absence of conversation interrupted by seizures of spastic pawing. What occasional gratification this gained me came at the expense of a growing reputation as some kind of pervert. One day I heard a girl with a fraternity pin glittering on her tit whisper loudly to a sorority sister as they passed: "It's always the quiet ones." I began hanging around with a bunch of fraternity boys who talked about visiting a whorehouse "to tear off a piece of ass," and even went with them once, with predictable results. To tell the truth I really did suspect myself of becoming some kind of pervert, and might well have become one, when I was unexpectedly saved by history.

By history, I say; by Hitler would be more to the point. Because it would seem that there was something in the genetic makeup of those European families who were producing children during the thirties, and who later had to flee their countries before, during, and after World War II, which caused them to be blessed with a disproportionately large number of girl children. And many of these children ultimately found their way to America, with or without their parents, and sometimes with one or both parents newly acquired in the general scramble. And most of these girls for some reason seemed to turn seventeen around 1950, and

171

a good number of them ended up as my undergraduate contemporaries on that old American campus, where they disguised themselves as girls from Forest Hills or Oneonta, or gathered in discreet cliques bound by a dislike for football rallies and a taste for intelligible conversation, or hid themselves in furnished rooms, starting at a knock on the door, or at thunder that sounded too much like an explosion. From France, from Poland, from Czechoslovakia they came to sit on my lap and share my bed, humane creatures, intelligent beings, angels who knew how to cook, who knew how to arrange little surprises, to buy little gifts, who knew how to be jealous, and how not to be jealous, and, through a remarkable heritage, who knew they were women. And, above all, who talked with me. Who talked with me, hour on hour, in bed, out of bed, after class, over coffee, drunk, sober, at parties, in cars, on the phone, about books, about friends, about teachers, about sex, about movies, about parents, about gossip, about restaurants, about life, about clothes, about religion, about talking, about Europe, America, animals, marriage, women, men, work, ideas, shopping, love, lingerie, pets, perfume, skiing, cheating, deodorants, desserts, dishonesty, brandy, bathing suits, traveling, so it seemed after a while that I had been mute for twenty years and had just begun to learn what talking was for.

A snapshot from the epoch shows a brunette with an elegant nose and Marlene Dietrich cheekbones, hair falling over one side of her brow, who seems to be saying to me: "Oh my goodness, what are you being so serious about? You're only twenty-one, after all." From another photo a pallid young woman with the intelligent nose of a French Jew gazes at me with ironic eyes. "Let me assure you, my friend," I can hear her saying with a bitter edge directed as much at herself as at me, "they do not award consolation prizes for bad luck. The world does not give one many presents." And here is another photograph, in color, showing a

172

girl with dark blond hair and a voluptuous peasant body, whose round cheeks and full lips say only one thing. And beside her I stand with my callow face and my asinine grin of embarrassment, thin, too thin, in sad-sack brown pants and blue sport shirt, yet with my arm rakishly around the blonde and in my free hand flaunting an enormous cigar, as if I were living a dream—yes—but not my own dream. And, in fact, at the left in the near background, just under my poised cigar, one sees a big, red Irish terrier, tail to the camera, urinating against a stone bench. Behind the bench, an ivied brick wall with a Gothic window, and at the far left an elm tree beyond which, in the distance, smooth green hills rising steeply out of a valley, blue sky, a vagrant puff of cloud: America. And if you look closely, you can see in an open half of the Gothic window, index fingers pulling down the corners of his mouth and red tongue protruding, Otis, staring like a gargoyle at the camera. (He disappears from the window—a moment later he emerges from the shadow of a Gothic arch—waving, grinning, cowboy thin, he approaches the girl, ignoring me—"What do you want to mess with cameras for?" he asks her—he rips a page out of his sketch book—"Here's the real thing," he says. "Never believe what a camera tells you, cameras won't tell you the truth. The truth, that takes an eye of genius if I may say so, an eye free of the banality of the mechanical of, literally, the cliché"—"My, Otis, you are a snob," she says—she takes the sketch from him—in it she seems womanly, defined, mature—"Why thank you Otis, that's very flattering"—she speaks English with a suggestion of hisses and lisps, of soft rubbery consonants, of odd gutturals, evocative of mazurkas, hussars, slivovitz, Mad King Ludwig, S. Z. "Cuddles" Szakall, and the easy carnality of a ripened civilization—"Hey, what about me?" I say, looking at the sketch—"You're not in this picture," says Otis pointedly. "Say how about coming up to do a little life modeling for me?" he asks the blonde—"Oh god, Otis, I'm talking to

173

Ronnie"—"Come on," he says, "you said you would"—"I never promised that"—"Come on, you're chicken. I'm talking about art"—"What are you kidding?" I say—"Ignore Sukenick's crude ideas," he says. "His mind lacks polish"—"No," she says firmly. "Now go away and leave us alone"—"Shit!" says Otis—he throws his pad on the ground, drops to the stone bench, and sits there head drooping, face like a tragic mask—"What are you kidding?" I say—she looks at him skeptically a minute, then looks at me, then back at Otis—she goes over to him and holds out her hand—"All right, Otis, come on," she says nodding—"Now?" says Otis—he jumps up grinning, and takes her hand—"What are you kidding?" I say—she shrugs—"What can you do," she says, "if it's that important"—she kisses my cheek as they pass me, walking off hand in hand—Otis waves gleefully—"You son of a bitch," I say. "You bitch. You son of a bitch. What are you kidding? Are you kidding? Are you kidding?") A second color photo, dated a week later, shows the same architecture, the same elm, the same cloud, a different dog, and me with my arm around either the same, or almost the same girl, in a vignette snapped by Otis who, in the interim, had bought a camera and become a photography nut. Here too, as in the first color shot, between the building and the elm, but so small you can see it only if you know it's there, just at the edge of the lawny slope, is the rock behind which on a spring night I first made love to that dark girl with the vacant eyes (the beautiful, disconsolate "gypsy" of my story, "The Sleeping Gypsy"—see *Epoch*, Spring 1959) who by contrast was so thoroughly American, an archtypical waste product of the neurotic fifties, who I thought I loved and learned you can't love someone who doesn't know who she is, because she isn't really there—hello, wherever you are. Speaking of that type, there are the slate steps where I was sitting in my senior year when a friend visiting from Boston told me, by the way, that he'd run into Slade in Cambridge did I know he was marrying my old high school girl friend?

Then we graduated. After that there was nothing to do. That was the fundamental thing one felt about 1955: there was nothing to do. So we all put ourselves on ice, some in the army, some on Mad Ave, some in grad school, some disappearing in the anonymous slums of the cities, and most of us haven't recovered yet.

She opened the door and let me in, examining me with a kind of stern curiosity. At first I was aware of nothing, and spoke mechanically: "Well! How are you?"

"So. Here you are again. Ronnie. What now?"

Then, unexpectedly, I saw she had changed. No. She hadn't changed really. The way I saw her had changed. There was no magic in my eye. She was a girl, like another.

"What now?" I repeated. "How do I know." I had the feeling we had resumed without surprise or hesitation a dialogue that had never really ended.

"You called." She shrugged as if she were still angry about something. Her well-known irate shrug.

"I don't know why I called Nancy. Just to see you. You should be flattered."

"Of course I'm flattered." She smiled her gallant smile as she had always smiled it. It seemed a little mannered. "It's been five years, hasn't it? Going on ten. Have you seen Ernie?"

"Slade, no. Not since you married him. No doubt he'll come to New York. We always turn up in the same places. Though at different times, it seems. Are you glad to see me?"

"I don't know yet," she answered. "Are you?"

"Yes." She was a girl like another. Probably a good fuck.

"Ronnie," she said, obviously trying to connect my

175

name with my presence. I suddenly felt there was no continuity between me and my adolescence.

"It's as if we were meeting for the first time," I said. I wanted to make that clear.

"Well then," she smiled, "let's pretend we are."

"How exciting." I immediately got an erection.

"Have I changed?" she asked.

"Yes. You're sexier."

She hadn't dressed for the occasion—a plain skirt, tight, but not too tight, and a sweater, loose, but showing the rise and division of her breasts. Her face, no makeup, suggestion of freckles, reminiscent of girlishness, but her body was riper—I imagined a voluptuous belly curve, deep creases under the ass.

"So are you, apparently," she responded. "Take your coat off." We were still standing by the door. It was a one-room apartment, a small room, in the East Sixties, smooth walls, doorman, probably paid over a hundred a month for that. We sat on opposite ends of the couch. The couch was also the bed.

"I was pretty surprised," I told her, "when I heard you married Slade—so much so that I wasn't very surprised to hear you got divorced."

"What was so surprising about it?"

"Well, I knew what little you knew of Slade in high school you didn't like very much."

"I guess you still don't know."

"Know what?"

"I slept with Ernie in high school. Toward spring of the last year."

"Oh. While you were going out with me?"

"I was always going out with you."

"Well. What do you know. How did that happen?"

"He came over one evening. He said he was looking for you. Later I found out he knew you were somewhere else. You'd come over to see me that afternoon and we'd had a

176

fight. As usual. My parents were out—I suppose he knew that too. Ernie is pretty methodical in such things—in most things. He got Dick Ricardo Sugar on the radio—you wouldn't remember him—you didn't like to dance."

"Couldn't dance."

"That kind of thing didn't interest you."

"What did you expect? It reminded me of Grossinger's. All right, I was a very square kid, I admit. I had other virtues."

"Such as."

"I don't remember."

"You were nice. I liked you. I probably loved you—or whatever adolescent equivalent. Anyway, he got me to dance with him. He started dancing pretty close. I was surprised. He was your friend after all. Then he kissed me and I just decided without thinking about it that I was going to let him do whatever he liked. Basically I think it was that I knew he could give me what I wanted without any complications. Ernie had a reputation you know—even then. It was curiosity really—just accumulated irresistible curiosity. I was sick of masturbation."

"You too?"

She made a face.

"I let him take my clothes off," she continued. "He wanted me to do it right there on the rug, but I took him upstairs. We did it in my parents' bed. It was bigger and more comfortable. That's pretty oedipal, I suppose. But then I am pretty oedipal. It was good. He did a good job. In fact he did it like a job, but then, that's Ernie. It was all very impersonal. I was glad I did it but I had no desire to sleep with him again. There was blood on the towel I'd spread on the bed, just like there's supposed to be."

"He probably added you to the total. He kept count you know."

"He still keeps count."

"Good christ. What's he up to?"

177

"He once calculated he slept with over a hundred girls. But he's also a liar. Don't believe anything he tells you."

"Then you met later in Cambridge?"

"Yes. I hadn't seen him since high school. It was my senior year. By that time I was really sick of the kinds of students you meet up there. Really sick. Ernie had taken up jazz. He played the drums and spent most of his time practicing. He was pretty good. He was going to enroll in some kind of jazz conservatory after he graduated, and he used to sit in at small clubs. He had a thing about Jewish girls at the time. He thought they made the best wives for gentile intellectuals. It was a theory, he had it all worked out. Then he decided to go to law school. He explained how it would be a good thing to have a Jewish wife in New York politics, and he also wanted my father's backing. My father had a fit. He told me if I married a goy I wouldn't see him again. We got married, he came to the wedding, and after that I didn't see him again. Not for a long time. I had no feelings about marrying a gentile. I never cared about being Jewish. That probably came from my mother, a German Jew, you know. She used to speak of 'the Jews.' "

"But why did you marry him?"

"Ernie could have been a hero. Just like he wants to be. He was the only man I'd met who behaved like that. He always acted on principle—on whatever principle he happened to believe in at the moment. I idealized him no doubt. I wanted to. He was strong. Physically strong, I mean. And he could really speak. You should have heard him addressing a rally in those days. We were active in the first CORE demonstrations in Boston. He knew what to say to a crowd. He had grown a goatee and bought himself a fur hat, and he used to cite parallels with Trotsky. And he could fight too, when he had to. He's a judo expert you know. One time this big guy molested me in a bar. Ernie took him outside and beat him half unconscious. Then we

178

picked the guy up and took him for a cup of coffee. He thanked us. He said he'd been drunk. He turned out to be a longshoreman who was drowning in debts to loan sharks. He was really pretty intelligent once he started talking. Ernie gave him a Veblen book he happened to be carrying. And he convinced him to go to the police. Later on we heard he'd been killed by the syndicate for squealing. I was terribly upset. That was the first time I began to think about what Ernie was doing. One thing about Ernie, when he does something he does it magnificently, even when it's stupid. Especially when it's stupid."

"He's always been like that," I said. I was a little jealous of Ernie from the way she'd described him. I was also pretty angry at her adolescent treachery with him. Ten years didn't make much difference. Had I only known I was being denied by the caprice of a deflowered virgin. How long had I wasted myself on the hypocrisy of disenchanted innocence? It was I who was the innocent. Me, with all my half-assed ideas about Life. Always. I was despicable.

But, curiously, I experienced a simultaneous arousal of sensuality. I had the sensation of being freed from something. The acknowledgment of her defloration by Slade had established for her in my eyes a retrogressive sexual identity. She was available. She was not the reluctant Nancy I had always retained in memory, but an exciting stranger. A stranger who nevertheless we both knew obviously owed me a lay.

"It's a shame," she said. "I feel sorry for Ernie. Basically he's a very confused person. He quit law school after the first semester. He decided it was political theory that reall; interested him. For two years he was the star of his graduate department. Suddenly he lost interest. About the same time he started fooling around with the co-eds. He'd get visits from this poor little bitch of a girl, one of his students, who didn't have the faintest idea she had a crush on him, he said. For him it was just a matter of her intellec-

179

tual development. He was being the teacher. In the fullest sense. One day I came in and found him on top of her on his desk. Ernie is the kind of a liar who doesn't even know when he's not telling the truth. They'd been having an affair for some time. When Ernie stood in front of me and told me it was all very innocent I think he really must have believed it. It all depended on your definition of innocent, he told me. After that he kept his little friends out of the house, at least. Then he started telling me I wasn't liberated. What he really wanted was to be liberated from me, but he didn't put it that way. Not Ernie. He gave me books to read and started lecturing me on the evils of monogamy. He encouraged me to have an affair. I didn't want to have an affair. He brought his friends around, and when I didn't like his friends, he started to bring strangers. He made me go to parties with nothing on under my dress, and tried to get me excited beforehand. He liked to feel me up in front of other men. Finally he told me I was frigid and he was tired of making love to me. This was a clinical observation, you understand. I didn't know anything about sex, I was too repressed. He stopped making love to me. He'd make me satisfy him, but he'd just tease me. One night he invited a young graduate assistant for dinner. I put on a sexy dress and had a lot to drink. While we were eating I flirted with him and rubbed my thigh against him under the table. I wanted to do the most obscene thing I could, out of spite. After dinner I danced with him so close that he began to get embarrassed, while my husband watched and made encouraging remarks. Then Ernie said he had to go out on an errand. So he went out and I got laid and I liked it. When Ernie came back I told him. He got red in the face, but he didn't say anything. Next day he tried to talk me out of doing it again. He'd revised his ideas, he said. But it was too late. I liked it. And besides, I was getting even. I used to meet the guy as often as I could, and then I'd tell Ernie I was too tired to make love. Finally Ernie got into a

fight with him and broke poor Alan's nose. I was watching.
Afterward I let Ernie screw me. My hero. I kept flirting
with men, Ernie kept getting into fights, and then I'd let
him screw me. It was really funny. I ended up practically
living with one man, dividing my time between him and
Ernie. Ultimately there wasn't much point to it, so I told
Ernie I wanted a divorce. He told me I was no damn good.
He called me a slut. And he gave it to me. What a comedy."

I took her hand. "Poor Nancy," I said.

She smiled at me. "Don't," she said.

I was immediately paralyzed by leaden memories. Then
I gave her a skeptical look and put my arm around her
shoulders.

"Don't," she said. "I'm not kidding."

"Come on," I said unceremoniously, and tried to kiss
her. She turned her head without otherwise moving.

"Cut it out," she said.

I tried to pull her against me. She scratched the back of
my hand. I cursed and held my hand up. There was a line
about an inch long that started between my first two
knuckles, red at one end and white at the other. A spot
of blood appeared where the skin was torn. "But why not
me?" I said.

"I'm sorry," she said. "You can hit me if you want."

"Why not me?"

"It would be too complicated. I don't want to get
involved."

"Fuck you. You already are involved."

"Oh." She smiled at me in an affected way, as if she
suddenly understood something. What, I don't know.

"Besides," I told her, "what I want from you isn't very
complicated."

"All right," she said. "If it's that important."

She started taking off her sweater.

"Wait a minute. What are you doing?"

"Isn't this what you want?" she asked.

181

She pulled the sweater over her head and sat there in her brassiere.

"Yeah, but, I mean you don't have to serve it up on a platter."

"I hate indirection. It makes you neurotic. If there's one thing I can't stand it's being neurotic."

She stood up and took off her skirt. Her breasts thrust forward as she reached behind to unhook her brassiere, then lowered one shoulder, and the other, as she freed herself of the straps. She turned her back to me as she slipped her panties off, let them fall to the floor, kicked them away with a quick movement of her leg, and turned again to me. At last. Beneath thin shoulders dazzling against a faded tan her implausibly large breasts with their perfect coned nipples, voluptuous belly curve, heavy creases under slim ass, between white thighs the golden crotch gleaming, radiant.

"Open the bed," she said.

It was some kind of convertible. I ran afoul of the mechanism after getting it half open.

"The hell with it," she said. "The rug is nice and thick."

"But wait . . ." I was fumbling with the bed.

"Come on," she urged. "I mean I haven't got all night."

Suddenly I was holding her body, swarming over it, like a man who wants to grab everything at once. She sank to her knees and kissed me. We both fell to the floor. "It's all right," she said. "I take pills." I wasn't asking. My penis felt heavy as a truncheon. I pushed into her without preliminary—the preliminaries were in my mind and generated a more than carnal urgency. I recognized across a decade two brown-blond hairs growing from the edge of her left nipple with the disinterest of a traveling salesman noting the scenery. It was a disappointing fuck. Too quick. And yet I wasn't disappointed.

We were lying side by side on the floor.

182

"Are you satisfied?" she asked.

I grunted, meaning yes.

"I'm glad *you* enjoyed yourself."

"What?" I asked.

"Nothing. I mean, I suppose this heals your ego. I'm glad it makes somebody happy."

She got up and put on her sweater and skirt, leaving her underwear where it had fallen. I zipped up and hoisted myself to the half-open couch. As I did so it opened fully into a bed. I fell back on it and stayed there.

"I suppose it did in a way. What do you expect? It took me more than ten years."

"Nothing. Only you didn't have to act as if I owed it to you."

"I'm sorry. Did I act that way?"

"You were taking advantage of our old relationship. I feel used."

"But you didn't have to do it, after all."

"Of course I didn't have to do it. I don't owe you a thing. I feel dirty."

Standing in front of me with her arms crossed over her breasts, clothes askew, hair tangled, her face screwed into a frown, she did in fact look dirty.

"I'm sorry," I said, sitting up, "but . . ."

"Never mind," she interrupted. "No intense little discussions. I've had enough of that. What we do we do. I believe in acting things out."

I shrugged. "Okay," I said.

She picked a pack of cigarettes off a table.

"Want one?" she asked.

"Thanks, I've stopped."

"What are you doing for a living?" she asked. "Are you a teacher?"

"No. I teach now and then."

"You don't want success?"

I shrugged.

183

"Why not? Too vulgar?"

"I haven't turned down any glittering opportunities."

"Don't you feel guilty?"

"No."

"So you've escaped too," she said, sitting down on the bed.

"What do you mean?"

"From Brooklyn."

"You never escape."

"Weren't you the one who was always talking about liberation? You and Ernie. And all your friends."

"Liberation maybe. Escape never. There's a big difference. It's a question of synthesis rather than negation."

"We've been out of school too long to quibble over words like that. All I know is I've changed my life so much that Gravesend doesn't seem real any more."

"Everything is real. Don't forget I'm a teacher. It's my business to quibble over words."

"I thought you weren't a teacher."

"I am and I'm not. Don't confuse me. What are you doing these days?"

"I'm a model."

"I wouldn't think you were skinny enough to be a model."

"Not a fashion model. A nude model."

"Oh. Isn't that a tough way to make a living?"

"No. I make a lot of money."

"Posing for artists?" I asked dubiously.

"Oh, I don't pose for artists any more. Except in special cases. It doesn't pay."

"What pays?"

"Photographers. Illustrators. Men's magazines."

"You don't mind it?"

"Mind what? It's better than eight hours a day in some phony office routine. Besides, I enjoy it. I have a good figure, why shouldn't I show it off? And I like making a

184

living with my body. It's healthier than most jobs, and more honest. It's wholesome."

"But, for example, you have pictures in the men's magazines?"

"Of course. Some of my friends were shocked. They tried to tell me the magazines are sick. But it's not girlie magazines that are sick. It's the people who look at them. I mean, do I strike you as a girlie?"

"But do you like the idea of exposing yourself to anyone who puts down the right change?"

"That depends. I once saw a very attractive guy next to me on the subway looking at one of my pictures. I enjoyed watching his face. I wondered what he'd do if I tapped him on the shoulder and said, That's me. But it's only a photograph that people see, don't forget. The photograph isn't me. What do I care who looks at it? I don't know the difference."

"What about your parents?"

"My father doesn't really mind as long as my identity isn't revealed. He seems to be sort of amused by it in fact. My mother flipped at first. It's not genteel you know. She spends all her money surreptitiously buying up the monthly supply of girlie magazines in Gravesend so they won't stray into the hands of her friends." She laughed. "The news dealers must think she's some kind of pervert. But they never use my real name in the captions. I always appear incognito."

"Can you appear incognito without any clothes on?"

"Oh sure. We're so used to recognizing one another by face and costume that your identity changes completely when you take your clothes off. You know that line from Lear? Take but my something away and so on. You'd be surprised. Your best friends don't recognize you when they see you nude. That's one reason I like it—it's like becoming a new person."

"Who do you become when you become a new person?"

185

"That depends on who you're with. I take on a new identity in response to the feelings of whoever is there. It's the same thing that happens with lovers. Only it happens with most people only two or three times in their lives. With me it happens every day. It doesn't necessarily have to do with love—it often doesn't with lovers."

"So you started by posing for artists?"

"Yes. That can be pleasant too. I really can't tell you how exhilarating it can be posing for the right kind of class. It's as if the concentration of the whole group on your bare flesh fills you up with energy. For a while I was going to graduate school and I'd go from a political science seminar to pose for an art class and I'd feel as if I were recharging myself. God, how much have I deprived myself through prudery. I've even considered becoming a nudist. I think we may be on the verge of rediscovering the human body. Would you like to see some of my pictures?"

"You bet."

She reached to a pile of magazines next to the bed and moved close to me so we could look at the pictures together.

"This one is funny," she said, turning the pages of a magazine. "You see I'm nude to the waist holding a tray of food below my breasts in front of a dinner table. The domestic type with overtones of Gauguin. The idea is I'm supposed to be serving dinner to my boyfriend."

Naughty Nanette, rich in racy recipes, serves up a spicy appetite rouser for the man of her dreams, the caption read.

"It's a series. In the first picture I have all my clothes on. See. I look quite formal. A little severe even. In the last picture I'm writhing naked in bed looking wanton."

She folded out the last picture. There she was, spread across three glossy pages in full color, lustier than life, indications of insatiable concupiscence gleaming from bared white cuspids.

"The boyfriend is always just outside the frame of the

186

picture," she said, flipping through other magazines. "The reader. The man of her dreams, and his. The stag, the stud, the yearling bull. The all-American adolescent. It's a lucrative business."

"A kind of prostitution, isn't it?"

"There's something to be said for prostitution, after all. You deliver what you're paid for. But this is all make-believe. The dream trade. None of it's real."

She handed me several paperbacks. *Prisoner of Lust:* through a virile triangle of blue-jeaned legs astride, a painted approximation of Nancy twisting nude on a bed, wrists lashed to bedposts at the mercy of another pair of blue jeans, muscular, stripped to the waist, a whip butt gripped in a brutal hand. *Executive Sweet:* the artist's conception of Nancy naked, nose pugged, face frecked, breasts enlarged, hair platinumed, perching crosslegged on a luxe free-form desk, gaily taking dictation. *Confessions of a Nude Model:* a photograph of an easel and canvas beyond which Nancy in a life pose, profile averted for anonymity.

"I really threw myself into that one." She laughed.

"Don't you ever get involved?" I asked.

"It's strictly professional," she snapped. "There's an invisible wall between you and the artist. Of course, I do get to feel pretty sexy sometimes—I'm not schizoid after all. But these guys are interested in money, not sex. Sometimes they try to come on after a session, but that's a different story. I never mix business and pleasure. Oh there have been exceptions. One time I was posing for a serious photographer. He was trying to get a picture representing ecstasy. I kept working myself up for him but he couldn't get the right shot. Finally we both got so excited we started making love. It seemed quite natural—I felt like a flower opening. I was on a table and he was standing up holding the camera switch. I told him when." She took a photography annual from the table and thumbing through it, opened to a full-page shot of her face.

187

"It's pretty obvious what this is," I observed.

"I'm not ashamed of my femininity."

"I wouldn't say so."

She took a cigarette and offered me one. "Thanks," I said, and took it. She lit it for me and then her own.

"I've also done a few nudies," she said.

"What are nudies?"

"Nudist films. Nature Camp. Naked Skis. Sun, Surf and Skin. The genre of nude tennis games. There's a big market for that in South America. Nothing pornographic of course."

By now I was becoming unbearably conscious of her nudity under her sweater and skirt. I put my arm around her shoulders.

"How did you get into that?" I asked.

"A man I know named Mr. Gerard. He's in the entertainment business. Very suave. He's always trying to get me down to his nightclub."

I moved my hand down toward her breast.

"Don't," she said.

"For christ sake, don't act like a high school girl."

"Oh, I see. You still resent that, do you. It's not enough that I let you make love to me. I suppose now you expect me to be at your disposal."

"Come on, don't give me that."

"I get it. This has all been a pornographic exhibition as far as you're concerned. You're incapable of a normal human conversation. You've always been a little oversexed if you ask me. Come on, what are you thinking? Keep me out of your unwholesome fantasies."

"You're still as frigid as ever if you want my opinion. Only a cold girl could do the kind of things you do with such aggressive innocence."

"You're corrupt. Not only corrupt but banal. You share the common reaction of dirty minds to sexual liberation. I suppose you think I'm some kind of slut."

188

"No. I know you're a nice girl. Who knows that better than me?"

"I'm not a nice girl. That kind of talk is a lot of crap. Why can't you understand that?"

"I understand it," I said. I got both my arms around her and managed to put a kiss on her lips while I groped the looseness of her breasts under the sweater.

"No. Please. Don't." I was trying to take off her sweater. "All you're after is a lay."

"I love you," I told her. This was a lie.

"You're lying," she said, but she let me take her sweater off.

"I swear it. I've always loved you."

"I know you're lying," she said, helping me take off her skirt. "Just give it to me and shut up."

"I ought to slap your silly face."

She covered her breasts. Her skirt had fallen to her ankles.

"Please," she breathed. "Don't hurt me."

That just egged me on. "And I don't love you," I added. "I never loved you. That was always a lie." Saying it, I immediately felt a tremendous relief.

"I don't care," she said. She opened her arms to me.

That was the right answer. It was as if she'd given me what I'd been trying to get from her for more than ten years.

This time it was completely different. She responded to me with exacting sensitivity. I felt that for her it was a kind of communication. "Make it last," she kept saying. But it was as if she were articulating with her body over and over something more like, Get through to me, Help me. I answered by moving slowly, carefully within her violence, like thought poised against mounting frenzy, until I felt we both moved within a furious meditation, and meditation rose darkly and broke in a wave of release.

189

I awoke looking into her face and, as I did so, she opened her eyes.

"Any complaints this time?" I asked.

"Are you kidding. I never had an orgasm like that."

"Congratulations."

"I'm quite serious. Thank you."

"You're welcome. If that's what you want."

"Why not? What do you want when you make love?"

"Whatever it is I guess you gave it to me."

"That's what a woman is for. I sense what you want and I give it to you."

"Was that the reason for showing me all your pictures?"

"If you liked them, so much the better."

"Why not just watch dirty movies in that case?"

"Why not?" She smiled.

I had to laugh at the way she had changed.

"So Brooklyn's finally come across," I said with possibly a remnant of anger in my voice.

"I sympathize," she said earnestly. "I want to come across." And then smiling whispered: "You deserve anything you get from me."

On that ambiguous note she rolled into my arms. We went to sleep.

"Ever rape a girl, Ron?"

"Why? What do you mean?"

"Rape," says Strop. "You know what that means, Ron. It means you get a girl so she's helpless, you stick your cock into her against her will, and you make her love it. That's the bit, sweetheart. Want to try it?"

"No!"

"Come on, sweetheart, they love it. Virile mastery. That's what they like. Don't you baby?" He looks toward a girl lying fully clothed, handcuffed to his desk. "Ask

190

Geraldine. Tell Ron you like to be raped, baby. Ask him to rape you."

Geraldine rolls her head from side to side and flutters her blond lashes.

"Come on, baby, or I'll have to give you another spanking. You don't want me to get out the whip, do you?"

She begins shaking her head faster. "No," she says in a curiously high-pitched little tremolo. "Please don't hurt me. I like to be raped. I love it. I'll do anything you tell me. Do it to me." She was looking right into my eyes and still shaking her head: no, no, no.

"I know you got eyes, sweetheart," Strop tells me. "I know it. When you got an itch, the thing to do is scratch it. So what if she's a little shy—you're not gonna hurt her. She'll learn. Come on, sweetheart. Live. Try anything once. Why not? Why not? You may never get another chance."

"I don't go in for that sort of thing, Strop."

"Don't tell me. Come on, come on, come on. You chicken? Don't worry, she won't complain, I got pictures I could send her husband. Don't be a sucker, don't be square. Wise up. It takes guts to get what you want in this world sweetheart. You got to grab, that's the way it works. She don't like it? So what. Come on come on come on. What the hell. What the *hell*."

I find myself walking toward Geraldine as if in a dream. She's still looking at me: no no no. It only eggs me on. She's wearing a loose cotton skirt snaked up to her stocking tops and revealing through thin cloth the bulge of her crotch. No no no. I moisten my parched lips. "Don't hurt me," she quavers in her little tremolo. I grab her hem and rip it upward. Wang! Out jumps this enormous cock erect, a purple, pulsing jack-in-the-box that almost hits me in the face as I jump back and, looking up I find Gerald his blond wig askew, raising himself from the desk on his elbows, camera in hands, snapping pictures like a maniac and saying, "That's right, Ron, watch the birdie." Click. "Hold

191

that a minute." Click click click. "Could you open your mouth a little more and look down at my cock that's it." Click click. "Oh boy, look at this god damn faggot, you know you're very photogenic sweetie" click click click "okay now stick your tongue back in your mouth" click click . . .

"All right, Gerald, that's enough."

"Okay, Mr. Banally. Say you wouldn't like to finish this would you honey?" Gerald asks me. "I could get some beautiful shots for my own album and maybe we'd go easy on you. I mean don't get me wrong I don't enjoy this kind of stuff what I like is pictures of it, tapes, movies, anything like that. I got a terrific collection come up and see it some time."

"Cool it Gerald. We got enough on him now. We got plenty. Now he's on our side."

"Okay Mr. Banally. These go into your file Ronnie. In case we ever need them."

"Just to make sure you're on our side," Strop says to me. "A formality, don't worry about it. It's just human nature. You can't go against human nature."

"What happened to that blonde you were going out with?" asked Slim. "The one you knew from high school."

"We broke up."

"Yeah? You wouldn't like to give me her number would you?"

"You got enough pussy on tap, pardner."

Slim had slept in my apartment. When he woke up he'd never bothered to put his clothes on—just stepped naked into his boots and drank his coffee that way. Now he put on his cowboy hat and turned around to me. His body was white and lean. He had, it seemed, a perpetual erection.

"Shucks, ah cain't never git enough," he said, thickening his accent for emphasis. "Hold me back, boys! Ahm a

192

wild stallion. Ahm a yearling bull. Hold me back or git outa mah way. Ahm a walking erection. Eeeee-yah-hoo! Jist imagine all the pretty gals out there jist a-waitin for ole Slim Sowbelly to come along and loosen their sweet chubby thighs."

He picked up his guitar and began strumming:

> *It's true that ah may stop a while,*
> *But yew know ah ain't stayin,*
> *Cause whisky is mah pardner,*
> *An women is mah frayun.*

The phone rang.

"If that's my mother," said Slim, "I ain't here. You haven't seen me, understand?"

"Hello."

"Ronnie, this is Aunt Theda. Did you see Stewart? I know he's in New York."

"No, I haven't seen him Aunt Theda."

"Just let him call me. That's all I ask. I don't even ask to see him. When did he come to New York?"

"I really don't know Aunt Theda."

"I just want to hear his voice. Believe me I wouldn't cause conflict. Why doesn't he write his mother a post card ask him. I only hear from him if he needs money. Two years ago from Wyoming yet he calls me to ask for a hundred dollars. That's the last time I heard his voice. Of course we play his record all the time. Have you heard his record? He has a wonderful voice. You know he was on the T.V. Monday afternoon. Imagine, a cowboy. Ronnie, tell him to call me up if he needs money. Only let him call in the day-time when Julius isn't home, or they'll have another fight. Ronnie, tell me, what does he want from me? Tell me what he wants and I'll give it to him. Only let him come and see us now and then. Ask what I did to him that was so terrible. Tell me, Ronnie, what did I do?"

193

"I don't know Aunt Theda. Look, if I see him I'll try and get him to call, I promise."

"Why don't you come out to dinner," she said. "You're becoming a stranger we haven't seen you for so long. It's the same thing with Sugar. You'd think their new house in Great Neck was a thousand miles away. Such a beautiful place. You should see the baby, it's the prettiest thing I ever saw, ask anybody. And smart? Like a whip. But what good does it do us, we never see them. Sugar has no consideration. Have you met her husband? He's a wonderful boy. Sterling Fixtures. Maybe you've heard of the firm. You should go visit them one day. Sugar would be happy to see you."

"Okay, Aunt Theda. Look, I have to go out now, but I promise I'll try and get Stewart to call if I see him."

"All right. I know you want to get rid of me. I'll hang up. I'm sure you're very busy. What are you doing now?"

"I'm teaching, but I'm taking a little vacation this term."

"Still in school. How come you don't find yourself a nice business?"

"I have to go now Aunt Theda."

"All right Ronnie. Don't forget to come to dinner."

"I will. Soon. Goodbye."

"You really ought to go over there," I told Slim.

"Shee-it!" he said playing with the guitar strings. He began strumming.

> I'm an oedipal cowboy from Brooklyn,
> I'm tall and I'm handsome to see,
> The girls they all say I'm good lookin,
> But that ain't why my mother loves me.

He laughed. I looked for traces of Stewart in Slim. The narrow face was still the same, but framed in his sideburns and bushy brown mustache the small nose looked like pure Texas.

There was a knock at the door.

"Oh christ," said Slim. "That must be that sucker to see the car. Just wait a second till I fix myself up proper here."

"Just a minute," I yelled.

Slim wriggled into his bowlegged jeans, slipped on a blue drip-dry plaid shirt, tied a green silk kerchief around his neck, put on his metal-buttoned denim jacket, turned the collar up, got back into his boots, adjusted his stetson, picked up his guitar, put one foot up on a chair and started tuning the strings.

"Okay," he said. "We're all set. Now remember. Don't you mention the damn axle. Or second gear. Or the crank case. Let him in."

He was a pudgy blond college kid, smooth-faced, with flushed cheeks, wearing chinos with a tweed jacket and a striped Italian shirt.

"Howdy pardner," said Slim with one ear to his guitar. "Set yerself down and have a cup a coffee, on the house."

"Thank you," said the kid. "My name's Bruce Barker."

"Well hi there Bruce. This here's Ronnie. An' mah name's Slim. Jist got inta town. Put 'er there."

"I called yesterday?"

"Didja now. That's nice."

"About the car."

"Oh the car, the car. Were you intrested in buying ole Em'ly?"

"Were you the one I talked to who was advertising a '53 Pontiac for three hundred dollars, perfect condition?"

"Yeah, that sounds like Em'ly. But yer too late mah frayun."

"You sold it already?"

"Nope. Ah decided not to sell it. Ah love that car. Ah jist cain't get mahself ta part company with it. Besides ahm

195

a-thinkin a headin back to Wyoming. The big city kinda
gits me down."

"Well, gee, you know I came all the way down here
from Forest Hills just to look at it."

"Say, ahm awful sorry. Ahl tell you what. Seein as ahm
sorta obliged to ya for subway fare an all, maybe we'll jist
go down an take a look at er. Fact is ah could use the money.
Ahm jist about hah an drah. Yew got the cayash on yew
mah frayun? None of this heah check writin stuff fer me.
Ah don't trust it. Ah don't even lak this paper money
yew folks use heah, the way it tears an crinkles up an
all."

"I have the cash," said the kid. "I even have the plate
from my old car."

"Well now, that's jist fahn," said Slim.

We went down to see the car, a fender-dented, rust-
eaten, paint-flaked sedan with Wyoming plates.

"I thought you said it was in perfect condition," said
the kid.

"Perfect *running* condition. It has to be. This car is used
to climbin up through the Grand Tetons. Start it up anything lower than the Rockies and it thinks it's goin down-
hill."

"What's the mileage?"

"The mileage. You can look at the mileage if yew
want." He opened the door. "Look at that, why she ain't
even got forty thousand on er. But it ain't the mileage. It's
the way it's been treated that counts. Out there a man
treats his car like he treats his hoss."

"Mind if I start it up?"

"Sure. Start it up." Slim gave him the key and he got in.
We raced around and got in the front seat through the
other door. The motor started okay.

"She's all right," said Slim. The kid was manipulating
the shift. "Wipers," said Slim. He reached over and turned
the wipers on, then turned on the heater. "Heater's good.

196

Even the radio works. Clock's broke, but you don't care bout that. Ah jist drove er all the way East an she never give me no trouble. That's a tough trip fer any car. Started way out in Cheyenne, through Laramie up to Billings, Montana. Ah was followin the cattle. Bet you never even heard a them towns."

"I heard of them," said the kid. He was trying to concentrate on the motor.

"That's a nice town, Billings. Very hospitable. They let me sleep in the town lock-up one night. Drunk an disorderly. From there ah cut down through the Badlands. They're gittin worse an worse. Down through Sioux City, Cimarron, had a hell of a time for myself in Dodge City. Boy, there's a tough town. Saw someone shoot a man who asked him if he was packin a gun. He got insulted. Pulled it out, let im have it, and said yeah. You wanna stay away from Dodge City, that's my advice."

"No kidding, they still carry guns out there? Say would you mind very much if I try it out?"

"Why, sure thing."

The kid drove around the block. "Look at that pick-up," Slim kept telling him. "With pick-up like that you don't even need second. Just shift right on into third."

When we got back the kid got out and looked under the hood. "Say, it's pretty oily in here, isn't it?"

"Yeah," said Slim. "Ah put oil in yesterday an it sorta slopped over everything. Ah didn't have a funnel."

"Well, it looks pretty good to me," said the kid.

"Ole Em'ly'll getcha there," said Slim.

"Only would you mind," said the kid, "if I took it in for my mechanic to look at?"

Slim looked at me. "His mechanic." He took off his stetson, ran his hand through his hair, and put it back on. "His mechanic," he repeated, turning red in the face. "I'll tell you what. You jist go right on back to Forest Hills and let your mechanic find you a car."

197

He slammed down the hood, kicked the doors closed, locked them, and started walking away.

"Hey, wait," the kid called after him. "What's wrong?"

"Look here," says Slim, turning around. "Ah never wanted to sell ya this here car nohow. Ah felt an obligation cause ah thought ah was dealin with a gentleman." He spoke as if he were spitting venom.

"Take it easy," I said.

"He mistrusts me. He wants to bring it to a mechanic. Ah take that as an insult. Ah have a good mind to . . ." He took a step toward Bruce Barker, who simultaneously took a step back.

"Easy," I said.

"I'm sorry," said the kid. "Forget it. A lot of people do that you know. It's very common." He looked at me in appeal.

"That's right," I said to Slim. "It's common practice. That's the way we do things in New York."

"Yew don't say," said Slim. "Well ahl be. Ah guess ah jist cain't git used to these big city ways. Fergit it pardner. I thought yew was jist tryin to insult me."

"That's okay."

"Ahm awful sorry. Ahl tell you what. Are you intrested in the car? Jist by way of makin up for our little misunderstandin, ahl let you have it for two fifty, drive it away right now."

"Two fifty?"

"Make it an even two. What do you say? Ah come down a hundred bills for you, friend. Wouldn't do that for everybody."

"Well . . ."

Slim shrugged his shoulders and started to walk away.

"Okay, I'll take it."

They signed the papers on the hood, the kid handed over the money, they changed the plates, and Slim gave him the keys.

198

"She's all yours," said Slim, shaking his hand.

The kid started the motor. "So long, Slim. And thanks."

"Adios, Bruce. An take good care of ole Em'ly," he said as the kid pulled away.

"A callow youth," Slim remarked as the car drove out of sight. He took out his cigarette tobacco.

"You're quite a salesman," I told him. "You ought to open a used car lot."

"Guys as dumb as that are just asking to be gypped. It's practically a public service. I can't stand college boys. Anyway, it's salesmanship that makes America what it is."

"What is it?"

"The great boomtown of history," he said, rolling his cigarette with the careless dexterity of a virtuoso at that art.

Upstairs Slim was playing with his guitar while I heated the coffee.

> *Ah woke up this mornin,*
> *Ah had the used car blues.*
> *Ah woke up this mornin,*
> *Ah had them used car blues.*
> *Mah crank case needed crankin,*
> *An mah brakes didn't have no shoes.*
>
> *Oh the paint looked nice an shiny,*
> *The upholstery was so clean,*
> *The paint looked so nice an shiny,*
> *The upholstery was real clean,*
> *But it didn't have no motor,*
> *Things ain't never what they seem.*
>
> *Ah went lookin for a sucker,*
> *Glad ah ain't in his shoes,*
> *Went lookin for a sucker,*
> *Glad ah ain't in Bruce Barker's shoes,*
> *Cause though you may not know it, Bruce,*
> *You got them used car blues.*

199

"What are you up to today?" I asked him.

"I'm splittin man. I got to do an integration rally. Ah don't know what the hell they're integratin, but they're always integratin some damn thing or other. Got to keep up my rating in the movement you know. They want me to make a trip down South, but I don't know if it's worth the chance of getting my ass knocked off.

> *Like a tree that's standin by the water,*
> *We shall not be moved.*

I won't be back here tonight. I can always find me a shack-up at one a them thar shindigs.

> *Ah never make much money,*
> *But ah know all the tricks,*
> *From integratin schwarzes,*
> *To livin off the chicks.*

Later that afternon I got a phone call from Julius.

"Ronnie, Stewart is in New York? Have you seen him?"

I hesitated.

"Don't worry," he said. "I wouldn't tell his mother. I'm calling from the place."

"Yes, I've seen him. He's okay."

"He's doing okay? He's got enough to live on? Where's he staying?"

"He stays with different friends. He gets along okay."

"What's he doing for money?"

"He gets a little from his record. He performs here and there."

"How much can he make? Listen, Ronnie, try and talk to him about the business. He wouldn't even have to work for me. I could get him a wonderful job with a friend, a wonderful opportunity. Later maybe he could take over here. I'm not getting any younger you know. You don't think he'd be interested in selling cars?"

200

"I don't think so, Uncle Julius. That's just not up his alley. He's set on his music."

"Ach, the entertainment business. What kind of future is that? There's no security. What can he make?"

"Some people make a lot of money at it."

"Of course, of course, you can hit it big in anything. Look at Harry Belafonte. He was on the T.V. the other day. Have you heard his record? 'Lonesome Stranger.'"

"I don't have a phonograph."

"So why doesn't he come and visit his mother? For myself I don't care. I'm his father, I can understand. He's young, he wants a little independence. But it breaks Theda's heart. He could at least call now and then. It's not right. Maybe you could try and talk to him."

"I'll try, Uncle Julius, but I can't promise anything."

"If he wants money he'll call, I can promise that. Once he called us from Wyoming he needs a hundred dollars right away."

"That was two years ago, Uncle Julius."

"Tell him if he needs money he should call. I'm always ready to help him out. If he wants to go to college even I'm willing to support him. Why does he want to ruin his life? He can go at night to finish high school. They can do that very fast nowadays. You think he wants to go to college?"

"I doubt it, Uncle Julius."

"Maybe you can talk to him about the business. He's got a wonderful selling personality, I can tell. Just let me show him the opportunities that exist today. He could make himself a fortune in no time. In no time."

"I'll try."

"Why doesn't he get in touch with his sister at least? Between me and Stewart I can understand, a little friction, we've had our quarrels, but what has he got against his sister? Theda tells me her husband is eager to set him up in something. His father is a wealthy man you know. We never

201

see them. They're too rich for our blood with their house in Great Neck."

"I don't know what to say, Uncle Julius."

"Well, it's not your problem, Ronnie. Try and talk to him a little. If anything comes up you can give me a ring."

A little later I got a call from Sugar.

"Mother said you wanted to talk to me," she said.

"I'm always glad to talk to you, Sugar. What did she say I wanted to talk to you about?"

"She didn't say."

There was a pause.

"It's a long time since we spoke to one another," she said. "What are you doing these days?"

"Nothing."

"You're not teaching?"

"No."

There was a pause.

"I thought you were writing a book."

"No."

There was a pause.

"Why don't you come out and see us some time? You never met my husband."

"When?"

"Any time you like."

"Tonight?"

"Well, we're busy tonight. I'll tell you what, I'll get in touch with you soon."

"Good. I'll be waiting by the phone."

She laughed. She had a coarse laugh.

"I mean it Ronnie. Life is dull out here."

"When life is dull it's dull anywhere."

"What do you mean by that?"

"I mean it's the same all over."

"Go on Ronnie. I'll ¹et you get your excitement. A bachelor in New York."

"It's like living on a roller coaster."

She laughed again.

"All right Ronnie. We'll be seeing you."

"Yeah, but, why the Cloisters?"

"Because that's where he has to meet his girl, he said,"
I said.

We were heading uptown on the West Side Drive in
Finch's car. Past his silhouette sped piers, masts, towering
prows and more slowly, the Hudson itself, factories on the
far shore, the Palisades. His face, I noticed, was starting to
paunch and jowl.

"Well why does he have to meet his girl at the Cloisters?" complained Finch. "I mean, couldn't they pick a
slightly more convenient rendezvous? Like, say, the top
of the Statue of Liberty, or Montauk Point maybe. Why
confine ourselves to the city limits?"

"How the hell do I know?" I said. "You know Slade.
He always liked a setting for himself. As if he were always
trying to assume the definitive pose."

"Ah, I think it's all a lot of crap. Look at Otis for example. He thrives on contradictions. You can't keep up
with Otis. Otis is a regular old chameleon. One day he tells
me all about Jung. Jung is the last word. So I go out and
buy *The Archetypes and the Collective Unconscious*, take
it home, and read it. Next week I go over there full of Jung,
and he tells me, Oh yeah, Jung. I had a Jung stage too.
What a farce. Why don't you try this. And he hands me a
copy of Wittgenstein. So I take it home, and I plow through
Philosophical Investigations and it was full of pubic hairs
too, like he must have been reading it in the can. Didn't
understand a word. Next week I come back full of questions, and he tells me, You know, I've become convinced I
don't really understand Wittgenstein. In fact I don't think

203

he can really be understood. I'd like to see anyone who can get ahead of Otis."

"Yeah, I know. One time I met him he looked like he'd suddenly lost about twenty pounds. He started explaining this great Zen diet he'd discovered—macrobiotic rice and whole wheat wafers, or something like that. He kept telling me to feel him between his thumb and index finger. See, no water, he'd say. I feel wonderful. I haven't fucked my girl for two weeks. If I try drinking a glass of beer I pass out. It's fantastic. I saw him a week later and I thought he was going to die. He was hobbling around on a cane and looked like he'd been in a concentration camp. He'd lost his job. His girl had left him. Luckily I managed to hook him on health food. I went to the library and found books for him on wheat germ recipes, vegetarianism, and organic produce. When he was ripe, I took him with me to a health food restaurant. He hadn't eaten anything but brown rice for weeks. His mouth began to water. I take it that vegetable cutlet there is supposed to be healthy? he says. Maybe I'll just taste a little piece. That was it. He gobbled everything I'd ordered. I had to restrain him. I was afraid his stomach would burst. That can happen, you know. A few days later I asked him about the diet. Oh yeah, the diet, he says. That was a gas. You ought to try it sometime."

"Otis is a real fuck-up," said Finch. "I never saw anything like it. Every time he seems about to get a show, or if it looks like he's making it with some girl, he starts getting depressed, and he's not happy again till he messes everything up."

"I think he does it for excitement," I said. "He has a morbid fear of success. I think he has the idea that if there's somewhere he's supposed to get, and he gets there, he might as well commit suicide. They say that's what happened to De Staël. Otis has the Romantic preference for the ever-receding goal. The effort rather than the victory. Like Wordsworth—the younger Wordsworth, of course."

204

"Like a god damn fool if you want my opinion," said Finch. "Otis is a nice guy. I admire him. But he'll never get anywhere. Of course I don't mean to imply that I'm getting anywhere. What a business. Now they've put me on a dog food account. Ritz Pet Treats. The canine caviar. The feline foie gras. How do you think that would go over? I mean imagine owning some kind of mutt for example. Something on the idea of a special treat every day in the week, only with a better rhyme. His tail will wag when you open the bag. He'll lick his chop when you take off the top. Your cat will smile when you feed her in style. A Ritz fed pet will cause you no sweat. They'll piss on the floor if you don't give them more. If they've got the shits, let them eat Ritz."

"Easy," I interrupted.

"Yeah, I know. I know. I can't help it. I've been working on that copy all week, it's overdue. You know I wouldn't mind if it were merely a fraud. I wouldn't mind being dishonest. But I mean slaving all day over dog food copy for christ sake. Oh it's a fairly valid way of making money compared to most. Full of many fine, intelligent people, people with talent, a really swell bunch. In any case where else would I go?"

"Why don't you look around?"

"Are you kidding. At my age I'm practically obsolescent. I'm past thirty now you know. The thing is with a kid I'm just going to have to make more money. You know I never really meant to marry Arlene. It just sort of happened, I've never been able to figure out exactly how. Of course I don't mean to say I'm unhappy with her. It's all a question of maintaining your freedom, that's all. And that takes money mainly, a lot of money. You know I've been thinking of going to see Yssis. He's a pretty big man now you know. A man like that could really do something for you if he felt like it. You think Yssis would remember me?"

"Come on Len. You're living in a dream."

"I'm just trying to be practical, that's all."

205

I was looking for Slade in a bar on Hudson Street where he'd asked me to meet him when this nut in an army surplus jacket and a lot of hair comes over and gives me a hug. Jesus, I thought, the queers are getting aggressive in this neighborhood. I really panicked when before I could get away he put his arm around my shoulder and, cursing, started pulling me toward the bar. "You lousy son of a bitch. Crazy asshole motherfucker. Say something you bastard. Bartender, two more. You like tequila?"

Suddenly peering at me from behind the drooping mustache and long, dark, curling, messianic beard, there he was. "Ernie Slade."

"Well who were you expecting, you bastard, Pope John the Twenty-Third?" His sentence exploded in rough laughter.

"No, but you look like you just came down out of the Sierra Maestra."

"Well, you know, the way you look is like a statement of position these days. Things have changed man. It's time to drop our incognitos and take a stand. You've got to identify yourself. Things are getting polarized. There are no neutrals. Looking nondescript just makes you everybody's enemy."

"I guess that makes me everybody's enemy."

He laughed.

"Why don't you grow a beard, Sukenick. It would do you good. It's like making up your mind. Well, salud!" He poured a little salt on the back of his fist, licked it off, gulped his tequila, and sucked a slice of lime. "Ah. Not bad. You can't get the really good stuff in this country. Hey, two more, will you. Have a cigar." He drew two enormous cigars from the pocket of his fatigue jacket and thrust one at me.

As he stood smiling around the cigar in his white teeth I realized why I hadn't recognized him. It wasn't the beard. It was that he looked famous. Last time I'd seen him he'd looked eminent without being eminent and apparently he had grown if not in reputation at least in prominence, and now looked famous without being famous.

"How's your magazine?" I asked him.

"*Secession?* Terrific. We've decided to publish monthly instead of quarterly. And we're going to Cuba for the first issue. We just flew down to Mexico City to make contacts."

"Who did?"

"Me and my girl. She's not in town yet. She's visiting her parents."

"How did you pull off a trip like that?"

"I just picked up the phone and made a reservation. Charged to her father's company. That's the way we do things in the big time, you bastard. The old man deducts it from taxes. He's always desperate for ways to lose money. And of course I draw expenses from the magazine. We've got to keep the editor alive if we're going to put the thing out you know." He smiled—an expression both of defiance and complicity.

"And who supports the magazine? Your girl?"

"There are others, there are others. You'd be surprised. Mexico is a great place, by the way. You can still feel the revolution in the air. We bought a car and drove around for a month. Yucatan, Tehuantepec, Acapulco. You ought to go there."

"Isn't it illegal to go to Cuba?"

"The State Department thinks so. But they don't stand a chance in the courts. We expect to get a test case out of the trip. Why don't you come along? We just want to see what's happening there. Castro's a damn fool. But he's got style. And it's the first real socialist state in the Western Hemisphere. That's quite a trick."

"I gather it's been pretty bloody."

He shrugged. "The capitalist press. Still, you can't expect a revolution without a little blood. Not a real revolution. Later on we project a fact-finding trip to China. Nobody in this country knows what the hell is going on

207

there. That's freedom of the press for you. You had dinner?"

"No."

"Come on."

"Where you going."

"I know a good Spanish restaurant on Fourteenth Street. It's an old anarchist hangout run by refugees from Franco."

"I don't have much money on me," I told him.

"Don't worry about it," he said.

We left our drinks on the bar and went outside where Slade pushed me into a potent little sports car. "A Da Pazzo Speziale," he said. "Competition model."

"Where'd you get a car like this?" I asked.

"I'm borrowing it from my girl." He turned the ignition and the motor detonated like muffled dynamite. "Though what the hell she needs it for I don't know. She drives like an old lady. Hold on." He leaned on the horn, peeled out, made a U turn in front of a taxi, and cut up a side street. "The toys of the rich," he remarked, obviously enjoying himself. We squealed around a corner. "I want to talk to that guy Williams. I hear he's in Havana. He's the guy who organized a community of Negroes in North Carolina and got them to use their rifles in self-defense. He had the Klan scared shitless. They ran the first time they heard a shot fired and they never came back. Then the F.B.I. framed Williams on some phony kidnaping charge and he had to leave the country."

We pulled into the curb at Fourteenth near Seventh.

"This is a no parking zone," I pointed out.

"Fuck it. I got Mass. plates."

Inside Slade greeted the headwaiter insouciantly, addressed our waiter as compañero and, dispensing with the menu, detailed a meal for us after exacting consultations in Spanish.

"Well," said Slade, tasting his sopa de ajo, "it beats the old high school cafeteria anyway."

208

"That's like a prenatal memory," I said. Noise, milk containers, gummy green table tops, everyone semiconscious in a trance of adolescent ignorance. A phrase came to mind: "The hell of innocence." I repeated it aloud.

"Speak for yourself," said Slade. "I knew what I was doing. I was fighting my way into Harvard. I had my finger on the trigger, man. I wasn't following anybody's rules."

"Maybe you were an exception."

"Maybe there were more than you think. A lot of those kids knew what they wanted. Kids who even at that age already knew how to use conformity as a mask, who discovered how to camouflage themselves in their own innocence. Take your super-square cousin for example."

"Sugar?"

"Christ, there was a hot little slut if there ever was one. I mean maybe nobody talked to you about it but she was really the world champ. No doubt she ended up marrying a bank account, but there was only one thing she was interested in while passing the time. Wake up man. That's the key to American life. Appearance is never reality. Girls know that by instinct. Nobody has to teach them a thing."

"So you screwed Sugar, did you?"

"Sure. She was a good lay too, you bastard. You should have tried her yourself. Or is that incest? Oh well, she would have found that an added attraction." He laughed coarsely.

"What about me?"

"You. You were always too fastidious. More wine? Camarero! Una otra botilla misma. Or too innocent. Take my sweet ex-wife. She learned to get what she wanted at a tender age, believe me. With her frigid moralism."

"Apparently," I said sourly. "Though I think she's changed in that respect."

"I'm sure she's changed. She's a shifty character, the bitch. I hear she's posing for dirty pictures and that kind of crap. She hasn't changed. She's just trying to prove it was

209

my fault. If I'd told her she was too promiscuous she would have become a nun. She's just turned herself inside out. You know there's nothing like an apostate puritan in the ranks of the sexual revolution. They become erotic terrorists. That started while we were still married. All her suppressed violence came crashing out. She liked getting me into fights. That got her excited. Someone in a carful of six guys would whistle at her and she'd say, Hit them. Hit them. Can you imagine that? Then she started fighting with *me*. And I mean real fights, man. Tooth and nail. Finally one night I really beat the ass off her. After that she was an angel for a while. Then she tried getting me to do it again. She started egging me on. It was impossible. I was getting exhausted. Anyway that wasn't the real trouble. The real trouble is she's hung up on her father. That'll never change. Ah. Calamares en su tinta."

The waiter set down our heaped curlicues of squid, rice blackened by the ink. He uncorked a bottle and filled our tumblers.

"I hear you've been seeing her."

"A little," I said.

"For old time's sake, huh? What did she say about me?"

"Not much."

"I'll bet. Listen, let me tell you something for your own good. I wouldn't call her a liar. If she were merely a liar it wouldn't be so bad. She's a raving maniac. She makes up her own version of everything as she goes along."

"Don't we all?"

"I hope not. Look, for your own good don't get involved with Nancy."

"She's living with me."

"Congratulations. May you live happily ever after."

"I don't know it's that serious."

"She always had a soft spot for you. After all, you were high school sweethearts. Have some more wine."

His voice was reduced to a croak. He looked as if some-

210

one had hit him in the face. I like Slade. That was the first
time I had the nerve to admit it to myself.

"A case of requited love I guess," he croaked. "It won't
last."

"Why?"

"You'll find out."

He drank his glass of wine and refilled it.

"You like to fuck her?"

"What do you think."

"To each his own. Has she gotten around to the handcuffs?"

"What handcuffs?"

"Never mind." He reached over the table and socked me
on the arm. "If you ever want to know how to get some
good mileage out of Nancy, just ask me. I know all her
tricks." Laughing coarsely, he filled my glass. What a son
of a bitch.

"Valdepeñas," said Slade, turning the half-empty bottle.
"You get good wine from Valdepeñas. They don't export
much." He filled his glass. "Thank god for good wine. Boy,
I'm sick of this country. Still, I'm damned if I'd go to Spain.
Much as I'd like to. I'll tell you something though, after
the Bay of Pigs I felt like leaving. A lot of people are thinking of emigrating to Australia. Escape the bomb at least.
White Australia. I'd probably end up living with the Bush-
men. It's getting hard to find a free country. Look at all the
places you can't go any more. Europe turning into a low-
grade America. Russia's an old story. The satellites are
enough to make you sick. Poland maybe. Cuba and China
they won't even give you a passport. That's a quarter of the
world right there, China. In South America they're still
castrating anarchists. Shoot down the workers every chance
they get. Peons in the feudal stage. Mexico's not so bad but
the American exiles are unappetizing."

"You've never gone anywhere except Mexico, have
you?"

211

"I don't need to. I don't have to go abroad to be an exile. I can stay right here. A utopian exile waiting for an impossible revolution. I feel like I was born a native of an America that never existed. We're stuck with this damn country in more ways than one, and the worst is in what we expect from it. The history of America is a progressively broken promise. But things are changing. We're going into the streets. And if they don't make good we'll go again. And again. And stay there. Till all promises are kept. I'll have a flan," he said to the hovering waiter. "Do you want dessert?"

"The same." I refilled our glasses with the last of the wine. "You're doing pretty well for a revolutionary," I said. "Are you going to pay with your girl friend's credit card?"

"It's easy to label every petty indulgence a betrayal. Bolshevik stolidness—as if happiness itself were betrayal. I wouldn't trust a grim revolution. There's going to be dancing in the streets man. A little adultery doesn't mean divorce. Betrayal is something absolute and irreversible. It's one thing to have an occasional affair and another to stop sleeping with your husband. It wasn't that she was making it with other men. I can take that sort of thing."

"Who, your girl?"

"Nancy. I encouraged it in fact. I take responsibility for that. What could I do? Anything to bring her to life. I tell you it got to be like fucking a dead animal. All clitoral, you know what I mean. She never felt anything beyond tickling the surface. So I encouraged it. It was for her sake. Then she becomes a god damn nymphomaniac and blames me for it. I don't know what she told you but that's what I call betrayal."

The waiter came with dessert. I ordered a couple of expressos.

"And now she's making it with my friends," said Slade. "It's all spite. Oh I don't blame you. I know how god damn attractive she can be. You were high school sweethearts. Only look out, that's all. I've known you a long time. She's

212

no damn good." He drew an enormous cigar from his pocket and stuck it in his mouth. The waiter appeared with a match. "Not that I give a fuck of course. It's your funeral. I had a hell of a time getting her to give me a divorce. She's all yours you bastard. I wish you luck. Well, to the revolution." He finished his wine.

"If people are going to insist on being barbarians," said Otis, "there's nothing much one can do. I mean you can either hit them over the head or make a point of your absence."

His face was a study of disdain. His nose seemed ready to bend backward in aversion. For the moment one lost sight of his yellow teeth, his unshaven, dirt-smudged face, his tangled hair. Otis had made a point of his absence at the Ritz Pet Hotel, an animal clinic and boarding establishment in the East Sixties where he had been working as an orderly. In fact he had just quit.

"Who was it that made the complaint?"

"It was this bitch of a woman in a flashy ermine coat." His lips writhed in scorn. "Obviously very parvenue. She walked in as I was taking her cat's temperature, a big white angora, a bitch of a cat, it kept scratching the hell out of me. Did you ever take a cat's temperature?"

"Can't say that I have." Otis had been going around with animal scratches on his hands and face for the last several months. One time he'd had to have stitches in his arm after a raccoon bite.

"Well it's not so bad once you get the hang of it. But this fucking cat just wouldn't stay still. The trouble was its fur was so long it took me about five minutes to find its asshole. Then every time I found it the cock sucker would start squirming and I'd lose it again. I'd been at it for a quarter of an hour when this bitch walks in. Every time I

213

found the cat's asshole it would throw a fit, and every time it threw a fit she threw a fit. You'd think it was her asshole I was after. Finally I said, madam, if you are familiar with your cat's rectum, perhaps you would like to try this yourself." Otis chuckled. "That didn't go down too well. Next thing I know the head vet corners me. Listen, Otis, he says, go get yourself a bath, a shave and a haircut. You're stinking up the place. This isn't a zoo, it's a pet hotel. The clients are afraid you're going to get their animals dirty. I was cleaning up a puddle of dog puke at the time, the contribution of an old moth-eaten St. Bernard. She's just sore about her cat, I told him. I don't care what she's sore about, he says. If the clients say you look dirty, then look clean, that's all I care about. How crass can you get?" asked Otis.

"Well you know maybe it's just as well. It sounds like a pretty trying job."

"What do you mean? It was a great job. I love animals. It was the people that got me down." His face was a tragic mask.

"Well, look, after all, you're not exactly cut out to spoil the pampered rich."

"It's not a question of rich people. I like rich people. I get along with them. It's the Boeotians who get my goat. The barbarians. The philistines. One day this chick walks in with a Chihuahua under her arm, dressed to the hilt, dragging some poor uncomfortable guy with her. Obviously some kind of hustler past her prime, a little tired around the eyes. She was really coming on. She wanted to board the dog so I asked her if it had shots. This dog, she says with incredible snot, is a pedigreed animal. I looked her right in the eye. Obviously two of a kind, I said. I thought it was going to be a real scene. This cunt was yapping her head off at me and the guy was making these sucky noises and kept saying, Come on Sugarplum, come on baby. I thought he was talking to the god damn dog. I figured I'd run into a couple of real maniacs. Then it turns out he's just trying to calm her down. By that time she was cursing both of us out and on top of everything else the poor dog was crying in terror. Never insult a whore. By the time he got her out of there the poor bastard was looking terribly sheepish."

"Well it's too bad when people don't know they have an Athenian in their midst. Maybe you should have told them that your ancestors fought in the Revolution."

"Yeah. For the English. Don't forget that. They had the right idea." He laughed. His expression was that of a gleeful gargoyle.

"How come you're not working today?" he asked.

"I was fired, in effect."

"Well. Welcome to the aristocracy of the unemployed. Where's your girl?"

"Nancy? How come you came over if you thought I wasn't going to be here?"

"Thought I'd take a chance. You haven't split up have you?"

"Listen Otis. If you start that crap again I swear." Otis had the habit of falling for his friends' girls (see pp. 173–174). I always associate his impulsive jealousies with the loss of his parents at an early age. His father, an amateur pilot, died attempting to fly under the Brooklyn Bridge on a bet in what Otis liked to call the first fatal airplane crash in the East River. His mother died shortly after in an Alpine climbing accident—on the day, as it happened, of the Munich Declaration. His father, a journalist, was so the story goes a drinking companion of F. Scott Fitzgerald, and was thought to be drunk on the occasion of his fatal flight. As a matter of fact Otis parted his hair toward the middle like an orphan of the boyish twenties and after a haircut always looked a little like F. Scott himself.

"It's a free country," Otis said. "And besides, you know very well I wouldn't screw around with a girl while you're going out with her. Competition in love is the ultimate

215

vulgarity as far as I'm concerned. But as long as you've broken up what the hell do you care?"

"She's moved back to her place, if that relieves your curiosity. And if you want her number it's not in the book."

"Don't be a bastard. I like to be around her, that's all. She's got style."

"Do you like to make a fool of yourself?" I asked.

"What the hell do I care what people think of me. I like what I like, that's all. And I like style. A villa on the Mediterranean. Over the bay at Lerici, where Shelley died. Blue sea, sails like stray sheep grazing. Or above Florence, like Berenson. Gardens laid out with compass and square rule. All geometry. Order. Beauty. One's life comes to more than a crude anecdote. Of course it's all a lot of shit, that kind of thing. Nevertheless, one feels a certain phony nostalgia. You know that story about Picasso? He'd come home late at night and find Max Jacob still working in his room. What are you doing, Max? he'd yell up. I'm searching for a style, Pablo, Max would say. There is no style, Picasso would yell back. There is no style—there you are. On the other hand, that's all there is. Especially for Picasso."

"Not all."

"No. Not all. In fact it's not even important. Luck is my good angel. One submits to chance and the gratifications of the moment. That's what I like about your friend Finch. He takes things as they come. He has no grandiose ambitions, no designs on the world. He doesn't think he's Napoleon, or Rembrandt, or Dostoevski, like all the other people I know."

"That's right, he's not fussy. All he wants to be is somebody else."

"Right. Anybody at all. I can understand that. Christ, don't you feel like a ghost sometimes? Literally a nobody? That's when I get the urge to join the Marines. The Foreign Legion. Anything with a uniform. The Salvation Army."

"Sure. That's what Wordsworth is talking about. He

tells how as a kid he had to grab hold of a wall to make sure the world was really there, but when he grew up the dead weight of reality almost crushed the sense of his own existence. It's when the world seems oppressive, dead, or to put it another way, unreal, that I get the feeling I'm walking around like a zombie."

"Well that's what art is all about, right? The discovery of reality."

"No. The invention of reality."

"You mean to say that a perfect description of a rose isn't in some sense a discovery of reality?"

"No. I mean it isn't art. We aren't botanists. Art seeks a vital connection with the world that, to stay alive, must be constantly reinvented to correspond with our truest feelings."

"The other night I fell into a vital connection with a girl in bed. Believe me art had nothing to do with my feelings."

"Sure. But you can't plug into everything with your cock. What people call the search for reality, vulgarity aside, is the search for that inner truth whose thread we trace through time the labyrinth. In following that we find ourselves. As we go along. In the sense that you find something not there before you started looking for it."

"Did you get that out of your notebook?"

"Yes. Art is a process of self-creation. It literally brings you to life. Wordsworth knew that. Or if he didn't it comes to the same thing because that's what he was up to. That's exactly the kind of thing you were talking about."

"It is?"

"Of course. You know Otis, sometimes when I talk to you I get the feeling that I'm talking with myself."

"Yeah. Frankly I get the feeling you're talking to Coleridge. See what I mean? I'm not even here. I'm a ghost, and somebody else's ghost at that. Now you take Finch. If he tells me he feels like a piece of ass, he doesn't have to compare himself to Baudelaire or Lord Rochester. That's the trouble with you and me. We're egomaniacs. We can't make simple statements. We're lost in our dreams. I wish I could get down to earth like Finch."

"Maybe you wish you could get down to earth, but not like Finch. I wonder if he knows about his wife?"

"What do you mean?"

"You don't know about his wife? She's been sleeping around ever since they got married. What a sow. That's exactly the word—sow. I don't know how Len can stand looking at her. And on top of that she's possessive as hell. If he looks at another girl she gets furious. Once I went to a ball game with Finch and he asked me to come home with him so Arlene wouldn't be suspicious."

"Too bad," said Otis. "No girl that fat has a right to be so fucking mean. What does Finch think about her?"

"Think about her? He doesn't think about her. He doesn't even see her. If Finch really thought about his life he'd have to do something about it, and that would be too much for him."

Otis looked grave.

"A sad case," he said. "By the way, that show didn't work out."

"Too bad. How come?"

"I lost the paintings."

"What do you mean you lost the paintings?"

"Well I was bringing them up to the guy see, and I left them on the sidewalk for a few minutes to pick up the car I'd borrowed."

"They were stolen?"

"Well it seems the garbage men came around."

"Oh no."

"I don't know. I don't really care that much. In fact I'm sort of relieved. I didn't really want a show. In fact I was getting pretty sick of those paintings."

"But the garbage for christ sake."

218

"Well what the hell do the garbage men know about art? In France, of course, it would never have happened. I'm sure in France the garbage men treat strayed paintings like lost children. Better than lost children. I've always felt myself out of step in this country. I think it all began when I was born left-handed. It always made me feel like I was working against the grain. My sympathy has always been for the oblique, the contrary, the perverse. The obvious leaves me cold. That's what always gets me into trouble. My appetite for anarchy. Still, it's a kind of freedom they don't allow in Europe. It doesn't matter how you're born, you learn everything righty like everyone else and that's that. If I were English I'd probably be some kind of eccentric. In America I'm a painter and for exactly the same reasons. Painting is just a state of mind for me, a position vis-à-vis the world. I don't really care about making it. I don't even care about painting if you really want to know the truth. Give me twenty thousand a year and a house in Westport, a yacht, good cigars, and a smart little cunt who learned how to wiggle her ass at Vassar—man, I wouldn't touch another brush."

"Come on, Otis."

"Oh of course I care about it, in a sense. But it's an ugly life, that's what grabs me. And I'm sick of it. I mean it. I'd give it up like that. I don't know. I don't even know whether I'm lying or telling the truth. And what the hell's the difference anyway. Hey, did I tell you what happened to me yesterday? I suddenly knew how Cézanne felt. Fantastic, I can't explain it—I simply knew how Cézanne *felt*. Listen, so long. I've got to beat it back to my place. You're wasting all my god damn time. Say, why don't you walk me over and look at my new paintings?"

I don't know why Otis never kept his door locked. He once tried to explain it to me—a complicated series of attitudes and counterattitudes beginning with casual negligence and growing increasingly removed from reality, the conse-

219

quence of which, in this neighborhood, would no doubt be burglary. But Otis also had an attitude toward burglary. "Everybody gets robbed around here. If you keep your door locked they'll come through the windows. Locking doors in this neighborhood is just a carry-over of the essentially bourgeois idea that you can control your fate. It's like living in a dream. Graduate from a good college, get into a good business, invest in a good insurance policy and you're set for life. Get your future behind you. Nonsense. We don't live in that world any more. Nobody does."

Otis' place consisted of three long rooms laid end to end without intervention of a door, a stove and refrigerator in the first, a cot in the second, paint and paintings in each— hung and stacked, left here and there, discarded and in progress—clothes, junk, curios, books, stale food scattered around, a few chairs, a table, various trunks and valises and little other furniture, the walls half this color, three quarters that color, pink, yellow, maroon, plaster peeled or shredded wallpaper.

The first painting was small, about a foot high. Otis looked at it speculatively. "It's called 'The Prisoners,'" he said. "I just made that up." Efflorescences of color emerging from dun chaos to assume bright, idiosyncratic shapes, like a combination of Gorky and Michelangelo's Prigionieri struggling to free themselves of the matter from which they spring, of which they consist, straining perpetually toward definitive form. "I think this is about the best thing I've ever done," said Otis.

The next one was in the same style, a variation on the first, about twice its size. "This one is my favorite," said Otis. "It's called 'The Prisoners, Two.'" The next was about four feet high, again a variation on the first two. "This is called 'The Prisoners' also. They're all called 'The Prisoners.'" He then led me to a huge canvas, about eight feet high, leaning against a wall, a gargantuan variation on the others. "This one is great," he said. "I really like this one."

220

After I had looked at it a while Otis pulled me by the elbow. "Now," he said, "come into the front room." We went into the front room. A whole wall was painted in an apparently ultimate interpretation of the theme. "Fantastic," I said. "Isn't it?" said Otis. "This is really the best one. I just finised it. After this one I had to stop. What I really want to do is rent a billboard. I don't want to stay cooped up in this place. I wouldn't give a shit if it burned down tomorrow. What I want is contact with the rest of the world. Help, let me out."

When I got home I found the door broken in, the place a shambles. Gone were my radio, my typewriter, my

father's gold watch
grandfather's stickpin
winter coat
suit
summer suit
six white shirts
silverware
the guitar I never learned to play
a bottle of bourbon
a desk lamp
a pair of cufflinks I never used
three sheets
two blankets
an alarm clock
a coffee pot
a leaky fountain pen
an old sweater
an iron
seven art books
a pound of hamburger
a pack of condoms
a bottle of athlete's foot lotion

which I'm sure I remembered seeing in the medicine chest. I went out and had a beer. Getting robbed gives you a heady

221

feeling. It's a relief in a way. You don't have to worry about getting robbed any more. It frees you from your possessions, it tends to flush you out of your hole. I had another beer and a third. After a while I realized I was quite happy about the whole thing. It was actually a stroke of luck. The only thing I was sore about was the drag of getting the door lock repaired.

"Let me ask you something," said Bernie running his thumb against the edge of the manuscript, "is this supposed to be finished?"

"Almost," I said. "Not quite."

"Well, frankly, I don't see how you're going to finish it. I don't think it can be finished. I don't want to discourage you, but actually I think the whole book may have been a mistake from the beginning."

"No reason why that should discourage me."

"Seriously, it doesn't go anywhere. I mean I'm not so antediluvian to require that a novel have a plot, but this is just a collection of disjointed fragments. You don't get anywhere at all. Where's the control, where's the tension? You can do a lot better than this Ronnie."

"Thanks," I said.

"For one thing, the chronology is completely screwed up. First you start going out with Nancy again. Then you tell Slim you've broken up with her. Then you tell Slade you're living with her. Then you tell Otis she's moved out. Then the next time she appears she's living with you. I mean what the hell is going on. When are you going with her and when did you break up?"

"Well you know maybe we broke up and reconciled several times. It's a very stormy relationship after all."

"But this is just the thing you see. The reader doesn't know this. You can't do that sort of thing."

"Why not? In books one isn't obliged to pursue the

222

banality of chronological order. What the fuck I'm not writing a timetable."

"You could at the very least indicate an underlying chronology."

"What for? It's just a sequence of words. The only thing that matters is the order of revelation in print."

"Sure. If you want to forgo verisimilitude, which unfortunately happens to be the essence of fictive writing."

"Nuts. Why should we have to suspend disbelief? It's all words and nothing but words. Are we children reading fairy tales or men trying to work out the essentials of our fate?"

"All right, look, it's one thing to be honest with the reader and another to play tricks on him. What about the Cloisters for example? You're driving up to the Cloisters with Finch to meet Slade and his girl, and that's the last we ever hear about it."

"Well I lost that scene actually."

"How do you mean?"

"I wrote a long elaborate Cloisters scene and then I left it in a book I returned to the library. I tried lost and found, everything, but I couldn't get it back."

"Couldn't you rewrite it?"

"I didn't have the heart. But I could tell you what happened essentially."

"Go on."

"Well we met in the cloister itself, that is, the thirteenth-century Trie Cloister from Bonnefort-En-Comminges. The formal garden, the porticoed gallery, the elegant yet restrained rhythm of the colonnade. Geometry, order, beauty, as Otis says somewhere. Slade steps into the garden, tweed jacket, foulard, white shoes. He affects a cane. Marietta walks at his side. She was beautiful. I hadn't thought of that. Stroking his well-trimmed beard and speaking quietly, Slade tells us he is thinking of renouncing politics."

"Slade? Fat chance. Listen, are you sure you're talking

about Slade? It doesn't sound like him."

"Look, you want to hear this or not?"

"Go on."

"As he confesses his feelings of futility about politics, he passes his hand slowly over his brow. He looks like he hasn't slept all night. There is a little in his ravaged face of Mann's Herr Peeperkorn."

"Come on. Slade?"

"Not much. Just a little. He has given up his magazine, he tells us."

"*Secession?* You're kidding."

"No. His new project is a colony to experiment with drugs, communal living, and the resuscitation of the aristocratic tradition."

"Oh for christ sake. Has he gone off his head?"

"I wouldn't know. Marietta walks at his side, her arm looped through his, almost protectively it seems. She is young, dazzlingly young. Fair, delicately flushed skin, but dark hair. Like almost a photographic negative of Nancy, get it?"

"You sound like you like her."

"Like her. I fell in love with her. She was so beautiful when I saw her I thought my teeth would fall out. That's the point. Oh I don't know if it's love exactly. But whatever it is it puts me in an extremely awkward position vis-à-vis Ernie, what with Nancy and all. I don't know what I'm going to do. In any case, as you can see, it's a pretty interesting scene. You think I ought to rewrite it?"

"I think you better leave it out. First of all it's improbable and second of all it makes things too complicated. I wouldn't mind meeting Marietta though."

"I'm sure you will. There's going to be a party at Finch's. You're invited."

"When?"

"I'm not sure yet."

"Speaking of Finch, I don't like the high school scene in

224

Fink's basement very much."

"How come?"

"For one thing you don't really get the old desperate feeling of always wanting to get better that we used to have, remember? The sense that we were trapped in a mediocre, unreal kind of life that we could only transcend by intense personal development. This was always the essential thing, it seems to me."

"It still is in a way. As part of a more general phenomenon, something a lot less private, a lot less the particular fault of Gravesend—the perpetual sedition of the spirit against the perpetual conspiracy of inappropriate institutions."

"Actually, yes. Why don't you put that in actually?"

"I just did."

"Come on. Don't get too coy."

"Now you want me to leave it out? Why don't you make up your mind?"

"It's your book, damn it. Look, you know, there are parts that aren't bad. I don't want to seem negative. This part where you're reading Hamstrung's manuscript. ' "Not bad," I said. "I especially like this part where Fletch traps Quinn, I mean Big Stoop, with the flamethrower. *Big Stoop was a screaming human torch, a flaming corpse who wouldn't go down."* ' That's good for a laugh."

"I'm glad you think it's funny."

"One thing though. I don't mind your quoting my articles, or even revealing details of my intimate life, but I really don't like Nancy accusing me of being queer."

"What are you talking about?"

"Right here," he said, flipping through the pages. "Here. 'What sex does he like anyway?' That's a catty thing to say. What the hell sex does she think I like. That's as good as saying I'm queer. What about that?"

"She is a bitch."

"You mean you actually think I'm homosexual?"

225

"I didn't say it—Nancy did."

"Come on."

"The opinions of the characters don't necessarily reflect the opinions of the author, you know that."

"Do you think I'm queer or not?"

"I think that's what Nancy thinks. Besides we haven't gotten to that scene yet and if you keep on talking about what's going to happen you'll spoil all the suspense. In any case this is exactly where I'd intended to put the Cloisters scene, in which case you wouldn't be here at all, so don't complain."

"Well if I say anything you don't like you can always delete it. ✳✳✳ ✳✳✳ ✳✳ ."

I don't know exactly how to begin   the thing is   not so much that I don't know the answer   as that I don't even know the problem   as Gertrude Stein dying what is the answer in that case what is the question   you see   everything was going along fine   as I remember   of course there was the Depression   the Depression was a long series of arguments between my mother and father   I'm still depressed   but things were sort of getting better   there was F.D.R.   and other initials initials proliferating optimistically all over the country   Howard Hughes flew around the world   things were picking up the Dodgers won the pennant   Reese Reiser Ducky Medwick Cookie Lavagetto   Dixie Walker's picky two step in the batter's box   the Series good as even   then Mickey Owen dropped the magic strike   Henrich landed on first   Casey blew up   Dimaggio's single Keller's double Poland Dunkirk Pearl Harbor Eddie Basinski playing the violin on second base barbed wire camps Owen sobbing in the clubhouse everything blew up Yankees pouring around the basepath sugar frozen life rationed black market conditions wait till next year wait till next year   if only he hung on to it   or at least found the ball and threw to first everything would have been different   that was where it began things were never the same after that   after that a certain kind of time ended   and another kind began   and left me still waiting for the solid final thunk in Owen's mitt   one time I remember   the heavy quiet of impending battle occasional flat note of artillery the muffled thud of shells toward the horizon   the password was Marilyn   it was either dawn or dusk   low gray sky red spilling from a slash over distant hills   occasional flat note of artillery the guns were clearing their throats one feels observed my escort the keen tension of impending battle one feels as an observer one knows the men are shitting in their pants   the password was Marilyn   I sucked a Tootsie Roll and worked my hand through her armpit toward her breast thinking the inadequacy of girls' names   Marilyn it should have been Dynamite Incredible Heaven-flesh   don't she said   guns rose ejaculated recoiled at random intervals planes scream overhead   cheer up you sadsacks says William Bendix I've had worse days driving a hack down Flatbush Avenue   jets rip through the air the whoosh whoosh whoosh of rockets   remember he said we're here to kill gooks   Marilyn said my escort a sentry snapped to attention with a smart salute   the bunker dug well into the hillside was said to contain a private swimming pool and tennis courts   here also "bivouacked" the nurses Wacs and U.S.O. personnel   for security reasons my escort informed me   a blonde rose from behind a typewriter high heels short shorts khaki shirt with colonel's insignia   yes sir said my escort he snapped to attention with a smart salute I'm not really a colonel she giggled the colonel lets me wear his shirts   she opened the door Colonel Banally she said we went in   rising wearily from behind immense desk piled maps banks of telephones passed hand through hair acknowledged sa-

227

lutes with boyish wink   is there anything I can do Colonel asked the blonde I don't know said Strop anybody feel like a piece of ass oh listen sweetie pie stick a few pins in that map there will you honey we got to mount some kind of attack today this is Marilyn he said and tell one of the girls to bring in the sunlamp he smiled boyishly and shook his head they don't let me get any sleep he said   on his desk a small printed sign in black letters KILL   some kind of attack he says let me think a minute   he lights a pipe lifts the seat of his swivel chair uncovering a built-in bed pan pulls down his pants sits a look of intense concentration puckers his face   push I say   harder   he grunts a knob bulges in his brow grows larger he moans curses grows larger push I say harder POP a puff of smoke a-a-a-h in the clearing cloud a lieutenant stands saluting rigid a little like Alan Ladd Strop wipes himself pulls up his pants   at ease lieu- tenant   yessir cigarette thankyousir now you see that map on the wall there we've got to take that pin today Fletch the men are getting jumpy this is a tough job Fletch you may get stuck I understand sir when do I start there's a campaign ribbon in this for you Fletch do you have your penknife your flamethrower now this is the plan we cover you with a barrage of shit and then you're on your own if you don't come back I mail this letter to a little girl back in Secaucus etc. okay boy shake hands good luck and try not to look so patriotic for god's sake it's depressing he salutes and exits Strop shakes his head they don't let me smile boyishly he says bunch of god damn tin heroes it's the brass back in HQ does all the real work the responsibility Marilyn for christ sake where's that goddam sunlamp   what prisoner oh yeah send him in   Hamstrung stumbles in between two giant Negro M.P.'s white hats billy clubs armbands   do you comprehend the nature of the crime of which you stand accused before this tribunal   I no I   you no you sir disobeying direct orders in the line of duty while under fire   I no I sir   shitting in your pants under fire how

many times do I have to tell you men you get up in the
morning you move your bowels you eat breakfast and that's
it haven't you been toilet trained private put him on latrine
duty   Hamstrung leans over the desk quickly just between you and me sir it's these coons sir they went to
Harvard actually Japs in black face working for secret Chi-
nese Zionists Strop pulls a blackjack from the desk slams
him across the face the M.P.'s catch him by the armpits
shoot him says Strop that's what happens to people who
don't cooperate they drag him out toes trailing gee I like
violence says Strop smiling boyishly   actually I said according to the Talmud I believe it's considered salubrious
to defecate at least seven times a day chuckling he tamped
his pipe while you undertake to wrongfully defend malefactors against authority who one wonders will take it upon
himself to defend you chuck-chuck these men I said are
studying under impossible conditions no toilet paper in
the latrines lapping from dog bowls on brink of slaughter
pit have you he says seen the sixth game of the 1947 Series
no was I supposed to if you had you would realize that
nothing is impossible you of course Professor Marsh appreciate the allusion of course says Bernie Yankees and Dodgers
Gionfriddo bottom of the sixth excellent says Whitebread
Blackhead he placed his heavy official hand on Bernie's
shoulder they turn away walking off Bernie looks back so
you want to be a journalist he says do you have an envelope
for me you promised I said why did I say that   I'll call
the police   hysteria around a dim slum corner   police
I'll call the police   slap   the police they'll fix your
wagon   slap   what's he doing to that chick asked
Slim   leave them alone I said   come on said Slim I
smell a little action   wait I said they're just having an
argument a lady in distress he said   hold on there stranger
what's the trouble here he says   who the hell are you
says the guy   I'll call the police says the woman   that
ain't a very nice way to treat a lady says Slim   help me

229

says the woman   what the hell business is it of yours says the guy   if you're smart you'll clear out of here mister says Slim this town ain't big enough for the likes of you   why you the guy lunges Slim side steps   before I can see what happened he has the guy balanced in midair he slams him against the sidewalk he leaves him there   police   the woman screams   easy there says Slim   police   easy says Slim   someone grabs my shoulder breathes whisky in my face socks me on the ear I bounce off the wall   the woman runs at me keep your hands off him she says police he's killing my husband she tries to scratch me I grab her wrists   the guy looks at us the hell with it he mutters he staggers off   hey here comes a cop says Slim police yells the woman rape police she slams me with her pocketbook   get her off me I say for christ sake rape she yells police I'm splitting baby says Slim ciao kee-mosabi he slips around the corner she's holding on my jacket rips the cop grabs me by the collar I can't breathe he throws me against the wall get your hands up his gun out don't move I'll blow your fucking head off   but I wasn't do I'll blow your fucking head off   police yells the woman   it's okay now lady so we finally caught up with you he says   caught up I say   police she yells it's okay lady I'm the police   help police he looks from her to me   lady I'm a policeman he says   the police she says what good are the police I demand satisfaction   now look lady   don't tell me I demand satisfaction what do you know about it   what's going on here he asks I shrug   don't tell me what's going on she says show me to the manager I demand satisfaction police help police   he gives her a slap in the face then you're not one of these beatnik sex fiends definitely not I say   help police she yells   he lets her have it with a left hook to the uterus she doubles over help she gasps he gives her a quick smash on the side of the skull with his pistol barrel resisting arrest he says she collapses   and remember he says

next time you have to slap a lady call a cop   from around
the corner I hear the thundering zoom-zoom-zoom of Slim's
cycle a cloud of fumes a flash of chrome a distant shout
of hi ho Silver   Theda opened the door and standing on
tiptoe gave me a wet kiss stranger she said   have a beer
said Julius balding a thin wreath clung to his skull rusty
gray   still in school Theda asked I gradually disappear into
no conflict upholstery   Julius cleared his throat   there
was a pause   so what's going to happen said Julius happen
I ask   I mean said Julius is there going to be a war or
not   I shrugged that's not my field I mumbled what do
you teach he asked   why don't you write a story like
Arthur Miller said Theda it's all true I knew the family just
put in a lot of sex they all do you can make a lot of money
on one story said Julius look at Harry Belafonte are you un-
easily writing about the family no I said   so what do you
hear from Stewart asked Theda you don't have to give away
any secrets I wouldn't cause conflict just tell me does he
need money you should visit Sugar Ronnie she'd love to
see you they have a beautiful house in Great Neck the father
is a wealthy man you know Sterling Fixtures   fixtures hell
says Julius he made his money on toilet seats   Julius please
says Theda   Sugar's told me an awful lot about you Ron
you're her cousin is that it   the kind of dark tall guy who
must have once looked good in a tennis outfit rich too
just what she wanted   we were heading for Long Island
stopped for a light he kept gunning the motor VROOM-
VROOM-VROOM   a red Corvette   I've always re-
gretted not having the time to meet more of Sugar's family
this god damned light that's why I leave the place early after
all to get ahead of the traffic it's about time VROOM we're
off   I'm crazy about driving   just give me a good car
look out mister   the traffic is disgusting move over bastard
he leaned on the horn   they ought to prohibit nonessen-
tial traffic during business hours   let them take the subway damn city government doesn't do a thing are you

231

kidding me   they ought to give tougher driving tests too
many incompetent drivers clean up the roads you son of a
bitch did you see that son of a bitch cut me off see what
I mean I'll catch up with that bastard oh my god a red light
what are you kidding me did you see that just as I get
to the intersection it turns red son of a god damn bitch
VROOM-VROOM they talk about taxi drivers believe me
hackies really know how to drive compared to most of these
morons sure they take chances their time is money but they
know what they're doing and let me tell you one thing you
never see a cab driver in an accident never you never see a
cabbie in an accident come on are you kidding me they must
have these lights timed for half an hour well we shouldn't
let it get on our nerves should we VROOM-VROOM-
VROOM you a college man Ron where'd you go   Cornell   oh the ghetto of the Ivy League hah hah hah I'm a
Colgate man myself here we go VROOM I guess we went
to the same football games didn't play football myself tennis
was my racket hah hah hah prick look where you're going
I swear they try to kill you they put these Puerto Rican
fellas into these trucks they don't give a damn it's not their
property they're driving around they ought to limit immi-
gration from that country I don't see why any illiterate
bastard who feels like it should have the right to come over
here and throw garbage in the streets of course they're good
workers I got plenty of Puerto Ricans working for me I
know every one of them by his first name Pedro hah hah I
mean I got nothing against them what I like about them is
they don't complain what I mean is they ought to have
some way of sifting out the good workers from these dirty
shiftless types jesus did you ever try one of those Puerto
Rican girls I mean I don't know anything about it firsthand
of course he winked but from what I hear they're really hot
stuff let me tell you they bite they scratch they scream they
squirm   I bet you know a lot of girls Ron   down in
Greenwich Village boy are you kidding me the artist's

life   didn't Sugar say you were some kind of artist   no
well just between you and me I mean we're both men of
the world right how come you don't get a haircut I mean
what do you get out of it   the girls like it I told him   oh
yeah now there's something I can understand he says say
Ron just between us maybe some time we can do the Village together meet some of your friends just for laughs all
on me of course   maybe I say   christ look at this are
you kidding me   we were on the thruway we'd hit a jam
up   they ought to keep the trucks off this damn road he
says   he jerked up the emergency brake with a vicious
rasp   how do they expect working people to get to their
jobs I tell you this city has gotten out of hand   crime
traffic corruption   what we need is a strong government that's willing to step in and enforce peace and order   someone who's willing to put his foot down   peace
and order   or else   VROOM-VROOM   VROOM-
VROOM-VROOM-VROOM   stranger said Sugar   she
was wearing too much makeup gone to fat a little tired
around the eyes   my hasn't he gotten nice looking she
kissed my cheek too bad we're relatives she laughed come
in   what will you have to drink Jer tell Leola to bring in
the drinks   her mouth looked too worn out to stay where
her makeup had put it   I wiped my cheek it was smeared
with lipstick disgusting   we went three steps down into a
huge living room approximate directoire real paintings on
the walls   we bought them on Beaut Moe Mart she said
last time we were in Europe the girl will be right in with
the drinks would you like to wash up I'm not dirty I said I
had the impression she was going to try and give me a haircut   the girl came in with cocktails a tray loaded with
herring lox chopped liver fish roe   the girl   dark smooth
skin delicate face elegant figure she walked through the
room like a queen placed the things on the table with incredible grace   Leola   would you like to see the baby
asked Sugar   no I said she was already half out of her

233

seat on the way upstairs   she sat down   you don't she laughed you were always an iconoclast she said how is that I asked she looked at me as if I were kidding her   I've been thinking about you a lot Ronnie I think I've come around to your way of thinking about convention you have yes and what way is that oh you know what I mean I mean why shouldn't we be unconventional if that's the way we feel about it you know what I mean you know I'm very envious of you Ronnie living alone in the city you can do anything you want you know what I mean she gave me a hard look in the eyes I felt she was estimating the size and capacity of my penis drawing conclusions about my experience I looked around Jer was washing up Leola appeared to announce dinner was ready I followed the regal undulations of her ass back to the kitchen   she's a gem said Sugar she is just a gem they're so hard to find today don't worry I pay her plenty she has a child you know she sees it on days off poor thing of course I wouldn't have it here shall we go in   I was already full by the time we finished soup Sugar and Jer really put it away they kept urging food on me we were all pretty high from the cocktails every time Leola bent over me to change a plate I had the impulse to lick her hand rub my head against her body she wouldn't look at me Sugar and Jer kept putting it away all the while I had the sense of Leola behind me silently waiting   so you're a professor now Ronnie no I said you know I sometimes regret not going to college   why I asked I was getting a headache   you're better off without it said Jer what do you need it for   I don't know it opens doors she said are you thinking of going to work said Jer I don't mean that she said maybe I was never that smart   are you kidding me listen there are more dopes that went through college said Jer I ought to know I was one of them hah hah hah isn't that right Ron   that's right I said   see the professor agrees with me   I was getting a headache I had stopped talking all the while I felt Leola behind me silent waiting

234

but not for me   why don't you stay over Sugar asked no
I can't it would be too much trouble don't be silly she said
we have fifteen rooms I'd meant trouble for me why travel
all the way back to the city tonight you can go in with Jer
in the morning   sure stay over Ron said Jer Jer has to go
out tonight she said it'll be cozy   yeah you can toast
marshmallows said Jer do we have any of those marshmallows left   no I can't   come on Ronnie it'll be just like
that summer remember that was ten years ago it'll be better
we'll have some privacy you know Ronnie I never got the
chance to talk to you the way I really wanted to I can't I
said sure you can Jer tell her to fix up a bedroom I was
getting a terrific headache would you like another drink she
asked no thanks Jer get Ronnie a drink Ronnie will go in
with you in the morning get me one too when are you
going out she asked about now he said Leola was bringing
coffee I knew if I could touch her my headache would go
away she wouldn't look at me   stick around Ron said Jer
I have to go out he winked Sugar got up from the table she
started swinging her heavy ass do you like to dance Ronnie
I'm a little tipsy   I have to go I said as soon as possible
why she asked I have a date a very important date I said
with a girl   oh she said a date well if it's a date she said
flatly that turned her off   I guess Jer can drive you to the
station is it an important date what kind of girls are you
going out with these days young ones I bet I'm envious
Ronnie she laughed the bachelor's life foot loose and fancy
free all I want is a little adventure let's go if you're going
said Jer I've got to go you've always got to go I got to meet
Gerard he said it's business oh sure Gerard what about you
he said let's not start that again   come again soon Ronnie
just call up don't be a stranger she kissed my cheek we left
I wiped my cheek with my handkerchief   it was smeared
with lipstick   you know I don't go in for that sort of thing
she said   she was making faces into a small mirror apply-
ing an impasto of lipstick on her writhing mouth   the

235

modern office the luxe free form desk   it's bread sweetie
pie said Strop a lot of it he zipped up his fly I thought you
needed a job I thought you were helping me find one said
Sugarplum   I am baby this is the only thing I know of
five hundred a shot what do you say don't be a bastard she
said you promised   look sweetheart you're not going to
find much else let's face it baby you're over the hill   the
answer is no I thought you'd do better by me Strop don't
be a bastard   it's better than hustling baby I could put
you in touch with Gerard again I told you no she said for
one thing I'm going to be married it's too risky all I want
is a home in the suburbs   yeah yeah okay sweetie pie if
you're going to be difficult about it but don't ask me for
any help at least I got one good flick out of you you're not
getting a cent for that if you're going to be so damn un-
cooperative of me she said what do you mean of me come
on baby I told you all about it don't play innocent with
me he turned off the light flicked a switch a screen opened
on the wall opposite the desk the coggy sound of a reel
turning the modern office the luxe free form desk the rug
covered with lumps of melting butter it solidifies heaves
into shapes figures emerge as from plastic from the sculptor's
block detach themselves Sugarplum naked racing backward
around the room the executive drawn toward her in reverse
doing an impossible back step Strop leaping back from the
office boy cock sticking out the office boy popping off
Nanette's prone body like a yo-yo Sugarplum does a back
flip onto the desk the two men punch one another on the
arm and laugh handcuff her to the desk show her a movie
camera and conceal it the screen goes black   you see
sweetie pie we even showed you the camera but you were
too busy to pay attention you bastard she says if you use that
you'll what you'll sue what are you going to do about it
baby now look all I want to be is a nice guy so if you'll make
another one I'll pay you for both otherwise you don't get
a cent you see what a nice guy I am please Strop his coarse

236

familiar laughter   I wiped my cheek with my handkerchief it was smeared with blood   they'll never make me
talk   next time they came it would probably be curtains   no more fooling around   though it was nice
talking to someone anyone at all torturer executioner how
long has it been no name in the grip of the present the
worst thing is the cold   no sun damp light through door
grill interesting rusticated stone wall patterns ceiling cracked
and seamed Frankenstein's face darkgray lightgray graygray
like living in a brain   I'll never talk   alphabetical order
pure chance click slap of boots in corridor occasional sobbing staccato of tommy gun fire incinerators like burning
fingernails rattle of key creak widening rectangle of light
four tired businessmen with preoccupied look of hurried
commuters   let's go   I'll never talk   through long
warm humid dim sloping tube distant merged glare of
yellow bulbs labyrinthine stairways always ascending to
heavy paneled door with black printed sign HEADQUAR-
TERS   we went in   behind her desk Miss Amnion so
you won't talk hey what's the matter too tough for you she
said remember I'm a squat article a member of the anti-
saloon league take him in   they shoved me into another
room glass cases chrome glistening steel white clad figures
white masked   one looks at me goes to a heavy round door
in the wall he opens it clouds of steam moist heat depth
darkness   he plunges in with a long pole he withdraws
a pair of rubber gloves hung limp from the pole hook he
puts them on looking at me his coarse familiar laughter   in
the middle of the room a cluster of white clad figures around
an operating table muttering   a man strides in white pants
white shoes he removes his surgical mask   Dr. Gerald he
says now I have all night if you want to waste my time and
yours turn on the tape recorder   I'll never talk   you intellectuals are pretty smart he says remember Camp Wackanooky and of course there's always Marie we got your file
up to date my friend two IBM cards punched full of data

237

one more and you hit bingo he gestures to the cluster in the middle of the room they fall back on the operating table an obviously female figure covered by a white sheet bulging at the abdomen they pull back the sheet revealing Nancy nude handcuffed to the table I'll talk I say name names anything you want   I knew you'd come around Ronnie let's get started it better be good   I don't know exactly how to begin   the thing is   not so much that I don't know the answer   as that I don't even know the question   as Gertrude Stein said the Depression was a long series of arguments between my mother and my father   then Howard Hughes flew round the world Owen dropped the bomb Munich Pearl Harbor Vichy Quisling Eddie Basinski playing the violin in black market conditions after that a certain kind of time ended I refer you to the Constitution or if you prefer the New Testament or Plato's *Apology* regarding truth order beauty since authority is not always legitimate and may be abused with the help of Musial and his degenerate fairies my father would have taken a strap to him for do we not in a sense sit at the very center of life amidst the poise of the elements or in Valéry's words pok: smack of ass hole through six orders of force and violence conspiring to overthrow culture anything lecher pervert parasite pacifist pinko beatnik   when I hear the word culture says Strop ripping off his mask I unzip my fly he unzipped it now he's on our side said Gerald unzip your fly I unzipped it her lids fluttered in her stained face she opened her eyes she looked at me   tell her she promised I said I have no condoms said Strop what the hell she's rich I said go on said Gerald heil Hitler said Strop   he went to the table his cock quivered like a blackjack guns rose ejaculated staccato of small arms fire she raised her feet to the stirrups her lids fluttered in her stained face she looked at me through the parenthesis of her thighs give it to me she said he plunges in withdraws lights a cigar you promised she says get this with the camera he says our boys need dirty movies there's a war on you know the rest of you line up size places   they tear off their masks and line up Zip Hunch Borneo Rivers Hamstrung the Roundtable Gents Sphincter Pete Uncle Mommy Gerald Slim with boots stetson swastika armband Slade with a big cigar Finch looking furtive Otis doing life sketches Waldo high collar vest watch chain Nifty plaid jacket red socks I looked at them you promised I said   Waldo pulls me aside this isn't for you son you're too young he says he tries to push me out of line go on says Nifty we're just having fun there's plenty for everyone what the hell she's rich I was ahead of him I said   Gerald taps me on the shoulder not you he says what do you mean not me why not me I say   Strop sticks it in push he says harder   here it comes hand me the forceps   desperate mooing sounds spasmodic bovine screams   voilà says Strop he pulls out a baby like a rabbit from a hat he holds it up   hey wait a minute I said that's me I looked at Nancy you promised I said   the hell with that says Strop your mother is dead   her skin was the color of clay jeweled with drops of moisture   I was repulsed by a strange shock of terror mixed with sexual impropriety drawn by trembling curiosity   her face had an expression of abandon and release   my mouth twisted my eyes began to sting tears tickled my cheeks   you promised I said   suddenly the lights went out   for a moment silence   then from somewhere outside beyond a tiny high pitched fluting expands in volume blossoms into a wail hopeless lost comes closer fractures into mooing sounds spasmodic bovine screams closer modulates to sobs sighs complaining obstinate comes close   she appears from head to foot wound in white bandages white rubber goggles with black lenses a monstrous bulge at the abdomen   you're not my mother I say   a torn bandage on the face began to flap slowly faster   no I said you don't look like her she never made those terrible noises when I was a kid she was beautiful she used to go out all the time with my father she said she loved me they used to leave me at home with the

239

lights off she said she wasn't going I ran away I hid in the lot it was dark I was scared why didn't she come for me she said she loved me you're not her where is she it's dark why doesn't she come get me besides she's dead who are you you're nothing like her you're too fat look at your stomach it's disgusting   she reached toward me the bandage began to flap fast fast faster mi mi mi mi muh mi muh mi muh mi   quiet I yelled get off my back what do you want now get out of my sight   in her goggles spokes of colored light revolved the bandage flapped the hollow sound of wind she reached toward me   you promised she said   leave me alone I screamed   she disappeared   wait I said tears tickled my cheeks where did you go it's dark I said come back I said you promised   I zeroed in through the sight   the anonymous brown figure helmet in hand swung from one side to the other as if uncertain where to turn   the bastards I muttered   he had no idea what was about to happen to him   I waited till I had his chest full in the cross hairs   the bastards I muttered   I squeezed the trigger   bomb away I yelled let's get out of here   the Superfort banked climbed steeply back over the sea   the weather was clear no flak no Zeroes   we could see the parachute flap open float down over the city   we had been warned not to look back at target I was staring out to sea suddenly there was an enormous flash it seemed to fill the sky   the sound of babies squalling came through plate glass   they kept bringing them in piled five or six to a stretcher they dumped them naked on the floor arms reaching legs kicking mouths gaping bellies swollen some already curled up quiet gray   we tapped on the plate glass no response   there's nothing we can do for them someone forgot the formula we might as well hang them from coat hooks   they kept bringing them in from all over the city from all over the world they kept coming soon they were dumping them in the corridor wailing gasping shrieking I was drowning in their cries   reports coming in on the wire

240

tickers women breeding like sows quadruplets the norm
mothers in area of Troy New York spawning broods of ten
dekapenduplets born in Jakarta all healthy and normal a
young girl near Lima Peru reported bearing single child
taken under protection of State baptized by President bom-
barded with subsidies endorsements discovered Mongoloid
not expected to live in Vatican pope gives birth to octuplets
issues bull legitimizing immaculate conception for clergy
authorizes artificial insemination for nuns doctors in Boston
report considerable success in experiments with male maternity through hormones plastic organs transplant hysterec-
tomies claim now men too can share joys of motherhood
dead babies clog Ganges causing disastrous floods drowning
millions famine spreads cannibalism in Pakistan in Germany babies bred for meat best breeders given ribbons extra
ration stamps Paris mobs riot in Les Halles report global
movement of urban populations into countryside pitched
battles between workers and peasants governments fall slow
hordes migrate in chaotic masses toward Free World rape
steal strip the earth eat their own dead gnaw rifle butts tank
treads digest opposing armies stumble through atomic dust
eating their own baked flesh   it's all a question of maintaining your freedom said Finch   one's life comes to more
than a crude anecdote said Otis   there's going to be dancing in the streets said Slade they promised   no true social
revolution without prior personal regeneration said Bernie
we must try to grasp a prophetic vision of the world based
on the profound nature of man   I think we may be on the
verge of rediscovering the human body said Nancy   the
perpetual sedition of the spirit against the perpetual conspiracy of inappropriate institutions I said art seeks a vital
connection with the world which must be constantly reinvented to correspond with our truest feelings the search
for reality is the search for inner truth   you mean to say
a description of a rose isn't a discovery of reality asked
Otis   it isn't art I said we aren't botanists   we aren't bot-

241

anists asked Otis   slow hordes mass   population armies stumble through opposing dust eating dead babies   the sedition of the spirit   the search for truth   I think we may be on the verge of rediscovering dead babies said Nancy   no true social revolution without stripping the earth said Bernie prophetic rifle butts   there's going to be dancing hordes said Slade promised flesh   one's life is baked anecdotes said Otis   gnaw freedom said Finch   hordes stumble in profound nature of dead baby sedition I said   rediscovering botanists Otis asked   roses gnawing perpetual rifle butts I said prophet flesh revolution I said search crude hordes I said baked botanists I said   eating dead babies I asked

Sunday evening. Outside a platonic rain heals the anarchic street. Its beat makes of the room an abstraction where, between paragraphs, one imagines gray-green billows from which, curtains of green-gray silk spilling. A key turned in the lock. A preliminary rattling of paper, bags and parcels.

"That you?"

"Hi."

She had already taken off her boots and, raincoat still dripping, was unloading jars and a variety of idiosyncratic shapes glistening in foil. Several soggy sections of the Sunday paper lay on the kitchen table, soggier still in consequence of wet weather: looking through I found the book review, the magazine, the news of the week, an investment come-on for an underdeveloped partner in the Free World (nice pictures), entertainment, and the bulky double news section (for the ads). She had been to dinner with her parents in Brooklyn.

"Quite a haul," I remarked.

"Don't you kiss me?"

I kissed her and ran my hand under her skirt for good measure.

242

"Nice to see you," I said.

"Cut it out," she said flatly. "Let me take off my coat." And glancing at the sink she added: "I thought you were going to do the dishes."

"So did I."

"Everything is filthy."

"Why don't you clean it up?"

"I have a job at nine tomorrow morning," she snapped. "You're not even working."

"You've been here three weeks, for christ sake, and you haven't even touched a broom."

"Oh, I have so." Her voice was full of indignant tears. "I swept last week." Since Nancy had moved in I'd discovered she cried very quickly. Tears for her were merely an extension of speech.

"Let's argue about it later. It's not important."

"It is important. I don't like it here."

"Since when?"

I'd already noticed that when she came back from her parents' she was filled with a kind of righteous egoism. Very conscious of her just desserts. Spoiled in fact.

"I never liked it here. It's just that my place is too small."

"What's wrong with it?"

"It's a slum. I don't see why I should have to live in a slum because of your romantic illusions."

"What illusions? Like low rent?"

"Oh, please. For someone with a Ph.D. low rent is merely an affectation. If not an impertinence."

"Well fuck you. You can always move out you know."

"Really, Ronnie. Look at all the people who just can't make any money. Why do you have to get stuck in a hole like this?"

"That it's a hole I have to admit, but insofar as being stuck, there I disagree. I can live on thirty dollars a week. That's the price of freedom."

243

"It's not freedom. It's subsistence. If it weren't for me you'd still be eating pork liver and beans every night. If that's your idea of freedom, it's not mine. My father always says that freedom is just money in the bank. Now I see what he means."

"You and your father. Grow up. Freedom is the power to do what you want. And I'm doing it. That's all. Everything else is bull."

"Oh, hell. You don't even see how ugly this place is." She was on the verge of tears again.

"I see it."

"You don't. Look at the walls. The paint is gray with age. The spots of pink where it's flaking remind me of raw flesh. There's never any sunlight. It's like living in a brain. The ceiling looks like it has varicose veins."

"More like Frankenstein's face, I've always thought."

"I can't stand it. The worst thing is the cold. They never give you enough heat. It's a dungeon. No wonder you complain about feeling isolated."

"Well I mean you have to pay for everything. But what you don't understand is that I like it here. I like uneven floors. I like cracked and bumpy walls. They have more character. The sterility of smooth plaster oppresses me. When I look up from my book I want to see a wall with an interesting pattern of cracks and seams. I want to see the scars of experience, not the blank of a cold innocence. A tenement is alive with the generations that have lived in it. The plumbing is tubercular, the woodwork groans, the accumulated filth is a chronicle. I enjoy the poverty. I like seeing old women fishing for food in garbage cans. I want to keep them in mind. The scabby children wandering around at night are a constant inspiration. The fights, muggings and murders are real violence not the psychosis of headlines. The drunks and maniacs are a perpetual sideshow. The street is a fiesta, noise, music, plenty of dirt, girls flirting, men whispering, whistling, kids screaming, the reek of food,

244

people eating as they walk, singing, yelling down from windows, beards, berets, yarmulkes, babushkas, bums like walking rummage sales, racketeers from George Raft movies, relics of Garibaldi in felt hats and mustachios, Ukrainians with suits circa Kiev 1935, the ethnic jabber—it reminds you, thank god, that America is still part of the world. A store sign in a foreign language suddenly makes me feel like a native. I don't know why it is. It must be my immigrant heritage. This is the only place in the country where I've ever felt at home."

"Very nice. Meanwhile I'm afraid to go out at night. Men talk to me in the street."

"What do you care? You don't understand Spanish."

"They try to touch me."

"If I saw you walking down the street I'd try to touch you myself. They don't mean anything, it's a type of compliment. How many times do I have to explain it to you?"

"I don't mind compliments in any language, but I don't like them when they verge on rape. That's going too far."

"You've been reading too many headlines."

"That's not true. Most rapes aren't even reported in the papers. Women don't want the publicity. A lot of them don't even get in touch with the police. The rapes we read about are only the visible part of the iceberg. Sexual assaults on women are going up every year. They say the best thing is not to show them you're scared. I'd just let him do what he wants and pray I get out of it with my life. Sometimes I think you'd like it if I got raped. Would it get you excited?"

"It would knock me out. While I'm waiting let me suggest that if you're going to go out without a brassiere in this neighborhood make an effort to keep your coat closed, especially when you're wearing high heels."

"What are you suggesting?"

"Merely discretion."

"Well, I suppose you have a point," she said, looking

245

as though she had been naughty. "If that's all you meant," she added quickly.

"That's all," I said. I picked up the magazine section and sat down on the sway-backed couch. That's the only part of the paper I like to look at—mostly to titillate myself with the glamor of products, including good-looking girls in underwear.

"Oh, by the way," said Nancy. "Your friend Bernie has an article in there."

"No kidding. Looks like he's working his way into the big time. What on?"

"Read it and see."

It was a back-of-the-book article of one column's width which, however, sank its narrow shaft through page after page of advertising.

LIBERATION TO WHAT?

LIBERATION TO WHAT?

By BERNARD MARSH

A Young Professor
Speaks For—and To—
The Arriving Generation

"That sounds like Bernie."

ASK AN

OLD GEEZER

LIKE ME

When it comes to

buying

your place in the sun

The youth of America is exploding. Looking back at what seems to some of them a decade of silence and a generation of hypocrites, our young people have precipitately refused to sit back and play a game whose rules have been dictated by their elders. They take nothing on authority. They are asking questions, and when they dislike the answers they get, they are capable of taking action, frequently in ways that are disconcerting to the establishment.

The youth of today is not rebellious—it is in revolt.

Bearded peaceniks
shown fighting police

A NEAT
FORMULATION

247

From the beatnik to the civil rights demonstrator it has shown an unprecedented disaffection with things as they are, and its responses range from "cool" contempt to hot indignation. And these youngsters are not rebels without a cause. They are aware of the causes of their discontent, and many are committed to doing something about them.

"Where does he get off with 'these youngsters' for christ sake? We're not that old."

"Bernie is," Nancy remarked.

"We're practically the same age."

"I didn't mean that."

(cont'd. from p. 13) ernments of the Diem type in Latin America, capable of pacifying the poverty-stricken from the barrios to the haciendas, while at the same time building the mil-

Unlike their predecessors in the twenties and thirties, these new insurgents are not merely concerned with personal liberation nor, on the other hand, do they place their faith in doctrinaire poli-

itary might to preserve at all costs the form of democratic instituions? The problem is a staggering one, and the administration, with its characteristic style, has recruited some of the best brain power in the nation to research it. These men have done their homework, and are now ready to (*cont'd. on p. 31*)

tics. They seem instinctively to recognize an inextricable connection between their personal freedom and that of society. In a sense one might say that they are already liberated, liberated from the old, but lack the social context in which to experiment with that liberation, test it, and turn it to new forms of freedom viable both for themselves and for the life of the community.

The question, then, is: liberation to what? It is here that we must turn to our great cultural prophets, figures such as D.H. Lawrence and Henry Miller, to such of their predecessors as Freud and Nietzsche, and to contemporary savants intent on discussing the problems they raised, like Norman O. Brown and Herbert Marcuse.

249

WHAT IS IT
THAT REALLY COUNTS?

URCO
ADDING MACHINES

For there can be no true social revolution without prior personal regeneration, the key to which lies in the deep psycho-sexual source of life that these men have begun to plumb. We must try to grasp a prophetic vision of the world, based on the profound nature of man. Such a truly humane insight would enable us to pro-

"I'll finish it later," I said. She was sitting next to me on the couch. I put my arm around her shoulders.

"Don't you like it? I thought it was pretty good."

"I'm sick of the word. I yearn for the flesh." I rubbed my finger against her cheek.

"What's Bernie up to lately?"

"Contemplating suicide."

"He ought to get married."

"To who? Besides he doesn't want to risk it in case he gets divorced. He has the theory that divorced people tend to kill themselves."

"What sex does he like anyway? Has he ever gone with a girl?"

"Once. The nut girl. I call her the nut girl because she used to threaten to bite his nuts off while he was asleep. Also because she was nuts. Bernie was terrified of her. He was in graduate school at the time and they were studying in the same department. She was smart and very competitive. After a while he became totally impotent. Then she left him. That was when he left graduate school. Since then anyone he's gone out with has been purely a question of intellectual companionship."

"I can't stand that kind of bitch."

"You said it."

"I don't want to castrate men. I want to do the opposite."

"You do, you do."

"By the way, I can't meet you at the museum tomorrow afternoon."

"Why not?"

"I have a date."

"What do you mean you have a date?"

"I have a date, I have a date. Don't you understand English?"

"You have a date with me. What about that?"

"I can't make it. I just told you that."

251

"Well where the hell do you get off making a date with someone else when you have a date with me?"

"I'm living with you, isn't that enough? Do you think you own me?"

"Who do you have a date with?"

"None of your business."

"All right. Either keep the date with me tomorrow or you can move out."

"Are you trying to get rid of me?"

"Keep the date or move out."

"You can't give me that kind of ultimatum. I'm a free agent."

"You do one or the other."

"You're a bully." Tears began to trickle from her eyes. "I won't do either."

I went into the bedroom and got her valise. "Pack up," I said, throwing it in her direction. I was really pissed off.

"I thought you believed in freedom."

"Don't give me that."

Sniffling, she went into the bedroom with the valise. I could hear her opening drawers and closets. A few minutes later she came out with her coat on, valise in hand.

"Is it still raining?" she asked.

"Where are you going?"

"To my place."

"Come on. Stick around."

"You're a bastard. I don't like it here."

"I don't want you to go."

"You're not running my life."

"Go on your date. Go to hell."

"Do you love me?" she asked.

"I hate your guts."

She dropped her valise and slipped her coat off. She wasn't wearing anything beneath it. Naked she sat on the couch and started crawling into my lap.

"Why don't you spank me?" she suggested. "I deserve it."

"The hell with that stuff. Last time you scratched the shit out of me."

"Maybe you ought to tie my hands up."

"A few minutes ago you were interested in freedom."

"I'm only kidding," she said.

I eased her off my lap and got up. She went to brush her teeth. I felt depressed. It was too exhausting to have her around all the time. I wished she would get the hell out.

I undressed and lay down on the bed in my pajama pants—she had appropriated the top—she came in with it on. It looked a lot better on her than on me, not quite long enough to cover two pale quarter moons of her jolies fesses. For bed she wore her hair in a loose braid, which was the way I liked it best.

"You're pretty," I told her. I pulled her onto the bed.

"Do you love me?" she asked.

"That's a complicated question."

"Not if you love me it's not. Sometimes I feel I'd just as well be a whore. It might be preferable in fact."

"How preferable?"

"Because it's completely straightforward. No misty abstractions. It's the act that counts. Concrete transactions. Completely honest. If only because there's nothing to be dishonest about."

"I guess we've known different whores."

"But I mean prostitution as an ideal. At its best there's a kind of purity involved."

"Come on. How bourgeois."

"I don't think so. Sometimes I feel I should make myself available to any man who wants me. Simply in response to the intensity of his desire. There's something really feminine in that. As an act of grace almost. Almost but not quite. I like the idea of getting paid—the money would establish my availability and in a funny way, the purity of the transaction. As if to say. All right, if everything has to be property, then I, at least, am common property."

"It sounds like a bad parody of socialism."

"Don't be rigid."

"Why don't you try it then?"

"I have. Of course it was with a guy I wanted anyway. But I didn't tell him that. That's the trouble though—you wouldn't be able to pick out the men you liked."

"Why don't you really try it?"

"Now you sound like Ernie. Always trying to get me to do things. Would you like to pimp for me?"

"Yes." I pulled her to me on the bed.

"No," she said, pushing me away. "I'll be damned if I'll cater to your fantasies. Ernie couldn't make love to me without having some kind of fantasy going."

"What do you mean, my fantasies?"

"That's right. I'm just responding to your needs."

"My needs?"

"Yes. And I'm sick of play-acting just to give you an erection. I'm through brutalizing myself for the amusement of perverts. It was the same thing with Ernie. He was completely impotent until I said the words he wanted to hear. I had to be a slut for him. That's why he always has to find new girls to sleep with. Girls he doesn't have to know. Ernie is afraid of women. He didn't want to love me. I'm not going to go through all that again."

"I don't want to love you either. You frighten the hell out of me."

"You see?"

"But I do."

"I don't believe it."

"But I really do."

"If you really love me how come you never asked me to marry you?"

"All right. Suppose I asked you to marry me?"

"I wouldn't marry you."

"What do you mean? What's wrong with me?"

"There's nothing wrong with you. It's just that I know it wouldn't work out. You'd get angry as soon as I slept with another man."

"No doubt."

"See what I mean? Marriage should be a union between free agents, not a matter of ownership. Jealously is so adolescent."

"Maybe. On the other hand I have some reservations about my wife behaving with the purity of a prostitute."

"Do you think I'm a bitch?" she asked.

"There's probably a more accurate name for it."

"You don't trust me. I can't really blame you. I don't want to be a prostitute or anything like that. I just want to be honest with you."

"Why don't you start by telling me who you have a date with tomorrow."

"Do you really want to know?"

"I want you to be honest with me, yes."

"All right. Ernie."

"Who? You're kidding."

"You made me tell you. Now you're going to get angry."

"All right. I'm not angry. How often do you see him?"

"I've only seen him a few times. It's hardly anything to make a fuss over."

"I'm not making a fuss. Did you go to bed with him?"

"You're not supposed to ask questions like that."

"Still. I want to know."

"Just once."

"You bitch." I rolled away from her on the bed. Soon I began to feel the mattress shake. She was crying.

"What are you crying about?"

"Because I allow you to invade my privacy and then you punish me for it. You're not fair."

"But why?"

255

"Did I sleep with him? It was like falling back into an old habit that's all. Nothing important."

"Did you like it?"

"It was nice. It was better than it used to be."

"How come?"

"Just because I hadn't made love with him for a long time. Essentially it was the same as ever. Sadistic fantasy. Same routine. I'm sick of that. Sometimes what I think I want most is someone who makes love like a machine. Like your cousin. Efficient, detached, unemotional. Keep imagination out of it. No involvement."

"How do you know how Slim makes love?"

"I know he makes it with a lot of girls. Anybody who makes it with that many girls must be pretty mechanical."

"Did you go to bed with Slim?"

"No."

"You're lying."

"All right have it your way. I'm lying."

"Then you did sleep with him."

"Why do you keep asking that stupid question. As if it were important."

"Did you?"

"Yes."

"How often?"

"Only once."

"How was it?"

"It was good. I liked it. He knows how to make love."

"But he's such an obvious, slimy type."

"I don't know. I think he's sort of attractive."

"Oh for god's sake."

"Don't worry. I'd never sleep with him again. There's nothing to it but the act. There's nothing left afterwards. I want to make love with someone I like." She pressed her body against me.

"Who's better, Slim or Ernie?"

"I don't think about it that way."

"How do you think about it?"

"Slim was better, if you have to know. Because he was nicer to me. It's part of his ego to satisfy a woman. Ernie just makes me suck his cock."

"Is that all?"

"Is that all what?"

"Is that all the men you've been sleeping with?"

"What do you want, a catalogue raisonnée of all the men I've slept with?"

"I mean recently. I mean my acquaintances. Which of my friends you've slept with, or maybe which you haven't, maybe that would be easier. We'd better get that straight right away."

"That's all."

"Are you sure?"

"I don't see why you think it's your business just because they're your friends. They're my lovers after all."

"Who else?"

She didn't answer.

"Who else?"

"I just told you. You're persecuting me."

"If I ever find out from one of them, I'll never see you again."

"All right. Len. You can't say I'm not being honest with you."

"Len!" I sat up in bed. "Finch. Oh no. Not Finch. You're crazy."

"It was very circumstantial. I couldn't really help it. I didn't want to."

"You're not going to tell me Finch raped you."

"I didn't say he raped me. I said I didn't want to."

"He hypnotized you? He slipped you a love potion?"

"Don't be sarcastic."

"I'm beginning to think you're some kind of nymphomaniac."

"That's not true." She sat up, holding the sheet over

257

her breast. "I didn't even like sleeping with him. He came over, I wasn't dressed, one thing led to another and it was too late to say no. If you can't understand that you're just being nasty."

"Why didn't you like sleeping with him?"

"He couldn't get an erection. I must have frightened him."

I laughed. "What a fiasco. You must have hated his guts."

"Not really. He's very appreciative."

"Oh. Is that so. Listen, don't you sometimes get confused with all these men?"

"Of course not. Because I know exactly how I feel about them. Ernie, for example."

"How?"

"Quite detached. Cool. A little nostalgic. Regretful maybe. Angry at times. Now and then I hate his guts. Sometimes there are whole days when I feel like I want to murder him."

"Very clear. What about me?"

"You know how I feel about you Ronnie." She leaned against me and kissed my neck. "It's Otis who confuses me."

"Otis? Otis too? Well that's about it. That just about finishes the list."

"Oh I haven't slept with Otis. I just like him. If I made love with him it would be too confusing. Things would get very complicated. It would spoil everything."

"But doesn't he bug you to go to bed with him?"

"No. He feels the same way."

"What would it spoil?"

"Everything. A lovely friendship with him. My relations with you."

"Why?"

"Among other things, once I slept with Otis I'd want to sleep with him again. I know that."

"You like him better than me?"

"Of course not. But I like him. I don't meet that many men I really like."

She was resting in my arms, all affection. We were quiet for a while. The sheet had slipped down exposing above my pajama tops part of her breast which I was stroking absently. I was no longer angry. I was jealous. She was pressing against me. I ran my hand along the curve of her thigh. Her fingers closed on my penis. I turned the light off. We slid down under the covers.

She was from the North she said. Valenciennes. She hadn't known about the Bal. She had inscribed only recently.

"Ça ne fait rien!" They pushed her out on the platform. She was blonde, about eighteen, freckles, très jeune fille.

"Otez!" they told her.

"Je vous en prie," she said looking back. "Je ne savais pas." She was starting to cry.

The drunken crowd gathered under the platform, their bodies painted red, green, blue, black, a color for each atelier, most naked except for loincloths.

They began to chant: "O-tez! O-tez! O-tez! O-tez!"

"Je vous en prie," she said looking back.

Someone reached out and ripped the top off her gown. She was dressed as a courtesan. The costume was of gauze and tore down to her panties. She wasn't wearing a brassiere. The crowd cheered at a glimpse of her smallish breasts as she covered them with her arms. A green boy was struggling up to the platform, fighting through our blues. "Marie! Marie!" he yelled. "Qu'est-ce qu'ils te font." He disappeared in a tangle of blue arms, blue bodies. Again the crowd took up its chant. She stood there with her arms covering her breasts, weeping. A blue arm reached out. The rest of her gown fell away. The crowd was applauding, chanting. A blue hand flicked out with a belt that whistled smack against her buttocks. She dropped her hands to her panties

259

and pulled them down. The crowd roared, applauded. She stood there weeping, head bowed, arms at her sides. A blue arm pulled her roughly back out of sight into the booth. "Too soon," Nancy said. "You're hurting me." I didn't answer. My penis was heavy with malice. They had spread a blanket on the floor. Her blond exhausted legs lay open incredibly thin arms outspread invisible veined breasts concealing childish rib articulations limp furrow of nubile pubis light blond. Nancy's dark gold. Her body was smudged with blue paint. "J'ai pas de capotes," I said to the type ahead of me. He was a leftist. "Moi non plus," he said shrugging. "Et alors? Elle est riche." Slow tangle of limbs limp furrow of nubile pubis staccato of small arms fire. "Ça va?" I asked. "Tu me fais mal," she said. "Nubile pubis," I said, light blond, my penis heavy, Nancy's dark gold. "How does it feel?" I asked. "You're hurting me." Brilliant light, a soundless roar, a pause. From somewhere outside, beyond, a tiny high-pitched fluting expands in volume, blossoms into a wail, hopeless, lost, fractures into dry sobs. "Je ne savais pas," she said. When we were done we lowered her by the legs to the mob. They fought over her for a while then she was pulled away by a crowd of blacks. I heard one final scream in the distance.

He raced wildly across the kitchen floor. I got ahead of him and let him have it right in the face, close range. The force of the spray sent him skidding backward. For an instant he rolled over on his back, then righted himself and headed toward the living room. He was a good two inches long and fast as a son-of-a-bitch. Again I got ahead of him and let him have it. This time he turned a quick circle and headed for the refrigerator. I had to cut him off before he got under there or I'd never get him out. I managed a quick spray toward the bottom of the refrigerator, enough to deflect him to a nearby chair leg. Now I had him. I let him climb for eight or ten seconds, then gave him a long sustained spray that stopped him in his tracks antennae waving. He was the biggest water bug I've seen for a long time. He dropped off the chair leg and fell with a heavy *plack*, rolled over and headed for the stove leaving a wet spot. Still moving fast, he made it to the space behind the stove before I could head him off. I saturated the area with a cloud of spray from above. Suddenly he scuttled out the other side and shot toward the sink but I was there ahead of him with the spray. He zigzagged across the linoleum, ran in a circle, headed for a crack under the bathroom door, and wedged himself in trying to hide. Now he was finished. I sprayed him point blank with short bursts. He backed out and rolled over, legs waving in the air. I stopped spraying. He turned over and ran back and forth in confusion. He was beginning to wobble. He rolled over again, righted himself, and began running in a small quick circle. He tipped, wobbled, extended a shiny brown wing. I held the spray at a range of about eight inches, pushed the button, and just held it there for about thirty seconds. I could see him flinch as it hit him, helpless to run away. Again he extended a wet, coppery wing, and without pulling it in, rolled over on his back, legs waving frantically. I kept the spray on him till he was lying in a pool of it. The fumes were so thick I could barely breathe myself. He was turning round and round on his back, his legs waving more slowly now. His underside was white and gluey, with pulsing vents. The extended wing lay paralyzed against the linoleum. One antenna groped slowly in the air, the other drooped like a wet hair into the puddle of spray. I could see his triangular head turning slowly on the whitish neck sinews, black eyes protruding. Little by little the legs stopped waving and began to curl up. One long back leg still pushed blindly against the linoleum. I went out to the front room and came back in about five minutes. The body was beginning to curl up. I pushed it onto a dust pan with a broom, and took it into the bathroom. Right side up it looked flattened out, but I noticed

261

the protruding back leg was still moving. I threw it into the toilet and flushed. The body floated round and round, slid limply into the whirlpool, and was swallowed up. I put on a jacket and went out.

People noise weather a big hand that slaps my cheek. Felt with body skin of face eyeballs teeth. Dazed yaw past housewives thread through shoals of darting schoolkids. Minnows dodge downstream. Car zoom truck fart. Street swings to composite pachanga blast from bodegas abogados cuchifritos. Blond squarehead Polack bulling past. On his way to a pogrom. Cop on the beat looks me over cold Ukrainian eyes. Headline from the *News* runs through his mind PERVERTS PINKOS DOPEFIENDS BEAT-NIKS. Three tall Negroes come stalking across the Avenue. Local bookie in his doorway jet hair white teeth lean hook nose. True dark Siciliano figures the odds on slipping a knife between my ribs. Has it in for me from when I saw him fix a parking meter dial. Drifting weightless insubstantial. Pervert pinko dopefiend beatnik. Float toward Tompkins Square a ghost haunted by people. BLAM the street jumps to gunshot blast of firecracker. Hemingway elephants me waterbugs. Pervert pinko dopefiend beatnik. A ghost haunted by people. Tompkins Square Spanish jabber rubbery sounds of Slavic pigeons shrieking chirping urchins. Keep moving. Pervert pinko dopefiend beatnik. Freeze and die asleep as in Arctic. Turn into tree rock pillar of salt. Blood thickens turns to Karo Syrup black strap molasses avocado paste barely oozing through my veins. Move with slow oafish steps like Frankenstein. Pulse beats with shock and rhythm of pile driver. Unable to regain mausoleum by cockcrow my body crumbles. Dessicates and blows away like Jello powder. Grains disperse to ends of earth ultimately go into orbit drawn through solar system by passing comet in direction of Mars Saturn Uranus Pluto to join a million light years later one of the stupendous cosmic clouds drift-

262

ing through the silence of the universe. BLAM. BLAM BLAM. Shock wave of pigeons rise in firecracker reverberation. Aged citizens convened in klatches babble argue poke and handle one another with non-Anglo-Saxon dexterity. Bohemian sex mothers play with babies and look at me around the corners of their eyes. Grizzly bum swings pint of wine does song and dance for oblivious companions. Puerto Rican kids big brown eyes scramble over my feet around my legs "Miramiramira!" Sky scratcher of Empire State. Tallest building in the world.

The playground. Softball game football catch a little stickball in a corner kids on bikes on chinning bars swinging on parallel bars throw dice pitch pennies rough one another up. The games stop. Kids freeze and look around. They slap one another on the arm and start circling across the pavement, urgent, faster, a centripetal movement sweeps through the playground. For a moment they circle ambiguously, an eddy of autumn leaves, trotting, bikes banked in steep turns, then peel off toward the Avenue at a fast run, cyclists peddling furiously. In thirty seconds there's not a kid in the playground. They draw me in their wake, two blocks down the Avenue, around a corner. A crowd is gathered in front of the brick wall of a tenement. At the center people are talking to a cop. A couple of patrol cars pull up simultaneously. The cops jump out and move toward the wall, dispersing the crowd. A boy is sitting against the wall, slumped forward, hands holding his abdomen. What happened. He was stabbed. It was a grudge fight. It was a gang fight. He was holding up a store. It was over a girl. He was robbing an apartment. He was a junkie. He wasn't a junkie. He was dead. He was still alive. A cop was writing things down on a pad. The boy wasn't paying attention to any of this. He was holding his abdomen. His chin rested on his chest and he was gazing upward as if he had something very important to think about. There was no blood on the sidewalk. The boy's face was the color of pale clay and he wasn't moving. He's unconscious, someone said. Go on, he's dead. No, he's still alive. His eyes were still open. He was concentrating on something very important. A big blond guy got up close, bent over, and stared into the boy's eyes from a distance of about four inches. I just want to see if I know the kid he said with unconvincing bravado. Curiosity about death. After a long time an ambulance came, siren screaming importantly. It backed up to the curb, the siren diminishing to a throaty purr. Two attendants fussed over the boy a minute or two, picked him up by the armpits and ankles, and laid him on the stretcher matter of factly. They put a blanket over him and pulled it up so it covered his face. One leg protruded from under the blanket, turned at an odd angle. What did I tell you, he's dead. No, I saw his leg move. It must have been a reflex. They shoved the stretcher into the ambulance and closed the doors. Again the siren screamed, the cops cleared a way, the ambulance rolled slowly down the Avenue and disappeared in the traffic.

I took a deep breath, and with it got the smell of a Polish restaurant on the corner. I was hungry. Enormously hungry. I hadn't been eating much lately. Keep that up too long you could dry up and blow away. I went into the restaurant and ate a plate of pirogi standing at the counter. Back out on the Avenue I found I was still hungry. I picked up a knish in a kosher delicatessen and ate it as I walked along. It seemed to increase my appetite. I stopped at a comidas criollas and bought a greasy cuchifrito, gulping it down almost before I'd stepped out of the restaurant. More ravenous still I hurried to a good pizzeria up the Avenue. The guy in the pizza parlor placed a slice on the counter, turning the crusty edge conveniently toward me with minute Neapolitan delicacy. I practically rammed it down my throat, and chased it with a Coke. Then I went

264

to the candy store across the street and ate a hot fudge sundae.

I couldn't stand the thought of going back to my apartment. Nancy had moved out. I had been spending a lot of time in cafeterias, bars, coffeehouses. Something tugged at my jacket. I was standing on a corner. I looked to the side—nothing—looked down—a little old lady smiling up at me, face withered as a prune. "Cross me?" she asked. "What?" "Cross me mister?" She held up her hand. No taller than a ten-year-old. We shuffled painstakingly across the Avenue, me holding her hand. "You get old you don't see so good," she said, grinning bashfully. "Thanks mister." She waved goodbye, looking highly pleased, and shuffled off, babushka, ragged overcoat, slow tiny steps. I had certain images of heroic isolation, types of exile and self-exile, Kafka, Joyce, Lawrence, Melville. The hell with it. Perverts pinkos dopefiends beatniks. I walked over to Otis' place.

"It's open," yelled Otis. I walked in. Otis, Nancy, Finch. They looked at me suspiciously.

"Don't you say hello," said Nancy.

"Hello," I said.

"What are you looking so suspicious about?" asked Otis.

"I don't look suspicious."

"How are you?" asked Finch.

"Not that great."

Finch and Otis looked at one another significantly, as if this had confirmed their expectations.

"Too bad," said Otis.

The three of them lapsed into impassive silence, as if I had intruded on a considered boredom.

"What's wrong?" I asked. "Are you angry at me or something?"

"You're the one who looks angry," said Otis.

265

"I don't look angry."

Nancy stirred uncomfortably on her chair. "Do you want some coffee?" she asked.

"Sure."

I followed her into the kitchen. She was wearing a loose white shift with big red polka dots under which I could see her body winking and nodding.

"Were you posing for Otis?" I asked.

"I told you I'm not sleeping with Otis."

"What about Finch."

"Or Len. Why don't you try and be civilized."

I went back to the other room.

"How's Arlene?" I asked Finch.

"On the point," he said. "Any day."

"How do you like the idea of being a father?"

"Oh, wonderful. Another little mouth to feed. Waking up at 5 A.M. to the howls of a dear familiar voice. Shit-filled diapers. No, I'm only kidding. Arlene will make a wonderful mother. Especially if I can afford to hire a couple of nursemaids. Which I can't. Seriously, I'm sure there's nothing like paternity. It's a full and rewarding experience. No, I really dig it, no kidding. It's really rich."

I looked at Otis. He was staring ostentatiously at the ceiling.

Nancy came in with coffee.

"Want some?" she asked Finch.

He smiled at her a certain way. "Thanks baby," he said. Prick.

"None for me," said Otis.

She gave me a dirty look and poured me a cup.

"The reason I came over here," said Finch, "is that I bought these kites."

"You don't have to explain why you came over here," I said. Finch looked disturbed.

"No one has to explain why he visits me," said Otis.

"Ronnie is in a bad mood," Nancy said. She put her hand on Otis' shoulder.

"I'm not in a bad mood." I wondered whether she was lying. I looked from Otis to Finch. "All right, so you got these kites. Terrific."

"Yeah. And I thought we could go down to the river and fly them."

"Sorry," I said. "I have to go home and play with my trains. By the way," I said to Nancy, "have you seen Slim?"

"No. Why should I see Slim?" I thought she was going to throw a cup of coffee at my head. Otis looked at her curiously.

"Don't get me wrong. I'm just trying to locate him. This poor girl keeps calling him at my place. She wants me to tell her where he is. She starts crying on the phone. I think he must have gotten her pregnant. I don't know where he is, I haven't seen him for weeks. He must have found a shack-up."

"That's a shame," said Nancy.

"What can you do?" I said. "He's invulnerable."

Otis shrugged. "I don't know. As far as I can see people betray one another because they betray themselves."

"Not Slim," I said. "He's got nothing to betray."

"Then stay away," said Otis. He looked at Nancy. She looked out the window.

"Still," I said. "I admire his lack of guilt. It's wholesome in a way."

"Yes," said Nancy. "There are too many things I'd prefer not to have done. I feel cluttered with them."

"Let's not get too complicated," said Finch. "It's a nice day. Who wants to fly a kite?"

Through the window you could see the midtown buildings. The Empire State was so clear it seemed as if there

267

were no atmosphere. From the top you'd see the docks, the harbor, three or four states. Ships in both rivers cutting their slow wakes. When the sun sets you can see the dust in the air below you tinted red, then purple. The lights go on in patterns. All the while a distant roar.

"You coming?" asked Otis.

"No. I don't have time for that sort of thing."

Flocks of pigeons wheeling from the roofs, racing and gliding in skidding circles, merged like intersecting schools of fish, then separated leaving confused stragglers. A jet arrowed up out of Idlewild.

"Why don't you come?" Nancy urged. She held out her hand. I took it.

"Okay," I said. "Let's go."

The walk along the East River, just north of the Williamsburg Bridge and the Brooklyn Navy Yard, three kites, a ripped up sheet, and twelve hundred feet of string. The weather was brisk. We kept our hands in our pockets and felt thick-fingered knotting kite strings. It took maybe ten minutes to make a kite. Little kids were already stopping to watch: "Hey mister, what you doin, flyin kites?" After a minute or two they would go about their own games, having lost interest in ours.

Across the chop and glint of opaque water, docks and factories on the Brooklyn-Queens waterfront. Ships pounded up and down the river washing the embankment, minutes later, with the waves of their wake: tugs, big freighters, tugs with lines of scows, a few motor yachts, tugs shouldering one or two barges, tankers sunk to the gunwales, barges with tracks of railroad cars. Bobbing gulls floated with the tide and garbage, settled on the walk, flapped and ruffled their feathers on the black iron railing. The weather had cleaned the air and you could distinguish the various stinks of the river—fishy, salt and dank, rotten hemp and rubbish—that came in gusts with the wind. A helicopter putted by over-

268

head, a jet out of Idlewild whistled over the city. The rumble of a subway train drifted across the water a mile behind our view of it crawling over the Williamsburg Bridge.

The wind was blowing out over the river. The first kite went up quickly, flapping and yawing, to about fifty feet where the string snapped and it settled into the water.

"More tail," said Otis. He started making the second kite, a red one. The passing kids were lingering to comment, advise, and generally join in. "Hey mister, it's too windy for kites."

"I think the kid's right," said Finch.

"You want to listen to these kids?" said Otis. "Get some sticks. We'll tie them to the tail."

We brought back some sticks. The kids, scouting around, started depositing twigs, small branches torn from trees, pieces of rusty metal, broken baseball bats, tin cans and bottles, rotting lumber. "Say mister, can I have a kite?"

"Let's give him a kite," said Nancy. "He's cute."

"What, are you joking?" I said. We looked at her murderously.

"Get your damn hands off there," said Otis.

The second kite, flapping its twig barbed tail, went up with the steady pull of a balloon. "Let it out, let it out," yelled Otis. Finch dropped the spool to let it unwind, I felt the string hissing through my fingers, then suddenly the cord slacked, the kite crumpled, and it collapsed broken-winged into the river.

"There's too much wind," said Finch. "It buckled."

"One more chance," I said.

"Strengthen the crosspiece with tape," said Otis.

We hauled our kite in like a dead fish. Then someone discovered that the spool with half our line had fallen

269

through the fence into the river. The string came up in a slimy complication of knots, loops and tangles.

"You might as well throw that part away," said Nancy.

"Are you kidding," I said, glaring at her. "Waste all that string?" Anybody could get a kite up five or six hundred feet. The hell with that.

We began working at knots with our fingernails and teeth, pulling at loops, unwinding tangles. From the big playing field on the other side of the walk came the sounds of a hardball game, solid thunk of ball in glove, smack of ash on horsehide, shouts of fielders and fans on the foul lines. Fifteen, twenty minutes, maybe a half hour later, after a lot of persistent, rather blind pulling, with luck, the line suddenly started to untangle.

We made the last kite, yellow, a hopeful color. It was Finch's turn. He held the kite up to the wind. I had the line. Otis and Nancy carried the extra spools. The wind sent the kite sailing low over the river, then—so fast nothing could be done—it took a nosedive right into the water.

"Well, that's that," said Otis, throwing down the spools.

"Shit!" said Finch, summing things up.

"Did it break?" I wondered.

"Pull it in."

"It's still in one piece."

"Careful, the line's stuck."

"It got a piece of seaweed."

"It's coming."

The kite came up whole, but dripping, dirty, wilted.

"Maybe we can dry it out," said Otis.

"Wait," I said. "Maybe it will go up anyway."

"Maybe it'll go up better," said Finch.

I grabbed the kite near the bridle and held it up. The damp string snapped taut and pulled through my fingers.

270

The kite disappeared. The line snaked around my ankle, caught at my shoelace.

"It's going up!" yelled Finch.

I was trying to free my ankle with one hand while I held the string with the other.

"Look out," yelled Otis, "it's tangling on your foot."

The string was sizzling through my fingers. I had the cord off my ankle but now it was around my wrist, hissing through the links of my watchband, pulling the watch right off my wrist. Would I have to let the watch go up?

"You got it you got it!" yelled Finch.

I was disentangled from the string but I couldn't find the kite.

"There she goes!" yelled Otis.

It was about two hundred feet high and going up like an elevator.

"Tie on more string, quick," I yelled.

"Let it out, let it out."

"Give it a tug."

"Hand me another spool."

The line was running out. Otis was trying to splice on another spool.

"You're out of string—hold it!"

I stopped the cord just before the end whipped through my hands. The kite, tugging hard, started to yaw and dive.

Otis was splicing the spool.

"Run with it."

I ran along the embankment in the direction of the kite's pull. Otis ran beside me fumbling with the lines.

"Hurry up."

"Okay. Let it go."

The line burned through my hands. The kite, low and way out over the river, began going up again. The spool,

271

dropped on the ground to spin freely, jerked and jumped like a landed fish as the string melted away from it.

"More string," I yelled.

"Where is it?"

"I don't know."

"Back there."

"Quick."

"Holy christ."

They ran back down the embankment. I held the string and again the kite started to dip and dive.

"Too much wind."

I tried tugging the string to make the kite rise. Each time I pulled it went up a bit, yawed, and took a sudden dive. It was like fishing in the sky.

Finch was back with another spool. We were trotting along the embankment.

"Slow down."

"Make it fast."

"You clumsy son of a bitch."

"Screw."

"Tug, give it a tug, god damn it."

"Run faster."

"Come on, you crazy bastard."

Everybody was cheering and cursing.

"Let it go!"

"Give it here."

I handed the line to Otis.

"Feel that pull, feel it," he yelled.

"Look at it go up."

"Miramira."

We had about eight hundred feet of line out. The kite was half way across the river and looked damn near as high as the bridge.

We tied the last two spools together and got them spliced onto the line. The kite took the full twelve hundred

272

feet of string we had. It was way the hell over the Brooklyn docks and much higher than the high piers of the Williamsburg Bridge. The line went out and up in a long white loop and disappeared against the sky's blue way before it reached the small yellow diamond of the kite.

We passed the line around so that each of us took it for a while, gingerly, incredulously, as though handling tangible evidence of a miracle. The kite zoomed about as if it were trying to get away, darting this way and that like a fish in a small tank. And, as I held the string, refrained from its dashing, playful motion for a long, solemn minute, stable, absolutely still, its long tail, just visible, hanging straight down.

"Gee," said one of the small boys gathered around us, "that fuckin kid can sure fly kites."

Then we noticed a high, black freighter, rust-flaked, greasy smoke boiling from the funnel, steering close in-shore. Suddenly someone shouted, "Watch the string."

We looked at the ship and back at the long, low parabola of the line curving up off the embankment.

"It's going to hit!"

"Tug it. Get it up."

"Pull in, pull it in."

Finch was playing the line. Otis grabbed it and began pulling in as Finch tugged and hiked the string. The rest of us, me, Nancy, and the kids, were shouting and waving our arms at the freighter.

"Get it up."

"Pull it in."

"Turn off, you bastard, turn off."

"Watch the masts."

The freighter was churning down the river full speed and close in-shore, but the kite was coming in, getting higher, the line straightening, getting taut.

273

"It's going to make it."

"Watch out, you mother fucker."

"A little more."

"Watch the mast."

The son of a bitch in the bridge was waving his arms in mock frenzy and pretending to spin the wheel. The line slipped over the high, black bow, over the foremast, the bridge, the belching funnel—and snagged the radar antenna at the very tip of the second mast.

The kite settled, dragging in the air after the freighter. We were cursing and shaking our fists. The pilot waved back, and we grew quiet, watching as the kite floated into the water way downstream. The last thing we could see, a sailor was pulling on the string and finally fished the kite onto the deck.

"Hell," said Finch.

"Tragedy," said Otis.

"A fitting end," I said.

And we went off together in the chill of late afternoon, projecting huge, beautiful homemade kites, hypothesizing an impossible, ultimate kite, heading for a local bar, happy, and nothing solved.

We walked to the end of the ill-lit hall. Miky, India, Ontouchables, Olympia y Victoria, Fuk all Vikings, Foxy & Helen in a heart, Manuel, Tiny, Gents. Kenny knocked on the door. After a minute it was opened by a little boy stretching to reach the doorknob. "Is your mother home?" Kenny asked. "She's workin." "Is your father here?" "I don't have no father."

An old woman came to the door.

"Bueno tarde," she said looking from me to Kenny. "Que quiere?"

"Quieren mama," said the boy.

The old woman looked frightened. "No aquí, no aquí. Trabajando."

"Mama is workin," said the boy.

"Por favor," said Kenny. "Es por una reunión por la huelga de alquiler. Venga si posible."

"Si. Gracia." She took the handbill Kenny gave her and closed the door.

"That covers this building," said Kenny. We were on the fifth floor. We went downstairs.

"Don't you get tired?" I asked. My feet were killing me.

"I'm used to it. It's just one more building anyway."

"So you never finished college?"

"I'll get there someday. I'm pretty close in terms of credits. You know I started at Brooklyn. Then there was the two years in prison during the Korean war. That was before they liberalized requirements for C.O. status. After that I went to City at night for a while. Then I quit to work for the Friends Service Committee. I did that for a few years. Then I got involved in CORE. I was going to City again when this thing started taking so much time so I took a leave of absence. I was almost finished."

We went outside and into the next building.

"What are you doing?" asked Kenny.

"Writing a novel."

"A novel?" He shrugged and looked blank. We knocked on a few doors and, getting no replies, slipped our handbill under them. On the second floor a woman's voice answered.

"Neighborhood Action Committee," said Kenny through the door. "Rent strike."

"Wait a minute," said the woman. We could hear sounds of splashing water inside.

After a while she opened the door. A Puerto Rican woman, thirty or forty. "Come in," she said. She seemed nervous. It was a clean, well-kept apartment. A little girl

275

and boy were standing naked in a tub and she rubbed them with a towel as she welcomed us.

"Sorry, I don't want them to catch cold. Say hello," she told them. They nodded at us uncertainly. "I'm glad you come today," she said. "The landlord come here. He say he goin to evict us."

"Now don't worry," said Kenny. "He can't evict you. Come down to NAC tomorrow. We have some legal help. He can't evict you unless he goes to court and gets an order to do it, and he knows he won't get one. He's just bluffing."

"But the woman upstairs she was evicted."

"That's because she didn't come to us soon enough. As long as we have your rent in escrow you won't be evicted."

"But he say he goin to throw us in the street. What are we goin to do?" Tears appeared in the corners of her eyes. She turned toward the kids and wiped them away with her fingertip. "Go get dressed," she told the kids. "Maybe we better give him the money."

"Believe me, I wouldn't let you do anything that would get you thrown out. Just come down to our office tomorrow. You can speak to our lawyer, and then you can decide if you want to give him the money."

She nodded. "And he took pictures of the whole apartment," she said.

"Pictures? What for?"

"I don't know what for. I fix up the whole place myself. He didn't do nothin. And the radiator don't work. What am I goin to do? I'm afraid the kids goin to get sick."

"You see? That's why you're not paying the rent. Let him fix the radiator and then you pay the rent. Right? You come down tomorrow. Next time he says he's going to throw you out tell him he's got to go to court and tell him you've

276

got a lawyer. And come to this meeting Saturday. We're going to make plans for a big demonstration."

"Okay, okay. I come tomorrow. I'm just afraid he goin to throw us out. Two three o'clock?"

"Okay. We'll be there."

"Okay. Goodbye. Thank you very much."

We went up to the next floor.

"I don't see why you'd want to write a novel," said Kenny. "In the current situation. What's needed is organization. Footwork, demonstrations."

"A novel is a demonstration," I said.

"I mean real demonstrations."

"A novel is real," I said.

"I don't understand you." He knocked on a door. A sharply dressed young guy opened it. Kenny explained about the meeting and gave him a handbill.

"Oh yeah. You from NAC," the guy said. "We fix them bastards, huh. We get em. Say, you want a beer?"

"Thanks," said Kenny. "We haven't got time."

"Sure, you got plenty time. You come in for a beer. I got a good idea I want to tell you. You have a big party see. We get some good music, we invite all the girls. Then you make your speeches, you ask for money and we all have a good time. Is better than a demonstration. What you say?"

"We'll take it under consideration. Meantime, come Saturday."

"Okay. You don't want no beer?"

"Thanks. We haven't got time."

We finished up the building and Kenny invited me over to the office of his organization. It was in a store front on one of the side streets. We found a guy named Adam there, a slim, bearded Negro. He was sitting thoughtfully on a desk.

"Well," said Adam, looking up as we came in, "they got our typewriter again."

277

"Again. Oh no. What are you gonna do. Anything else?"

"What else is there? They got the rest last time."

"How did they get in?"

"The back window."

"Did you call the police?" I asked.

"The cops? Hell no. Whose side do you think we're on? People would stop talking to us if we called the cops. Anyway they're not going to be any help."

"It's our third robbery," said Kenny.

"You got any idea who did it?" I asked.

"We better call José," said Adam.

"Who's José?" I asked.

"José is the guy who knows who knows who did it," said Adam.

"Last time we got the typewriter back for twenty bucks," Kenny explained.

"It's getting to be like part of the rent," said Adam.

"We can't afford it," said Kenny.

"Of course we can't afford it," said Adam. "But then we can't even afford the office, so what the hell."

"You see what we're up against," said Kenny. "We get it from both sides. Last week an old Puerto Rican guy we talked into giving out literature for us was arrested and beaten up by the cops. Why don't you come down and help us out some time? You know any Spanish?"

"A little."

"We could use someone to write handbills. It has to be done in two languages. In fact we're even thinking of starting a little sort of mimeographed weekly. And of course we always need people for work door to door."

"I'll do what I can."

"Good. That's the kind of work that's needed at this stage. Practical stuff. Concrete action. I don't know why you'd want to write a novel."

"That's okay," I told him.

278

On the occasion of Arlene's accouchement, our hero received an urgent phone call from the expectant sire, pleading with him in the name of loyalty, humanity, and common sense, to come over and provide aid and comfort in the hour of his sore trial. On his arrival at the Finch homestead, briefly delayed by a pint purchase of an old Kentucky remedy deemed effective for such troubles, Ronnie found to his amaze a rare festive atmosphere pervading the premises. Indeed it seemed that Len had issued his clarion call to all the forces of friendship who, in unhesitating response, had foregathered together with their women and their bottles in mighty conclave to outface the event. Nor was gaiety ruled out of order in a company so quick to make merry with femme and flask. Many and often were the trips to the wassail bowl and the toasts to the host's pending paternity. The latter was himself in a fine state of exhilaration and despair greeting Ronnie at the threshold.

"I don't know how I got mixed up with all these people," said Len. "All I did was make a few phone calls."

Len had a glass in hand, and judging from outward signs, was already well into that state which the Italians call "umbriago."

"What news?" queried solicitous Ron.

"Any minute, any minute. She already got the first pains. I think I better check the hospital."

With this the two travelers parted company, Len wending his way toward the telephone, and Ron keeping his course through the general hubble and bubble.

"Suicides on Sunday mornings in November are least likely to succeed. Think about that for a minute."

"The important thing is . . ."

"Honeywell?"

"Jist got inta town."

"Do you want to be a shmuck?"

"Neurosis is an internalized false situation."

You got to shake it shake it shake it.

279

Above the beat of the phonograph, Ronnie discerned the tone of Otis' aggressive gentility, Kenny's furry baritone, Bernie's assertive nasalities. His heart leaped hearing Nancy's low-pitched laughter as a record changed, then fell when he found her tête à tête with Otis. There was Slim, there a girl whose name slipped his mind, and many another face both familiar and unfamiliar. Our hero made his way to the wassail board and poured himself a stiff one. Slim ambled over.

"Hey there. Jist got inta town. I hear some chick's been tryin to get a hold a me. Next time she calls invite her over. She's a hot lay if it's the babe I'm thinkin of. Chick named Doris?"

"No. Helen."

"I don't know. I can't keep up. Uh oh. Here comes the sexual revolution."

An ingenuous blonde approached, fresh, buxom, full of wheaty innocence.

"This here's Edna," said Slim.

"Etta."

"Sorry honey. Etta. From Iowa."

"Etta Farrow," she said in a voice without hill or vale. "Pleased to make yr acquaintance."

"She's yours if you want her," said Slim, patting her buttocks. "I call her Sooie." He raised his voice in a piercing cry. "So-o-o-ie! So-o-o-ie! Sooie sooie sooie!" Unable to contain his vast amusement, he laughed and slapped his thigh, then hers.

"Oh Slim," said Etta with a little titter.

"She'll do anything," said Slim. "She's had three abortions."

"Oh Slim. You don't have to tell that to everyone," she said blandly.

"You should be proud, honey. You're the sexual revolution. On the hoof."

280

"Oh Slim. Yr such a card. What's the sexual revolution?" she asked blondly.

"Whut kin yuh do?" asked Slim. He ambled off.

Etta, smiling expectantly, stood close. But such was Ronnie's tactical ineptitude that he soon brought the engagement to a pass from which there was no course but oafish retreat, the sexual revolution still in doubt. Lackluster Ron. He mumbled excuses and moved away.

"Say, Ron. How're you doing?" asked Kenny. "Did you ever hear what happened to Myrna Melman? She left Radcliffe in her sophomore year to marry a doctor. I just heard."

"Myrna Melman?"

"Yeah. She has four kids."

"Frankly, this doesn't come as a surprise," said Bernie. "No surprise at all. Say, you want to hear something fantastic. Suicide is the fourth largest killer among men between twenty-five and forty. Isn't that something? The whole network of society is breaking down. We already have mass neurosis and this is just the beginning. It's still private. There's going to be an explosion. It's fantastic. I'm doing an article on it. By the way, did I tell you I got a contract to write a book? *The Vital Tradition.* Whitman, Lawrence, Miller, that line. A neo-Reichian analysis of modern literature."

"Congratulations."

"Thanks. Actually I've decided there's more need today for good criticism than anything else. One begins to note an orgiastic admiration of the ersatz. I'm going to use it for a Ph.D. thesis actually. What the hell. I might as well get the damn thing. I mean, speaking practically."

"Why not?"

Nancy smiled across the room. Ronnie went over to where she was talking with Otis. He wondered whether she was lying. Lovelorn Ron.

"America exists in terms of a false situation," said Otis.

281

"It's inside all of us. No John F. Kennedy or any other president can do anything about that. We're living in a dream."

"Well, he's got almost seven years," said Nancy. "How are you?"

"Looks like I'm going to have to get a job," said Ronnie.

"Too bad," said Otis. "Why don't you try the Ritz Pet Hotel?"

"I'm glad," said Nancy. "It will do you good."

"Sure," said Ronnie. "I suppose you'd like to see me become a professor and move to the Five Towns. That's your style."

"I beg your pardon. Let's say Bucks County and Central Park East."

"Yeah. A Bucks County beatnik. Charity drives and discreet orgies. Plenty of high culture. A gilded butterfly."

"Can I get anyone a drink?" asked Otis. He slipped off.

"You're a puritan at heart," said Nancy.

"Yes, I'm a puritan at heart," said Ronnie. "And a bourgeois like you. And an artist like Otis, and a rebel like Slade, and a failure like Finch, and an emasculated Jew like Bernie, and a bastard like Slim, and a sensualist like everyone, and a lot of other things, if you want to go into what I am at heart."

"I'm not a bourgeois," said Nancy. "Why can't you understand that?"

Just then Slim ambled over.

"Ciao baby," he said, giving Nancy a squeeze around the waist. "Jist got inta town."

She gave him a certain kind of smile. Bitch.

"Ronnie's trying to tell me I'm middle class." She laughed boldly.

"There's nothing middle class about you in bed baby," said Slim. "She likes everything."

"You're a liar," snapped Nancy.

"Shucks, ma'am, I didn't mean to offend no one. This

282

here's Edna. She's had three abortions. She's a girl who likes everything, ain't you honey?"

"Well gee whiz, once you get into bed with a man. Like the time I was raped by three sailors."

"We already heard that story," said Slim.

Ronnie hadn't, but he tried to imagine it.

You got to shake it shake it shake it.

The doorbell rang. Len opened and, behold, on the threshold the lady Marietta, she of the stately mien and gracious manner, yet youthful withal, the fair, flushed face untouched by cosmetic, fresh and well frecked, the lustrous locks gathered in two girlish bunches. Poised in the portal, large eyes aglow, porting gem nor adornment, graceful form cloaked in simple fur-trimmed suede, she removed a glove in a gesture of incomparable délicatesse and, with the generosity so natural to her, candidly offered the host her bared left hand. He took it. Behind her solemn Slade, looking thinner, beard trimmed to D. H. Lawrence proportions, his face that of one who hasn't slept all night. Enchanting Marietta, with the artless grace that was her birthright, unbuttoned her coat, and her goodly escort drawing it off from behind, thereby revealed a form whose divine proportions, though veiled in unassuming sweater and skirt, drew forth an entranced sigh from the pious assembled there, and not least from lovestruck Ronnie.

"Hey Slade's here," called Len advancing unsteadily. "I just spoke to the hospital. She's in labor. Here's to Len Junior," he said, raising his glass. "You're all invited to the briss. We'll serve sliced brisket." He wobbled on.

"I ever tell you what happened with that there Bruce Barker?" asked Slim. "He got in touch with me through my agent. Said he wanted to see me. Course I knew what was up but I said okay, what the hell. Thought I'd teach him a little lesson. He tells me the car's a total wreck. That so I say. He's gonna have to junk it he says. Too bad I say, next time be more careful. You must a known what shape it was

283

in he tells me. You callin me a crook? I ask him. Yes he says. That's all man. I let him have it. A left to the gut a right to the teeth and forget it. He was finished right there. But I wasn't lettin him off so easy. I hit him with a fast karate chop and bring him down with my blackjack and I got in a few quick kicks for good measure." Ronnie looked down at Slim's pointed, high-heeled boots. "He was all bloody man. I left him on the sidewalk. That'll learn him to call people crooks. Man I hate these college boys. They think everyone's gotta treat them with kid gloves."

"Do you like to hurt people?" asked Nancy.

Slim looked at her. "Yeah, I enjoyed myself."

"I had enough of that with Ernie," she said. "I haven't got any patience for the exhibitionism of amateur hoods."

"You liked my prick though."

"Are you going to stand there and let him say that to me?" she asked Ronnie.

Ronnie thought about it. "No," he said. He walked away.

You got to shake it shake it shake it.

Slade held a bottle up at him.

"Drinking bourbon?" He filled Ronnie's glass.

"What's new?" Ronnie asked.

"Nothing's new you bastard. I'm a little itchy, that's all. Can't sleep. I haven't slept for forty-eight hours. I'm going through a transition phase. Have you met Marietta? Oh yeah the Cloisters. Didn't I tell you she was a beautiful chick. I love her. I tell you rich people start out three jumps ahead of us man. Look at her, she's only nineteen. It's the rich people who are going to save the world man, don't kid yourself. Because they're free. They don't have to fight freedom wars for desperate Pyrrhic victories. They grow up with it. Get them while they're young, find the ones with good instincts. Am I talking too much?"

"No. Are you still off politics?"

"No, I'm not off politics. I'm just off the magazine,

that's all. I'm on a new kind of politics. I've just given up working around the fringes of established institutions. It's futile, in the long run it's futile, and in the short run it's worse. Remember, we live in an occupied country. Power's just going to swallow you up man. The hell with that. Renunciation is the thing. No one can be a wise observer of human life but from the vantage of voluntary poverty. Thoreau. I'm in a withdrawal phase man, but I'm going to come out fighting a kind of psychic guerrilla war. Nothing's going to change unless people change. First the leaders, then through them the people. Personal regeneration. It's going to be fantastically hard. We've got to change our reflexes. Contact others, people like us, people ready to change, young people, under thirty, under twenty preferably. Then organization, agitation, transformation. That's what I call power. Oh man am I talking too much? I heard you broke up with Nancy. Too bad. I thought you might salvage her. But nobody's going to save anyone else. We've each got to do it ourselves. Sauve qui peut. Oh we can help one another a little bit. That day when the great vacuum of our lives suddenly rises before us and we really start to sweat. Then that contact is all we've got. And it only helps a little bit. Touch me, hold my hand. It helps. We've got to work on that. Oh man will you shut me up. Who's that, Kenny Malcolm? I haven't seen him for years. Hey Kenny, good to see you."

He put down his drink, grabbed Kenny by the shoulder, and shook hands with him. It looked like he was going to hug him. Kenny seemed a little surprised. He stepped back a bit.

"Hi Ernie," he said quietly. He stood there sort of shuffling his feet, looking this way and that. Slade looked at him, his smile hardening into a grimace that gradually disappeared. "I hear you're involved in community stuff," said Slade.

"Yeah. I hear you're starting a magazine."

285

"No, I dropped that."

Kenny nodded as if he'd expected it. They both looked at Ronnie, nothing to say. Slim wandered over.

"Say pardner, I remember you. You were the class pacifist. The school saint."

"Who's this?" asked Kenny.

"My cousin, Slim. You didn't know him."

"No, I wasn't in the brain trust. I was younger."

"Slim's a cowboy singer," said Ronnie.

"That's interesting," said Kenny.

"Sometimes it is and sometimes it ain't. What's your bag?"

"My what?"

"What are you doing," said Ron.

"Oh. I didn't tell you," said Kenny. "I'm going to Mississippi. They want to see if they can start organizing for voter registration."

"No kidding," said Ron.

"Good luck," said Slade. "I might be able to give you a few contacts when you go."

"Thanks," said Kenny.

"Yeah, good luck," said Slim. "You'll need it man. Those coyotes'll kill you."

"I've thought about that," said Kenny.

"You better think again. They're a gonna kill you. They're gonna hang you from a tree."

"It's a risk I'm willing to take."

"They're gonna cut your balls off. If you want to be a martyr there must be an easier way of doing it," said Slim.

"I don't intend to be a martyr."

"What are your politics?" asked Slade.

"I don't mix in politics, pardner. I'm just waitin for the Mafia to throw out that bastard Castro and open up Havana again. That's my politics. What a scene that used to be. The Mafia and the C.I.A. If you think Vito Genovese is

286

goin to take the Bay of Pigs lyin down you're loco mister. Plumb loco."

"I don't think that's very fair."

The high clear tones of virgin-voiced Marietta came like a fresh breeze at the end of a hot summer's day when the toil-weary straphanger, taking his sweaty path to the subway station, passes an air conditioned apartment house lobby whence the thin-clad goddess sends a blessed blast of air as she trips coolly out the door, and he pauses to puzzle out the imperious ways of the Olympians.

"I don't think that's very fair," said Marietta.

"Ma'am?" inquired Slim.

"It's not fair to make fun of someone about to risk his life for others. I'm sure you aren't serious about the things you're saying. I don't think you really believe that."

"Oh I don't, I don't," said Slim.

"I don't know who you are," she said going up to Kenny, "but we all admire what you're doing." She kissed him on the cheek.

Kenny drew back. "I'm not asking for admiration," he said bluntly.

"Kenny Malcolm," said Slade. "Marietta Honeywell."

"Where'd this come from?" asked Slim, looking her up and down.

"Calm down," advised Ronnie.

"What's the matter, you got eyes?" said Slim. "Scuse me, ma'am, mah name's Slim. Jist got inta town. Ah know ole Slim gits a little ornery from time to time but he don't mean nothin by it. It's a vice in me ah know. Takes a pretty woman ta say whut no man would tell me. Ah don't know why ah was saying such things why, ahm a headin down South mahself pretty soon. Some of us maybe won't be comin back ah misdoubt. We ain't skeered but yuh git ta feelin kinda edgy an lonesome."

Slade laughed. "Oh man, listen to this cat talk. He talks

287

more than I do. You must be a drugstore cowboy man. What are you riding?"

"Shh, quiet," crooned Marietta. She put her hand to the back of Slade's neck and massaged gently. "Quiet. Don't talk. Aren't you hungry yet?"

Slade shook his head no. "I won't be down till I'm out of gas," he said.

"So that's the scene," Slim said to Ronnie. "Why the fuck didn't you clue me?" He went off.

You got to shake it shake it shake it.

"I'm awfully glad to see you again," smiled Marietta, offering her hand.

"Are you really?" asked Ronnie. He shook her hand. He wanted to kiss it. "Me too," he said.

Len came over and filled their glasses.

"You know I did go and see Yssis, did I tell you?"

"You went?" said Ronnie. "What's he doing?"

"He's a big man now, you know. In cybernetics. But you'd never guess who his boss is. Eugene."

"You're kidding."

"I swear to god. Eugene. He directs some kind of data analysis program. Research, Interpretation, Trending, Systems—the RITS Corporation. Trend prediction, computers, public management. Can you imagine that shmuck?"

"Come on, Len," said Kenny. "You sound envious."

"I'm not envious, but he's such a shmuck."

"Well, he's a shmuck. Do you want to be a shmuck?"

"I don't know, it's such a load of shit," said Finch. "Yssis remembered me very well. He said he'd see what he could do. Don't call me I'll call you. Still, between him and Eugene, who knows? We're going to need more money now you know. But what the hell, we'll make out. We have a very good relationship, Arlene and me. It's not perfect, but it's what I call a very good relationship. We have our ups and downs but basically we understand one another. That's the important thing. You know we didn't plan on

288

having a kid but now that we're having one I sort of like the idea. A miniature Len running around the house you know, teach him how to play ball, tell him about girls, it's like a new start. Christ I'm getting high. I better check the hospital again."

"Where's my coat?" asked Kenny. "I got to beat it."

"Come on, I'll give it to you."

"Be seeing you," said Ronnie.

"Right," said Kenny. He went off with Len.

"There's something sort of old-fashioned about Kenny, isn't there?" asked Slade. "Something basically stodgy. There's something contradictory about a revolutionary being stodgy. Man you can keep that revolution. Look at the way he walks—he walks like a robot. He's cut off from his own body. The revolution of the robots. No man, there's got to be dancing in the streets."

Etta, sidling by, smiled at Slade. "Do you like dancing?" she asked.

"It's all right. Why?"

"Oh, I like dancing."

"I don't think we've met. I'm Ernie Slade."

"I'm Etta Farrow." She tittered.

"You're a little goose," said Slade. "Why don't you give me your phone number?"

Etta tittered. "I might." She glanced at Marietta. Marietta smiled at Ronnie. "They can't stay away from him," she said. "And he can't stay away from them. That's Ernie."

"Is that you?" asked Bernie. "I didn't recognize you actually."

"Say, it's the well-known critic and polemicist," said Slade. "I've been reading your stuff."

"I feel like I can't stay away from you," said Ronnie. "If you don't mind my saying so."

"I don't think I've seen you since the bad old days," said Bernie.

289

"Of course not. Why should you have to stay away from me?"

"No man, I guess you haven't. How you doing? Say how about that slip in the Nixon book?"

Ronnie shrugged. "I don't want to interfere with a friend," he said. The liar.

"About the Hiss typewriter? It doesn't prove a thing."

"You mean Ernie and me? I don't think people ever belong to one another in that sense, do you?"

"What do you mean it doesn't prove anything? It can prove he's not guilty man."

"I don't, no."

"That remains to be seen, actually. But one must make a distinction. I mean after all he was up to his neck in the Party in any case."

"Neither does Ernie."

"You're too much. And you're the guy who makes a living writing for the so-called radical press."

"Look it's not a moral issue," said Bernie. "It's a matter of fact."

Suddenly Marietta raised her hand and started stamping her foot impatiently. "It's a moral issue, it's a moral issue. It symbolizes the fraudulence of McCarthyism."

"Put your hand down, for christ sake," said Slade. "This isn't Poly Sci One."

She put her fingers to her mouth. "Sorry." Her cheeks turned an attractive pink.

Nancy and Otis came over.

"What's all this?" asked Nancy.

"Nothing," said Slade. "Just talk. Hello honey." He kissed her on the mouth. The son of a bitch. Then why get divorced?

"Just talk is right," said Otis. "You intellectuals. You never get past the words you use. You miss life itself."

"Meaning?" inquired Slade.

"Meaning light sound space color touch the air you breathe."

"That's all very pretty. But what about Hitler's twenty million, Franco's camps, Siberia."

"I'm sorry," said Nancy. "I didn't mean to cause trouble with your cousin."

"That's all right," said Ronnie. "Have you met Ernie's girl friend?"

"She's a lovely little girl."

"What about Greek prison islands, torture in Haiti, American oppression, six million murdered in Red China, needless famine. Those are the brute facts of our life man. Don't give me that stuff."

"I agree. Only stop talking and go do something about it."

"Come on," said Ronnie.

"I want to listen," said Marietta.

"Fine. But we also have to construct a program, formulate an identity. The ultimate war won't be fought between countries but between kinds of people. Your image of yourself is important too you know."

"Shit!" With a brief violent motion of the forearm Otis threw his drink against the floor where it smashed on the wood in a splatter of glass, ice cubes and liquid. "That's my image. I'm the guy who threw his glass on the floor."

"You're drunk."

"Of course."

Slade shrugged. "Etta." He took her hand. "Here's the girl to talk to about life itself."

Etta tittered. Ronnie took Marietta by the arm. "Come with me a minute."

He steered her into the darkened bedroom and put his arms around her. She looked up at him inquiringly. He started kissing her.

"Hey, wait a minute," she said.

291

Oblivious, Ronnie eased her down on the coat-covered bed. She had her arms around him. He was feeling her under her clothing.

"Wait a minute," she breathed. "You can't do this."

"I love you," he said.

"That's not true."

"It's half true. I want you to come home with me. Can we shake Ernie?"

"No we can't shake Ernie. I'll ask him if he minds."

"Why ask?"

"Because it's good manners. You're Ernie's ex-wife, aren't you?"

Ronnie looked over his shoulder. Nancy was watching them. "Hey, come on," he said. "What are you doing here?"

"I'm glad to meet you," said Nancy. "Ernie's taste isn't always this good."

"Thank you," said Marietta.

"Come on," said Ronnie. He still had his hands under her clothes.

Nancy patted him on the head. "Excuse me," she said. "Don't get up." She turned and left the room. Ronnie started to get up but Marietta held him.

"You're going out with her, aren't you?"

"I was."

"I think she's nice."

Slade's silhouette appeared in the light coming through the doorway. Ronnie, as matter of factly as he could under the circumstances, got up off the bed. Impossible to see the expression on Slade's shaded face.

"We were looking for something," Ronnie said.

"Oh Ronnie." Marietta sprang off the bed and took Slade's hand. "Ronnie wants to make love with me," she said, taking his hand as well. "Isn't that beautiful?"

"Cool," said Slade. He disengaged his hand and left the room.

292

"I suppose that's what they call candor in finishing school," said Ronnie.

"I didn't go to finishing school," she said reproachfully. "Excuse me. I think I had better speak to Ernie." She went out. Ronnie went back to the party. He noticed Nancy laughing in a corner with Otis. God damned Otis. Was she lying? Len weaved over carrying a bottle and filled Ronnie's glass with an unsteady hand.

"You know," he said, "to tell you the truth we didn't actually plan on having a kid. But we have a good understanding, that's the important thing. The truth is I'm not really sure it's mine. But that's not the important thing. The important thing is to teach him to play baseball, tell him about girls. Avoid your mistakes. It's like a new start. The important thing is . . . I forget. To tell you the truth I'm really drunk. Oh yeah, the important thing is we're going to need a little more money now. I got it all figured out. I'm going to do the barking for the dog food commercials. What did you think, they depend on real dogs to do that? They can't depend on dogs to do that. You have to get just the right bark at just the right time. That stuff really pays. I've been practicing, you want to hear?"

"Gee Len, I'd like to, but not right now. I have to get a cigarette from Nancy."

"Take one of mine."

"No, I have to get one from Nancy."

Nancy was alone in her corner watching Slade and Marietta with an appraising look.

"Let me have a cigarette will you?"

She smiled and gave him the pack. The match she held up seemed to sway back and forth in front of his nose several times before he managed to get a light. Or was it Ronnie who was swaying?

"I want to ask you something," he said.

"What?"

293

"Let's get married."

"Ronnie. We know it won't work. You know how spoiled I am. Maybe that's unreasonable. But then I am unreasonable. Maybe what I need is a rich old man. A rich old man with elegant manners who can understand a woman better than she understands herself. Who won't mind when I go away and who I can always come back to. Isn't that silly? But it's sweet of you to ask Ronnie, I really love you."

"Are you sleeping with Otis?"

She sighed. "Weren't you just making out with Ernie's girl friend in the bedroom?"

"That's different. Ernie doesn't mind. Besides, she's rich."

"She's a perfectly lovely girl and I think that's a very coarse thing to say."

"You're right. I'm sorry."

"You act like an absolute bastard and then you expect everybody to treat you with kid gloves. Here's Otis. Why don't you ask him? Ronnie thinks we're sleeping together."

Otis shrugged. "Maybe we are. What's it to you? Why do you have to know what everybody does? I'll tell you why. It's because you want to control everything. You don't want friends, you want slaves. You're afraid to let things happen."

"In a sense I'm letting everything happen."

"Don't fend me off with jokes. That's just the trouble. You treat people as comic characters. You refuse to see their anguish. You don't take anyone seriously but yourself."

"Am I that bad?"

"You're worse. I'm sick of your condescension. I'm tired of catering to your problems. I have my own life you know.

"Do you think you're being entirely fair?"

"Christ, Ron, you just don't realize what an egomaniac you are."

"Gee I'm sorry Otis. I didn't realize. What can I do?"

"I don't know. Maybe it's my hang up. I always feel I

294

have trouble getting people to acknowledge my existence. Forget it. What a life. I feel like a ghost." His face was a tragic mask.

"But that's ridiculous. You're Otis."

He shrugged. "Who's Otis?"

"Otis." Ronnie grabbed his shoulder and shook him a little. "Otis. Otis the painter. Otis the contrary. Otis the nut. My old friend, Otis."

"Otis the nut. See, there you go again. You're an egomaniac. I'm going to announce it to everybody. HEY, EVERYBODY."

"Wait a minute," said Ronnie. "You can't do that."

"Who says so? HEY, EVERYBODY. LISTEN."

"Come on, cut it out."

"SUKENICK IS A TERRIFIC EGOMANIAC. EVERYBODY WATCH OUT." Otis broke down in laughter. Applause, cheers, a few boos.

"*Sieurs et dames*," said Ronnie. He took a bow. Someone pulled his elbow from behind.

"Hey, come here," said Slade. "Want to split a joint?"

"Sure."

"Come on."

They went into the bathroom. Slade locked the door and pulled the joint out of his breast pocket. "This is good stuff," he said. "Acapulco Gold." He lit it and handed it to Ronnie. They took alternating drags in silence.

"Hey," said Ronnie. "I hope you weren't sore about Marietta."

"Come on, you bastard. This is Ernie Slade you're talking to. Old Slade's thrown that garbage overboard a long time ago. You turn each other on so you turn each other on. Crazy. Glad you dig her. She's a beautiful chick. She wants to make it with someone that's up to her. You can't keep sex in jail man. You can't control a river in flood, it goes where it wants to. Unless you dam it up altogether. Say that's a nice pair a shoes man."

295

"Thanks."

"Yeah. Now if it were someone I didn't like that might present a problem. I don't know what Slade would do, he'd have to think about that one. Though we usually dig the same people. I mean sex aside. Though I can see why she goes for you. We've got this sexual empathy going. It's like doubling your sex life. Tune in to her station and turn on to what she turns on. That's a funny phrase turn on, isn't it. Turn on the radio, turn on the light. Turn on. Turn. I like your shoes man. Wait a minute, I got a pin."

He impaled the end of the cigarette on a pin and handed it to Ronnie who took a drag.

"Yeah she's a beautiful girl," Ronnie said. "She's rich. I mean she's got a rich face. I mean I could look at her face and tell you she's rich. There's something about a rich girl's face. All that money behind it. It arouses my instincts to rape."

"No forget that stuff man. She's a good girl. She's the best. You take care of her. We need girls like that man."

"Don't get me wrong," said Ronnie. "I love her. She's beautiful. I mean she looks a little insubstantial when she stands next to Nancy but for a kid that age."

"That's the difference between being and becoming man. Nancy's all there and that's all there's going to be there. Marietta's still in process. That's why she's more exciting. Nobody knows what she's going to be yet, especially her. Where'd you get square shoes like that?"

"France."

"Gee, square shoes. I like your shoes man."

"Yeah, they're nice shoes. What's between you and Nancy now?"

"Oh I love Nancy. Nancy is a beautiful girl. She was a phase. I'll never love anyone in quite the same way I love Nancy. Which is just as well. She's a hell of a bitch."

"She needs a rich old man," said Ronnie.

"A rich old man. Perfect. Her father. Listen, take it easy with Marietta, you bastard." He put his hand on Ronnie's shoulder and squeezed. "I know you will. She's just a kid. We got to be careful with kids like that. And keep our fingers crossed. Sometimes with her you get a feeling. A feeling of a place where you can breathe more easily, where you move without effort, and everything is perfect. And that's where Ernie Slade is heading for."

"And I wish him luck," said Ronnie. He offered his hand to Slade who stared at it a minute, then took it. They shook hands.

"Say where'd you get shoes like that?" asked Slade.

"France."

"Yeah I like those shoes. Did I say that?" He laughed. "Say haven't we been in here a long time. Christ we been in here a hell of a long time. We been in here a long time. I'll open the door."

"Go ahead."

"Go ahead? With what?"

"With the door."

"Oh yeah, the door. I forgot the door. Say that's funny man." He laughed. "I forgot the door. Can you imagine forgetting the door." He laughed. "Say we been in here a hell of a long time man. I think I'll open the door." He unlocked the door. They came out.

"Say we were in there a long time man. Did I say that?"

Ronnie thought a minute. "No," he said.

"Hey, you guys hear?" asked Len. "It's a girl."

"Hey great. No kidding." Ronnie slapped him on the back, Slade shook his hand.

"I wanted a boy," said Len.

"Oh. Too bad. What the hell, a girl's not so bad."

"Oh well," said Len, "that's not the important thing. The important thing is, the important thing is, the important thing is that I forget the important thing."

297

"Have you got a name picked out?"

"Arlene likes the name Iris. It means messenger of the gods." He trudged off.

Ronnie leaned against the wall. The people seemed indefinite, moving fluidly, fish in a tank. As they spoke their faces underwent exaggerations, deformations, their figures shrank, grew, metamorphosed, they became extensions of themselves. Bernie lectures thick-lipped static finger gesture, Otis' comic face turns tragic comic tragic, Slim's bowlegged jeans from behind flexing pumping posting, Etta's pale plump cheeks twitch, dilate, Len shifts through the crowd in an aimless dance, Slade freezes in the bleak pose of a Renaissance monument, Nancy and Marietta talk earnestly within a nimbus of light, their bodies merge, coalesce in curves, Mancy, Narietta. Objects themselves turn to molecules contained in shapes of couch, piano, table, fluid in the drift of time, allowing Ronnie to perceive for a moment the slow millenarian flow of one thing into another.

"Quite a party."

Ronnie turns to his side. Leaning against the wall next to him a natty figure, profile cut from cardboard.

"You look familiar," says Ronnie.

He turns full face. The bright green eyes. "Hi," he says. His coarse familiar laughter.

"What are you doing here?"

"Oh I know Len Finch. Ritz Enterprises. That's my company. I get my finger in a lot of things." He laughs again.

"Frankly, I'm a little surprised."

"What's the matter? Didn't you think I was real?"

"Yeah I knew you were real all right. In a sense I thought you were too real to show up here."

He laughs. "You're too much baby," he says, shaking his head at Ronnie's naïveté. "I know a lot of people here. I'm good friends with your cousin."

"You know Slim?"

298

"Are you putting me on sweetheart? He records on the Ritz label."

"Well I can believe that."

"Sure. I see a lot of familiar faces. That fellow there."

"Otis?"

"Yeah, that's the name. I had him working for me a while didn't I? We had him taking care of the animals. We like to get types like that to do our dirty work. And that stud there. Ernie Slade. I know him from somewhere. Etta Farrow. She's what you might call a protégée. And your friend Bernie. Who do you think got him into Columbia?"

"You got Bernie into Columbia?"

He laughs. "That piece over there, blondie. I got eyes for her sweetheart. I'm working on her. She's been down to my club."

"What club?"

"Oh it's just a little key club. We call it our thing. It's run by a friend of mine named Gerard."

"Keep your hands off of Nancy."

He shrugs. "People come to me. Who are you going home with baby? That sweet young thing over there? That's about your speed. Man I'd like to have her tied to a table."

"No that's Slade's girl. I'm keeping my hands off. He's too involved with her."

"Yeah? That's not the way I case it."

People were dancing to the phonograph. Slade was doing a rock with Etta Farrow. Slim was talking to Marietta. Otis and Nancy were laughing together.

"He's too involved with her," Ronnie says, "what the hell. Besides I want to go home with Nancy. I can't go home with both of them after all."

"Why not? That would be a great scene. That's the kind of scene that sells a novel you know. Or even better, suppose I go home with both of them. I'd know what to do with them baby. Your friend blondie has real possibilities. I bet I could get her interested in doing a little performance

299

at my club. And your sweet young thing. I'd like to have her tied to a table baby. These nice girls, that's the time to get them you know, when they're spoiled and young. Teach them to enjoy rape. It's simple Pavlov, reward and punishment. Work on their reflexes. Once you cultivate that craving you got them hooked sweetheart. The volupté of masochism, the itch for total subjection. Forced prostitution, naked girls kissing swastikas in Nazi slave brothels. A thirst for cruelty, betrayal, a taste for violence. I once got this girl to where she liked masturbating with a loaded pistol. Loathesome but beautiful. You get the scene baby? Now that's what sells a novel. I'll tell you all about it sweetheart you just write it down. Or you can come along if you want. We can make a movie out of it. You know I think you have an admirable manuscript here. Sure, Bernie showed it to me, what did you think? Just spice it up a little bit and we're going to have a hot property on our hands. A few scenes like the one I'm suggesting and a title like *I Was an Egghead Nymphomaniac* or whatever it is, you can make it up. That's the way it works baby, that's the way it works. Put in a few good jokes, a little satire, a typographical trick or two, and call it avant garde. I run a little-known but highly lucrative publishing house and I'm in a position to know that you stand to make a lot of money sweetheart. That means you'll be famous. You'll be a great writer. That's what you want, isn't it? Now you just leave the girls to me, that's the least of it. What do you say?"

Ronnie is drenched in sweat. Strop looks at him his green eyes glittering, his bold smile that fixed grimace which is simultaneously a challenge, an insult, and a gesture of complicity. "Pardon me sweetheart," he says. He makes his way toward Marietta and Slim. Ronnie follows. Strop taps Slim on the shoulder. "Move over, Slim," he says.

Slim whirls around pugnaciously. "What are you kid . . ." Strop looks at him. "Oh excuse me Mr. Banally. I didn't know it was you. I didn't know you were here. Sorry."

300

"You interested in that gig in Vegas?" asks Strop. "Come around and talk to me."

"Oh, gee, thanks a lot Mr. Banally. I'll come in to-morrow."

"Not tomorrow. Sometime next week. Call my secretary."

"Okay Mr. Banally, whatever you say. Thanks Mr. Banally." Slim disappears.

"I'm Strop Banally," he says to Marietta. "I'm an old friend of Ronnie's. Would you like to dance?"

She looks up, fascinated. "Certainly Mr. Banally."

"Call me Strop."

He puts his arm around her waist, steers her to the middle of the floor, and draws her to him. For a minute Ronnie watches them dance. Then he starts toward them. He moves in a dream of rage. He is gigantic. He grabs Strop by the arm. "I'm cutting in," he says quietly. Strop looks at him. His green eyes glitter. Then he raises his eyebrows nonchalantly and smiles a smile that this time is more nearly a grimace.

"Not bad baby," he says. He hands her to him. Ronnie pulls Marietta against him and dances off with her.

"Who is that nice sexy man you chased away from me?" she asks reproachfully.

"Never mind," says Ronnie. "He's an old friend."

She touches Ronnie's cheek with her fingers. "Green eyes," she says.

shake it shake it shake it

They were dancing to heavy beat teen-age music. Marietta claps, stamps, wriggles, breaking loose.

"What's the step?" Ronnie asks.

"There's no step. Just do it do it do it."

shake it shake it shake it

Ronnie lets her go and dances in an orbit around her doing his own step.

you got to shake it shake it shake it

301

"That's right, do it do it do it," Marietta claps.

shake it shake it

Marietta stamps wriggles shakes. Her breasts quiver, her hair bunches whip around, her pelvis undulates, she laughs and claps.

you got to shake it

Ronnie shakes it. He feels like he's shaking out of a crust. He feels like he's shaking something off.

you got to shake it

"Feel the beat," says Marietta. "Feel your body. Do it do it do it."

you got to sha-a-ake it

Nancy dances up to Ronnie. "I thought you didn't know how to dance," she says.

"I'm making it up," says Ronnie. "You got to sha-a-ake it."

SHAKE it SHAKE it SHAKE it

He dances with Nancy. He switches back to Marietta. Then he dances by himself between Nancy and Marietta.

SHAKE it SHAKE it SHAKE it

you got to shay a AKE it

Smiling, the two girls dance to one another. Ronnie cuts back in. Finally the three join hands and dance together.

you got to sha-a-ake it

The record ends. For a moment they stand holding hands grinning gleefully, secretively at one another.

Suddenly a deep woofing noise breaks out, a St. Bernard barking.

"What the hell," says Ronnie.

Again the woofing followed by a series of lap-dog yaps.

"What's going on? Oh no. Len."

Finch is on the other side of the room nose in the air, now howling like a hound at the chandelier.

"Owoo-o-o-o. Ow ow owoo-o-o-o. Woof, woof. Yap yap. Yip yap yap. Aroof aroof. Roof roof. Oaf oaf oaf. Aroo-o-o-o. Aroo-o-o-o. Oaf oaf aroo-o-o-o-o."

302

Ronnie goes over. Otis is already there trying to calm him down.

"Come on Len. Cut it out. Easy, will you. Take it easy."

"Rarrarrarr," says Len. "R-r-r-r. R-r-roof. Groof groof gruff groof."

"Throw im a hunk a meat," yells Slim.

"Easy Len, easy boy. Come on fella."

"Ark ark ark ark ark. Rarrarruff. Gruff gruff gruff. Arf arf aroo-o-o-o aroo-o-o-o-o."

"Come on Len. Down boy. Easy."

"R-r-r-rarroof. Grarrarf."

Marietta comes over and going up to Len puts her hand on his head. "Come on now Len," she says. She strokes his head, runs her hand through his hair, down his back. Len begins to whine and whimper. Tears appear in the corners of his eyes. "Come on now," says Marietta, rubbing the back of his neck. "It's all right, it's going to be all right." Len begins to pant and sob. His lips contort in spasms. A moan of grief tears loose from his chest and he throws himself into Marietta's arms crying like a baby.

"What happened?" asks Otis.

"I'm sick," cries Len. "Oh god, I don't f-f-feel well."

"Do you want to go to the john?" asks Nancy.

"N-no. I w-w-want, I w-want, I don't kn-know," he wails.

"Easy," says Marietta, rubbing his neck. "We all love you."

"You d-do?" asks Len.

"Yes we do," says Marietta.

"I'm drunk," says Len. "I feel sick. I just wanted to show Banally."

"Show him what?"

"How I could bark. For his dog food commercials. B-but he l-l-left right away. He didn't give me a ch-ch-chance. Oh god. Everything's going around."

"Let me help him to the john," says Nancy. She gets

303

his arm over her shoulders and stumbles off with him. Otis catches up and takes the other arm.

"I guess it's about time to go," Ronnie says to Marietta. She takes his hand.

"Let's go tell Ernie," she says.

Slade sits on the arm of Etta's chair, fondling her, whispering in her ear. She sits up in the chair with a drink in her hand, tittering and looking straight ahead.

Holding Ronnie's hand Marietta caresses Slade's shoulder, the back of his head. She smiles at him. "Ronnie's taking me home," she says.

"Cool," says Slade looking up from Etta.

"You don't mind, do you?" asks Marietta. She strokes his head, runs her hand through his hair, down his back.

"When Slade says cool he means cool," croaks Slade.

"I'll call you in the morning," Marietta says. She squeezes the back of his neck.

"Cool," croaks Slade.

Ronnie goes with Marietta to the bedroom to get their coats. There he embraces her in a long kiss. Nancy comes in.

"Are we going?" she asks. "Bernie's staying with Len." She smiles at Marietta. Ronnie looks from one to the other.

"Guess so," he says.

Out in the street they each take one of Ronnie's arms. "Where are we going?" he asks.

"That's up to you," says Nancy.

"My place, then," he says.

"Is it big enough?" asks Marietta. She giggles. "Shall we take a cab?"

"Well . . ." begins Ronnie.

"Here, wait a minute." She opens her purse and hands Ronnie a bill. He hails a cab. Marietta gets in first, then Ronnie, then Nancy. They each lean against him. He puts his arms over their shoulders. Marietta looks up at him. He kisses her. Then he kisses Nancy. Then Marietta while she and Nancy hold hands in his lap. At a red light the cabbie thrusts his big meaty face over his shoulder. "Ey," he says. "Save some fuh tumarra."

They pull up at Ronnie's house. Marietta and Nancy go inside while he pays the cabbie who looks at him, nodding. "Have a good time," he says.

He did.

The professor walks into class. He wears his perpetual brown tweed jacket and his face looks like he forgot to get up this morning. On the other hand, his violet and orange tie, cheap display of sartorial self-expression. Glancing quickly at the class, he sits down at the desk and pulls from his briefcase a thickness of index cards sandwiched in a green textbook. He scans through the cards nervously, as if he hasn't looked at them since his doctoral examination. Suddenly he gets up and walks to the window, then back to his desk, then back to the window. This continues as the classroom fills up.

Worse looking specimens have stood before their classes at this large, second-rate university. Dark, obviously Semitic face, widow's peak, heavy brows, large eyes, lips indicating a weakness, perhaps, in the direction of the sensual, narrow, tense body. First-day students, usually relieved by his relative youth, always give him nonetheless, possibly due to his unofficial manner, an erratic and therefore dangerous, psych-out profile. What does he want of us? What if he doesn't know?

The bell rings. He sits down at his desk, opens his book, and looks up. "Now the figure we are about to consider is usually made to seem the dullest of the great poets, the least romantic of Romantics, the stodgiest of men."

He looks around at the class. They slouch in their seats, fiddle with their pens, doodle in their notebooks. The sexy girl in the front row stretches and crosses her legs, staring at him with big, drippy eyes. An athlete half dozes in the

305

back, small head cocked in large hand as if he were ready to toss it down field. A girl with a fraternity pin hanging from a tit shaped like a nose cone smirks at her neighbor. A boy dressed like the banker in an old melodrama blows smoke rings at the NO SMOKING sign. Mr. Selznick, who writes the good papers and never talks, stares disconsolately out the window.

"Let me describe, then, a man who was a political, moral, and poetic revolutionary, a pantheist visionary, who joined his sympathies with the first great modern revolutionary movement and was very likely an activist in that movement, who fathered a bastard by his French mistress, Annette, who felt alienated by the advancing English industrial culture and concocted a poetry and a poetic of that alienation, who with Coleridge created a new poetry that was in important ways the first modern poetry and which produced the first literary avant garde in the sense which we attach to that phrase today, wrote what we now would call a manifesto for that movement, and provided it with models of indisputable greatness whose possibilities, it seems to me, have yet to be exhausted."

The young banker drops his cigarette and steps on it. The girl with the nose cones peers around and smirks. Mr. Selznick looks glumly attentive. The sexy girl raises her hand.

"Yes?"

"Aren't you going to take attendance, Mr. Sukenick?"

"No." He gets up and starts pacing beside his desk. "Of course it is true that Wordsworth died forty years too late, just as Keats died forty years too soon. But those are the chances we take. We have to be grateful for what we get. England had declared war on France. The Terror reigned in Paris. Wordsworth's radical allegiance was thrown in doubt. He resorted to abstract speculation, then in despair of strictly intellectual pursuits, he retired to the countryside to cultivate his visionary relationship with nature, and thereby to write his great poetry. Around him he had Coleridge, his sister, his circle, but his poems strike the note of solitude, elevate the solitary communion with nature. Perhaps it was a brilliant way out. Perhaps it was still possible. D. H. Lawrence was forced to deal more with the city. Perhaps it was still possible. Perhaps it wasn't. For one thing he got caught up in the reaction to the French Revolution, the disillusionment and long crack-down that accompanied recognition of the nationalist, imperialist, totalitarian aspects of the Napoleonic sequel to the movement from which men of good will had expected so much. The ground was cut from under them. Does this begin to sound slightly familiar? In any case Wordsworth's politics, his religion, became more and more conventional, more and more conservative, his poetry more and more empty. He became an ex-radical, an ex-visionary, and, finally, an ex-poet. Thirty or forty years of stasis more or less, a public monument. Naturally, they made him Poet Laureate."

The banker boy raises his hand. "Is this going to be on the mid-term?" he asks.

"Everything up to the middle of the term will be on the mid-term." The nose cones suddenly zero in on a notebook, then after a moment alter trajectory toward a neighbor. "What'd he say?" she whispers. Sukenick sits down again behind his desk.

"It is, in a way, a poetry of reconcilement, an autotherapeutic poetry. Its intense autobiographical character, its interest in the genesis of the poet himself, represents an attempt, through introspection, to find within the ego sources of power, harmony, affirmation, denied by the conditions of social reality." He addresses himself to Mr. Selznick. "It is a way, through the synthesizing and projective powers of the imagination, of warding off what Wordsworth called the 'universe of death,' that positivist reality devoid of value, interest, or humanity and totally unresponsive to the momentous needs of the ego. It is a way of confirming

307

the value of the self and then of projecting that self into reality to find the world suddenly responsive and fraught with value. This is not a poetic trick but a primal psychic function."

Mr. Selznick raises his hand. This is the first time Mr. Selznick has raised his hand. "Is it like Proust?" he asks. Titters from the class.

"Yes, in a way it is like Proust. Unity of experience equals reality of self and that alone is a tremendous source of self-affirmation."

Mr. Selznick nods. Pens whir in notebooks.

"Thus the confessional and auto-therapeutic nature of Wordsworth's poetry stands as a great paradigm. The so-called healing power of his verse has been widely noted. Of course you may object that poetry doesn't cure anything. You're right. Poetry doesn't cure anything—except the mind. And the mind cures—through acts. It would be hard to overestimate the importance of the imagination in confronting and even creating the world in which we live. But you're still right." Sukenick gets up and begins pacing beside his desk, gesturing, waving his finger. "Poetry itself is capable only of affective resolutions, momentary harmonies which dissolve, like the masque in *The Tempest*, while the world remains the same. It is only through concrete actions that we change the world and thereby change our lives. Perhaps what we need is a poetry that moves us to act, that points an accusing finger like the biblical prophets, a poetry that persuades, arouses, has its effect in the polling booths, gets us into the streets. Because we can write poems till the world ends, shout till we're blue in the face, set fire to ourselves and jump screaming from the top of the Empire State Building and no one is going to pay any attention. Nothing is going to change, not one chairman of one board will bat an eyelash, not one politician will lift a hand, not one bureaucrat will drop a tear, not one landlord will give a fart. Corporations get away with murder, the government thrives

308

on hypocrisy, wealth breeds wealth and smugness or sheer arrogance in turn. Nobody's going to risk what he's got. And the helpless get it up the ass and always will, you know it's true.

> It's the same the whole world over,
> The poor man gets the blame,
> The rich man gets the pleasure,
> Ain't that a bloody shame?

What are you going to do? If you don't learn anything else here today I want you to remember this—there comes a time when life is not worth living for enough people all over the world. That's all. There comes a time. And we're getting close to that time. Until you recognize that your lives will have no meaning. You're young, you can change, there's hope. You're not that committed. Don't sell yourselves so cheap. Don't sell yourselves at all. Don't listen to what they tell you, don't even listen to me. Forget about mid-terms, about grades. Pick up what you can, say what you think, and don't be afraid to do what you god damn well please. Half of this country is now in its twenties or younger. Or younger! It's all yours kids. I mean right now. Let's get the hell out there and *fight!*"

The class rises as one. "FREEDOM!" they yell, and dashing helter-skelter through the classroom, race pell-mell out the door. Cut to New York Public Library. A huge crowd blocks Fifth Avenue as a hundred banjos assembled on the steps bang out "Happy Days Are Here Again," only to be drowned in a scattered, suddenly amplifying, quickly thunderous chant: "Free-DOM, Free-DOM, Free-DOM." From the lower Avenue, from Forty-second East and West, the crowd floods into upper Fifth, heading for Bonwit Teller's. A squad of mounted police reins up, fires a volley in the air, mills about, turns tail and scatters in panic. Past Korvette's, past Rockefeller Center, past Tiffany's, past Jen-

309

sen's, past the Hallmark Greeting Card temple they go, a solid mass from curb to curb swollen by throngs at each cross street, chanting, singing, laughing, fist shaking, invincible. The lunch crowd from Chock Full o' Nuts pours out to join them waving shrimp salad sandwiches. The entire staff and clientele of the Librairie de France, singing the Marseillaise, comes out to join them. Tourists flow out of transistor clearance sales to join them. Fat housewives from the Bronx sweat up subway steps to join them. A heckler on a soapbox holds up a sign that says FUCK YOU. "Fuck you!" he screams. "Fuck you! Fuck you!" His face turns red, purple, with each shout another pimple bursts until, out of pimples, he submerges in the crowd as into a sea. Word spreads that similar demonstrations are taking place in Paris, Moscow, Peking. The marchers are now backed up down to Fourteenth Street. Squads of squat women from Klein's bring up the rear. Above the demonstrators bobs a mobile forest of banners and placards: FREEDOM, PEACE NOW, HADASSAH MOTHERS AGAINST THE DRAFT, LEGALIZE POT, END THE ARMS RACE, RICHMOND LOCAL OF FEDERATED PENCIL SHARPENERS—NOW! SHARE THE WEALTH, WE WANT WILKIE, CUT UP THE PIE, INTERNATIONAL ASSOCIATION OF AMALGAMATED TOOTHPICK WORKERS—NOW! NATIONALIZE ROCKEFELLER, PACEM IN TERRIS, FREEDOM FOR THE ARTS, THE ANACHARSIS CLOOTS DELEGATION TO THE FIRST CONGRESS OF THE FOURTH INTERNATIONAL—NOW! MAX SHACHTMAN IS NOT A SHACHTMANITE, FREE SILVER, LEGALIZE PROSTITUTION, REPEAL! ONE WORLD, WOBBLIES FOR PEACE, ANARCHISTS FOR GESTALT THERAPY, BALLING IS FUN, LSD SAVES, HANDS OFF LENNIE BRUCE, ONE MAN ONE VOTE—NOW! MAKE LOVE NOT WAR—NOW! AFFILIATED REPRESENTATIVES OF THE UNREPRESENTED AND UNAFFILIATED—NOW! STUDENTS AGAINST THE DEATH INSTINCT—NOW! LOVE CONQUERS ALL—NOW! At Fifty-ninth Street the crowd moving uptown meets the vanguard of the contingents coming down from Harlem. Everyone converges on Grand Army Plaza where a rock 'n' roll band wails from an improvised bandstand. Irregular guerrilla groups of teen-age liberation commandos slip through the crowd into the center and begin to dance. Everybody claps in rhythm. The banners and placards disappear. Bit by bit the whole huge crowd begins to move in rhythm. Everybody starts to rock. Everyone rocks. Come on everyone rocks. You got to shake it shake it shake it. Everyone rocks. Come on shake it. Everybody dances. The whole huge crowd, the streets, the midtown buildings themselves, everybody rocks. Blind undulations, slow tangle of limbs, flesh comforts flesh. Voices mingle in endearments, whispers end in sighs, sighs in belly grunts. Hands grope smooth skin, breasts, bodies coalesce, indistinguishable, Marietta's souplesse, Nancy's volupté. "Sergeant Vack!" barks Gerald. "Yes sir," calls Sergeant Vack. He has blank eyes like Little Orphan Annie. "Ask Colonel Banally to come in. Tell him we're ready." He looks significantly at Marietta, tied to a table, then at Ronald sitting bound in a corner. "We're going to make him watch," says Gerald. "Yes sir," says Sergeant Vack. "And Sergeant," continues Gerald. "You get eggies." "Thankyousir!" says Sergeant Vack. He takes a huge rusty key from his belt, unlocks the creaking cell door, and goes out. "Ronald!" cries Marietta. "Don't worry," says Ronald. To himself he says, ("Looks like we're goners, unless . . .") Garbage tangle of naked arms and legs. From the courtyard staccato of small arms fire. They're mowing them down, he said. They had no right to pitch to Musial, no right. Mi muh mi muh mi. Iron gull Stukas dive screaming. Ack-ack syncopation. Indistinguishable endearments delight slow flesh tangle. The cell door creaks, brutal fluorescent light rapes the shadows. Banally comes in, leading Nancy. "It's curtains for you, Ronald," he says. "But first we're going to have a little fun." He turns to Nancy. "Isn't that right sweetheart?"

311

Nancy nods like a drugged slave. "Ronald!" cries Marietta. "What have they done to her?" "You'll find out," says Strop. "Sergeant, set up the camera. Our boys need dirty movies. There's a war on, you know. It's the final solution." He turns to Nancy. "Take off your clothes," he says. Slowly, as in a trance, she starts to unbutton her cardigan. Sergeant Vack stops to watch. Eyes snap into his head like lemons in a slot machine. ("Now's my chance,") thinks Ronald. Unknown to his captors, Ronald has secretly gnawed through the ropes that bound his hands and feet. He springs up, swings Sergeant Vack around by his shoulder, and punches him in the jaw. "Pardon my fist," he says. Lemons, cherries, oranges roll through Sergeant Vack's eyes until they go blank and he collapses. "Ach du lieber!" says Gerald. He pulls a Luger from his pocket. But Ronald, too quick for him, grabs Vack's combat knife and hurls a bull's eye at Gerald's jugular. "Argh!" says Gerald. Clutching his throat he goes pffffft! and deflates like a balloon. "$*#@¢!" says Strop. He runs out the door for help. "Hurry," says Ronald, "the secret passage!" Releasing Marietta, he takes Nancy by the hand and they crawl through a long dim damp humid sloping narrow tunnel lined with hairy vegetation. They emerge at the bushy crotch of a gully opening into a green field. At one end stands an old DC-3. "Come on," says Ronald, "it's our only chance." They climb aboard. "Do you know how to fly?" asks Marietta. "I was a member of Captain Midnight's Secret Squadron," says Ronald. What would Wrong Way Corrigan do? he wonders. He experiments with the controls. The motors whine, sputter, roar to life. A patrol emerges from the trees. The plane goes bumping slowly across the field amidst staccato of small arms fire. They gather speed. The trees loom ahead. Banally races into the middle of the field and stands directly in front of the plane spraying bullets at them with a submachine gun. Ronald touches the controls. The plane veers

312

slightly to the side and catches Banally with one of its propellers. He disintegrates like watermelon in a fan. At that instant the plane bounds into the air. The trees tower before them. Ronald pulls back on the joystick. The engines roar, the plane climbs heavily into the sky. "Whew!" says Ronald. "I guess that spells finis for Strop Banally." Nancy stirs and moans. He opens his eyes. Half light of dawn. Nancy lies arms crossed between breasts, covers slipped off. "Cold?" he asks. The heavy fringed lids flutter. He pulls the blankets over her. The eyes blink open, look into his face, narrow, fall closed. Marietta sleeps prone, arms at sides, chin cocked up as if she were floating noseward through the air. He touches her back under the covers. She turns her head slightly and smiles. Between warmth and warmth he drowses. The large warmth of the sun the small warmth of the stones.

the large warmth of the sun the small warmth of the stones suk sukno sukiennice across the arroyo a flight of birds rises from behind a stand of cypress dead green on luminous blue he raises his hand the falcon hurls itself into the air suk sukno sukiennice Ducho el Viejo shuffles through the geometry of the garden coming up from the suk below the Alhambra across the arroyo plaintive from the hill of the Generalife a burro trumpets Ducho el Viejo stands next to him on the walls nodding shaking his head ay! Don Renaldo do you know the verses of de Icaza give alms lady for there is in life nothing like the pain of being blind in Granada cypress cedar eucalyptus plaintive from the hill of the Generalife a cock crows nodding he continues from Granada one can look both backward and forward city of the Jews suk sukno sukiennice noon quiet of cypress cedar eucalyptus the cante jondo sobs in the air on the high horizon the Sierra Nevada shimmers white mysterious he raises his hand the falcon hurls itself into the air Jews from Morocco from Exodus possessions in pillowcases seasick in

313

the crossing to Gibraltar old man calm prophetic fingers raises hand beard white mysterious ellos han matado el Re quién es el Re

Slade opens the door he wears a maroon dressing gown

my dear he says to Nancy he kisses her cheek he puts his arm around Ronnie's shoulders how are you this morning he asks a little tired says Ronnie but all here

Slade turns to Marietta it's good to see you he says they hug he gives her a long kiss on the mouth she responds with a luxuriant embrace the other two watch smiling

I think it's warm enough for coffee on the terrace says Slade the terrace coffee on the table rolls beyond the river bridge green wall of Palisades

how are you feeling asks Slade I'm all here says Ronnie I've never been so totally here warmth of sun warmth of coffee the feel of the table pale sky river glitter there are times says Nancy when civilization comes down to small amenities

Slade smiles let's simply say there are moments when life composes itself one could wish says Marietta that there were more of them

no says Ronnie I have no such wish it's not a question he says of moments one goes along one looks both backward and forward it's a question of being totally here a question of response concentration the feel of things like the landscape from a car like continual improvisation like he half rises like he sweeps his arm through the air like he sits down like he pauses impossible to explain he frowns

Marietta leans over and kisses his lips he glances at Slade who smiles he looks at Nancy whose responding smile flashes among them a perfect metaphor of their common secret

l'chaim says Julius   Sugar Stewart Jer Theda all lift their glasses and drink their beer   on this Thanksgiving says Julius being all together let's stop for a minute before eating to remember the poor and the helpless to think about

314

the people all over the world who have nothing to thank
god we have enough and above all to remember the per-
secutions of our people and in that memory to pledge
sympathy and help to the outcast the deprived and the
victimized let's eat   not too much for me says Stewart Jer
and I have to go off to a CORE meeting   that's nice says
Theda don't waste time here wait I'll make you a sandwich
you can eat on the way   you want me to come dear asks
Sugar no says Jer you take care of the kid   don't neglect
the business says Julius don't worry says Jer since turning it
into a workers' co-op it practically runs itself   what's this
thing you're working on asks Julius   it's called the Gravesend Neighborhood Project says Stewart we're trying to
subsidize low income minorities to integrate into the neighborhood   I'll tell you says Theda it's a wonderful thing
just like FDR   Grave's End   look says Hunch the boys
elected me head of this shop so from now on anyone who
ain't nice to Zip answers to me you wanna make something
of it   sure Hunch sure says Borneo   of course says Black-
bread Whitehead final decision in such matters always rests
with the instructor and frankly I admire your impulse to
defend your students from the heavy official hand of the
administration for nota bene Mr. Sukenick nota bene there
is no such thing as standardized education that is a blatant
paradox personally I like to teach my students the fart in
Chaucer a fascinating subject incidentally with profound
ramifications especially regarding the religious institutions
of the fourteenth century do you recall the summoner's tale
for example let me summarize   Stoopnagel shuts off his
transistor okay you guys cool it you're gonna follow Kenny
into these buildings we're gonna clean things up a little
around here the Roundtable Gents split into work squads
clean up the streets organize the tenants salvage good
buildings demolish hopeless tenements   say Ronnie says
Hamstrong how about helping me out a little with my
homework I got a night school class tomorrow sure Ham-

315

strong says Ronnie sit down have a drink no thanks says
Hamstrong I'm on the wagon besides I got to help the lady
next door fix up her place a little she got a bad heart you
know I'm sending up a little extra heat for these old buz-
zards lately what the hell Slumski will never know the difference   what you got rats says Slumski and you didn't
tell me you should have told me I'll call the exterminator
right away wait I'll go after them myself   Henry Sliesinger
reports the news we have just received word that the space
capsule on its way back from Mars is approaching Earth
and is about to execute re-entry we switch you to the space
control center which is now in direct radio contact with
the astronaut over do you read me up there over   roger a
little Jello a nice can of soup   what what you're not
coming through do you read me   a little Jello I said I read
you already   roger listen Ace what's it like coming back
from man's first flight to Mars over   Mars what Mars
Venus over   Venus come on Ace don't put us on you
made a right didn't you out away from the sun toward the
stars   what out in   come on Ace you mean you were
going in when you were supposed to be going out quit your
kidding Ace gee whiz I told you to keep an eye on the instruments you went to Venus these hot pilots always flying by
the seat of their pants they always have to improvise   listen
here's the General he looks a little sore Ace   he says he
wants his space ship back wait a minute he wants to talk
to you   snotty fuck ass meat beating jerkoff son-of-a-bitch
bastard come back here with that mother fucking equip-
ment you little prick   we're on the air General you remember what happened to Uncle Don   uh   do you read
me Colonel   I want to tell you we consider this the most
significant achievement of our space program to date a
major step forward I have congratulations from the President only it was programmed for Mars for Mars for Mars
do you read me Colonel for Mars now you're not going
to tell me you went to Venus are you come on Colonel

over over   Ace   come on boy you know me this is
the General   the old General   listen a little coopera-
tion up there what are you trying to give me a heart attack   listen   shmuck   you went to Venus wait till I
get him into debriefing Venus that's all that's it court mar-
tial drum him out drum him out rip off his wings his
medals all his buttons off off what's he trying to do to
me   roger all right all right already so I made a little
mistake don't hock me will you you can't hang a man
for making a mistake I'm a space hero ain't I okay you
mother fuckers power dive I'm coming down eeeeeeeeeeeeeeeooowoo o o o o o o o OOM

317

uP

s

t

r

a

drift
turn
wheel
float
in
huge
spirals
fall
away
ran
dom
dis
tant
un
in
tell
i
gible
whirl
heave
clump
cluster
patterns
galaxies
constellations
big bear
water carrier
archer
twins

uP

                 pok
             the ball
         disappeared
           over the rim
             of the stadium
               one watched
                 with detached curiosity
                   the figure running wildly
                     toward the leftfield bull pen
                       Dimaggio was between second and third
                     ahead of him gray hair wasted love bankruptcy
                 of suicide the fielder's glove came down in a
             swatting motion he doubled over the bullpen fence
       Dimaggio jumped in the air hands to his head
       Gionfriddo got him to autograph the ball

                              r

                   s   *a*

                        t

"Rats?" says Slumski. "You got rats? There are no rats
in this building. We have no rats here. Unless you brought
them in with you. That's the trouble with you people.
You're dirty. If you're gonna have filth you're gonna have
rats. A complaint? Go on, complain to the mayor for all I
care. Listen I'll give you rats. I'll throw you right out on the
street. So you see a lousy rat you get hysterical. They don't
bother you. What do you want me to do? Buy a cat. What
can I tell you? If you don't like it move out."

Slade opens the door in a T-shirt, barefoot, unshaven.
"Well," he says. "The morning after. You must be tired,"
he says to Sukenick.

320

"A little," says Sukenick. "But I feel good."

"I'll bet," says Slade. "Hi," he says to Nancy. He looks inquisitively at Marietta. "It's good to see you," he says, keeping his distance.

She gives him a kiss on the cheek. "It's good to be back."

"Glad to hear it. Well, don't just stand around. Make yourselves comfortable. The entire resources of the Slade household are at your disposal." He pulls the covers up on the bed and brings a chair in from the kitchen. "I have some instant coffee," he says.

They sit uncomfortably in a congealing silence. A pregnant roach scuttles across the floor. They watch it attentively. Suddenly Slade's foot shoots out and comes down on it. Everybody jumps. Slade lifts his foot up uncovering the roach flattened in the center of a brown-white stain. "Ugh," he says. He scrapes the ball of his foot against the floor.

"I could use some coffee," says Ronnie.

"You want to make it?" Slade asks Nancy.

"No," she says.

"I'll make it," says Marietta, getting up. "Let's put the light on. It's always so gray in here." She puts it on.

"I'll help," says Nancy.

"It was my idea that we come here all together," Sukenick tells Slade. "It seemed crucial."

"Well frankly man, if you didn't come I wouldn't have sent an invitation."

"That's why I came."

"Okay. Cool. How do you feel?"

"Free."

"Free? From what?"

"Free of you. Free of Nancy. And of Marietta. Free of Otis, Len, Bernie. And I love you all. You're all part of me."

"Cool," says Slade.

They come in with the coffee. "There's no milk," says

321

Marietta. "Here's sugar. And there are only two cups. We can share them."

"Thanks," says Ronnie. "It's great to have coffee."

"There are times," observes Nancy, "when civilization comes down to small amenities."

"Very small," says Slade.

"Almost nonexistent," says Marietta.

"There are times," says Sukenick, "when we define civilization as we go along."

Slade shares a cup with Marietta, Sukenick with Nancy. Slade and Marietta sit on the bed. She touches his shoulder. He puts his arm around her.

"I think it's time we go," Nancy says to Sukenick.

"Okay," says Sukenick.

They get up to go. Sukenick holds out his hand to Slade. Slade takes it, then pats Nancy on the head. Marietta looks at him. She gets up to kiss Sukenick goodbye and, going to Nancy, hesitates, murmurs something, and kisses her quickly on the lips.

"I should call Otis," says Nancy as they walk downstairs. "He must have gone home alone last night."

"Sure," says Sukenick. Was she lying? Who cares. They start down the last flight. He feels his weight coming down on the step. High specific gravity. But he moves lightly, breathes easily, in another element. Thin air, æther. The way they moved on Olympus. If she lies she has her reasons. Need for privacy. Preservation of appearance. Defense against me. My fault. To lie is human. Socrates lies Socrates is human. Animals can't lie. My body, my animal. Each breath a satisfaction. His weight comes down on each stair. Specific gravity. Her body jolts a bit with every step. High heels. She was part of him. After first time all night with a girl. Reflection, expansion, affirmation. Each for the other, like mirrors. Nancy, Ronnie, Marietta, Ernie, even Otis. Sukenick to the fifth. This contact. Inadequacy of sex. This contact. With or without. Walls crumble. A means

322

among others. What others? He bounces down the last of the stairs, through the hall. Dim yellow bulb illumines grime stained peeling walls. He raps his knuckle against cracking plaster—there with gratifying solidity. They were all part of him. He wanted nothing of them but that they exist. He was free of them. Let them lie or not lie, make love or not make love. He loved them all. Triviality of sex. He steps onto the sidewalk. Specific gravity. Would the ground support him? The street glitters with clarity, inexhaustible detail. Inexhaustible interest. See, hear, smell. Unequivocal. Has no meaning. The opacity of experience. He takes her hand. Moist, warm. Think. How long will it last? Think. How did it happen, how again? Get it down. Think. Make a movie of it, put it on tape. Record luminous thoughts. Futile. Never twice the same. Shifts, changes. Even as it happens. Even as. Even as. An old woman drops a coin. A boy mounts his bike. "There's a phone booth," she says. A truck roars by.

I'm having a party. To celebrate the end of my novel. Everyone's here. We're all drinking champagne. I love champagne, I'm a real champagne head. My place is jammed, people are hanging from the fire escape, cheering at pedestrians. In the living room we're dancing like maniacs, music blasting from the tape recorder, the kind of music I like at parties, Chuck Berry, Bo Diddley, Ray Charles, Olatunji and His Drums of Passion, Mongo Santamaria, Greek bouzouki music, The McCoys, The Rolling Stones. Len, Otis, Ernie, Bernie are here. Nancy and Marietta are here. There's Strop—hello sweetheart. There's Hamstrung. Slim, Sugar, Sugarplum, Jer, Gerald, Zip, Hunch, Borneo, Yssis, Eugene, Kenny, Adam, Nanette, Etta Farrow, Oola Wonderleigh, Slumski, Sergeant Vack, the Gents, Waldo, Nifty, they're all here. Even Bill Davies is here. Swaying in his tight pants, he lifts a limp toast to

323

me. "Landsman!" he says. I didn't forget you Bill. You shmuck. Otis dances over holding up a champagne glass. "It's pure life," he yells. Julius and Theda just popped in, looking lost. They can only stay a minute. They're dragging Herm and Irma along. Hi Herm, hi Irma. "Hey," says Otis, "I know that guy." He points to Jer. "He's the guy who came into the Pet Hotel that time with the crazy hooker and her Chihuahua. Remember?" Sugarplum sidles up to Jer. "Hi, Jer," she says. "Remember me? The Pet Hotel? Gerard?" "What are you kidding me," says Jer. "I never saw you before." He moves off. Sugar gives him one of the meanest looks I ever saw. Now Sukenick is holding a champagne glass in the air and doing his own crazy dance to Greek bouzouki music. He must be drunk already. Live it up Ron boy, the book's almost over. Hey, where did they come from? Grandpa suddenly appears at the edge of the dancers, spats, cane, ruby stickpin, goatish beard white-yellowed, raising a champagne glass to the one that Ronnie holds. Dutchik el Viejo is at his side, straight, spare, severe, dressed in black. They start clapping to the rhythm and the rhythm changes, the beat quickens, Greek to Slavic, Sukenick steps faster, "Hi!" shouts Grandpa, clapping, and Ronnie tosses his glass over his shoulder, crosses his arms, leaps into a squatting position and kzatzchas across the floor, back straight, legs shooting in and out, slapping his heels like a cossack, as the onlookers applaud. Dutchik steps forward and begins clapping and stamping with his heel in a slow, steady rhythm like the pulse of one's blood. Sukenick straightens, throws his head back, and hands on hips steps gravely across the floor on his heels flaunting pride like a red banner. The clapping comes faster, starts to syncopate, Sukenick stands still, erect, and allows his heels to explode in a quickening burst of controlled percussion as Dutchik shouts "Olé! Olé!" Then Grandpa steps up with Dutchik and they begin a new rhythm, intricate, sinuous, stately, oriental. Ronnie's hips swing, his trunk sways, he

324

flexes his shoulders, his arms, he snaps his fingers. Grandpa and Dutchik move into the dance as the beat quickens, and for a moment the three of them move in a rhythmic circle then, the old men disappear and Sukenick is alone on the floor dancing to the theme from *Never On Sunday*. Everyone applauds. "Terrific, Ron," says Otis. "Olé!"

"It's pure life," says Ron. He wipes his brow, stands still and holds up his hands.

"Hold it, quiet everybody, quiet please. If you will allow me just a few minutes, it seems only appropriate here that I read the Author's Dedication to this book."

"Oyez oyez!" cries Finch.

Sukenick fishes through his clothing, finally pulls a piece of folded typing paper from his back pocket and opens it. He reads:

" 'First of all come my mother and father, may they live in health and happiness. Then my Uncle Benny, who used to read the Sunday comics to me becoming my first literary influence. To my sister, with love, she deserves special credit. To Dave Behrens, Phil Green, Ronnie Hafter, Marty Washburn, Norm Rush, Pete Marin, Al Amateau, Adek Zylberberg, Serge Doubrovsky, Beby Spina, and all my indispensable pals. To Steve Katz here briefly on a special guest appearance from his own novel with a team of his tumbling mild-nosed Egyptian spotted rabbits, take a bow Steve. To all the women who helped me out, you know who you are—I love you all. To the three and three fourth teachers who helped me along. And above all, to Lynn, my wife.' I notice there is also appended here a malediction 'conscribing to ignominy all those who have hated, thwarted, and doublecrossed me,' followed by a long list of names, which, however, seems a little inapropos at this time. Instead, I would now like to present a brief entertainment that some of us have worked up for you. You want to back us up here Slim?"

Len, Bernie, Slade and Otis join Sukenick in the middle

325

of the room. Slim strikes a chord on his guitar, "Hit it boys," says Ronnie, and the five join in relatively close harmony.

> *We hope the hell you like us*
> *Now that the book is through,*
> *We hope the hell you dig us,*
> *We sure as hell dig you,*
> *We know that life is perfect,*
> *And novels should be too,*
> *But if it's not quite perfect,*
> *At least it's all quite true,*
> *It was lots of fun to write it,*
> *And lots of sweating too,*
> *So we hope the hell you like it,*
> *And if you don't the hell with you.*

Cheers and applause, a few boos. A pretty girl, fired no doubt by the champagne, races up to Slim, big eyes blazing, snatches the guitar from him, and begins banging out the chords of an Italian folksong. She starts to sing. Sukenick joins her, loud and off key. He must be bombed out of his head.

> *Olimpia Olimpia Olimpia tu me tradise,*
> *Me dise che te vegne in veste Pise.*

After a few choruses the girl starts singing a sad wild song in Russian which Sukenick, thank god, doesn't know. Instead he turns to greet a slim blond guy with a distinguished mustache. This is Marty, and the singing girl, Nora Kersh Spina who along with Al Amateau and Lynn were in the original kite flying incident a few years ago. Al, however, with his impeccable taste, declined coming on grounds of aesthetic propriety, so he isn't here. Marty carries a small airlines bag with him, expecting the trip to London I promised to give him in the book. Ronnie makes his apologies.

326

It didn't fit in. It would have been too expensive. What can I do? I plumb my imagination. "Oh, Nanette. Nanette, je te présente Marty Washburn. Il est très fort. Un peintre merveilleux. Un esprit formidable." Marty bows slightly. "Mademoiselle, charmé."

Suddenly a hush spreads through the company. All heads turn toward a sweeping baroque stairway at the top of which Lynn has just appeared, all aglow, and begins descending step by stately step. Her dark hair is piled high on her head and she wears a long clinging white gown gathered below the breast, with a deep, daring scoop neck, charmingly exaggerated by a plunging notch at the cleavage. Her arms are sheathed in long white gloves. The men sigh with each step she takes, the women are lost in abject admiration. Ronnie greets her at the bottom with a glass of champagne, from which she takes a sip. They dance off together to the strains of a waltz as the awed company claps politely. Nancy smiles as they dance by.

"Who's that?" asks Lynn.

"Nancy."

"So that's the one," she says.

"It's only a novel don't forget."

"I understand that very well, but don't say only. It's been three years of our life. Anyway I thought she'd be prettier."

"It's a matter of taste. Excuse me a minute. I've got to talk to Slade."

Slade seems to be in a bad mood. Ronnie greets him and holds out his hand. Slade just stands there with his drink swaying belligerently back and forth.

"So it looks like you wind up with all the girls," he says. "All right man, some day you'll come down my street."

"What do you mean, Ernie?"

"I thought you were going to introduce me to Nanette."

"Okay, okay. Where's Marietta?"

"Off in some corner with Otis. Say, what's the matter

327

with that character man? Can't you guys find your own girls? I suppose you know he's been making it with Nancy."

"That son of a bitch! How do you know?"

"It's obvious man. Wise up."

Sukenick goes over to Otis who is talking to Marietta in a corner.

"Say, listen," says Sukenick. "What the hell you think you're doing. Making it with everybody's girl. That's not the kind of thing I expect from you, Otis. It's too much. You're what I call a bad character. You've got no verisimilitude. Screwing around like that. What kind of novel you think this is anyway?"

"Oh!" says Marietta. "I don't think that's very fair."

"Don't worry about Ron," says Otis. "Ron is just fond of displaying that streak of vulgarity which so often marks the coarse vitality of genius."

"Hardly," says Bernie. "Not if he insists on destroying his own novel this way. I mean you don't expect anyone to swallow this kind of thing actually."

"Ah novels are a load of crap anyway," says Len.

All right, the party is over. I've had enough of this. All I want to do is end the book. If I'm lucky maybe I'll manage it today, that would be nice. Before Friday in any case. Friday is New Year's Eve. Sometime in these five days, by god, I'm going to finish this. Though frankly I'm tired. My eyes are shot. Then there are the interruptions. Pachangas blasting out of hi-fi windows on the courtyard. The furniture refinishing place downstairs sending up paint fumes and gassing us out of our apartment, I'll have to call the Health Department. Sometime before Friday we have to go eat with my parents in Brooklyn. Then there are all the friends in for the holidays, people from Boston, Ithaca, Chicago, California, Nova Scotia. And I have to write for jobs this week. Without fail. Without fail. We're scraping the bottom of the barrel. And I'm really sick of this neighborhood, man, five years of slum life, I've had it. The thing is

328

any move you make you've got to triple your rent. At least. Look, encourage your friends to buy this book, no kidding. I never made a cent off writing, they could throw it away worse places. Or perhaps you aren't interested in this variety of personal confession. That's not our problem, tell us a story. Or maybe you've begun to notice certain discrepancies, speaking of the story. I thought you weren't married, I thought your parents were dead. Very sharp. Very perceptive. Well this is just to let you know that I have my secrets too, ladies and gents. I'm not an exponent of indecent public exposure. You want to find out about my personal life give me a ring I'm in the book. I have nothing better to do than make intimate revelations to the idly curious, tourists of my soul. I'm going to finish this today, the hell with it. I've had enough of this. I'm just playing with words anyway, what did you think I was doing? Just playing with words ga-ga-ga-ga-ga-ga-goo-goo-gig-geg-gug-gack. I'm thirty-three I've got more important things to attend to, money, career, women, hobbies, vacations, lots of things, really good ones, I got a list somewhere. Nel mezzo del cammin di nostra vita—mi frega niente. I just make it up as I go along, the hell with it, I'm finishing today. Though it's all true what I've written, every word of it, I insist on that. Bernie, Finch, Sukenick, Slade, Otis, they have, at least, the courage of my contradictions. Comic characters under sentence of death. Maybe I better keep it up a while longer, what am I going to do when I'm done? No, impossible. It's dissolving into words, script on paper. Time to leave my cave, these scenes, the magic paintings on my rocky walls figure in figure in figure, Lascaux, the potent hunters, the bulls dreaming across the centuries. Forget it. Exist, subsist, resist. That's all. That's the plot, the subplot, and the counterplot. End quickly, quietly. Nothing dramatic. I light a pipe. I go to the window. It's four in the afternoon, wintry outside, getting dark. Down at the corner I can see a brick wall plastered with scaling, ragged,

329

multicolored layers of old billboard posters. Their odds and ends of remnant lettering seem to spell out an undecipherable message. On the corner a young woman and an older man meet, stop, speak a moment, and the woman goes running back down the Avenue. The light starts to empty from the sky, ragged overcast patched with blue. On the tenement roof above the corner, among television aerials, a boyish figure raises a long, bare pole. He holds it above his head, moves it in a slow circle, and lowers it again. No sequel in the vacant air, no signal comes. He raises the pole, moves it in a circle, and lowers it again. The light is emptying from the sky. He raises the pole, moves it in a circle, lowers it again. The light is emptying from the sky. He raises the pole, moves it in a circle, lowers it. He raises the pole, moves it in a circle, lowers it. He raises the pole, moves it in a circle, lowers it. Again. Again. Again. The light empties from the sky.

CPSIA information can be obtained at www.ICGtesting.com
Printed in the USA
BVOW03s0901030816

457801BV00001B/36/P